KU-220-235

For Kristi,
Confidante, companion, best friend, bride.
They're all for you.

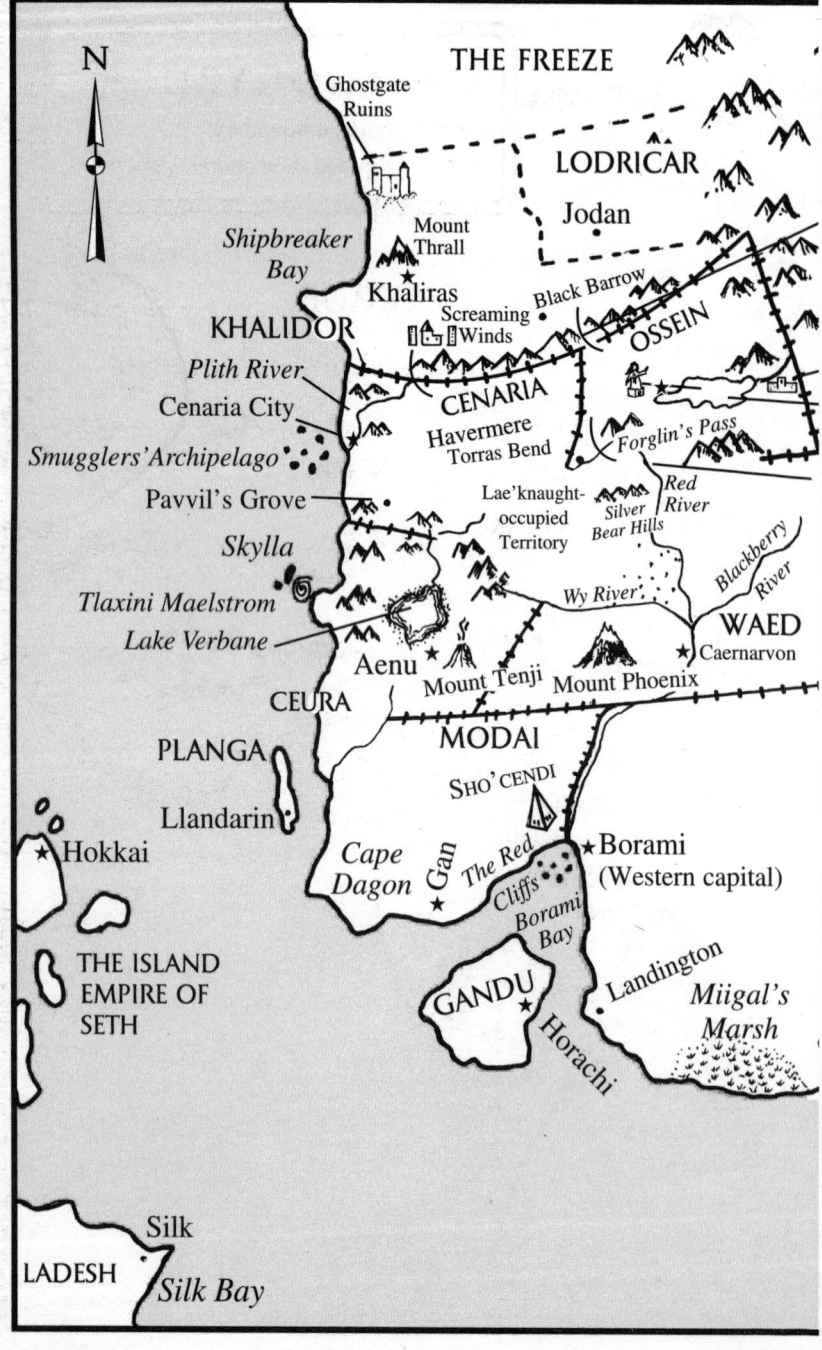

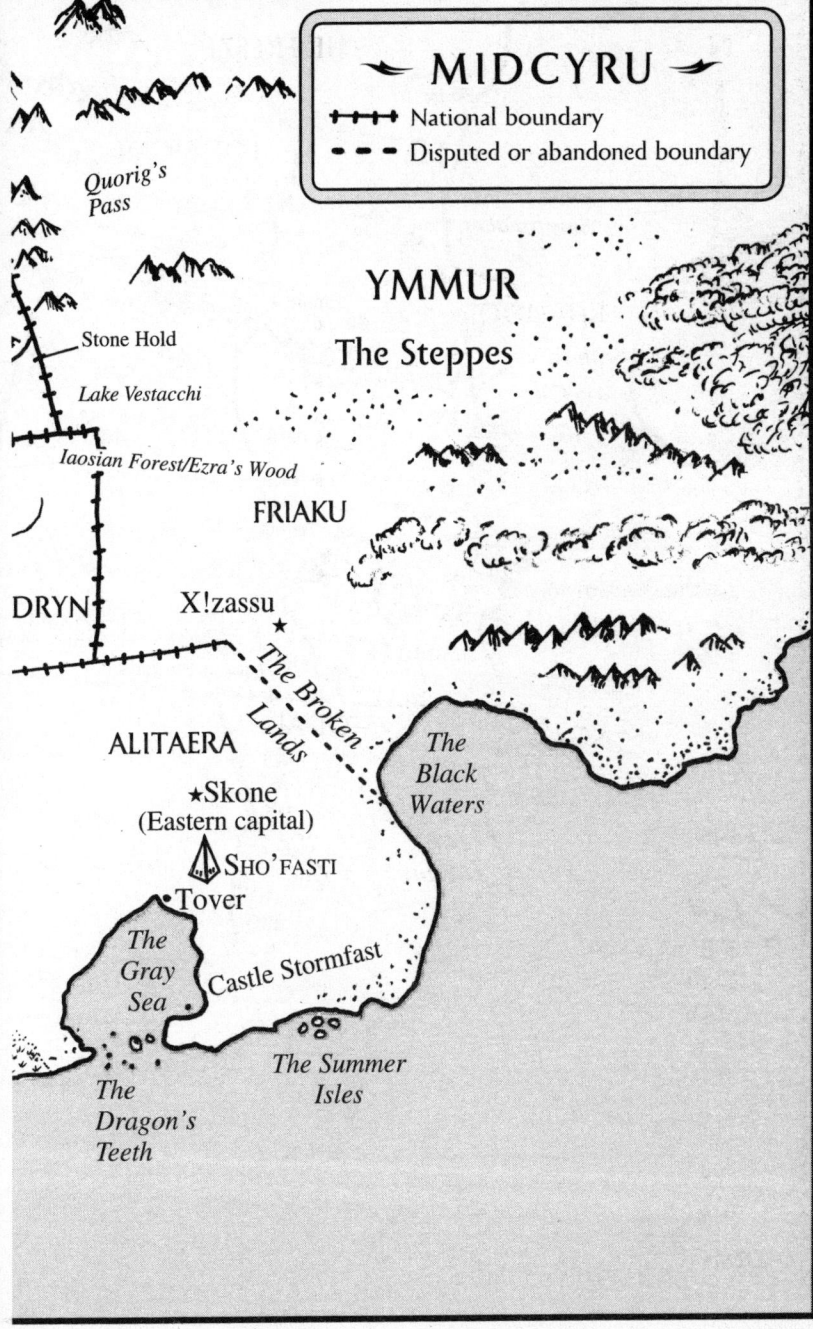

1

*A*zoth squatted in the alley, cold mud squishing through his bare toes. He stared at the narrow space beneath the wall, trying to get his nerve up. The sun wouldn't come up for hours, and the tavern was empty. Most taverns in the city had dirt floors, but this part of the Warrens had been built over marshland, and not even drunks wanted to drink standing ankle-deep in mud, so the tavern had been raised a few inches on stilts and floored with stout bamboo poles.

Coins sometimes dropped through the gaps in the bamboo, and the crawlspace was too small for most people to go after them. The guild's bigs were too big and the littles were too scared to squeeze into the suffocating darkness shared with spiders and cockroaches and rats and the wicked half-wild tomcat the owner kept. Worst was the pressure of the bamboo against your back, flattening you every time a patron walked overhead. It had been Azoth's favorite spot for a year, but he wasn't as small as he used to be. Last time, he got stuck and spent hours panicking until it rained and the ground softened beneath him enough that he could dig himself out.

It was muddy now, and there would be no patrons, and Azoth had seen the tomcat leave. It should be fine. Besides, Rat was collecting guild dues tomorrow, and Azoth didn't have four coppers. He didn't even have one, so there wasn't much choice. Rat wasn't understanding, and he didn't know his own strength. Littles had died from his beatings.

Pushing aside mounds of mud, Azoth lay on his stomach. The dank earth soaked his thin, filthy tunic instantly. He'd have to work fast. He was skinny, and if he caught a chill, the odds of getting better weren't good.

Scooting through the darkness, he began searching for the telltale metallic gleam. A couple of lamps were still burning in the tavern, so light filtered through the gaps, illuminating the mud and standing water in strange rectangles. Heavy marsh mist climbed the shafts of light only to fall over and over again. Spider webs draped across Azoth's face and broke, and he felt a tingle on the back of his neck.

He froze. No, it was his imagination. He exhaled slowly. Something glimmered and he grabbed his first copper. He slithered to the unfinished pine beam he had gotten stuck under last time and shoveled mud away until water filled the depression. The gap was still so narrow that he had to turn his head sideways to squeeze underneath it. Holding his breath and pushing his face into the slimy water, he began the slow crawl.

His head and shoulders made it through, but then a stub of a branch caught the back of his tunic, tearing the cloth and jabbing his back. He almost cried out and was instantly glad he hadn't. Through a wide space between bamboo poles, Azoth saw a man seated at the bar, still drinking. In the Warrens, you had to judge people quickly. Even if you had quick hands like Azoth did, when you stole every day, you were bound to get caught eventually. All merchants hit the guild rats who stole from them. If they wanted to have any goods left to sell, they had to. The trick was picking the ones who'd smack you so you didn't try their booth next time; there were others who'd beat you so badly you never had a next time. Azoth thought he saw something kind and sad and lonely in this lanky figure. He was perhaps thirty, with a scraggly blond beard and a huge sword on his hip.

"How could you abandon me?" the man whispered so quietly Azoth could barely distinguish the words. He held a flagon in his left hand and cradled something Azoth couldn't see in his right. "After all the years I've served you, how could you abandon me now? Is it because of Vonda?"

There was an itch on Azoth's calf. He ignored it. It was just his imagination again. He reached behind his back to free his tunic. He needed to find his coins and get out of here.

Something heavy dropped onto the floor above Azoth and slammed his face into the water, driving the breath from his lungs. He gasped and nearly inhaled water.

"Why Durzo Blint, you never fail to surprise," the weight above Azoth said. Nothing was visible of the man through the gaps except a drawn dagger. He must have dropped from the rafters. "Hey, I'm all for calling a bluff, but you should have seen Vonda when she figured out you weren't going to save her. Made me damn near bawl my eyes out."

The lanky man turned. His voice was slow, broken. "I killed six men tonight. Are you sure you want to make it seven?"

Azoth slowly caught up with what they'd been saying. The lanky man was the wetboy Durzo Blint. A wetboy was like an assassin—in the way a tiger is like a kitten. Among wetboys, Durzo Blint was indisputably the best. Or, as the head of Azoth's guild said, at least the disputes didn't last long. *And I thought Durzo Blint looked* kind?

The itch on Azoth's calf itched again. It wasn't his imagination. There was something crawling up the inside of his trousers. It felt big, but not as big as a cockroach. Azoth's fear identified the weight: a white wolf spider. Its poison liquefied flesh in a slowly spreading circle. If it bit, even with a healer the best an adult could hope for was to lose a limb. A guild rat wouldn't be so lucky.

"Blint, you'll be lucky if you don't cut your head off after all you've been drinking. Just in the time I've been watching, you've had—"

"Eight flagons. And I had four before that."

Azoth didn't move. If he jerked his legs together to kill the spider, the water would splash and the men would know he was there. Even if Durzo Blint had looked kind, that was an awful big sword, and Azoth knew better than to trust grown-ups.

"You're bluffing," the man said, but there was fear in his voice.

"I don't bluff," Durzo Blint said. "Why don't you invite your friends in?"

The spider crawled up to Azoth's inner thigh. Trembling, he pulled his tunic up in back and stretched the waist of his trousers, making a gap and praying the spider would crawl for it.

Above him, the assassin reached two fingers up to his lips and whistled. Azoth didn't see Durzo move, but the whistle ended in a gurgle and a moment later, the assassin's body tumbled to the floor. There were yells as the front and back doors burst open. The boards flexed and jumped. Concentrating on not jostling the spider, Azoth didn't move, even when another dropping body pushed his face briefly under water.

The spider crawled across Azoth's butt and then onto his thumb. Slowly, Azoth drew his hand around so he could see it. His fears were right. It was a white wolf spider, its legs as long as Azoth's thumb. He flung it away convulsively and rubbed his fingers, making sure he hadn't been bitten.

He reached for the splintered branch holding his tunic and broke it off. The sound was magnified in the sudden silence above. Azoth couldn't see anyone through the gaps. A few feet away, something was dripping from the boards into a puddle. It was too dark to see what it was, but it didn't take much imagination to guess.

The silence was eerie. If any of the men walked across the floor, groaning boards and flexing bamboo would have announced it. The entire fight had lasted maybe twenty seconds, and Azoth was sure no one had left the tavern. Had they all killed each other?

He was chilled, and not just from the water. Death was no stranger in the Warrens, but Azoth had never seen so many people die so fast and so easily.

Even taking extra care to look out for the spider, in a

few minutes, Azoth had gathered six coppers. If he were braver, he would have looted the bodies in the tavern, but Azoth couldn't believe Durzo Blint was dead. Maybe he was a demon, like the other guild rats said. Maybe he was standing outside, waiting to kill Azoth for spying on him.

Chest tight with fear, Azoth turned and scooted toward his hole. Six coppers was good. Dues were only four, so he could buy bread tomorrow to share with Jarl and Doll Girl.

He was a foot from the opening when something bright flashed in front of his nose. It was so close, it took a moment to come into focus. It was Durzo Blint's huge sword, and it was stuck through the floor all the way into the mud, barring Azoth's escape.

Just above Azoth on the other side of the floor, Durzo Blint whispered, "Never speak of this. Understand? I've done worse than kill children."

The sword disappeared, and Azoth scrambled out into the night. He didn't stop running for miles.

$\mathcal{F}$our coppers! Four! This isn't four." Rat's face was so rage-red his pimples only showed as a scattering of white dots. He grabbed Jarl's threadbare tunic and lifted him off the ground. Azoth ducked his head. He couldn't watch.

"This is four!" Rat shouted, spit flying. As his hand slapped across Jarl's face, Azoth realized it was a performance. Not the beating—Rat was definitely hitting Jarl—but he was hitting him with an open hand. It was louder that way. Rat wasn't even paying attention to Jarl. He was watching the rest of the guild, enjoying their fear.

"Who's next?" Rat asked, dropping Jarl. Azoth stepped forward quickly so Rat wouldn't kick his friend. At sixteen, Rat was already as big as a man and he had fat, which made him unique among the slaveborn.

Azoth held out his four coppers.

"Eight, puke," Rat said, taking the four from Azoth's hand.

"Eight?"

"You gotta pay for Doll Girl, too."

Azoth looked around for help. Some of the bigs shifted and looked at each other, but no one said a word. "She's too young," Azoth said. "Littles don't pay dues till they're eight."

Attention shifted to Doll Girl, who was sitting in the dirty alley. She noticed the looks and withered, shrinking into herself. Doll Girl was tiny, with huge eyes, but beneath the grime, her features were as fine and perfect as her namesake's.

"I say she's eight unless she says different." Rat leered. "Say it, Doll Girl, say it or I'll beat up your boyfriend." Doll Girl's big eyes got bigger and Rat laughed. Azoth didn't protest, didn't point out that Doll Girl was mute. Rat knew. Everyone knew. But Rat was the Fist. He only answered to Ja'laliel, and Ja'laliel wasn't here.

Rat pulled Azoth close and lowered his voice. "Why don't you join my pretty boys, Azo? You'll never pay dues again."

Azoth tried to speak, but his throat was so tight that he only squeaked. Rat laughed again and everyone joined him, some enjoying Azoth's humiliation, some just hoping to put Rat in a good mood before their turn came. Black hatred stabbed through him. Azoth hated Rat, hated the guild, hated himself.

He cleared his throat to try again. Rat caught his eye and smirked. Rat was big, but he wasn't stupid. He knew how far he was pushing Azoth. He knew Azoth would crumple, afraid, just like everyone else.

Azoth spat a wad of phlegm onto Rat's face. "Go bugger yourself, Ratty Fatty."

There was an eternity of stunned silence. A golden moment of victory. Azoth thought he could hear jaws dropping. Sanity was just starting to reassert itself when Rat's fist caught him on the ear. Black spots blotted out the world as he hit the ground. He blinked up at Rat, whose black hair glowed like a halo as it blocked the noon sun, and knew he was going to die.

"Rat! Rat, I need you."

Azoth rolled over and saw Ja'laliel emerging from the guild's building. His pale skin was beaded with sweat though the day wasn't hot. He coughed unhealthily. "Rat! I said now."

Rat wiped his face, and seeing his rage cool so suddenly was almost more frightening than seeing its sudden heat. His face cleared, and he smiled at Azoth. Just smiled.

"Hey-ho, Jay-Oh," Azoth said.

"Hey-ho, Azo," Jarl said, coming to join Azoth and Doll Girl. "You know, you're about as smart as a box of hair. They'll be calling him Ratty Fatty behind his back for years."

"He wanted me to be one of his girls," Azoth said.

They were propped against a wall several blocks away, sharing the stale loaf Azoth had bought. The smells of baking, though less intense this late in the day, covered at least some of the smells of sewage, rotting garbage piled on the banks of the river, and the rancid bite of the urine and brains of the tanneries.

If Ceuran architecture was all bamboo and rice fiber walls and screens, Cenarian architecture was rougher, heavier, lacking the studied simplicity of Ceuran design. If Alitaeran architecture was all granite and pine, Cenarian architecture was less formidable, lacking the deliberate durability of Alitaeran structures. If Osseini architecture was airy spires and soaring arches, Cenarian architecture only soared above one story in a few nobles' manses on the east side. Cenarian buildings were everything squat and dank and cheap and low, especially in the Warrens. A material that cost twice as much was never used, even if it lasted four times as long. Cenarians didn't think long term because they didn't live long term. Their buildings frequently incorporated bamboo and rice fiber, both of which grew nearby, and pine and granite, which were not too far away, but there was no Cenarian style. The country had been conquered too many times over the centuries to pride itself on anything but survival. In the Warrens, there wasn't even pride.

Azoth absently ripped the loaf into thirds, then scowled. He'd made two about the same size, and one third smaller. He put one of the bigger pieces on his leg and handed the other big piece to Doll Girl, who followed him like a shadow. He was about to hand the small piece to Jarl when he saw Doll Girl's face pucker in disapproval.

Azoth sighed and took the small piece for himself. Jarl didn't even notice. "Better one of his girls than dead," Jarl said.

"I won't end up like Bim."

"Azo, once Ja'laliel buys review, Rat'll be our guild head. You're eleven. Five years till you get review. You'll never make it. Rat'll make Bim look lucky compared to you."

"So what do I do, Jarl?" Ordinarily, this was Azoth's favorite time. He was with the two people he didn't have to be afraid of, and he was silencing the insistent voice of hunger. Now, the bread tasted like dust. He stared into the market, not even seeing the fishmonger beating her husband.

Jarl smiled, his teeth brilliant against his black Ladeshian skin. "If I tell you a secret can you keep it quiet?"

Azoth looked from side to side and leaned in. The loud crunching of bread and smacking of lips beside him stopped him. "Well, *I* can. I'm not so sure about Doll Girl."

They both turned toward where she sat, gnawing on the heel of the loaf. The combination of the crumbs stuck to her face and her scowl of outrage made them howl with laughter.

Azoth rubbed her blonde head and, when she kept scowling, pulled her close. She fought against him, but when he let his arm drop, she didn't scoot away. She looked at Jarl expectantly.

Jarl lifted his tunic and removed a rag he'd had tied around his body as a sash. "I won't be like the others, Azo. I'm not just going to let life happen to me. I'm gonna get out." He opened the sash. Tucked within its folds were a dozen coppers, four silvers, and impossibly, two gold gunders.

"Four years. Four years I've been saving." He dropped two more coppers into the sash.

"You mean all the times Rat's slapped you around for not making your dues, you've had this?"

Jarl smiled and, slowly, Azoth understood. The beatings were a small price to pay for hope. After a while, most guild rats withered and let life beat them. They became animals. Or they went crazy like Azoth had today and got themselves killed.

Looking at that treasure, part of Azoth wanted to strike Jarl, grab the sash, and run. With that money, he could get out, get clothes to replace his rags, and pay apprentice fees somewhere, anywhere. Maybe even with Durzo Blint, as he'd told Jarl and Doll Girl so many times.

Then he saw Doll Girl. He knew how she'd look at him if he stole that sash full of life. "If any of us make it out of the Warrens, it'll be you, Jarl. You deserve it. You have a plan?"

"Always," Jarl said. He looked up, his brown eyes bright. "I want you to take it, Azo. As soon as we find out where Durzo Blint lives, we're going get you out. All right?"

Azoth looked at the pile of coins. Four years. Dozens of beatings. Not only did he not know if he would give that much for Jarl, but he'd also thought of stealing it from him. He couldn't hold back hot tears. He was so ashamed. He was so afraid. Afraid of Rat. Afraid of Durzo Blint. Always afraid. But if he got out, he could help Jarl. And Blint would teach him to kill.

Azoth looked up at Jarl, not daring to look at Doll Girl for fear of what might be in her big brown eyes. "I'll take it."

He knew who he'd kill first.

3

*D*urzo Blint pulled himself on top of the small estate's wall and watched the guard pass. *The perfect guard,* Durzo thought: a bit slow, lacking imagination, and dutiful. He took his thirty-nine steps, stopped at the corner, planted his halberd, scratched his stomach under his gambeson, checked in all directions, then walked on.

Thirty-five. Thirty-six. Durzo slipped out of the man's shadow and eased himself over the edge of the walkway. He held on by his fingertips.

Now. He dropped and hit the grass just as the guard thumped the butt of his halberd on the wood walkway. He doubted the guard would have heard him anyway, but paranoia begat perfection in the wetboy's trade. The yard was small, and the house not much bigger. It was built on the Ceuran design, with translucent rice paper walls. Bald cypress and white cedar formed the doors and arches and cheaper local pine had been used for the frame and the floors. It was spartan like all Ceuran houses, and that fit General Agon's military background and his ascetic personality. More than that, it fit his budget. Despite the general's many successes, King Davin had not rewarded him well—which was part of why the wetboy had come.

Durzo found an unlocked window on the second floor. The general's wife was asleep in the bed: they weren't so Ceuran as to sleep on woven mats. They were, however, poor enough that the mattress was stuffed with straw rather than feathers. The general's wife was a plain woman, snoring gently and sprawled more in the middle than to one side of the bed. The covers on the side she was facing had been disturbed.

The wetboy slid into the room, using his Talent to soften the sound of his footsteps on the hardwood floor.

Curious. A quick glance confirmed that the general hadn't just come for a nocturnal conjugal visit. They actually shared the room. Perhaps he was even poorer than people thought.

Durzo's brow furrowed under his mask. It was a detail he didn't need to know. He drew the short poisoner's knife and walked toward the bed. She'd never feel a thing.

He stopped. The woman was turned *toward* the disturbed covers. She'd been sleeping close to her husband before he got up. Not on the far side of the bed, the way a woman merely doing her marital duties would.

It was a love match. After her murder, Aleine Gunder had planned to offer the general a quick remarriage to a rich noblewoman. But this general, who'd married a low-born woman for love, would react quite differently to his wife's murder than a man who'd married for ambition.

The idiot. The prince was so consumed with ambition that he thought everyone else was, too. The wetboy

sheathed the knife and stepped into the hall. He still had
to know where the general stood. Immediately.

"Dammit, man! King Davin's dying. I'd be surprised if
he's got a week left."

Whoever had spoken was mostly right. The wetboy
had given the king his final dose of poison tonight. By
dawn, he would be dead, leaving a throne in contention
between one man who was strong and just, and another
who was weak and corrupt. The underworld Sa'kagé was
not disinterested in the outcome.

The voice had come from the receiving room downstairs. The wetboy hurried to the end of the hall. The
house was so small that the receiving room doubled as
the study. He had a perfect view of the two men.

General Brant Agon had a graying beard, close-
trimmed hair that he didn't comb, and a jerky way of
moving, keeping his eyes on everything. He was thin and
sinewy, his legs slightly bowed from a life in the saddle.

The man across from him was Duke Regnus Gyre. The
wing-backed chair creaked as he shifted his weight. He
was a huge man, both tall and wide, and little of his bulk
was fat. He folded ringed fingers on his belly.

*By the Night Angels. I could kill them both and end the
Nine's worries right now.*

"Are we deceiving ourselves, Brant?" Duke Gyre
asked.

The general didn't answer immediately. "My lord—"

"No, Brant. I need your opinion as a friend, not as a
vassal." Durzo crept closer. He drew the throwing knives
slowly, careful with the poisoned edges.

"If we do nothing," the general said, "Aleine Gunder
will become king. He is a weak, foul, and faithless man.

The Sa'kagé already owns the Warrens; the king's patrols won't even leave the main roads, and you know all the reasons that's only bound to get worse. The Death Games entrenched the Sa'kagé. Aleine doesn't have the will or the inclination to oppose the Sa'kagé now, while we can still root them out. So are we deceiving ourselves in thinking that you'd be a better king? Not at all. And the throne is yours by rights."

Blint almost smiled. The underworld's lords, the Sa'kagé Nine, agreed with every word—which was why Blint was making sure Regnus Gyre didn't become king.

"And tactically? We could do it?"

"With minimal bloodshed. Duke Wesseros is out of the country. My own regiment is in the city. The men believe in you, my lord. We need a strong king. A good king. We need you, Regnus."

Duke Gyre looked at his hands. "And Aleine's family? They'll be part of the 'minimal bloodshed'?"

The general's voice was quiet. "You want the truth? Yes. Even if we don't order it, one of our men will kill them to protect you, even if it meant hanging. They believe in you that much."

Duke Gyre breathed. "So the question is, does the good of many in the future outweigh the murder of a few now?"

How long has it been since I had such qualms? Durzo barely stifled an overpowering urge to throw the daggers.

The suddenness of his rage shook him. *What was that about?*

It was Regnus. The man reminded him of another king he'd once served. A king worthy of it.

"That's for you to answer, my lord," General Agon said. "But, if I may, is the question really so philosophical?"

"What do you mean?"

"You still love Nalia, don't you?" Nalia was Aleine Gunder's wife.

Regnus looked stricken. "I was betrothed to her for ten years, Brant. We were each other's first lovers."

"My lord, I'm sorry," the general said. "It's not my—"

"No, Brant. I never speak of it. As I decide whether to be a man or a king, let me." He breathed deeply. "It's been fifteen years since Nalia's father broke our betrothal and married her to that dog Aleine. I should be over it. I am, except when I have to see her with her children and have to imagine her sharing a bed with Aleine Gunder. The only joy my marriage has given me is my son Logan, and I can scarce believe her own has been better."

"My lord, given the involuntary nature of both of your weddings, could you not divorce Catrinna and marry—"

"No." Regnus shook his head. "If the queen's children live, they will always be a threat to my son, whether I exile them or adopt them. Nalia's eldest boy is fourteen—too old to forget that he was destined for a throne."

"The right is on your side, my lord, and who knows but that answers unforeseen may arise to these problems once you sit on the throne?"

Regnus nodded unhappily, obviously knowing he held hundreds or thousands of lives in his hands, not knowing he held his own as well. *If he plots rebellion, I'll kill him now, I swear by the Night Angels. I serve only the Sa'kagé now. And myself. Always myself.*

"May generations unborn forgive me," Regnus Gyre said, tears gleaming in his eyes. "But I will not commit murder for what may be, Brant. I cannot. I will swear fealty."

The wetboy slid the daggers back into their sheaths, ignoring the twin feelings of relief and despair he felt.

It's that damned woman. She's ruined me. She's ruined everything.

Blint saw the ambush from fifty paces away, and walked right into its teeth. The sun was still an hour from rising and the only people on the twisting streets of the Warrens were merchants who'd fallen asleep where they shouldn't have and were hurrying home to their wives.

The guild—Black Dragon from the guild glyphs he'd passed—was hiding around a narrow choke point in the alley where guild rats could spring up to clog both ends of the street and also attack from the low rooftops.

He had affected a bad right knee and pulled his cloak tight around his shoulders, the hood pulled low over his face. As he limped into the trap, one of the older children, a *big* as they called them, jumped into the alley ahead of him and whistled, brandishing a rusty saber. Guild rats surrounded the wetboy.

"Clever," Durzo said. "You keep a lookout before dawn when most of the other guilds are sleeping, and you're able to jump a few bags who've been out all night whoring. They don't want to explain any bruises from fighting to their wives, so they hand over their coins. Not bad. Whose idea was that?"

"Azoth's," a big said, pointing past the wetboy.

"Shut up, Roth!" the guild head said.

The wetboy looked at the small boy on the rooftop. He

was holding a rock aloft, his pale blue eyes intent, ready. He looked familiar. "Oh, now you've given him away," Durzo said.

"You shut up, too!" the guild head said, shaking the saber at him. "Hand over your purse or we'll kill you."

"Ja'laliel," a black guild rat said, "he called them 'bags.' A merchant wouldn't know we call 'em that. He's Sa'kagé."

"Shut up, Jarl! We need this." Ja'laliel coughed and spat blood. "Just give us your—"

"I don't have the time for this. Move," Durzo said.

"Hand it—"

The wetboy darted forward, his left hand twisting Ja'laliel's sword hand, snatching the saber, and his body spinning in. His right elbow cracked against the guild head's temple, but he pulled the blow so it wouldn't kill.

The fight was over by the time the guild rats flinched.

"I said I don't have time for this," Durzo said. He threw back his hood.

He knew he was nothing special to look at. He was lanky and sharp-featured, with dark blond hair and a wispy blond beard over lightly pockmarked cheeks. But he might have had three heads from the way the children shrank back.

"Durzo Blint," Roth murmured.

Rocks rattled to the ground.

"Durzo Blint," the name passed through the guild rats in waves. He saw fear and awe in their eyes. They'd just tried to mug a legend.

He smirked. "Sharpen this. Only an amateur lets his blade rust." He threw the saber into a gutter clotted with sewage. Then he walked through the mob. They scattered as if he might kill them all.

Azoth watched him stride into the early morning mists, disappearing like so many other hopes into the sinkhole of the Warrens. Durzo Blint was everything Azoth wasn't. He was powerful, dangerous, confident, fearless. He was like a god. He'd looked at the whole guild arrayed against him—even the bigs like Roth and Ja'laliel and Rat—and he'd been amused. Amused! *Someday,* Azoth swore. He didn't quite dare even think the whole thought, lest Blint sense his presumption, but his whole body yearned for it. *Someday.*

When Blint was far enough away not to notice, Azoth followed.

4

The bashers guarding the Nine's subterranean chamber eyed Durzo sourly. They were twins and two of the biggest men in the Sa'kagé. Each had a lightning bolt tattooed down his forehead.

"Weapons?" one said.

"Lefty," Durzo said in greeting, removing his sword, three daggers, the darts strapped to his wrist, and a number of small glass balls from his other arm.

"I'm Lefty," the other one said, patting down Blint vigorously.

"You mind?" Durzo asked. "We both know if I wanted to kill anyone in there I could, with or without weapons."

Lefty flushed. "Why don't I ram this pretty sword—"

"What Lefty means is, why don't you pretend not to be a threat, and we'll pretend we're the reason," Bernerd said. "It's just a formality, Blint. Like asking someone how they are when you don't care."

"I don't ask."

"I was sorry to hear about Vonda," Bernerd said. Durzo

stopped cold, a lance twisting through his guts. "Really," the big man said. He held the door open. Glanced at his brother.

Part of Durzo knew he should say something cutting or threatening or funny, but his tongue was leaden.

"Um, Master Blint?" Bernerd said. Recovering, Durzo stepped into the Nine's meeting room without raising his eyes.

It was a place to inspire fear. Carved from black fire-glass, a platform dominated the room. Nine chairs sat on the platform. A tenth chair sat above them like a throne. There was only bare floor facing the chairs. Those the Nine interviewed would stand.

The chamber was a tight rectangle, but it was deep. The ceiling was so high it disappeared in the darkness. It gave those questioned the feeling of being interrogated in hell. That the chairs, walls, and even the floor were carved with little gargoyles, dragons, and people, all screaming, did nothing to cool the effect.

But Durzo walked in with an easy familiarity. The night held no terrors for him. The shadows welcomed his eyes, hid nothing from him. *At least that much is left me.*

The Nine had their cowls on, except for Momma K, though most knew there was no hiding their identities from Durzo. Above them, the Shinga, Pon Dradin, sat in his throne. He was as still and silent as usual.

"Ith the wife dead?" Corbin Fishill asked. He was a fashionable, handsome man with a reputation for cruelty, especially toward those children in the guilds he managed. The laughter his lisp might have provoked somehow dried up under the ever-present malice on his face.

"Things aren't as you expected," Durzo said. He gave his report briefly. The king would soon die, and the men whom the Sa'kagé had feared would try to succeed him would not press their claim. That left the throne to Aleine Gunder, who was too weak to dare interfere with the Sa'kagé.

"I would suggest," Durzo said, "that we make the prince promote General Agon to lord general. Agon would keep the prince from consolidating his power, and if Khalidor makes any move—"

The tiny former slave master interrupted, "While we acknowledge your . . . complaint against Khalidor, Master Blint, we aren't to squander our political capital on some general."

"We don't have to," Momma K said. The Mistress of Pleasures was still beautiful, though it had been years since she was the city's most celebrated courtesan. "We can get what we want by pretending someone else asked for it." Everyone stopped and listened. "The prince was willing to buy off the general with a political marriage. So we tell him that Agon's price is a political appointment instead. The general won't ever know, and the prince isn't likely to ask about it."

"And that gives us leverage to reopen the slavery issue," the slave master said.

"I'll be damned if we turn slavers again," another said. He was a big man gone to fat, with heavy jowls, small eyes, and scarred fists befitting the master of the Sa'kagé's bashers.

"That converthation can wait. Blint doethn't need to be here for that," Corbin Fishill said. He turned his heavy-lidded eyes to Blint. "You didn't kill tonight." He let the statement hang, unadorned.

Durzo looked at him, refusing to take the provocation. "Can you thtill do it?"

Words were useless with a man like Corbin Fishill. He spoke the language of meat. Durzo walked to him. Corbin didn't flinch, didn't turn aside as Durzo came toward the platform, though several of the Nine were clearly nervous. Under Fishill's velvet trousers, Blint could see his muscles bunch.

Corbin kicked at Durzo's face, but Durzo had already moved. He slammed a needle deep into Corbin's calf and stepped back.

A bell rang and a moment later, Bernerd and Lefty burst into the room. Blint crossed his arms and made no move to defend himself.

Blint was tall, but his mass was all lean muscle and sinew. Lefty charged like a warhorse. Durzo merely extended both hands, unclenched, but when Lefty crashed into him, the impossible happened. Instead of crushing the smaller man, Lefty's sprint ended instantly.

His face stopped first, his nose popping against Durzo's open hand. The rest of him continued forward. His body lifted parallel to the ground, then crashed to the stone floor.

"Thtop!" Corbin Fishill shouted.

Bernerd skidded to a halt in front of Durzo and then knelt by his brother. Lefty was moaning, his bleeding nose filling the mouth of a rat carved into the rock floor.

Corbin pulled the needle out of his calf with a grimace. "What ith thith, Blint?"

"You want to know if I can still kill?" Durzo put a small

vial in front of the basher. "If that needle was poisoned, this is the antidote. But if the needle wasn't poisoned, the antidote will kill you. Drink it or don't."

"Drink it, Corbin," Pon Dradin said. It was the first time the Shinga had spoken since Blint entered. "You know, Blint, you'd be a better wetboy if you didn't know you were the best. You are—but you still take your orders from me. The next time you touch one of my Nine, there will be consequences. Now get the hell out."

The tunnel felt wrong. Azoth had been in other tunnels before, and if he wasn't exactly comfortable with moving through the cloying dark by touch, he could still do it. This tunnel had started out like any other: rough cut, winding, and of course dark. But as it plunged deeper into the earth, the walls got straighter, the floor smoother. This tunnel was important.

But that was different, not wrong. What was wrong was one step in front of Azoth. He squatted on his heels, resting, thinking. He didn't sit. You only sat when you knew there was nothing you'd have to run away from.

He couldn't smell anything different, though the air was as heavy and thick as gruel down here. If he squinted, he thought could see something, but he was pretty sure that was just from squeezing his eyes. He extended his hand again. Was the air cooler just there?

Then he was sure he felt the air shift. Sudden fear arced through Azoth. Blint had passed through here twenty minutes ago. He hadn't carried a torch. Azoth hadn't thought about it then. Now he remembered the stories.

A little puff of sour air lapped at his cheek. Azoth

almost ran, but he didn't know which way was safe to run. He had no way to defend himself. The Fist kept all the weapons. Another puff touched his other cheek. *It smells. Like garlic?*

"There are secrets in this world, kid," a voice said. "Secrets like magical alarms and the identities of the Nine. If you take another step, you'll find one of those secrets. Then two nice bashers with orders to kill intruders will find you."

"Master Blint?" Azoth searched the darkness.

"Next time you follow a man, don't be so furtive. It makes you conspicuous."

Whatever that meant, it didn't sound good. "Master Blint?"

He heard laughter up the tunnel, moving away.

Azoth jumped to his feet, feeling his hope slip away with the fading laughter. He ran up the tunnel in the dark. "Wait!"

There was no response. Azoth ran faster. A stone grabbed his foot and he fell roughly, skinning his knees and hands on the stone floor. "Master Blint, wait! I need to apprentice with you. Master Blint, please!"

The voice spoke just over him, though when he looked, Azoth could see nothing. "I don't take apprentices. Go home, kid."

"But I'm different! I'll do anything. I've got money!"

But there was no response. Blint was gone.

The silence ached, throbbed in time with the cuts on Azoth's knees and palms. But there was no help for it. He wanted to cry, but crying was for babies.

Azoth walked back to Black Dragon territory as the sky lightened. Parts of the Warrens were shaking off their drunken slumber. Bakers were up, and smiths' apprentices were starting forge fires, but the guild rats, the whores, the bashers, and the sneak thieves had gone to sleep, and the cutpurses, cons, sharps, and rest of those who worked the daylight were still asleep.

Usually, the smells of the Warrens were comfortable. There was the permeating smell of the cattle yards over the more immediate smells of human waste glooping through wide gutters in every street to further foul the Plith River, the rotting vegetation from the shallows and backwaters of the slow river, the less sour smell of the ocean when a lucky breeze blew, the stench of the sleeping never-washed beggars who might attack a guild rat for no reason other than their rage at the world. For the first time to Azoth, rather than home, the smells denoted filth. Rejection and despair were the vapors rising from every moldering ruin and shit pile in the Warrens.

The abandoned mill here, once used for hulling rice, wasn't just an empty building the guild could sleep in. It was a sign. Mills on the west shore would be looted by those so desperate they'd break past whatever bashers the mill owners hired. It was all garbage and rejection, and Azoth was part of it.

When he got to the guild home, Azoth nodded to the lookout and slipped inside with no attempt at stealth. The guild was used to children getting up to piss in the night, so no one would think he'd been out. If he tried to sneak in, he'd just draw attention to himself.

Maybe that was what furtive meant.

Lying down in his usual spot next to the window, he slipped between Doll Girl and Jarl. It got cold here, but the floor was flat and there weren't many splinters.

He nudged his friend. "Jay-Oh, you know what furtive means?"

But Jarl rolled away, grunting. Azoth poked him again, but Jarl wouldn't move. *Long night, I guess.*

Like all the guild rats, Azoth, Jarl, and Doll Girl slept close to each other for warmth. Usually Doll Girl got the middle because she was small and got cold so easy, but tonight Jarl and Doll Girl weren't lying close to each other.

Doll Girl scooted close and wrapped her arms around him, squeezing tightly, and Azoth was glad for her warmth. A worry gnawed at the back of his mind like a rat, but he was too tired. He slept.

$\underline{\underline{5}}$

*T*he nightmare started when Azoth woke.

"Good morning," Rat said. "How's my favorite little guttershite?" The glee on Rat's face told Azoth that something was seriously wrong. Roth and Harelip stood on either side of Rat, almost bursting with excitement.

Doll Girl was gone. Jarl was gone. Ja'laliel was nowhere to be seen. Blinking against the sunlight streaming through the guild home's torn roof, Azoth stood and tried to orient himself. The rest of the guild was gone, either working, scavenging, or just deciding that now would be a good time to be outside. So they'd seen Rat come in.

Roth stood by the back door, and Harelip stood behind Rat in case Azoth ran for the front door or a window.

"Where were you last night?" Rat asked.

"I had to piss."

"Long piss. You missed the fun." When Rat spoke like that, totally flat, no affect in his voice, Azoth felt a fear too deep to shiver out. Azoth knew violence. He'd seen sailors murdered, had seen prostitutes with fresh scars, had a friend die from a vendor's beating. Cruelty walked the Warrens holding hands with poverty and rage. But the dead look in Rat's eyes marked him as more of a freak than Harelip. Harelip had been born without part of his lip. Rat had been born without a conscience.

"What did you do?" Azoth asked.

"Roth?" Rat lifted his chin at the big.

Roth opened the door, said, "Good boy," as if speaking to a dog, and grabbed something. He hauled it inside, and Azoth saw that it was Jarl. Jarl's lips were swollen, both eyes black and so big he could barely see through the slits. He was missing teeth and he had crusted blood on his face from where his hair had been pulled so hard his scalp bled.

He was wearing a dress.

Azoth felt hot and cold tingles on his skin, a rush of blood to his face. He couldn't show Rat weakness. He couldn't move. He turned so he wouldn't throw up.

Behind him, Jarl let out a little whimper. "Azo, please. Azo, don't turn away from me. I didn't want—"

Rat struck him across the face. Jarl fell to the ground and didn't move.

"Jarl's mine now," Rat said. "He thinks he'll fight every night, and he will. For a while." Rat smiled. "But I'll break him. Time's on my side."

"I'll kill you. I swear it," Azoth said.

"Oh, are you Master Blint's apprentice now?" Rat smiled as Azoth shot Jarl a look, feeling betrayed. Jarl turned his face to the floor, his shoulders shaking as he cried silently. "Jarl told us all about it, sometime between Roth and Davi, I think. But I'm confused. If Master Blint apprenticed you, why are you here, Azo? You come back to kill me?"

Jarl's tears stilled and he turned, grasping at straws.

There was nothing to say. "He wouldn't take me," Azoth admitted. Jarl slumped.

"Everyone knows he doesn't take apprentices, stupid," Rat said. "So here's the deal, Azo. I don't know what you've done for him, but Ja'laliel's ordered me not to touch you, and I won't. But sooner or later, this'll be my guild."

"Sooner, I think," Roth said. He wiggled his eyebrows at Azoth.

"I have big plans for Black Dragon, Azo, and I won't let you get in my way," Rat said.

"What do you want from me?" Azoth's voice came out thin and reedy.

"I want you to be a hero. I want everyone who doesn't dare stand up to me themselves to look at you and start to hope. And then I will destroy everything you've done. I will destroy everything you love. I will destroy you so completely that no one will ever defy me again. So do your best, do your worst, do nothing at all. I win no matter what. I always do."

Azoth didn't pay dues the next day. He hoped Rat would hit him. Just once, and he'd be off the pedestal, he'd just be another guild rat. But Rat didn't hit him. He'd raged and swore, his eyes smiling, and told Azoth to bring double next time.

Of course, he brought nothing. He merely extended an empty hand, as if already beaten. It didn't matter. Rat raged, accused him of defying him, and didn't lay a hand on him. And so it was, every dues day. Gradually, Azoth went back to work and started accumulating coppers to put in Jarl's pack. The days were awful: Rat didn't let Jarl speak to Azoth, and after a while, Azoth didn't think Jarl even wanted to speak to him. The Jarl he knew disappeared by slow degrees. It didn't even help when they stopped making him wear the dress.

The nights were worse. Rat took Jarl every night while the rest of the guild pretended not to hear. Azoth and Doll Girl huddled together and in the quiet punctuated by low weeping afterward, Azoth lay on his back for long hours, plotting elaborate revenge that he knew he'd never carry out.

He became reckless, cursing Rat to his face, questioning every order the boy gave and championing anyone Rat beat. Rat swore back, but always with that little smile in his eyes. The littles and the losers in the guild started deferring to Azoth and looking at him with worshipful eyes.

Azoth could feel the guild reaching a critical mass the day two bigs brought him lunch and sat with him on the porch. It was a revelation. He'd never believed that any of the bigs would follow him. Why would they? He was nothing. And then he saw his mistake. He'd never made plans for what to do when bigs joined him. Across the yard, Ja'laliel sat, miserable, coughing blood and looking hopeless.

I'm so stupid. Rat had been waiting for this. He'd arranged for Azoth to be a hero. He'd even told him. This wasn't going to be a coup. It was going to be a purge.

"Father, please, don't go." Logan Gyre held his father's destrier, ignoring the predawn chill and holding back tears.

"No, leave it," Duke Gyre told Wendel North, his steward, who was directing servants with chests full of the duke's clothing. "But I want a thousand wool cloaks sent within a week. Use our funds and don't ask for repayment. I don't want to give the king an excuse to say no." He clasped gauntleted hands behind his back. "I don't know what shape the garrison's stables are in, but I'd like to have word from Havermere of how many horses they can send before winter."

"Already done, milord."

On every side, servants were coming and going, loading the wagons that would travel north with provisions and supplies. A hundred Gyre knights made their own last-minute preparations, checking their saddles, horses, and weapons. Servants who would be leaving their families said hurried goodbyes.

Duke Gyre turned to Logan, and just seeing his father in his mail brought tears of pride and fear to Logan's eyes.

"Son, you're twelve years old."

"I can fight. Even Master Vorden admits that I handle a sword almost as well as the soldiers."

"Logan, it isn't because I don't believe in your abilities that I'm making you stay. It's because I do. The fact is, your mother needs you here more than I need you in the mountains."

"But I want to go with you."

"And I don't want to leave at all. It doesn't have anything to do with what we want."

"Jasin said Niner is trying to embarrass you. He said it's an insult for a duke to be given such a small command." He didn't mention the other things Jasin had said. Logan didn't consider himself quick-tempered, but in the three months since King Davin had died and Aleine Gunder had assumed the title Aleine IX—known condescendingly as Niner—Logan had been in half a dozen fights.

"And what do you think, son?"

"I don't think you're afraid of anyone."

"So Jasin said I was afraid, did he? Is that where you got the bruises on your knuckles?"

Logan grinned suddenly. He was as tall as his father, and if he didn't have Regnus Gyre's bulk yet, their guards master Ren Vorden said it was only a matter of time. When Logan fought other boys, he didn't lose.

"Son, make no mistake. Commanding the garrison at Screaming Winds is a slight, but it's better than exile or death. If I stay, the king will give me one or the other eventually. Each summer, you'll come train with my men, but I need you here, too. For half the year you'll be my eyes and ears in Cenaria. Your mother—" he broke off and looked past Logan.

"Thinks your father is a fool," Catrinna Gyre said, coming up behind them suddenly. She had been born to another ducal family, the Graesins, and she had their green eyes, petite features, and temper. Despite the early hour, she was dressed in a beautiful green silk dress edged with ermine, her hair brushed glossy. "Regnus, if you get on that horse, I never want to see you come back."

"Catrinna, we aren't having this discussion again."

"That jackal will hurl you against my family, you know that. Destroy you, destroy them—he wins no matter what."

"*This* is your family, Catrinna. And I've made my decision." Duke Gyre's voice carried with a whip crack of command, an edge that made Logan want to shrink and not be noticed.

"Which of your harlots are you taking with you?"

"I'm not taking any of the maidservants, Catrinna, though some of them will be hard to replace. I'm leaving them here out of respect for your—"

"How stupid do you think I am? You'll just find sluts there."

"Catrinna. Go inside. Now!"

She obeyed and Duke Gyre watched her go. He spoke without turning toward Logan. "Your mother . . . there are things I'll share with you when you're older. For now, I expect you to honor her, but you will be Lord Gyre while I'm gone."

Logan's eyes went wide.

His father clapped him on the shoulder. "That doesn't mean you get to skip your lessons. Wendel will teach you everything you need to know. I swear the man understands more about running our lands than I do. I'm only a four-day ride away. You have a fine mind, son, and that's why you have to stay. This city is a vipers' nest. There are those who would destroy us. Your mother has seen hints of that, and it's been part of her troubles. I'm gambling with you, Logan. I wish I didn't have to, but you're the only piece I have left to play. Surprise them. Be smarter, better, braver, and faster than anyone expects. It's not a fair burden for me to put on you, but I must. I'm counting on you. House Gyre is counting on you. All our retainers and vassals are counting on you, and maybe even the kingdom itself."

Duke Gyre swung up onto his huge white destrier. "I love you, son. But don't let me down."

6

The darkness was as close and cold as the dead's embrace. Azoth squatted against the alley wall, hoping the night wind covered the sound of thunder in his heart. The fifth big who'd joined him had stolen a shiv from Rat's weapons cache, and Azoth clutched the thin metal so tightly his hand hurt.

There was still no motion in the alley. Azoth stuck the blade in the dirt of the alley and put his hands in his armpits to keep them warm. Nothing might happen for hours. It didn't matter. He was running out of chances. He'd wasted too much time as it was.

Rat wasn't stupid. He was cruel, but he had plans. Azoth didn't. He'd been flailing in his fear for three months. Flailing when he could have been planning. The Fist had declared his intentions. That made it easy enough. Azoth knew some of what he was planning; all he had to do was piece together how. Now, as he thought, he could feel himself slipping into Rat's skin all too easily, thinking Rat's thoughts.

A purge isn't good enough. A purge will give me safety for a couple of years. Other guild heads have killed to keep their power. Killing doesn't make me different. Azoth worked on the idea. Rat didn't have small ambitions. Rat had bottled up his hatred for three months. Why would he be willing to not even hit Azoth for three months?

Destruction. That's what it came down to. Rat would destroy him in spectacular fashion. He would sate his own cruelty and advance his power. He would do something so awful that Azoth would become a story the guilds would tell. He might not even kill him, just leave him maimed in some horrific way so that everyone who met Azoth would fear Rat more.

There was a shuffling sound in the alley and Azoth tensed. Slowly, so slowly, he pulled out the shiv. The alley was tight, the buildings sagging so close a grown man could touch both walls at the same time. Azoth had chosen it for that reason. He wouldn't let his quarry slip past him. But now the walls seemed malevolent, stretching hungry fingers toward each other, closing out the stars, grabbing for him. Wind muttered over the roofs, telling tales of murder.

Azoth heard the shuffle again and relaxed. A scarred old rat emerged from under a pile of moldering boards and sniffed. Azoth held still as the rat waddled forward. It sniffed at Azoth's bare feet, nudged them with a wet nose, and sensing no danger, moved forward to feed.

Just as the rat moved to bite, Azoth buried the shiv behind its ear and into the ground beneath. It jerked but didn't squeak. He withdrew the thin iron, satisfied with his stealth. He checked the alley again. Still nothing.

So where am I weak? What would I *do to destroy me if I were Rat?*

Something tickled his neck and he brushed it away. *Curse the bugs.*

Bugs? It's freezing out here. His hand came down from his neck warm and sticky.

Azoth turned and lashed out, but the shiv went spinning from his hand as something struck his wrist.

Durzo Blint squatted on his heels not a foot away. He didn't speak. He just stared, his eyes colder than the night.

There was a long pause as they stared at each other, neither saying a word. "You saw the rat," Azoth said.

An eyebrow lifted.

"You cut me where I cut it. You were showing me that you're as much better than me as I am better than the rat."

A hint of a smile. "A strange little guild rat you are. So smart, so stupid."

Azoth looked at the shiv—now magically in Durzo's hand—and felt ashamed. He *was* stupid. What had he been thinking? He was going to threaten a wetboy? But he said, "I'm going to apprentice with you."

Blint's open hand cracked across his face and sent him sprawling into the wall. His face scraped against rock and he landed heavily.

When he rolled over, Blint was standing over him. "Give me one good reason why I shouldn't kill you," Blint said.

Doll Girl. She wasn't only the answer to Blint's question, she was Azoth's weakness. She was where Rat would strike. A wave of nausea swept over Azoth. First Jarl and now Doll Girl.

"You should," Azoth said.

Blint raised an eyebrow again.

"You're the best wetboy in the city, but you're not the only one. And if you won't apprentice me and you don't kill me, I'll train under Hu Gibbet or Scarred Wrable. I'll spend my life training just for the moment I have my chance at you. I'll wait until you think I've forgotten today. I'll wait until you think it was just a dumb guild rat's threat. After I'm a master, you'll jump at shadows for a while. But after you jump a dozen times and I'm not there, you won't jump just once, and that's when I'll be there. I don't care if you kill me at the same time. I'll trade my life for yours."

Durzo's eyes barely had to shift to go from dangerously amused to simply dangerous. But Azoth didn't even see them through the tears brimming in his own eyes. He only saw the vacant look that had come into Jarl's eyes and imagined seeing it in Doll Girl's. He imagined her screams if Rat came and took her every night. She'd scream wordlessly for the first few weeks, maybe fight— bite and scratch for a while—and then she wouldn't scream anymore, wouldn't fight at all. There would just be grunting and the sounds of flesh and Rat's pleasure. Just like Jarl.

"Is your life so empty, boy?"

It will be if you say no. "I want to be like you."

"No one wants to be like me." Blint drew a huge black sword and touched the edge to Azoth's throat. In that moment, Azoth didn't care if the blade drank his life's blood.

Death would be kinder than watching Doll Girl disappear before his eyes.

"You like hurting people?" Blint asked.

"No, sir."

"Ever killed anyone?"

"No."

"Then why are you wasting my time?"

What was wrong with him? Did he really mean that? He couldn't. "I heard you don't like it. That you don't have to like it to be good," Azoth said.

"Who told you that?"

"Momma K. She said that's the difference between you and some of the others."

Blint frowned. He pulled a clove of garlic from a pouch and popped it into his mouth. He sheathed his sword, chewing.

"All right, kid. You want to get rich?" Azoth nodded. "You're quick. But can you tell what your marks are thinking and remember fifty things at once? Do you have good hands?" Nod. Nod. Nod.

"Be a gambler." Durzo laughed.

Azoth didn't. He looked at his feet. "I don't want to be afraid anymore."

"Ja'laliel beats you?"

"Ja'laliel's nothing."

"Then who is?" Blint asked.

"Our Fist. Rat." Why was it so hard to say his name?

"He beats you?"

"Unless you'll . . . unless you'll do things with him." It sounded weak, and Blint didn't say anything, so Azoth said, "I won't let anyone beat me again. Not ever."

Blint kept looking past Azoth, giving him time to blink

away his tears. The full moon bathed the city in golden light. "The old whore can be beautiful," he said. "Despite everything."

Azoth followed Blint's gaze, but there was no one else in sight. Silver mist rose from the warm manure of the cattle yards and coiled around old broken aqueducts. In the darkness, Azoth couldn't see the Bleeding Man freshly scrawled over his own guild's Black Dragon, but he knew it was there. His guild had been losing territory steadily since Ja'laliel got sick.

"Sir?" Azoth said.

"This city's got no culture but street culture. The buildings are brick on one street, daub and wattle the next, and bamboo one over. Titles Alitaeran, clothes Callaean, music all Sethi harps and Lodricari lyres—the damn rice paddies themselves stolen from Ceura. But as long as you don't touch her or look too close, sometimes she's beautiful."

Azoth thought he understood. You had to be careful what you touched and where you walked in the Warrens. Pools of vomit and other bodily fluids were splattered in the streets, and the dung-fueled fires and fatty steam from the constantly boiling tallow vats covered everything with a greasy, sooty sheen. But he had no reply. He wasn't even sure Blint was talking to him.

"You're close, boy. But I never take apprentices, and I won't take you." Blint paused, and idly spun the shiv from finger to finger. "Not unless you do something you can't."

Hope burst into life in Azoth's breast for the first time in months. "I'll do anything," he said.

"You'd have to do it alone. No one else could know.

You'd have to figure out how, when, and where. All by yourself."

"What do I have to do?" Azoth asked. He could feel the Night Angels curling their fingers around his stomach. How did he know what Blint was going to say next?

Blint picked up the dead rat and threw it to Azoth. "Just this. Kill your Rat and bring me proof. You've got a week."

7

Solon Tofusin led the nag up Sidlin Way between the gaudy, close-packed manses of the great families of Cenaria. Many of the houses were less than a decade old. Others were older but had been recently remodeled. The buildings along this one street were qualitatively different from all the rest of Cenarian architecture. These had been made by those hoping their money could purchase culture. All were ostentatious, trying to rival their neighbors by their exotic design, whether in builders' fantasies of Ladeshian spires or Friaki pleasure domes or in more accurately articulated Alitaeran mansions or perfect scale imitations of famous Ceuran summer palaces. There was even what he thought he recognized from a painting as a bulbous Ymmuri temple, complete with prayer flags. Slave money, he thought.

It wasn't slavery that appalled him. On his island, slavery was common. But not like it had been here. These manses had been built on pit fighters and baby farms. It had been out of his way, but he'd walked through the

Warrens to see what the silent half of his new home city was like. The squalor there made the wealth here obscene.

He was tired. Though not tall, he was thick. Thick through the stomach and, mercifully, still thicker through the chest and shoulders. The nag was a good horse, but she was no warhorse, and he had to walk her as often as he rode.

The large estates loomed ahead, differentiated from the others not so much by the size of the buildings as by the amount of land within the walls. Where the manses were packed side by side, the estates sprawled. Guards presided over gates of ironwood rather than intricate grillwork— gates built long ago for defense, not decoration.

The gate of the first estate bore the Jadwin trout inlaid with gold leaf. Through the sally port, he saw a lavish garden filled with statues, some marble, some covered with beaten gold. *No wonder they have a dozen guards.* All the guards were professional and a few furlongs short of handsome, which gave credence to the rumors about the duchess, and he was more than happy to pass the Jadwin estate. He was a handsome man with olive skin, black eyes, and hair still black as a night untouched by the gray shadows of dawn. Sharing a house with a voracious duchess whose husband left on frequent and lengthy embassies was trouble he didn't need.

Not that I'll find less where I'm going. Dorian, my friend, I hope this was genius. He didn't want to consider the other possibility.

"I am Solon Tofusin. I'm here to see Lord Gyre," Solon said as he arrived in front of the Gyre estate's gate.

"The duke?" the guard asked. He pushed his helm back and scraped a hand across his forehead.

The man's a simpleton. "Yes, Duke Gyre." He spoke slowly and with more emphasis than was necessary, but he was tired.

"That's a crying shame," the guard said.

Solon waited, but the man didn't elaborate. *Not a simpleton, an ass.* "Is Lord Gyre gone?"

"Nawp."

So that's what this is about. The red hair should have tipped me off. Solon said, "I know that after millennia of being raided, the smarter Ceurans moved inland, leaving your ancestors on the coast, and I realize that when Sethi pirates raided your village they carried off all the presentable women—again leaving your ancestors—so through no fault of your own, you're both stupid and ugly. But might you attempt to explain how Lord Gyre is both gone and not gone? You can use small words."

Perversely, the man looked pleased. "No marks on your skin, no rings through your face, you don't even talk like a fish. And you're fat for a fish, too. Let me guess, they offered you to the sea but the sea gods wouldn't take you and when you washed up on the beach you were nursed by a troll who mistook you for one of her own."

"She was blind," Solon said, and when the man laughed, he decided he liked him.

"Duke Gyre left this morning. He won't be back," the guard said.

"He won't be back? You mean ever?"

"Not my place to talk about it. But no, not ever, unless I miss my guess. He's gone to command the garrison at Screaming Winds."

"But you said Lord Gyre isn't gone," Solon said.

"The duke named his son the Gyre until he returns."

"Which will be never."

"You're quick for a fish. His son Logan is the Gyre."

Not good. For the life of him, Solon couldn't remember if Dorian had said Duke Gyre or Lord Gyre. Solon hadn't even considered that there might be two heads of House Gyre. If the prophecy was about Duke Gyre, he needed to get riding, now. But if it were about his son, Solon would be leaving his charge at the time he needed him most.

"May I speak with Lord Gyre?"

"Can you use that steel?" the guard asked. "If you can't, I'd suggest you hide it."

"Excuse me?"

"Don't say I didn't warn you. Come with me." The guard called to another atop the wall, who came to hold the gate while the Ceuran led Solon into the estate. A stable boy took the nag, and Solon kept his sword.

He couldn't help but be impressed. The Gyre estate had a permanence about it, the deliberate gravitas of an old family. Acanthus was planted inside the walls and out, growing from red soil Solon knew must have been brought in especially for the purpose. The thistly plants hadn't just been chosen to keep beggars or thieves from the walls, they also had long associations with Alitaeran nobility. The manse itself was similarly daunting, all heavy stone and broad arches and thick doors that could withstand a siege engine. The only compromise strength had made with beauty were the climbing blood roses that framed each door and every ground floor window. Against the backdrop of black stone and iron-barred windows, their perfect red hue was striking.

Solon didn't pay attention to the ringing of steel until the guard walked past the entry to the manse and around to the back of the building. Here, with a view across the Plith to Castle Cenaria, several guards were watching as two men bundled in practice armor pummeled each other. The smaller man was retreating, going back in circles as the larger man's blows thudded on his shield. The smaller man stumbled, and his opponent bull-rushed, leveling him with a shield like a ram. The man raised his sword, but the next blow sent it flying and the next rang his helmet like a bell.

Logan Gyre tore off his helmet and laughed, helping the guard to his feet. Solon's heart sank. This was Lord Gyre? He was a child in a giant's body, baby fat still on his face. He couldn't have been more than fourteen, probably younger. Solon could imagine Dorian laughing. Dorian knew he didn't like children.

The Ceuran guard stepped forward and spoke quietly to Lord Gyre.

"Hello," the boy lord said, turning to Solon. "Marcus tells me you fancy yourself quite a swordsman. Are you?"

Solon looked at the Ceuran, who gave him a self-satisfied smile. *His name is Marcus?* Even the names in this country were a mess. With little regard for people's origins, Alitaeran names like Marcus or Lucienne mixed freely with Lodricari names like Rodo or Daydra, Ceuran names like Hideo or Shizumi, and normal Cenarian names like Aleine or Felene. About the only names most people wouldn't name their children were the slaves names common in the Warrens, like Scar or Harelip. "I can hold my own, Lord Gyre. But it is words I wish to exchange with you, not blows." *If I go now, my old mare and I can make it to the garrison in six, maybe seven days.*

"We will speak then—after we spar. Marcus, get him some practice armor." The men looked pleased, and Solon saw that they loved this young lord like he was their own son. And laughed too easily and spoiled him. He was suddenly the Gyre, and the men were still entranced by the novelty of the idea.

"I don't need it," Solon said.

The chuckling stopped and the men looked at him.

"You want to spar without armor?" Logan asked.

"I don't want to spar at all, but if it is your will, I shall consent—but I won't fight with a practice blade." The men hooted at the prospect of seeing this short Sethi fight their giant, unarmored. Only Marcus and one or two others looked troubled. With the thick armor Logan wore, there was little danger that he would be seriously injured, even with a sharp sword. But the danger was there. In his eyes, Solon saw that Logan knew it too. He was suddenly doubting if he should have been quite so brash with someone who he knew nothing about, someone who might well wish him harm. Logan was looking again at Solon's stocky build.

"Milord," Marcus said, "maybe it would be best if—"

"Agreed," Logan said to Solon. He pulled his helmet on and locked the visor. He unlimbered his sword and said, "Ready when you are."

Before Logan could react, Solon jabbed his fingers through the boy's visor and grabbed the nosepiece. He yanked Logan forward and twisted. The boy slammed into the ground with a grunt. Solon drew a knife from Logan's belt and held it to the boy's eye, his knee resting on the side of Logan's helmet, holding it in place.

"Do you yield?" Solon asked.

The boy's breaths were labored. "I yield."

Solon released him and stood, brushing the dust from the leg of his breeches. He didn't offer to help Lord Gyre stand.

The men were quiet. Several had drawn swords, but none moved forward. It was obvious that if Solon had meant to kill Logan, he would have already done it. No doubt they were thinking about what Duke Gyre would have done to them if such a thing had happened.

"You're a fool boy, Lord Gyre," Solon said. "A buffoon performing for men you may one day have to ask to die for you." *He said Duke Gyre, surely Dorian said* Duke *Gyre. But he sent me here. Surely he would have sent me to the garrison directly if he meant the duke. The prophecy wasn't about me. Dorian couldn't have known that I would be held up, that I would get to the city this late. Could he?*

Logan removed his helmet, and he was red-faced, but he didn't let his embarrassment flare into anger. He said, "I, I deserved that. And I deserved the manhandling you just gave me. Or worse. I'm sorry. It is a poor host who assaults his guests."

"You know they've been losing on purpose, don't you?"

Logan looked stricken. He glanced at the man he'd been fighting as Solon arrived, then stared at his own feet. Then, as if it took an effort of will, he raised his eyes to Solon's. "I see that you speak true. Though it shames me to learn it, I thank you." And now his men looked ashamed. They'd been letting him win because they loved him, and now they had shamed their lord. The men weren't just pained, they were in misery.

How does this boy command such loyalty? Is it just loyalty to his father? As he watched Logan look at each of the men in turn—staring until each met his gaze and then looked away—Solon doubted that. Logan let the pained silence sit and grow.

"In six months' time," Logan said, addressing the men, "I will serve at my father's garrison. I will not sit safely in the castle. I will fight, and so will many of you. But since you seem to think sparring is entertainment, very well. You will entertain yourselves by sparring until midnight. All of you. Tomorrow, we will start training. And I expect all of you to be here an hour before dawn. Understood?"

"Yes, sir!"

Logan turned to Solon. "Sorry about that, Master Tofusin. About all of it. Please call me Logan. You'll stay for dinner, of course, but can I also have the servants prepare a room for you?"

"Yes," Solon said. "I think I'd like that."

8

*E*very time Vürdmeister Neph Dada met with Rat, it was in a different place. Rooms in inns, cellars of boat shops, bakeries, east side parks, and dead-end alleys in the Warrens. Ever since Neph had figured out that Rat was afraid of the dark, he'd made sure they always met at night.

Tonight, Neph watched Rat and his bodyguards enter the tiny old overfull graveyard. It wasn't as dark as Neph would have hoped; taverns and game halls and whorehouses huddled not thirty paces away. Rat didn't dismiss his bodyguards immediately. Like most parts of the Warrens, the graveyard was less than a foot above the waterline. The Rabbits, as the natives of the Warrens were called, buried their dead directly in the mud. If they had the money, they erected sarcophagi above ground, but ignorant immigrants had buried their dead in coffins after some riot or another years ago, and the ground had swollen above those graves as the coffins fought to float to the surface. Several had broken open, their contents devoured by feral dogs.

Rat and his bodyguards looked sick with fright. "Go on," Rat finally said to his bigs, nonchalantly picking up a skull and tossing it at one of them. The boy stepped back quickly and the skull, weak with age or disease, shattered on a stone.

"Hello, child," Neph rasped into Rat's ear. Rat flinched and Neph smiled his gap-toothed smile, his long, sparse white hair falling in a greasy trickle to his shoulders. Neph stood so close the boy took a step back.

"What do you want? Why am I here?" Rat asked.

"Ah, petulance and philosophy all bound up in one." Neph shuffled closer. He'd grown up in Lodricar, east of Khalidor. The Lodricari thought men who distanced themselves so much that you couldn't even smell their breath were hiding something. Merchants in Cenaria who dealt with the Lodricari complained bitterly about it, but stood close eagerly enough when Lodricari coins were at stake. But Neph didn't stand close for cultural reasons. He hadn't lived in Lodricar for half a century. He stood close because he liked to see Rat's discomfort.

"Ha!" Neph said, exhaling a gust of rotten air over Rat's face.

"What?" Rat said, trying not to edge back.

"I haven't given up on you yet, you great stupid boy. Sometimes you manage to learn despite yourself. But that's not what I'm here for. Not what you're here for, either. It's time to move. Your enemies are arrayed against you but not yet organized."

"How do you know that?"

"I know more than you think, Ratty Fatty." Neph laughed again, and spittle flew onto Rat's face. Rat almost struck him then, Neph could tell. Rat had become a guild Fist for a reason. But of course he'd never hit Neph. The old man knew he looked frail, but a Vürdmeister had other defenses.

"Do you know how many boys your father has whelped?" Neph asked.

Rat looked around the graveyard as if Neph hadn't already checked for anyone eavesdropping. The boy was hopelessly stupid. Stupid, but capable of cunning, and utterly ruthless. Besides, Neph didn't have many choices. When he'd come to Cenaria, he'd been placed in charge of four boys. The most promising one had eaten some bad meat in the first year and died before Neph had even known he was sick. This week, the second had been killed in territory fight between guilds. That left Neph with only two. "His Holiness has fathered one hundred and thirty-two boys the last time I counted. Most of those lacked Talent and were culled. You are one of forty-three who are his seed. I've told you this before. What I haven't told you is that each of you is given a task, a test to prove your usefulness to your father. If you pass, you may one day become Godking yourself. Can you guess what your task is?"

Rat's beady eyes glittered with visions of opulent splendor.

Neph slapped him. "Your task, boy."

Rat rubbed his cheek, trembling with rage. "Become Shinga," he said quietly.

Well, the boy aimed higher than Neph would have guessed. Good. "His Holiness has declared that Cenaria will fall, as will all the southlands. The Sa'kagé is the only real power in Cenaria, so, yes, you will become Shinga. Then you will give your father Cenaria and everything in it—or, more likely, you will fail and die and one of your brothers will do this."

"There are others in the city?" Rat asked.

"Your father is a god, but his tools are men, and thus fail. His Holiness plans accordingly. Now my little failure-in-waiting, what is your brilliant plan to deal with Azoth?"

Rage roared high in Rat's eyes once more, but he controlled it. One word from Neph, and Rat would be one more corpse floating in the Plith by morning, and they both knew it. In truth, Neph was testing him. Cruelty was Rat's greatest asset—Neph had seen Rat's bloodthirstiness cow older boys who might have killed him—but it was worthless if he couldn't control it.

Rat said, "I'll kill Azoth. I'll make him bleed like—"

"What you can't do is kill him. If you do, he will be forgotten; another will take his place. He must live broken, where all the world can see him."

"I'll beat him in front of everyone. I'll break his hands and—"

"What happens if his *lizards* rush to defend him?"

"They, they wouldn't. They're too afraid."

"Unlike other boys I know," Neph said, "Azoth isn't stupid. He knew what it meant when those bigs came to him. He may have even been planning for this all along. The first thing he'll expect is that you'll get scared and try to beat him. So he'll have a plan for it."

Neph watched the realization settle on Rat that he might actually lose control of the guild. If he lost the guild, he'd lose his life.

"But you have a plan," Rat said. "A way I can destroy him, don't you?"

"And I might even share it," Neph said.

*   *   *

It was coming. Azoth could feel it as he lay on the floor, surrounded by his lizards, his guild. *His.* Fifteen littles and five bigs. Half the littles in Black Dragon and a quarter of the bigs were his now. They slept peacefully around him, probably even Badger, who was supposed to only be feigning sleep.

Azoth hadn't slept for four days. The night he'd come home from talking to Blint and every night since, he'd lain awake, plotting, doubting, feverish with excitement about a life without Rat. And the rising light of day had melted his plans with the fog. He'd called those who stood with him his lizards as a joke—they certainly weren't dragons—but the children had taken the name proudly, deaf to the despair in the label.

During the days, he'd acted, given orders, formed his pathetic lizards into a force, done anything to keep his mind off killing Rat. How long would Rat wait? The time for a purge was now. Everyone was waiting to see what Rat would do. Everyone was still sure that he would do something. If he didn't, though, and soon, his faithful would start to doubt him, and he'd lose the guild in an instant.

Azoth had even given orders for three of the littles he trusted most to guard Doll Girl at all times. Then he'd doubted himself. It wasn't a good use of the strength he had. He needed those littles bringing him information: listening to the others in the guild, searching the other guilds to see if any of the neighboring guilds would like the lizards to join them. Besides, what could three littles do against all of Rat's bigs? Children who were eight, ten, and eleven respectively weren't going to stop Rat's fifteen- and sixteen-year-olds. He'd ended up assigning two of the bigs who had joined him first to watch over her, and had kept her close during every waking hour.

He was slipping, though. The nights without sleep were catching up with him. His mind was a muddle. It was only a matter of time until he made a stupid mistake. And all of it was because he didn't have the guts to kill Rat.

He could do it tonight. It would be easy, really. Rat had gone out before midnight with two bigs, but when they got back, he'd fall asleep instantly. The bastard never had trouble sleeping. Azoth had the shiv. He even had a real knife that one of the bigs had stolen. All he had to do was walk up to Rat and stick it in him. Anywhere in the stomach would work. Even if Rat's dragons were loyal enough to take him to a healer, they'd certainly take all of his money. What healer was going to work for free on a guild rat? All Azoth had to do was wait until five minutes after Rat got back, then get up to piss. On his way back in, he'd kill him.

It was the only way Doll Girl would ever be safe.

He knew what becoming a wetboy would mean. Everything would change. Wetboys were knives in the dark. Azoth would learn how to fight, how to kill. He wouldn't just learn how, he'd do it. Blint would expect him to kill. That niggled at him like a stare from Doll Girl that wouldn't really count unless he met her eyes. But he didn't think much about the specifics of murdering. He held onto that image of Durzo Blint, laughing at the entire guild. Durzo Blint, laughing at Rat and his little army. Durzo Blint, fearless. Durzo Blint, who Azoth could *be*.

Blint would take him away. Azoth wouldn't lead Black Dragon. He wouldn't even lead his lizards. But he didn't want to. He didn't want the littles looking at him like he was their father, the bigs who towered over him looking at him like he knew what he was doing, like he would keep them all safe. He couldn't even keep himself safe. This was all a fraud. He was a fraud. He'd been set up, and they didn't even see it.

The unmistakable sound of the front door being moved aside heralded Rat's return. Azoth was so scared he would have wept if he hadn't told Badger to stay awake. He couldn't weep in front of his bigs. He was sure Rat would come over to him, have the bigs lift him up, and take him away to some horrific punishment that would make Jarl's look easy. But true to form, Rat pushed into his harem, lay down, and was asleep in seconds.

A wetboy wouldn't cry. Azoth tried to slow his breathing, tried to listen to see if Rat's bodyguards were asleep, too.

Wetboys weren't afraid. They were killers. Other people were afraid of them. Everyone in the Sa'kagé was afraid of them.

If I lie here and try to sleep again, I might sleep here with nothing happening for another night or another week, but Rat will get me. He'll destroy everything. Azoth had seen the look in his eyes. He believed Rat would destroy him, and he didn't believe that it would be a week before he did. *It's either that or I kill him first.* In his mind, Azoth saw himself as a hero, like something out of a bard's tale: giving Jarl his money back, giving Ja'laliel enough to buy review, everyone in the guild loving him for killing Rat, and Doll Girl speaking for the first time, approval glowing in her eyes, telling how brave he was.

It was stupid, and he couldn't afford stupidity.

He had to piss. Azoth got up angrily and walked out the back door. Rat's bodyguards didn't even shift in their sleep as he walked past them.

The night air was cold and rank. Azoth had been spending most of the collection money to feed his lizards. Today, he'd bought fish. The ever-hungry littles had gotten into the entrails and eaten them and gotten sick. His urine arcing into the alley, he thought that he should have had someone watching out for that. It was just something else he'd missed.

He heard a scuffing sound from inside and turned, lacing his breeches up. Looking into the darkness, though, he saw nothing. He was losing it, jumping at sounds when there were three score guild rats pressed together in the house, sleeping, moaning on empty bellies, and rolling into their neighbors.

Suddenly, he smiled and touched the shiv. There might be a hundred things he didn't know and a thousand more he couldn't control, but he knew what he needed to do now.

Rat had to die; it was that simple. What happened to Azoth after he did it didn't even matter. Whether they thanked him or killed him, he had to kill Rat. He had to kill him before Rat got to Doll Girl. He had to kill him now.

And with that, the decision was made. Azoth held the shiv up along his wrist and stepped inside. Rat would be sleeping wedged in with his harem. It would only be two steps out of Azoth's way. Azoth would pretend to stumble in case the bigs were watching, and then plunge the shiv into Rat's stomach. He would stab him over and over until Rat was dead or he was.

Azoth was within four steps of his attack when he came in sight of his own sleeping space.

Badger was lying on his back in the darkness, a thin line drawn across his neck, black on white skin. His eyes were open, but he wasn't moving.

Doll Girl's space was empty. She was gone, and so was Rat.

$$\underline{\underline{9}}$$

$\mathcal{H}$e lay in the darkness, too stunned to weep. Even in his sudden blind shock, Azoth knew that Rat's bigs couldn't be asleep. This was what they had been waiting for. Azoth had left for the barest minute, and they had taken Doll Girl. It wouldn't even do him any good to wake the whole guild. In the darkness and confusion, he'd never know just which of Rat's bigs was gone. And what would he do even if he knew? Even if he knew who was gone, he wouldn't know where they'd gone. Even if he knew where they'd gone, what would he do?

He lay in the darkness, stumbling over thoughts, staring at the sagging ceiling. He'd heard them. Damn him forever. He'd heard the sound and didn't even go look.

He lay in the darkness, finished. The watch changed. The sun rose. The guild rats stirred, and he stared at the sagging ceiling, waiting for it to collapse on him like everything else. He couldn't have moved if he wanted to.

He lay in the light. Children were shrieking, littles pulling at him, shouting something. Something about Badger.

Questions. It was all words. Words were wind. Someone shook him, but he was far away.

It wasn't until long after that that he woke. There was only one sound that could have brought him out of his trance: Rat, laughing.

Tingles shot across his skin and he sat upright. He still had the shiv. There was dried blood on the floor, but Azoth barely saw it. He stood and started walking toward the door.

That terrible laugh rang out again, and Azoth ran.

The moment he stepped through the door, out of the corner of his eye he saw the shadow of the doorframe elongate and snap forward. It was as fast as a trapdoor spider he'd once seen, and just as effective. He slammed into the shadow like he'd run into a wall. His head rang as he was pulled back into the deep shadows between the guild building and the ruin next to it.

"So eager for death, little one?"

Azoth couldn't shake his head, couldn't shake loose. The shadow had a hand like iron over his face. Slowly, he realized it was Master Blint.

"Five days, kid. Five days you had to kill him." He was whispering in Azoth's ear, the faintest hint of garlic and onions laced through his breath. In front of them, Rat was talking with the guild, laughing and making them laugh with him. Some of Azoth's lizards were there, laughing too, hoping to escape Rat's notice.

So it begins already. Whatever Azoth had accomplished was already coming apart. The rest of the lizards were gone. Doubtless they'd come crawling back later to see what had happened. Azoth couldn't even be mad at them for it. In the Warrens, you did what you had to to survive. It wasn't their failure; it was his. Blint was right: the bigs on either side of Rat were ready. Rat himself was ready. If Azoth had charged out there, he would have died. Or worse. All the time he'd had to plan, and he'd done nothing. He would have deserved that death.

"Calm now, kid?" Blint asked. "Good. Because I'm going to show you what your hesitation cost."

Solon was ushered in to dinner by an old man with a stooped back and a smartly pressed uniform adorned with gold braid and the Gyre's soaring white falcon on a field sable, which over the centuries had become barely recognizable as the gyrfalcon it was. A northern falcon. And not Khalidoran or even Lodricari, gyrfalcons were only found in the Freeze. *So the Gyres are hardly more native to Cenaria than I am.*

Dinner was set in the great hall, a strange choice to Solon's mind. It wasn't that the great hall wasn't impressive—it was too much so. It must have been almost as large as Castle Cenaria's own great hall, adorned with tapestries, banners, shields of long-dead enemies, enormous canvasses, statuary in marble and gold leaf, and a ceiling mural depicting a scene from the Alkestia. In the midst of such grandeur, the table was dwarfed to insignificance, though it was fifteen paces long.

"Lord Solon Tofusin, of House Tofusin, Windseekers of Royal House Bra'aden of the Island Empire of Seth," the old man announced. Solon was pleased that the man had either known or dug up the appropriate titles, even if Seth was scarcely an empire these days. Solon walked forward to greet Lady Gyre.

She was an attractive woman, stately, with the dark green eyes and the dusky skin and delicate bones of House Graesin. Though she had an admirable figure, she dressed modestly by Cenarian standards: the neckline high, the hemline coming down almost to her slim ankles, the gray gown fitted but not tight.

"Blessings, my Lady," Solon said, giving the traditional Sethi open-palmed bow, "may the sun smile upon you and all storms find you in port." It was a little much, but so was having three people dine in a hall large enough to have its own weather.

She hmmphed, not even bothering to speak to him. They sat and servants brought out the first course, a mandarin duck soup with fennel. "My son warned me of what you were, but you speak quite well, nor have you seen fit to put metal through your face. And you're wearing clothes. I'm quite pleased." Evidently the good duchess had heard about her son's luck with sparring Solon and didn't appreciate having her son humbled.

"Is it true, then?" Logan asked. He was at one end of the table, his mother at the other, and Solon unfortunately in the middle. "Do the Sethi really go naked on their ships?"

"Logan," Catrinna Gyre said sharply.

"No. If I may, Lady Gyre, that's a common misperception. Our island splits the hottest current in the Great Sea, so it's quite warm there even in the winter. In the summer, it's nearly intolerable. So though we don't wear as much clothing or as heavy clothing as people do here, we aren't without our own standards of modesty."

"Modesty? You call women who run about on boats

half-naked modest?" Lady Gyre asked. Logan looked enrapt by the idea.

"Not all of them are modest, of course. But to us, breasts are about as erotic as necks. It might be pleasant to kiss them, but there's no reason to—"

"You go too far!" Lady Gyre said.

"On the other hand, a woman who shows her ankles is obviously hoping not to go below decks alone. Indeed, Lady Gyre," he lifted an eyebrow and pretended to look at her ankles, though they were too far away and on the other side of table legs. "Sethi women would think you quite brazen."

Catrinna Gyre's face went ashen.

Before she could say anything, though, Logan laughed. "Ankles? Ankles? That's so . . . dumb!" He wolf-whistled. "Nice ankles, mother." He laughed again.

A servant arrived with the second course, but Solon didn't even see him set it down. *Why do I do this?* It wouldn't be the first time his sharp tongue had cut his own throat.

"I see that your lack of respect isn't confined to striking Lord Gyre," the duchess said.

Now he's Lord Gyre. So, the men weren't stupid; they weren't babying Logan; she'd probably ordered them not to hit Logan in practice.

"Mother, he was never disrespectful to me. And he didn't mean to disrespect you, either." Logan looked from his mother to Solon, and found stony gazes on each. "Did you, Lord Tofusin?"

"Milady," Solon said, "my father once told me that ~~are~~ no lords on the practice field because there are ~~n~~ the battlefield."

"Nonsense," she said. "A true lord is always a lord. In Cenaria we understand this."

"Mother, he means that enemy swords cut nobles as surely as they cut peasants."

Lady Gyre ignored her son and said, "What is it that you want from us, Master Tofusin?"

It was a rude thing to ask a guest, and not least for addressing him as a commoner. Solon had been counting on the Gyres' courtesy to give him long enough to figure out that very thing. He had thought that he could watch and wait, dine with the Gyres at every meal, and be afforded a fortnight or two before he announced any intention of his plans. He thought he might like the boy, but this woman, gods! He might be better off with the Jadwin seductress.

"Mother, don't you think you're being a little—"

She didn't even look at her son; she just raised her palm toward him and stared at Solon, unblinking.

So that's how it is.

Logan wasn't just her son. For all that he was only a boy, Logan was Catrinna Gyre's lord. In that contemptuous gesture, Solon read the family's history. She raised her hand, and her son was still young enough, still inexperienced enough, that he went silent like a good son rather than punished her like a good lord. In that contempt and the contempt she'd greeted him with, Solon saw why Duke Gyre had named his son Lord Gyre in his own absence. The duke couldn't trust his own wife to rule.

"I'm waiting," Lady Gyre said. The chill in her voice made his decision.

Solon didn't like children, but he loathed tyrants. Damn you, Dorian. "I've come to be Lord Gyre's adviser," he said, smiling warmly.

"Ha! Absolutely not."

"Mother," Logan said, a touch of steel entering his voice.

"No. Never," she said. "In fact, Master Tofusin, I'd like you to leave."

"Mother."

"Immediately," she said.

Solon didn't move, merely held his knife and two-pronged fork—he was glad he remembered how the Cenarians used the things—over his plate, willing himself not to move.

"When are you going to let Lord Gyre act like Lord Gyre?" he asked her.

"When he's ready. When he's older. And I will not be questioned by some Sethi savage who—"

"Is that what the duke commanded you when he named his son lord in his absence? Let Logan be lord once he's ready? My father once told me that delayed obedience is really disobedience."

"Guards!" she called.

"Dammit, mother! Stop it!" Logan stood so abruptly his chair clattered to the ground behind him.

The guards were halfway to Solon's chair. They suddenly looked caught, conspicuous. They looked at each other and slowed, vainly tried to approach quietly, their chain mail jingling with every step.

"Logan, we'll speak about this later," Catrinna Gyre said. "Tallan, Bran, escort this man out. Now."

"I am the Gyre! Don't touch him," Logan shouted.

The guards stopped. Catrinna's eyes flashed fury. "How dare you question my authority. You second-guess your mother in front of a stranger? You're an embarrassment, Logan Gyre. You shame your family. Your father made a terrible mistake in trusting you."

Solon felt sick, and Logan looked worse. He was shaken, suddenly wavering, about to fold. *The snake. She destroys what she should protect. She shatters her own son's confidence.*

Logan looked at Tallan and Bran. The men looked wretched to be so visibly witnessing Logan's humiliation. Logan shrank, seemed to deflate.

I have to do something.

"My Lord Gyre," Solon said, standing and drawing all eyes. "I'm terribly sorry. I don't wish to impose on your hospitality. The last thing I would wish to be is an occasion for strife in your family, and indeed, I forgot myself and spoke too frankly to your mother. I am not always attuned to . . . tempering the truth for Cenarian sensibilities. Lady Gyre, I apologize for any offense you or your lord may have taken. Lord Gyre, I apologize if you felt I treated you lightly and will of course take my leave, if you will grant it." A little twist on the *if you will grant it.*

Logan stood straighter. "I will not."

"My lord?" Solon painted puzzlement on his face.

"I've found too much tempering and not enough truth in this house, Lord Tofusin," Logan said. "You've done nothing to offend me. I'd like you to stay. And I'm sure my mother will do all she can to make you feel welcome."

"Logan Gyre, you will not—" Catrinna Gyre said.

"Men!" Logan said to the guards loudly to cut her off. "Lady Gyre is tired and overwrought. Escort her to her chambers. I'd appreciate it if one of you would watch her door this night in case she requires anything. We will all dine in the usual room in the morning."

Solon loved it. Logan had just confined his mother to her chambers and put a guard on the door to keep her there until morning, all without giving her an avenue for complaint. *This boy will be formidable.*

Will be? He already is. And I've just chained myself to him. It wasn't a comfortable thought. He hadn't even decided to stay. Actually, half an hour ago, he'd decided not to decide for a few weeks. Now he was Logan's.

Did you know this would happen, Dorian? Dorian didn't believe in coincidences. But Solon had never had his friend's faith. Now, faith or no faith, he was committed. It made his neck feel tight, like wearing a slave collar two sizes too small.

The rest of an excellent meal passed in silence. Solon begged his lord's leave and went looking for the nearest inn that served Sethi wine.

10

*H*er face was destroyed. Azoth had once seen a man kicked square in the face by a horse. He'd died wheezing on broken teeth and blood. Doll Girl's face was worse.

Azoth looked away, but Durzo grabbed a handful of his hair and turned him back. "Look, damn you, look. This is what you've done, boy. This is what hesitation costs. When I say kill, you kill. Not tomorrow, not five days later. You kill that second. No hesitation. No doubts. No second thoughts. Obedience. Do you understand the word? I know better than you do. You know nothing. You are nothing. This is what you are. You are weakness. You are filth. You are the blood bubbling out of that little girl's nose."

Sobs burst from Azoth's throat. He thrashed and tried to turn away, but Durzo's grip was steel. "No! Look! This is what you've done! This is your fault! Your failure! Your deader did this. A deader shouldn't do anything. A deader is dead. Not five days from now—a deader is dead as soon as you take the contract. Do you understand?"

Azoth threw up, and still Durzo held his hair, turning him so his vomit didn't splatter on Doll Girl. When he was done, Durzo turned him around and let go. But Azoth turned away, not even wiping the puke from his lips. He looked at Doll Girl. She couldn't last long. Every breath was labored. Blood welled, dribbled, dripped, slid onto the sheets, onto the floor.

He stared until her face disappeared, until he was only seeing red angles and curves where once that doll-pretty face had been. The red angles went white-hot and branded his memory, searing him. He held perfectly still so the scars on his mind would give a perfect image of what he'd done, would perfectly match the lacerations on her face.

Durzo didn't say a word. It didn't matter. He didn't matter. Azoth didn't matter. All that mattered was the bloody little girl lying on bloody sheets. He felt something inside collapsing, something squeezing the breath out of his body. Part of him was glad; part of him cheered as he felt himself being crushed, compacted into insignificance, into oblivion. This was what he deserved.

But then it stopped. He blinked and noticed there were no tears in his eyes. He *wouldn't* be crushed. Something in him refused to be crushed. He turned to Durzo.

"If you save her, I'm yours. Forever."

"You don't understand, boy. You've already failed. Besides, she's dying. There's nothing you can do. She's worthless now. A girl on the street is worth exactly what she can get for whoring. Saving her life is no kindness. She won't thank you for it."

"I'll find you when he's dead," Azoth said.

"You've already failed."

"You gave me a week. It's only been five days."

Durzo shook his head. "By the Night Angels. So be it. But if you come without proof, I'll end you."

Azoth didn't answer. He was already walking away.

She wasn't dying fast, but she was certainly dying. Durzo couldn't help but have a certain detached professional rage. It had been sloppy, cruel work. With the horrible wounds on her face, it was obvious that she had been intended to live and live with hideous scars that would forever shame her. But instead, she was dying, wheezing out her life through a broken bloody nose.

There was nothing he could do for her, either. That was quickly evident. He'd killed both of the bigs who had been guarding her after the butchery, but he suspected that neither of them had been the cutter. They had both seemed a little too horrified at the evil they were part of. Some part of Durzo that still had a shred of decency demanded he go kill the twist who had done this immediately, but he'd tended to the little girl first.

She was lying on a low cot in one of the smaller safe houses he owned in the Warrens. He cleaned her up as well as he could. He knew a lot about preserving life: he'd learned that as he learned about killing. It was just a matter of approaching the line between life and death from the opposite side. So it was quickly apparent that her wounds were beyond his skills. She'd been kicked, and she was bleeding inside. That would kill her even if the blood she was losing from her face didn't.

"Life is empty," he told her still form. "Life is worthless, meaningless. Life is pain and suffering. I'm sparing you if I let you die. You'll be ugly now. They'll laugh at you. Stare at you. Point at you. Shudder. You'll overhear their questions. You'll know their self-serving pity. You'll be a curiosity, a horror. Your life is worth nothing now."

He had no choice. He had to let her die. It was only kind. Not just, perhaps, but kind. *Not just.* The thought ate at him, and her ugliness and blood, her wheezing, ate at him.

Maybe he needed to save her. For the boy. Maybe she would be just the goad to move him. Momma K said Azoth might be too kind. Maybe from this Azoth would learn to act first, act fast, kill anyone who threatened him. The boy had already waited too long. It was a risk either way. The boy had sworn himself to Durzo if he saved her, but what would having this cripple around do to a boy? She'd be a living reminder of failure.

Durzo couldn't allow Azoth to destroy himself over a girl. He wouldn't allow it.

The wheezing decided him. He wouldn't kill her himself, and he wasn't such a coward that he'd run away and let her die alone. Fine. He'd do what he could to save her. If she died, it wasn't his fault. If she lived, he'd deal with Azoth.

But who the hell could save her?

Solon stared at the dregs of his sixth glass of, to be charitable, lousy Sethi red. Any honest vintner on the island would have been ashamed to serve such dreck at their least favorite nephew's coming of age. And dregs? The glass must have been at least half dregs. Someone needed to tell the innkeeper this wine wasn't meant to be aged. It was supposed to be served within a year. At the outside. Kaede wouldn't have tolerated it.

So he told the innkeeper. And realized from the look on the man's face that he'd already told him. At least twice.

Well, to hell with it. He was paying good money for bad wine, and he kept hoping after a few glasses he might not notice just how bad it was. He was wrong. Every glass just made him a little more irritable about the poor quality. Why would someone ship a bad wine all the way across the Great Sea? Did they actually make a profit on it?

As he put down another silver, he realized it was because of homesick fools like himself that they made a profit on it. The thought made him sick. Or maybe that was the wine. Someday he'd have to convince Lord Gyre to invest in Sethi wines.

He slumped further in his chair and waved for another glass, ignoring the few other patrons and the bored innkeeper. This was really an inexcusable exercise in self-pity, the likes of which he would have whipped out of Logan Gyre if he saw him indulging in something so juvenile. But he'd traveled so far, and for what? He remembered Dorian's smile, that mischievous little grin the girls never stopped cooing over.

"A kingdom rests in your hands, Solon."

"What do I care about Cenaria? It's half a world away!"

"I didn't say the kingdom was Cenaria, did I?" That damn grin again. Then it faded. "Solon, you know I wouldn't ask this if there were any other way—"

"You don't see everything. There's got to be another way. At least tell me what I'm supposed to do. Dorian, you know what I'd be leaving. You know what this will cost me."

"I do," Dorian said, his aristocratic features showing the pain a great lord might feel when sending men to their deaths to accomplish some necessary goal. "He needs you, Solon—"

Solon's memories were abruptly cut short with the jab of a dagger into his spine. He sat bolt upright, sloshing the dregs of his seventh glass onto the table.

"That's enough, friend," a low voice said into his ear. "I know what you are, and I need you to come with me."

"Or else?" Solon asked, dizzy. Who could know that he was here?

"Yes. Or else." Amused.

"Or else what? You're going to kill me in front of five witnesses?" Solon asked. He rarely drank more than two glasses of wine at any time. He was too impaired for this. Who the hell was this man?

"And you're supposed to be smart," the man said. "If I know what you are and still threaten you, do you think I lack the will to kill you?"

He had Solon there. "And what's to stop me—"

The dagger jabbed his spine again. "Enough talk. You've been poisoned. You do what I say and I'll give you the antidote. Does that answer the rest of your questions?"

"Actually—"

"You'll know you're really poisoned because any time now your neck and armpits will start itching."

"Uh-huh. Ariamu root?" Solon asked, trying to think. Was he bluffing? Why would he bluff?

"Plus a few other things. Last warning."

His shoulder started itching. Damn. He could have

taken care of ariamu root by itself, but this . . . "What do you want?"

"Head outside. Don't turn, don't say anything."

Solon walked to the door, almost trembling. The man had said "what you are" not "who you are." That might have referred to being Sethi, but his other comment obviously didn't. The Sethi might be famous or infamous for many things, but rightly or wrongly, intelligence wasn't one of them.

He'd barely touched the street when he felt the dagger jab his spine again. A hand drew his sword from the scabbard. "That won't be necessary," Solon said. Was that his imagination, or was his neck itching? "Show me what you want."

The poisoner led him around the building where two horses were waiting. Together they rode south and then across the Vanden Bridge. They were swallowed by the Warrens, and though Solon didn't think the man had been taking turns solely to get him lost, he soon was. Damn wine.

Finally, they stopped in front of one tiny shack among many. He dismounted unsteadily and followed the man inside. The poisoner wore dark clothes and a voluminous gray-black cloak with its hood up. All Solon could see was that he was tall, obviously athletic, and probably thin. The man nodded toward the door, and Solon stepped inside.

The smell of blood hit him instantly. A little girl was lying on a low bed, barely breathing, barely bleeding, her face a gory mess. Solon turned. "She's dying. There's nothing I can do."

"I did what I could," the man said. "Now you do what you do. I've left all the tools you may need."

"Whatever you think I am, you're wrong. I'm no healer!"

"She dies, you die." Solon felt the weight of the man's eyes on him. Then the poisoner turned and left.

Solon looked at the closed door and felt despair rising like twin waves of darkness coming from each side. Then he shook himself. Enough. So he was tired, still drunk, poisoned, itchy, and never had been much good at healing to begin with. Dorian had said that someone here needed him, hadn't he? So surely Solon couldn't die yet.

Unless, of course, just making Logan stand up to his mother was all that Solon had been needed for.

Well. That's the problem with prophecy, isn't it? You never know. Solon knelt by the little girl and began working.

11

$\mathcal{M}$omma K crossed her legs in the absently provocative way that only a veteran courtesan could. Some people fidgeted habitually. Momma K seduced habitually. With a figure most of her girls could only envy, she could pass for thirty, but Momma K was unashamed of her age. She'd thrown a huge party for her own fortieth birthday. Few of those who'd told her she outshone her own courtesans had been lying, for Gwinvere Kirena had been the courtesan of an age. Durzo knew of a dozen duels that had been fought over her, and at least as many lords had proposed to her, but Gwinvere Kirena would be chained to no man. She knew too well all the men she knew.

"He really does have you nervous, this Azoth. Doesn't he?" Momma K said.

"No."

"Liar." Momma K smiled, all full red lips and perfect teeth.

"What gave me away?" Durzo asked, not really

interested. He *was* nervous, though. Things had spun suddenly out of control.

"You were staring at my breasts. You only look at me like I'm a woman when you're too distracted to keep your guard up." She smiled again. "Don't worry—I think it's sweet."

"Don't you ever stop?"

"You're a simpler man than you like to think, Durzo Blint. You really only have three refuges when the world overwhelms you. Do you want me to tell you what they are, my big, strong wetboy?"

"Is this the kind of thing you talk about with clients?" It was a cheap shot. Moreover, it was the kind of comment a whore would have been hit with enough times that she was well armored against it now.

She didn't even blink. "No," she said. "But there was a rather pathetically endowed baron who liked to have me pretend I was his nursemaid and when he was naughty, I'd—"

"Spare me." It was a loss to have her stop, but she'd have gone on for ten minutes, and not skipped a single detail.

"Then what do you want, Durzo? Now you're staring at your hands again."

He *was* staring at his hands. Gwinvere could be more trouble than she was worth, but her advice was always good. She was the most perceptive person he knew and smarter than he was by a long shot. "I want to know what to do, Gwinvere." After a long moment of silence, he looked up from his hands.

"About the boy?" she asked.

"I don't think he has it in him."

* * *

When Azoth came around the corner, Rat was sitting on the back porch of the ruin the guild called home. Azoth's heart seized at the sight of the ugly boy. Rat was alone, waiting for him. He was spinning a short sword on its point. Spots of rust interplayed with the winking of the waning moon on bright steel as it spun.

In this unguarded moment, Rat's face seemed as mutable as that spinning steel, one moment the monster Azoth had always known, the next moment an overgrown, scared child. Azoth shuffled forward, more confused and frightened by that glimpse of humanity than soothed. He'd seen too much.

He came forward through the stench of the alley that the whole guild used as their toilet. He didn't even care to watch where he put his feet. He was hollow.

When he looked up, Rat was standing, that familiar cruel grin on his lips, the rusty sword pointing at Azoth's throat.

"That's far enough," Rat said.

Azoth flinched. "Rat," he said, and swallowed.

"No closer," Rat said. "You've got a shiv. Give it to me."

Azoth was on the verge of tears. He took the shiv from his belt and held it out, handle first. "Please," he said. "I don't want to die. I'm sorry. I'll do whatever you want. Just don't hurt me."

Rat took the shiv.

"I'll give him that he's smart," Durzo said. "But it takes more than intelligence. You've seen him here with all the

other guild rats. Does he have that . . . ?" He snapped his
fingers, unable to find the word.

"Most of them I only see in the winter. They sleep on
the streets the rest of the year. I give them a roof, Durzo,
not a home."

"But you've seen him."

"I've seen him." She would never forget him.

"Gwinvere, is he cunning?"

Rat tucked the shiv in his belt and patted Azoth down. He
found no other weapons. His fear dissolved and left only
exultation. "Don't hurt you?" he asked. He backhanded
Azoth.

It was almost ridiculous. Azoth practically flew from
the force of the blow. He sprawled in the dirt and got up
slowly, his hands and knees bleeding. *He's so small!*

How did I ever fear this? Azoth's eyes bled fear. He was
crying, making little whimpers in the darkness. Rat said,
"I'm going to have to hurt you, Azoth. You've made me. I
didn't want it to be this way. I wanted you with me."

It was all too easy. Azoth had come back to the guild
already destroyed. Rat didn't like it. He wanted to do
something to seal Azoth's humiliation.

He stepped forward and grabbed Azoth's hair. He
pulled him up to his knees, enjoying the little cries of pain
the boy gave.

He owed what would come next to Neph. Rat didn't
particularly like boys more than girls. He didn't see much
difference. But Rat never would have thought of this as
a weapon if Neph hadn't told him how much it broke a
person's spirit to be forced.

It had become one of Rat's favorites. Anyone could make a girl scared, but the boys in the guild feared him more than they had ever feared anyone. They looked at Bim or Weese or Pod or Jarl and they melted. And the more he had done it, the more it stirred him. Just looking at Azoth now, on his knees, eyes round with fear, made Rat's loins stir. There was nothing like watching the fire of defiance roar high and then, quickly or over many nights, die, flare up again, and die forever.

"A wetboy has to lose himself," Durzo said. "No, abandon himself. To be a perfect killer, he has to wear the perfect skin for each kill. Gwinvere, you understand, don't you?"

She recrossed her long legs. "Understanding is what sets courtesans apart from whores. I get under the skin of every man to walk through my doors. If I know a man, I know how to please him. I know how to manipulate him so that he'll try to buy my love and become competitive with the others trying to do the same thing, but not become jealous of them."

"A wetboy has to know his deaders like that," Durzo said.

"And you don't think Azoth can do that?"

"Oh no. I think he can," Durzo said. "But after you know a man or a woman like that—after you wear their skin and walk a few miles in it, you can't help but love them—"

"But it's not real love," Gwinvere said quietly.

"—and when you love them, that's the moment a wetboy has to kill."

"And that's what Azoth can't do."

"He's too soft."

"Even now, even after what happened to his little friend?"

"Even now."

"You were right," Azoth said through his tears. He looked up at Rat standing over him, moonlight throwing his shadow over Azoth. "I knew what you wanted, and I wanted it, too. I just . . . I just couldn't. But I'm ready now."

Rat looked down at him, a faint light of suspicion blooming in his eyes.

"I found a special place for us . . ." Azoth stopped. "But it doesn't matter, we can do it here. We should do it here." Rat's eyes were hard, but unreadable. Azoth stood slowly, holding on to Rat's hips. "Let's just do it here. Let the whole guild hear us. Let everyone know."

His whole body was shaking and there was no way to hide it. Revulsion was arcing through him like lightning, but he kept his face hopeful, pretended his trembling was pure naive uncertainty. *I can't. I can't. Let him kill me. Anything but . . .* If he thought, if he considered anything for another second, he was lost.

Azoth reached a trembling hand up to Rat's cheek, and stood, then stood on tiptoe and kissed him.

"No," Rat said, slapping him. "We do this my way."

"To ply this trade, a man has to value nothing, has to sacrifice . . ." Durzo trailed off.

"Everything?" Gwinvere asked. "Like you've done so well? My sister might have words about that."

"Vonda's dead because I didn't," Durzo said. He wouldn't meet Gwinvere's gaze. Out the window, night was just beginning to lose its hold on the city.

Looking at Durzo there, his hard, pockmarked face glowing yellow sorrow in the lamplight, Gwinvere softened. "So you fell in love, Durzo. Not even wetboys are immune. Love is a madness."

"Love is failure. I lost everything because I failed."

"And what do you do if Azoth fails?" Gwinvere asked.

"I let him die. Or I kill him."

"You need him," she said gently. "You told me yourself that he'll call a ka'kari to you."

Before Durzo could say anything, there was a knock at the door.

"Come," Momma K said.

One of Gwinvere's maids, obviously a former courtesan herself, now too old for the brothels, poked her head in the door. "There's a boy to see you, milady. His name is Azoth."

"Show him in," Gwinvere said.

Durzo looked at her. "What the hell is he doing here?"

"I don't know." Gwinvere was amused. "I suppose that if he's the kind of boy you can mold into a wetboy, he can't be without certain resources."

"Damn, I left him not three hours ago," Durzo said.

"So?"

"So I told him I'd kill him if I saw him without proof. You know I can't make idle threats." Durzo sighed. "You might have been right, but it's out of my hands."

"He's not here for you, Durzo. He's here to see me. So why don't you do your little shadow thing and disappear?"

"My little shadow thing?"

"Now, Durzo."

The door opened and a bleeding, wretched boy was shown in. But even beat up as he was, Gwinvere would have picked him out from a thousand guild rats. This guild rat had fire in his eyes. He stood straight even though his face was abraded, his mouth and nose dribbling blood. He looked at her unabashedly, but was either young enough or smart enough that he looked at her eyes rather than at her cleavage.

"You see more than most, don't you," Momma K said. It wasn't a question.

He didn't even nod. He was too young to be mocking her tendency to state questions, so there was something else in that flat stare he was giving her.

Of course. "And you've seen something terrible, haven't you?"

Azoth just looked at her with big eyes, trembling. He was a picture of the naked innocence that died every day in the Warrens. It stirred something in her that she'd thought long dead. Without so much as a word, she knew she could offer the boy a mother's arms, a mother's embrace, a safe place. She could give a refuge, even to this child of the Warrens, who'd probably never been held in his life. A soft look, a touch on his cheek, and a word, and he would collapse into her arms and cry.

And what will Durzo do? Vonda had barely been dead three months. He'd lost more than lover when she'd died, and Gwinvere didn't know if he'd ever recover. *Will he understand that Azoth's tears don't make him weak?*

To be honest with herself, Gwinvere knew that holding Azoth wouldn't be just for Azoth. She couldn't remember the last time she'd held someone who hadn't paid for the privilege.

And what will Durzo do if he sees real love now? Will it make him be human, or will he tell himself Azoth is too weak and kill him rather than admit that he needs him?

It all took her just a second to read the boy and weigh her options. There was too much at stake. She couldn't do it.

"So, Azoth," she asked, folding her arms under her breasts, "who'd you kill?"

The blood drained from Azoth's face. He blinked as fear suddenly cleared his eyes of the tears that were threatening.

"First kill, too," Momma K said. "Good."

"I don't know what you're talking about," Azoth said, too quickly.

"I know what a killer looks like." Her voice was sharp. "So who did you kill?"

"I need to talk to Durzo Blint. Please. Where is he?"

"Right here," Blint said, behind Azoth. Azoth flinched. "And since you've found me," Blint continued, "someone better be dead."

"He . . ." Azoth looked at Momma K, obviously wondering if he could speak in front of her. "He is."

"Where's the body?" Blint demanded.

"It's, it's in the river."

"So there's no proof. How convenient."

"Here's your proof," Azoth shouted, suddenly furious.

He threw what he was holding at Durzo. Durzo snatched it out of the air.

"You call this proof?" Durzo asked. He opened his hand and Momma K saw he held a bloody ear. "I call it an ear. Ever known a man to die from losing an ear, Gwin?"

Momma K said, "Don't you put me in the middle of this, Durzo Blint."

"I can show you the body," Azoth said.

"You said it's in the river."

"It is."

Durzo hesitated.

"Damn you, Durzo. Go," Momma K said. "You owe him that much."

The sun sat fully above the horizon when they arrived at the boat repair shop. Durzo went inside alone and came out ten minutes later, rolling down a wet sleeve. He didn't look down at Azoth as he asked, "Son, he was naked. Did he . . ."

"I got the noose around his foot before, before he could . . . I killed him before." In cold and distant tones, Azoth told him everything. The night was fading like a bad dream, and what he remembered doing, he couldn't believe he had done. It must have been someone else. As he told his story, Blint looked at him in a way no one ever had before. It might have been pity. Azoth didn't know. He'd never seen pity before.

"Did Doll Girl make it?" Azoth asked.

Durzo put his hands on Azoth's shoulders and looked into his eyes. "I don't know. She looked bad. I got the best person I could find to try to save her. Kid," Blint looked away, blinking. "I'm going to give you one more chance."

"Another test?" Azoth's shoulders slumped. His voice was flat, deflated. He couldn't even spare the energy for outrage. "You can't. I did everything you said."

"No more tests. I'm giving you one more chance to reconsider. You've done everything I asked. But this isn't the life you want. You want off the street? I'll give you a bag of silver and apprentice you to a fletcher or an herbalist on the east side. But if you come with me, you trade everything for it. Once you do this work, you'll never be the same. You will be alone. You will be different. Always.

"And that's not the worst of it. I'm not trying to scare you. Well, maybe I am. But I'm not exaggerating. I'm not lying to you. The worst of it, kid, is this: Relationships are ropes. Love is a noose. If you come with me, you must forswear love. Do you know what that means?"

Azoth shook his head.

"It means you can bang as many women as you want, but you can never love one. I won't allow you to ruin yourself *over a girl,*" Durzo's voice filled with violence. His hands were claws on Azoth's shoulders, his eyes predator's eyes. "Do you understand?"

"What about Doll Girl?" Azoth asked. He must have been tired. He knew mentioning her was a mistake before he finished the question.

"You're ten, eleven years old? You think you love her?"

"No." *Too late.*

"I'll let you know if she lives, but if you come with me, Azoth, you will never talk to her again. You understand? You apprentice to my fletcher or the herbalist, you can see her as much as you want. Please, kid. Take it. This might be your last chance for happiness."

Happiness? I just don't want to be afraid anymore. Blint wasn't afraid. People were afraid of him. They whispered his name in awe.

"You follow me now," Blint said, "and by the Night Angels, you *belong* to me. Once we start, you become a wetboy or you die. The Sa'kagé can't afford to do it any other way. Or you stay, and I'll find you in a few days and take you to your new master."

Blint stood and brushed his still-damp hands as if washing them of the matter. He turned abruptly and strode into the shadows of an alley.

Stepping out from the niche he'd been standing in, Azoth looked down the street toward the guild home, a hundred paces away. Maybe he didn't need to go with Blint now. He'd killed Rat. Maybe he could go back and everything would be all right.

Go back to what? I'm still too little to be the guild head. Ja'laliel's still dying. Jarl and Doll Girl were still both maimed. There would be no hero's welcome for Azoth. Roth or some other big would take over the guild, and Azoth would be afraid again, as if nothing had ever happened.

But he promised me an apprenticeship! Yes, he'd promised, but everyone knew you didn't trust adults.

Blint was still confusing. It didn't sound right how he talked about Doll Girl, but just now Azoth had seen something in the wetboy. There was something in him that cared. There was something in the legendary killer that wanted the best for Azoth.

Azoth didn't believe that Doll Girl was worthless just

because she wasn't pretty anymore. He didn't know if he could kill again. He didn't know what Blint would do to him or why. But whatever that something was that he had seen in the wetboy, it was far more precious to Azoth than all his doubts.

Down the street, Jarl stepped out of the guild home. He saw Azoth, and even from that distance, Azoth saw him smile, white teeth brilliant against his Ladeshian skin. From the blood on the back porch and Rat's absence, they must have guessed that he was dead. Jarl waved and started hurrying toward Azoth in the dazzling sunlight.

Azoth turned his back on his best friend and stepped into the shadows' embrace.

12

"Welcome home," Master Blint's voice was tinged with sarcasm, but Azoth didn't hear it. The word *home* held magic. He'd never had a home.

Durzo Blint's house crouched deep in the Warrens underneath the ruins of an old temple. Azoth stared in open wonder. From the outside, it looked like there was nothing here, but Blint had several rooms—none of them small.

"You'll learn to fight here," Blint said, locking, unlocking, and relocking each of three bolts on the door. The room was wide and deep, and crammed with equipment: various targets, pads filled with straw, and every kind of practice weapon, beams suspended above the ground, strange tripods with wood appendages, cables, ropes, hooks, and ladders.

"And you'll learn to use those." Blint pointed to the weapons lining the walls, each neatly outlined in white paint. There were weapons of every size and shape from single-edged daggers to enormous cleavers. Blades straight or curving, one- or two-edged, one- or two-handed, with different colors and patterns of steel. Swords with hooks, notches, and barbs. Then there were maces, flails, axes, war hammers, clubs, staves, pole arms, sickles, spears, slings, darts, garrotes, short bows, longbows, crossbows.

The next room was just as amazing. Disguises and equipment lined the walls, each painstakingly outlined. But here there were also tables covered with books and vials. The books bristled with bookmarks. The jars covered a huge table and were filled with seeds, flowers, leaves, mushrooms, liquids, and powders.

"These are the base ingredients for most of the poisons in the world. As soon as Momma K teaches you how to read, you'll read and memorize most of what's in these books. The poisoner's art *is* an art. You will master it.

"Yes, sir."

"In a couple of years, when your Talent quickens, I'll teach you to use magic."

"Magic?" Azoth was feeling more exhausted by the second.

"You think I accepted you because of your looks? Magic is essential to what we do. No Talent, no wetboy."

Azoth started to totter, but before he could collapse, Master Blint grabbed him by the back of his ragged tunic and guided him to the next room. There was only one pallet and Blint didn't set him on it, but guided him instead to a spot by a small fireplace.

"First kills are hard," Blint said. He seemed to be speaking from far away. "Some time this week, you'll probably cry. Do it when I'm gone."

"I won't cry," Azoth vowed.

"Sure. Now sleep."

*   *   *

"Life is empty. When we take a life, we aren't taking anything of value. Wetboys are killers. That's all we do. That's all we are. There are no poets in the bitter business," Blint said.

He must have left while Azoth slept, because Azoth now held a sword small enough for an eleven-year-old in his fist, feeling awkward.

"Now attack me," Blint said.

"What?"

The side of Blint's sword smashed into Azoth's head.

"I order. You obey. No hesitations. Got it?"

"Yes, sir." Azoth climbed to his feet and picked up the sword. He rubbed his head.

"Attack," Blint said.

Azoth did, wildly. Blint deflected his blows or stepped to one side so that Azoth fell over from the force of his own swings. All the while, Blint spoke.

"You aren't making art, you're making corpses. Dead is dead." He parried quickly and Azoth's blade went skittering across the floor. "Grab that." Blint walked after Azoth and engaged him again. "Don't play with your kills. Don't go for the one-thrust beautiful finish. Cut someone twenty times and let them collapse from blood loss—then finish them. Don't make it beautiful. You aren't making art, you're making corpses."

And so the lessons continued, physical action with a continuously running monologue, each lesson summarized, demonstrated, and summarized again.

In the study: "Never taste death. Every vial, every jar in here is death. If you're working with death, you'll get powders, pastes, and salves on your hands. Never lick the death on your fingers. Never touch death to your eyes.

You'll wash your hands with this liquor and then this water, always into this basin which is used for nothing else and will only be emptied where I show you. Never taste death."

On the street: "Embrace the shadows. . . . Breathe the silence. . . . Be ordinary, be invisible. . . . Mark the man. . . . Know every out. . . ."

When he made mistakes, Blint didn't yell. If Azoth didn't block correctly, he was merely drawing his wage when the wood practice sword crashed into his shin. If he couldn't recite the lessons of the day and expand on any that Blint asked about, he got cuffed for every one he forgot.

It was all even-handed. It was all fair, but Azoth never relaxed. If he failed too much, just as dispassionately as Master Blint cuffed Azoth, he might kill him. All it would take would be for Blint to not pull one blow short. Azoth wouldn't even know he'd failed until he found himself dying.

More than once he wanted to quit. But there was no quitting. More than once, he wanted to kill Blint. But trying would mean death. More than once, he wanted to cry. But he'd vowed he wouldn't—and he didn't.

"Momma K, who's Vonda?" Azoth asked. After his reading lessons, she took a cup of ootai before they started on politics, history, and court etiquette. After he trained with Blint all morning, he studied with her through the afternoon. He was exhausted and sore all the time, but he slept through the whole of every night and woke warm, not shivering. The gnawing voice and debilitating weakness of hunger was only a memory.

He never complained. If he did, they might make him go back.

Momma K didn't answer immediately. "That is a very delicate question."

"Does that mean you won't tell me?"

"It means I don't want to. But I will because you may need to know, and the man who should tell you won't." She closed her eyes for a moment, and when she continued, her voice was flat. "Vonda was Durzo's lover. Durzo had a treasure and Khalidor's Godking wanted it. You remember what I taught you about Khalidor?"

Azoth nodded.

Momma K opened her eyes and lifted her eyebrows.

He grimaced, then recited. "Khalidor is our northern neighbor. They've always said Cenaria and most of Midcyru is theirs, but they can't take it because Duke Gyre and his men guard Screaming Winds."

"The pass at Screaming Winds is highly defensible," Momma K suggested. "And the prize?" When Azoth looked at her blankly, she said, "Khalidor could go around the mountains the long way, but they don't because . . ."

"Because we're not really worth it, and the Sa'kagé runs everything."

"Cenaria is corrupt, the treasury is empty, the Ceurans raid us from the south—and the Lae'knaught holds our eastern lands, and they hate Khalidorans even more than they hate most mages. So yes, we're not worth taking."

"Isn't that what I said?"

"You were right, but not for all the right reasons," she said. She sipped her ootai again, and Azoth thought she'd forgotten his original question, or that she hoped he had. Then she said, "To get Durzo's treasure, the Godking kidnapped Vonda and proposed a trade: the treasure for Vonda's life. Durzo decided that his treasure was more important, so he let her die. But something happened, and Durzo lost his treasure too. So Vonda died for no reason whatsoever."

"You're mad at him," Azoth said.

Momma K's voice had no inflection whatever, and her eyes were dead. "It was a great treasure, Azoth. If I were Durzo, I might've done the same, except for one thing. . . ." She looked away. "Vonda was my little sister."

13

Solon caught the edge of the halberd with his long sword and heaved it aside, then stepped in and kicked one of Logan's men in the stomach. A few years ago, that kick would have reached his helmet. He supposed he should be thankful that he could beat the Gyre's guards at all, but that was what came of having as his best friends a prophet and a second-echelon blade master. *Feir would have words about how fat I've let myself get. And slow.*

"My lord," Wendel North said, approaching the fighting men.

Logan stepped away from a match he was losing and Solon followed him. The steward gave Solon a flat stare, but didn't protest his presence. "Milord, your mother has just returned."

"Oh? Where was she, Wendel, uh, I mean, Master North?" Logan asked. With the men, he did better, but acting the lord to a man who had probably been in charge of spanking him a few weeks ago was beyond Logan right now. Solon didn't allow himself to grin, though. Let Lady

Gyre undermine Logan's authority. He would have no part of that.

"She spoke with the queen."

"Why?"

"She put forth a petition for guardianship."

"What?" Solon asked.

"She is asking the crown to appoint her to be duchess until the duke returns, or until my lord reaches the age of majority—which in this country, Master Tofusin, is twenty-one."

"But we have my father's letters appointing me," Logan said. "The king can't interfere with a house's appointments unless they're guilty of treason."

Wendel North pushed his glasses up his nose nervously. "That's not altogether true, milord."

Solon looked back at the guards, who were beginning to quit sparring and drift closer. "Back to it, dogs!" They jumped to obey.

"The king may appoint a guardian to an underage lord if the previous lord of that house hasn't left the necessary provisions," Wendel said. "It comes down to this: your father left two copies of the letter appointing you lord in his absence. He gave one to your mother, and the other to me. As soon as I heard where Lady Catrinna went, I checked my copy, which I kept under lock and key. It's gone. Forgive me, Lord Gyre," The steward flushed. "I swear I had no part in this. I thought I had the only key."

"What did the queen say?" Solon asked.

Wendel blinked. As Solon had guessed, Wendel knew, but he hadn't wanted to let Solon know how extensive his network of eyes-and-ears was. After a moment, the steward said, "The matter might have been handled fairly easily, but the king doesn't let the queen make any decisions without him. He interrupted them while they were speaking. He said that he would take the matter under advisement. I'm sorry. I don't know what that means."

"I'm afraid I do," Solon said.

"What?" Logan asked.

"Who's your family's solicitor?"

"I asked you first," Logan said.

"Boy!"

"Count Rimbold Drake," Logan said, sulking a little.

"It means we need to speak with Count Drake. Now."

"Do I have to wear the shoes?" Azoth asked. He didn't like shoes. You couldn't feel the ground to know how slick it was, and they pinched.

"Nah, we'll go see Count Drake with you wearing a nobleman's tunic and barefoot," Durzo said.

"Really?"

"No."

For all the times Azoth had envied the merchants' and lords' sons at the markets, he'd never thought of how uncomfortable their clothes were. But Durzo was his master now, and he was already impatient with how long it was taking Azoth to get ready, so Azoth kept his mouth shut. He hadn't been Durzo's apprentice for long, and he still worried the wetboy would throw him out.

They walked across Vanden Bridge to the east side. To Azoth, it was a revelation. He'd never even tried to cross Vanden Bridge and hadn't believed the guild rats who claimed to have made it past the guards. On the east side of the river, there were no ruins, no empty buildings at all.

There were no beggars on the streets. It smelled different, foreign, alien. Azoth couldn't smell the manure of the cattle yards at all. Even the gutters were different. There was only one every third street, and none in the major streets. People didn't just throw their slops and sewage out the windows and let them accumulate until they gradually flowed away. Here, they carried them to the third street and dumped them there to flow down stone channels in the cobblestone streets so that even those streets were safe to walk in. Most alarming, though, was that the people smelled wrong. Men didn't smell of sweat and their labors. When a woman passed, she smelled only lightly of perfume rather than overpoweringly of it with the stale odors of sweat and sex laced underneath. When Azoth asked Blint about it, the wetboy just said, "You're going to be a lot of work, aren't you?"

They passed a wide building that was billowing steam. Glistening, perfectly coifed men and women were emerging. Azoth didn't even ask. "It's a bath house," Blint said. "Another Ceuran import. The only difference is that here the men and women bathe separately, except in Momma K's, of course."

The owner of the Tipsy Tart greeted Blint as Master Tulii. He answered her with an accent and an effete attitude and ordered his carriage brought around.

Once they were under way, Azoth asked, "Where are we going? Who's Count Drake?"

"He's an old friend, a noble who has to work for a living. He's a solicitor." When Azoth looked puzzled, Master Blint said, "A solicitor is a man who does worse things within the law than most crooks do outside it. But he's a good man. He's going to help me make you useful."

"Master?" Azoth asked. "How's Doll Girl?"

"She's not your problem anymore. You're not to ask about her again." A minute passed as the streets rolled by. Durzo finally said, "She's in bad shape, but she'll live."

He said nothing more until they were shown into the count's tiny estate.

Count Drake was a kindly-looking man of perhaps forty. He had a pince nez tucked in a pocket of his vest and he limped as he closed the door behind them and took a seat behind a desk piled high with stacks of papers.

"I never thought you'd take an apprentice, Durzo. In fact, I seem to remember you swearing it—and swearing at great length," the count said.

"And I still believe every word I said," Durzo said gruffly.

"Ah, you're either being terrifically subtle or making no sense at all, my friend." Count Drake smiled, though, and Azoth could tell it was a real smile, without malice or calculation.

Despite himself, Durzo smiled, too. "They've been missing you, Rimbold."

"Really? I wasn't aware of anyone shooting at me for some time." Durzo laughed, and Azoth almost fell out of his chair. He hadn't thought the wetboy was capable of laughter.

"I need your help," Durzo said.

"All I have is yours, Durzo."

"I want to make this boy new."

"What are you thinking?" Count Drake asked, looking at Azoth quizzically.

"A noble of some sort, relatively poor. The kind who gets invited to social events but doesn't attract attention."

"Hmm," Count Drake said. "The third son of a baron, then. He'll be upper nobility, but nobody important. Or wait. An eastern baron. My second cousins live two days' ride beyond Havermere, and most of their lands have been seized by the Lae'knaught, so if you want an ironclad identity, we could make him a Stern."

"That will do."

"First name?" Count Drake asked Azoth.

"Azoth," Azoth said.

"Not your real name, son," the count said. "Your new name."

"Kylar," Durzo said.

The count produced a piece of blank paper and put on the pince nez. "How do you want to spell that? K-Y-L-E-R? K-I-L-E-R?"

Durzo spelled it and the solicitor wrote it down. Count Drake grinned. "Old Jaeran punning?"

"You know me," Durzo said.

"No, Durzo, I don't think anyone does. Still, kind of ominous, don't you think?"

"It fits the life."

For about the hundredth time, Azoth felt like he was not simply a child but an outsider. It seemed everywhere there were secrets that he couldn't know, mysteries he couldn't penetrate. Now it wasn't just muted conversations with Momma K about something called a ka'kari, or Sa'kagé politics, or court intrigues, or magic, or creatures from the Freeze that were imaginary but Durzo insisted did exist, or others that he insisted didn't, or references to gods and angels that Blint wouldn't explain to him even when he did ask. Now it was his own name. Azoth was about to demand an explanation, but they were already moving on to other things.

The count said, "How soon do you need this and how solid does it have to be?"

"Solid. Sooner is better."

"I thought so," the count said. "I'll make it good enough that unless the real Sterns come here, no one will ever know. Of course, you're still left with a rather significant problem. You have to train him to be a noble."

"Oh no I don't."

"Of course you . . ." the count trailed off. He clicked his tongue. "I see." He adjusted his pince nez and looked at Azoth. "When shall I take him?"

"In a few months, if he lives that long. There are things I need to teach him first." Durzo looked out the window. "Who's that?"

"Ah," Count Drake said. "That's the young Lord Logan Gyre. A young man who will make a fine duke one day."

"No, the Sethi."

"I don't know. Haven't seen him before. Looks like an adviser."

Durzo cursed. He grabbed Azoth's hand and practically dragged him out the door.

"Are you ready to obey?" Durzo demanded.

Azoth nodded quickly.

"See that boy?"

"You call that a boy?" Azoth asked. The young man the count had called Logan Gyre wore a green cloak with black piping, fine black leather boots polished to a high sheen, a cotton tunic, and a sword. He was twenty paces from the door and was being shown in by a porter. His face looked young, but his frame made him look years older than Azoth. He was huge, already taller than Azoth would probably ever be and thicker and wider than anyone he knew, and he didn't look fat. Where Azoth felt awkward and clumsy in his clothes, Logan looked comfortable, confident, handsome, lordly. Just looking at him made Azoth feel shabby.

"Start a fight with him. Distract the Sethi until I can get out."

"Logan!" a girl cried out from upstairs.

"Serah!" Logan called, looking up.

Azoth looked at Master Blint, but he was gone. There was no time to say anything. It didn't matter whether he understood or not. There were mysteries he wasn't allowed to understand yet. He could only act or wait, obey or disobey.

The porter opened the door and Azoth stepped back around the corner, out of sight. As Logan stepped inside and looked up the stairs, a smile curving his lips, Azoth stepped around the corner.

They collided and Azoth landed on his back. Logan almost tripped over him as Azoth rolled to the side and caught Logan's foot in the stomach.

"Oof!"

Logan caught himself on the banister. "I'm so sorry—"

"You fat ape!" Azoth staggered to his feet, holding his stomach. "You clumsy guttershite—" he cut off as he realized all the curses he knew would mark him as coming from the Warrens.

"I didn't—" Logan said.

"What's going on?" the girl asked from the top of the

stairs. Logan looked up, a guilty look flashing across his face.

Azoth punched him in the nose. Logan's head rocked back.

"Logan!" the Sethi man shouted.

But Logan's mild expression was gone. His face was a mask, intense, but not furious. He grabbed Azoth's cloak and lifted him off the ground.

Azoth panicked; he threw punches blindly, screaming, his fists grazing Logan's cheeks and chin.

"Logan!"

"Stop it!" Logan shouted in Azoth's face. "Stop it!" Azoth went crazy, and Logan's intensity flashed into fury. He shifted his hands and held Azoth off the ground with one, then buried his other fist in Azoth's stomach once, twice. The wind rushed from Azoth's lungs. Then a fist the size of a sledge flattened his nose, blinding him with instant tears and pain.

Then, amid distant shouting, he felt himself being spun in a tight circle and—briefly—flying.

Azoth's head slapped against hardwood and the world flashed bright.

14

Logan had insisted on going upstairs to help the countess take care of young Kylar Stern. He was mortified, and
apparently not solely because he'd lost his temper in front
of Count Drake's pretty daughter. For Solon, it had been
an instructive ten seconds.

Count Drake and Solon were left alone. The count led
him to his office. "Why don't you sit down?" the count
said, taking his own seat behind his desk. "Where are you
from, Master Tofusin?"

It was either courtesy or bait. Solon chuckled. "That's
the first time I've been asked that question." He gestured
to himself as if to say, *Just look at my skin.*

The count said, "I don't see any clan rings, or any scars
where they've been removed."

"Well, not all Sethi wear the rings."

"I was under the distinct impression that they did,"
Count Drake said.

"What is this? What are you after?"

"I'm curious about who you really are, Master Tofusin.

Logan Gyre is not only a fine young man whom I regard almost as a son, he's also suddenly the lord of one of the most powerful houses in the land. I've never seen you or heard of you, and suddenly you're his adviser? That strikes me as peculiar. I don't care that you're Sethi—if you are—but I've spent some time on Hokkai and Tawgathu, and the only Sethi who don't pierce their cheeks are the exiles stripped of clan and family. But if you are an exile, you should have scars from your rings being torn out, and you have none."

"Your knowledge of our culture is admirable, but incomplete. I am of House Tofusin, Windseekers of the Royal House. My father's appointment was to Sho'cendi."

"An ambassador to the red mages?"

"Yes. Sho'cendi accepts students from all over the world. As I had no magical talent, I received my education among the merchants and nobles, who are not as tolerant. Not having the rings made life a little easier. There's more to it than that, but I don't think the rest of my story is any of your business."

"Fair enough."

"What took you to Seth?" Solon asked.

"Slavery," the count said. "Before I became fully part of the movement that finally ended slavery here seven years ago, I thought a more moderate path might work. I went to Hokkai to see if I could learn ways to make slaves' lives better."

From the small size of his house—which was very small for a noble, even one as low as a count—Solon knew that Count Drake hadn't been one of the slavers who felt guilty about his newfound wealth. He must have been a real crusader all along.

"It's totally different in Seth," Solon said. "The Year of Joy changes everything."

"Yes, I advanced the idea here, even got the law passed, but the Sa'kagé immediately suborned it. Instead of every slave being freed on the seventh year, slaves were to be freed seven years from the beginning of their indenture. The Sa'kagé claimed it was simpler, that it would be ridiculous to buy a slave in the sixth year and own them for only a month or a week. Of course, in practice, the Sa'kagé's people kept the records, so where in your country, the seventh year is full of celebration as every slave is freed, here the years passed and slaves were never freed. Slaves became slaves for life. They were beaten, scourged, given to the Death Games, their children sent to the baby farms."

"I've heard those became truly awful," Solon said.

"The Sa'kagé set them up, saying that they would be places where the children of prostitutes might be redeemed. Slaves, true, but redeemed. It sounded good, but it gave us places like the House of Mercy. Sorry, I shouldn't go on. It was a dark time. Is that boy ever coming down?"

"Maybe we should get started," Solon said. "I don't think this will wait, and from the way Logan was looking at your daughter, they might be talking a while."

The count chuckled. "Are you testing me now?"

"Does Duke Gyre know?"

"Yes. He and I are friends. Regnus is loath to demand control of Logan's flirtations, given the circumstances of his own marriage."

"I'm not familiar with those. Can you enlighten me?" Solon asked.

"It's not my place. Anyway, Logan and Serah will grow out of it. What appears to be the problem?"

"Catrinna Gyre."

"Careful," the count said.

"Did the duke give you letters that declared his son Lord Gyre in his absence?"

"He spoke of it, but he had to leave quickly. He said his steward would bring them."

"Lady Gyre has stolen the letters and destroyed them. Then she went to the queen."

"She went to whom?" The count was astonished.

"Is that unusual?"

"They have no love for each other. What happened?" Count Drake asked.

"Lady Gyre asked to be made Logan's guardian. The king overheard them. He came in and said he would take it under advisement. What does that mean?"

Count Drake removed his pince nez and rubbed the bridge of his nose. "It means that if he acts quickly, he can appoint a guardian for Logan."

"Will Catrinna Gyre do such a poor job?" Solon asked.

Count Drake sighed. "Legally, the king can put anyone in Logan's place that he wants so long as they're related to him, which means almost anyone in the nobility. And once he's got a guardian in place, even Regnus won't be able to rescind the appointment. Catrinna has just delivered House Gyre to the king."

"But you're Duke Gyre's solicitor—and he told you his wishes. Doesn't that carry any weight?" Solon asked.

"If the king were interested in the truth, yes. As is, to save the Gyres, we'd need the Gyre family parchment, the duke's Great Seal, and a reckless willingness to forge a state document. The king holds court in half an hour. I'd guess this will be the first item on the agenda. There's just no time."

Solon cleared his throat and produced a roll of heavy parchment and a large seal.

Count Drake grinned and snatched the parchment. "I think I suddenly like you, Master Tofusin."

"Wendel North helped me with the wording," Solon said. "I thought I'd leave the signature and the seal to you."

Count Drake rummaged through his desk, found a letter from the duke, and laid it on top of the writ of guardianship. With quick, sure strokes, he forged the duke's signature flawlessly. Count Drake looked up guiltily and said, "Let's just call it an artifact of a misspent youth."

Solon dribbled sealing wax on the parchment. "Then here's to misspent youth."

"Next time you'll move," Blint said as Azoth groaned his way back into consciousness.

"I don't think I'll ever move again. My head feels like someone threw it against a wall."

Blint laughed, the second time Azoth had heard him do that recently. He was sitting on the edge of Azoth's bed. "You did well. They thought you were embarrassed because you got knocked down in front of Drake's daughter, so they decided it was all harmless kid stuff. The young lord Gyre was mortified that he hit you—apparently he's a real big friendly giant, never loses his temper. The fact you're about a quarter his size and Serah was furious with him also helps. They were all quite impressed."

"Impressed? That's stupid."

"In their world fighting has rules, so fighting means risking embarrassment and pain and at worst risking your looks if you get a broken nose or an unfortunate scar. It doesn't mean dying or killing. In their world, you can fight a man and then become his friend. In fact, you're going to play it so Logan does become your friend, because with a man like him, you can only come out of this as a great friend or a terrible enemy. Do you understand that, *Kylar?* We'll work together on your new identity soon."

"Yes, sir. Sir, why didn't you want Master Tofusin to see you? That's why you made me fight Logan, isn't it? To be a distraction?"

"Solon Tofusin is a magus. Most magi—that's male mages—can't tell if you're Talented just by looking at you. On the other hand, most magae—female mages—can. There are disguises against their sight that I'll teach you later, but I didn't have the time to do it and I didn't feel like going upstairs and jumping out a window."

Azoth was confused. "But he doesn't act like a mage."

"And how would you know?" Durzo asked.

"Uh . . ." Azoth didn't think saying, "He isn't like the mages in stories" was going to please Durzo.

"The truth is," Durzo said, "Solon hasn't told Logan or anyone else that he's a mage, and you won't tell anyone either. When you know a man's secrets, you have power over him. A man's secret is his weakness. Every man has a weakness, no matter . . ." Master Blint's voice dropped to nothing, his eyes suddenly distant, lifeless. He stood and left without a word.

Azoth closed his eyes, confused. He wondered about his new master. He wondered about the guild. He wondered if Ja'laliel had bought review. He wondered how Jarl was doing. Most of all, he wondered about Doll Girl.

"Hey-ho, Azo."

"Hey-ho, Jay-Oh," Azoth said. Even as he gave the words the same stress he always had, Azoth felt part of himself die. This was supposed to be one of his last outings as Azoth. Soon, he would have to become Kylar. He would walk differently, talk differently. He wouldn't ever visit his old neighborhoods in the Warrens. But now he saw that Azoth's world was already dying, that he would never connect with Jarl again. It had nothing to do with the lies Kylar would tell, and everything to do with Rat. It was different now. It always would be.

Azoth and Jarl looked at each other for a long moment in the common room of Momma K's house. It was almost midnight, and the guild rats would soon be shooed out of the house. They were welcome in the common room all day, but they were allowed to sleep here only in the winter, and then only if they obeyed her rules: no fighting, no stealing, no going anywhere but the kitchen and the common room, and no bothering the adults who visited. Any guild rat who broke the rules got his entire guild banned from Momma K's for the winter. Usually, it was a death sentence for the offender, because it meant the whole guild would have to sleep in the sewers to stay warm, and they would kill him for that.

Still, the place was always crowded. There was a fireplace and a floor covered with soft rugs good for sleeping on. Those rugs had once been clean, but were now stained from their filthy bodies. Despite the damage, Momma K never got mad at them—and every few months, new rugs showed up. There were durable chairs the guild rats were allowed to sit on, toys, dolls, and piles of games they could play. Sometimes Momma K even brought them treats. Here they gambled and bragged and gossiped freely with anyone who was here, even children outside their own guild. It was the only place the guild rats were allowed to resemble children. It was the only safe place they knew.

Coming back, it looked different. What had seemed so recently the very lap of luxury now was just a plain room, with plain furnishings and simple toys because the guild rats would ruin anything better. They would stain everything and break anything delicate, not from malice but from ignorance. The place was the same; it was Azoth who had changed. Azoth—or Kylar, whichever he was—marveled at the stench of the guild rats. Didn't they smell themselves? Weren't they ashamed, or was it just him, ashamed to see what he had been?

As he always did after his reading lesson with Momma K, Azoth had looked for Jarl. But now that they were face to face, neither could find anything to say.

"I need your help," Azoth said finally. There was no way to cover what he wanted. He wasn't here to visit a friend. He was here to do a job.

"My help?"

"I need to know what's happened to Doll Girl. Where is she? And I need to know what's happening with the guilds."

"I guess you wouldn't know."

"No." Guilds weren't part of his life now. Nothing was like it used to be.

"Your master hit you?" Jarl asked, looking at Azoth's black eyes.

"I got this in a fight. He does hit me, but not like—" Azoth cut off.

"Not like Rat?"

"How is he?" Azoth said, trying to cover.

"Why don't you tell me? You're the one who killed him."

Azoth opened his mouth, but seeing two littles in Momma K's front room, stopped.

"Blint made you kill Rat to see if you could do it, didn't he?" Jarl asked, his voice low.

"No. Are you crazy?" In his head, he could hear the echoes of Master Blint's voice from their training: "Word gets out. Word always gets out."

Hurt filled Jarl's eyes, and he said nothing for a long time. "I shouldn't push, Azoth. I'm sorry. I should just thank you. Rat . . . he messed me up bad. I'm so confused all the time. I hated him, but sometimes. . . . When Rat disappeared and I saw you walking away with Blint . . ." Jarl blinked rapidly and stared away. "Sometimes I hate you. You left me with no one. But that's not right. You didn't do anything wrong. Just Rat . . . and me."

Azoth didn't know what to say.

Jarl blinked furiously again. "Shut up, Jarl. Shut up." He dashed the tears from his eyes with fists. "What do you need?"

There was something Azoth should say, he knew it. Some assurance he should give, but he didn't know what it was. Jarl had been his friend—was his friend, wasn't he?—but he'd changed. Azoth had changed. He was supposed to be Kylar now, but instead, he was just a fraud straddling two worlds and trying to hold on as they tore apart. Whatever the cataclysm named Rat had left Azoth holding onto, one thing was certain. A chasm had opened between him and Jarl, and Azoth was afraid to even approach it, didn't understand what it was, didn't know anything except that it made him feel dirty and scared. Jarl was letting him put the walls back up by asking his simple question—a simple question that could be answered simply, a problem that they could actually resolve.

"Doll Girl," Azoth said. He felt relieved to back away from his once-friend and guilty that he felt relieved.

"Oh," Jarl said. "You know she got . . . ?"

"Is she all right now?"

"She's alive. But I don't know if she's going to make it. They make fun of her. Without you around, she isn't like she used to be. I've been sharing my food with her, but the guild's falling apart. Things are too bad. We don't have enough food."

The guild, not our guild. Azoth kept his face blank, refused to show how much that hurt. It shouldn't have hurt. He was the one who'd wanted out, he was the one who left, but it still made him feel empty.

You will be alone. You will be different. Always.

"Ja'laliel's almost dead; turns out Rat stole his review money. And now they lost the waterfront to Burning Man, and others are closing in."

"They?"

Jarl's face twisted. "If you've got to know, they threw me out of Black Dragon. Threw us all out. Didn't want buggers and Rat-lovers, they said."

"You don't have a guild?" Azoth asked. It was a disaster. Guild rats without a guild were fair game for anyone. That Jarl had stayed alive since being expelled was surprising, that he'd had food to share with Doll Girl was amazing, and that he was willing to was humbling.

"Some of us have banded together for a little while. They call us the Buggers. I'm going to try to join Two Fist on the north side. Rumor is they might get the market on Durdun soon," Jarl said.

That was Jarl. Always had a plan.

"They're willing to take Doll Girl, too?"

He was answered with guilty silence.

"I asked. I did, Azoth. They just won't do it. If you—" Jarl's mouth opened to say more, then closed.

"I'm not going to make you ask, Jarl. I've been looking for you to give it back." Azoth lifted his tunic and unwrapped the sash full of coins. He handed it to Jarl.

"Azoth, this—this is twice as heavy as it was."

"I'll take care of Doll Girl. Give me a couple weeks. Can you take care of her for that long?"

Jarl's eyes were filling with tears, and Azoth was afraid his would too. They called each other Jarl and Azoth now, not Jay-Oh and Azo.

Azoth said, "I'm going to tell Momma K how smart you are and see if she has work for you. You know, if things don't work out with Two Fist."

"You'd do that for me?"

"Sure, Jay-Oh."

"Azo?" Jarl said.

"Yeah?"

Jarl hesitated, swallowed. "I just wish . . ."

"Me too, Jarl. Me too."

15

The price of disobedience is death. The words kept running through his head every day as Azoth planned his disobedience.

Azoth's training was brutally hard, but it wasn't brutal. In the guilds, a Fist might beat you to make a point and make a mistake that left you permanently maimed. Master Blint never made mistakes. Azoth hurt exactly as much as Blint wanted him to. Usually, that was a lot.

But so what? Azoth had two meals a day. He could eat as much as he wanted, and Blint worked the soreness out of his muscles every day as they trained.

At first everything was curses and beatings. Azoth couldn't do anything right. But curses were just air, and beatings were just momentary pain. Blint would never maim Azoth, and if he chose to kill him, there was nothing Azoth could do to stop him anyway.

It was the closest thing to safety he'd ever known.

Within weeks, he realized he liked the training. The sparring, the blunted practice weapons, the obstacle

courses, even the herb lore. Learning reading with
Momma K was hard. *But so what?* Two hours of frustration a day was nothing. Azoth's life was good.

Within a month, he realized that he was talented. It
wasn't obvious, and if he hadn't been so keyed in to Master Blint's every mood and reaction, he would never have
noticed, but now and then, he'd see a faint look of surprise
as he mastered some new skill more quickly than Master
Blint had expected.

It made him work all the harder, hoping to see that look
not once a week, but once a day. For her part, Momma
K made him decipher squiggles for longer than he could
imagine. She had a way of smiling and saying just the right
thing that it pulled him along through the hours. Words were
power, she said. Words were another sword for the man who
wielded them well. And he would need them if the world
was to believe that he was Kylar Stern, so Momma K worked
with him on his alternate identity, quizzing him with likely
questions other nobles would ask, helping him come up
with harmless stories about growing up in eastern Cenaria,
and teaching him the rudiments of etiquette. She told him
Count Drake would teach him the rest once he went to live
with the Drakes. When Azoth walked in the Drakes' door,
she said, he would be Kylar forever after. Blint would train
him in a safe house on the east side. Momma K would meet
with him in one of her homes on the east side. Only when
he started accompanying Blint on jobs would he return to
the Warrens.

Azoth worked hard for her and without complaint except for one time when he got disgusted at his own stupidity and threw a book across the room. He worked in
the hell of Momma K's displeasure for a week until he

brought her some flowers he'd stolen and she forgave him.

He'd given Jarl plenty of money to take care of Doll Girl, but Jarl wouldn't be able to just give her the money; someone would steal it. The worst part of it was that she was alone. Mute and with a horribly beaten face, she wouldn't be making any friends, either.

The price of disobedience is death, Master Blint had said. And he'd forbidden him to see Doll Girl again. Ever.

Momma K told Azoth that Master Blint would eventually come to like him and trust him, but that when he said things like that, for now Azoth should take it as law. That made Azoth hopeful—until she clarified: street law, which was immutable and omnipotent; not the pathetic king's law. It was a shame, because Azoth had to see Doll Girl one last time.

When he did get his chance, it was through no guile of his own. Master Blint had a job, so he simply left Azoth to his own devices. He left a list of chores, too, but Azoth knew that if he hurried, he could finish all the chores and still have several hours before he was supposed to meet with Momma K for his reading lesson.

He threw himself into his work with a fury. He dusted the weapons room, climbing up on a ladder to reach the higher rows of weapons and the equipment out of his reach. He checked and cleaned the wood practice weapons. He oiled and cleaned the weapons Master Blint had used recently. He worked a different kind of oil into the leather targets and dummies that Master Blint made him attack by the hour. He checked the seams on the ones Master Blint himself had kicked, and finding several burst, sewed them shut again. He wasn't very good with a needle, but Master Blint tolerated less than perfect work here—if nowhere else. He swept the floor, and as always, didn't throw the dirt out into the street, but collected it in a small bin. Master Blint didn't want him to leave the safe house. Not ever, unless he was under direct orders.

He found himself cleaning one of Blint's daggers a second time. It was a long thin blade with tiny gold filigree. Through chance or age, the gold was thin in the grooves that had been etched for it, so blood had collected in every narrow groove of the filigree—Blint had used this blade recently, and he must have been in a hurry when he sheathed it. So Azoth found himself using the point of another fine dagger to pick out the blood.

He should have soaked the blade in water and then scrubbed it vigorously, but this was his last chore. It was still three hours until he was supposed to be at Momma K's. If he had to work on chores until then, it wouldn't be his fault that he didn't leave.

"What happens if you do nothing? Blint had asked him. Nothing. There's a price and a terrible freedom to that, boy. Remember it." Master Blint had been speaking of making your move on a deader when things looked risky, but Azoth could feel the burden of those words now.

If I do something, what's the worst that could happen? Master Blint kills me. That was pretty bad. The odds of it were low, though. Unlike other wetboys who might spend their whole lives in the Warrens, Master Blint only took jobs from people who could afford his prices. That usually meant nobles. That always meant east side. So he'd be on the opposite side of the city from Azoth.

The real worst case if I do nothing? Doll Girl dies.

He put down the dagger with a grimace.

Finding Doll Girl was easier said than done. The Black Dragon guild had ceased to exist. It was just gone. Kylar went to their old territory and found that it had been swallowed by Red Hand, Burning Man, and Rusty Knife. The old Black Dragons scrawled on buildings and aqueducts were already fading. He wore a pair of daggers, but he didn't have to use them. Once, he was stopped by some Burning Men, but one of the bigs used to be one of his lizards. The boy spoke a few words to the others who were about to try to rob Azoth, and they eased away. The lizard never said a word to him.

He crisscrossed their old territory half a dozen times, but he never found Doll Girl. Once, he thought he saw Corbin Fishill, someone he'd always known was important, and who he now knew—Master Blint had told him—was one of the Nine. But all the guild rats he saw kept their distance.

Time was running out when Azoth finally thought of the old bakery. Doll Girl was there, alone. She had her back to him, and for a moment, he paused, afraid to get her attention. Then she turned.

Rat's sadism was evident. A month hadn't been long enough for her wounds to heal. It had only been long enough to show both what her face must have looked like for the last weeks, and what it would look like for the rest of her life. Rat had beaten her first, just beat her into submission or unconsciousness. Then he'd taken a knife to her face.

One deep cut looped from the corner of her left eye to the corner of her mouth. It had been stitched with dozens of tiny stitches, but the resulting scar would tug the corner of Doll Girl's mouth up into an unnatural grin forever. Her other cheek bore a broad X-shaped cut, which was matched again by a smaller X across her lips in front. Eating, smiling, frowning—moving her mouth at all must have been excruciating. One of her eyes was still swollen, and Azoth wasn't sure if she'd ever be able to see out of it again. The rest of the wounds looked like they would fade. A scab on her forehead, the barest yellow around her other eye as the black faded, and a nose that must have been reset because Azoth was sure Rat had broken it.

All in all, her face was, and was supposed to be, a testament to cruelty. Rat wanted anyone who ever looked at Doll Girl to know that she hadn't just had an accident. He wanted everyone to know that this had been done deliberately. For a moment, Azoth wished Rat's death had been even more horrible.

Then time seemed to start again. He was staring at Doll Girl, staring at his friend's face with open horror. Her eyes, that had been so full of surprise and sudden hope, brimmed full with tears. She covered herself and turned away, crying silently, her thin shoulders shaking.

He sat next to her. "I came as soon as I could. I've got a master now and I had to disobey him just to be here, but I couldn't leave you here. Things have been bad, huh?" She started sobbing.

He could just imagine the names they must have called her. Sometimes he wanted to kill everyone in the Warrens. How could they make fun of Doll Girl? How could they hurt her? It was a miracle she was still alive. A miracle, and Jarl. Jarl must have risked his life a dozen times.

Azoth scooted over and pulled her close. She turned

and clung to him as if her tears would wash her away. He held her and cried.

Time passed. Azoth felt like he'd been squeezed dry. He wasn't sure how long he'd held her, but he knew it had been too long. "I have good news," he told her.

She looked up at him with those big brown eyes.

"Come with me," he said.

Doll Girl followed him out of the Warrens, over the Vanden Bridge, and to Count Drake's. Her eyes widened as they headed toward the count's house, and further when the old porter opened the door for Azoth and showed them in.

Count Drake was in his office. He rose and ushered them in, somehow not even registering surprise at how awful Doll Girl's face looked. He was a better person than Azoth.

"Has Azoth told you why you're here, young lady?" the count asked. The name was a deliberate choice, Azoth saw. Doll Girl was part of Azoth's life—she wouldn't be part of Kylar's. She wasn't going to know his new name.

Doll Girl shook her head shyly, clinging to Azoth.

"We've found a family for you, Doll Girl," Count Drake said. "They want you to come and be their daughter. They're going to take care of you. You'll never have to sleep on the streets again. They serve in a house here on the east side. If you don't want to, you never have to go back to the Warrens ever again."

Of course, it had all been a little more involved than that. Count Drake had known the family for some time. They had taken in other slaveborn orphans over the years, but couldn't afford to feed another. So Azoth had sworn that he would provide for her out of his wages, which were already generous, and which Master Blint had told him would increase as he became more useful. Count Drake hadn't been enamored of keeping any secret from Master Blint, but after Azoth had explained what had happened, he'd been willing to help.

Doll Girl clung to Azoth, either not understanding or not believing what the count had just said.

Count Drake stood. "Well, I'm sure you have some things you probably wish to tell her, and I need to get the coach in order, so if you'll excuse me?" He left them alone, and Doll Girl looked at Azoth with accusing eyes.

"You never were dumb," he said.

She squeezed his hand, hard.

"My master ordered me not to see you. Today is the last time we ever get to see each other." She tugged on his hand, face pugnacious. "Yes, ever," he said. "I don't want it to be this way, but he'll kill me if he finds out I defied him even this much. I'm sorry. Please don't be mad at me."

She was crying again and there was nothing he could do.

"I have to go now. He might be back any time. I'm sorry." He tore his eyes from her and stepped toward the door.

"Don't leave me."

The voice sent a lance of ice down his spine. He turned, incredulous. It was a little girl voice, exactly like you'd expect if you didn't know Doll Girl was a mute.

"Please?" Doll Girl said. It was a pretty voice, incongruous coming out of a beaten mask of a face Rat had left her.

Azoth's eyes filled with tears again, and he ran out the door—

Straight into someone tall and lean and as hard as if he'd been cut out of solid rock. Azoth fell on his butt and stared up in horror.

Master Blint's face was purple with fury. "You dare?" he shouted. "After all I've done for you, you defy me? I just killed one of the Nine and what do you do? You walk around the killing ground for two hours, so everyone knows Blint's apprentice was there. You may have cost me everything!"

He swept Azoth off the ground as if he were a kitten and hit him. Azoth's tunic tore in Blint's hand as he fell back from the force of the blow. But Blint came forward, and this time his closed fist crashed against Azoth's jaw.

Azoth's face rebounded off the count's floor and he barely saw Doll Girl flying at Master Blint as the huge black sword cleared its sheath.

"Don't hurt her!" Azoth shouted. Insanely, he threw himself at Blint and grabbed Retribution's blade, but Blint was a force of nature. He didn't even slow as he scooped Doll Girl up and deposited her in the hall. He locked the door, unlocked it, and relocked it in rapid succession. He turned back to Azoth, but whatever he was about to say died. The great black sword was still locked in Azoth's hands, cutting to the bone. Except that now it wasn't black. The blade was glowing blue.

Incandescent blue fire surrounded Azoth's hand, burning cold into his cut fingers, spreading down the blade—

"No, not that! It's mine!" Blint cried. He flung the sword aside as if it were an adder, away from both of them. If there had been fury in his eyes before, now it turned to absolute unreasoning rage. Azoth didn't even see the first blow. He didn't even know how he'd reached the floor again. Something wet and sticky was blocking out his vision.

Then the world faded into repeated heavy blows and exploding light and pain and the sharp garlicky breath of Master Blint and distant shouting and banging on a door that seemed further and further away.

16

Durzo gazed into the frothy brown ale as if it held answers. It didn't, and he had a choice to make. The usual
forced gaiety of the brothel swirled around him, but nobody male or female bothered him. Perhaps it was Retribution unsheathed on the table in front of him. Perhaps it
was merely the look on his face.

Don't hurt her! Azoth had yelled. As if Durzo would
murder some seven-year-old girl. What kind of a monster
did the boy think he was? Then he remembered beating
the shit out of the boy, artlessly pounding that yielding
child flesh, beating him unconscious before Count Drake
broke the door down and grabbed him. He'd almost killed
Count Drake for that, he'd been so wild. The count had
fixed such a look on Durzo—damn Count Drake and his
damn holy eyes.

That incandescent blue. Damn it. Damn all magic. In
that flash of blue on Retribution, he'd seen his hope die.
The hope had been dying since Vonda died, but that blue
was a door slamming shut forever. It meant Azoth was

worthy as Durzo was not, as if all of Durzo's years of service were worth nothing. The boy was taking from him all that made him special. What did that leave for Durzo Blint?

Ashes. Ashes, and blood, and nothing more.

Suddenly the sword Retribution before him seemed a mockery. *Retribution? Giving people what they deserve? If I really did that, I'd shove that damn blade down my own throat.*

The last time he'd been so close to madness had been when Vonda died, four months and six days ago. Sighing, he swirled the ale around in the glass, but he didn't drink. Time enough for that later. Later, after he made his decision, he'd need a drink. He'd need twelve, no matter what he decided.

He'd drunk a lot with Vonda. It pissed her sister off. Of course, the whole relationship had pissed Momma K off. She'd forbidden Durzo to see her innocent little sister. She'd forbidden Vonda to see the wetboy. Momma K, so smart in other matters, had probably done more to get their relationship going than anything. Surrounded by easy flesh, whether he paid for it or not, Gwinvere's little sister was suddenly intriguing. He wanted to know if the virginal bit was an act.

It was. He'd been disappointed but had hidden it. It was hypocrisy, anyway, and she'd had plenty of other mysteries. Vonda didn't always treat him well, but at least she didn't fear him. He didn't think she understood him enough to fear him. She seemed to just glide along on the surface of life while others had to plunge into the sewer water. Durzo hadn't understood her, and it had entranced him.

After their affair started, he might have kept it secret.
He could have; he knew Gwinvere's schedule well enough
that they could have kept things going for years. Even
with Gwinvere's insight, Durzo knew how to be inscru-
table. But it hadn't happened. Vonda had told her. Probably announced it immediately, if Durzo knew Vonda. It
might have been a little callous, but Vonda didn't know
what she was doing.

"End this now, Durzo Blint," Gwinvere had told him,
quite calmly. "She'll destroy you. I love my sister, but she
will be your ruin." It had all been words. Words to get
Gwinvere's way, as always. With all her power, it infuriated her that she couldn't run the lives of those she really
wanted to.

She'd been right, of course. Maybe not in the way she
had meant it, but she'd been right. Gwinvere always had
understood him better than anyone else, and he'd understood her. They were mirrors to each other. Gwinvere Kirena would have been perfect for him—if he could love
what he saw in the mirror.

*Why am I thinking about this? It's all old shit. It's all
finished.* There was a choice to be made: did he raise the
boy and hope, or did he kill him now?

*Hope. Right. Hope is the lies we tell ourselves about
the future.* He'd hoped before. Dared to dream about a
different life, but when it came time—

"You look pensive, Gaelan Starfire," a Ladeshian bard
said, seating himself across from Durzo without waiting
to be asked.

"I'm deciding who to kill. Call me that again and you
jump to the front of the list, Aristarchos."

The bard smiled with the confidence of a man who

knows he has perfect white teeth that only set off a handsome face. By the Night Angels.

"We've been awfully curious about what's been happening for the last few months."

"You and the Society can go to hell," Durzo said.

"I think you like the attention, *Durzo Blint*. If you wanted us dead, we'd be dead. Or are you really bound by this code of retribution? It's of considerable debate in the society."

"Still fighting over the same questions, huh? Don't you all have anything better to do? Talk talk talk. Why don't you do something productive for once?"

"We're trying, Durzo. In fact, that's why I'm here. I want to help you."

"How kind."

"You've lost it, haven't you?" Aristarchos asked. "Have you lost it, or has it abandoned you? Do the stones really choose their own masters?"

Durzo noticed he was spinning the knife from finger to finger again. It wasn't to intimidate the Ladeshian—who laudably enough didn't even glance at it—it just kept his hands busy. It was nothing. He stopped it. "Here's why I've never been friends with any of you, Aristarchos: I don't know if your little circle has ever been interested in me, or if it's only interested in my power. Once, I was almost convinced to share some of my mysteries, but I realized that what I share with one of you, I share with all of you. So tell me, why would I give my enemies such power?"

"Is that what we've come to?" Aristarchos asked. "Enemies? Why then do you not wipe us from the face of the earth? You're uniquely suited to such a task."

"I don't kill without cause. Fear isn't enough to motivate me. It may be beyond your comprehension, but I can hold power without using it."

Aristarchos stroked his chin. "Then you are a better man than many have feared. I see now why you were chosen in the first place." Aristarchos stood. "Know this, Durzo Blint. I am far from home and have not the means I might wish, but if you call on me, I will give you what help I can. And knowing that you have deemed the cause just will be enough explanation for me. Good day."

The man walked out of the brothel, smiling and winking at the whores who seemed disappointed to lose his business. He wore his charm like a mask, Durzo saw.

The masks change, but the masquers remain the same, don't they? Durzo had lived with the bilge waste of humanity for so long, he saw filth in every heart. He knew the filth was there; he was right about that. Filth and darkness were even in Rimbold Drake's heart. But Drake didn't act from that darkness, did he? No. That masquer—if only that one—had changed.

Fear isn't enough to motivate me, he'd said—while planning to murder a child. *What kind of a monster am I?*

He was caught now. Truly and desperately caught. He'd just killed Corbin Fishill. The man's death had been sanctioned by the Shinga and the rest of the Nine. Corbin had been managing the guilds as if he were in Khalidor, setting guild against guild, encouraging open war between them and doing absolutely nothing to regulate brutality within the guilds. Khalidorans did such things in the belief that the best would naturally rise. But the Sa'kagé wanted members, not monsters.

Worse, they now had some indication that Corbin actually had been working for Khalidor. That was inexcusable. Not taking the work, but taking it without reporting it to the rest of the Nine. Loyalties had to be to the Sa'kagé first.

The kill had been sanctioned, and it had been just. That didn't mean that Corbin's friends would accept it. Durzo had killed members of the Nine before, but he always took extra care to conceal whose work it was. Now Azoth had tromped around his killing grounds for hours, a little before the job was done and a lot after. Enough people knew or guessed Durzo had taken Azoth as his apprentice that they couldn't fail to link the two. It was sloppy wet work, they'd say. Maybe Durzo Blint is slipping.

Being the best made him a target. The appearance of weakness gave every second-rate wetboy hope that they could move up. Azoth couldn't have known, of course. Still didn't know so many things. But in that flash of blue light from Retribution's blade, Durzo had seen his own death. If he let the boy live, Durzo would die. Sooner or later.

And there it was. The divine economy. For someone to live, someone had to die.

Durzo Blint made his decision, and started drinking.

"Master Blint hasn't come to see me."

"No," Momma K said.

"It's been four days. You said he wasn't mad anymore," Azoth said, making fists with his hands. He thought he had cut them, but they were fine. Lots of other places on his body hurt, so he hadn't just imagined being beaten, but his hands were fine.

"Three days. And he's not mad. Drink this."

"No. I don't want any more of that stuff. It makes me feel worse." He regretted the words as soon as he said them. Momma K's eyebrows went up and her eyes went cold. Even huddled in warm blankets in a spare bedroom here in her house, when her eyes turned frosty, nothing could make you feel warm.

"Child, let me tell you a story. Have you ever heard of the Snake of Haran?"

Azoth shook his head.

"The snake has seven heads, but each time you cut one head off, two more grow in its place."

"Really? There's really such a thing?"

"No. In Haran they call it the Snake of Ladesh. It's imaginary."

"Then why did you tell me about it?" Azoth asked.

"Are you being deliberately obtuse?" When he didn't answer, she said, "If you'll let me finish, you'll see the story is an analogy. Analogies are lies grown-ups tell."

"Why?" Being stuck in bed was making Azoth petulant.

"Why does anyone tell lies? Because they're useful. Now drink your medicine and then shut your mouth," Momma K said.

Azoth knew he was pushing it, so he didn't ask any more. He drank the thick mint-and-anise-flavored brew.

"Right now the Sa'kagé has its own Snake of Haran, Azoth . . . *Kylar.* Do you know Corbin Fishill?"

Azoth nodded. Corbin was the handsome, impressive young man who had sometimes come and talked to Ja'laliel.

"Corbin was one of the Nine. He ran the children's guilds."

"Was?" Azoth almost squeaked. He wasn't supposed to know Corbin was even important, much less how important.

"Durzo killed him three days ago. When the baby farms were shut down, the Sa'kagé was given a chance to literally raise its own army. But Corbin was allowing or encouraging guild war that was wiping out the slaveborn. And he was a spy. The Sa'kagé thought he was a Ceuran spy, but now they think he was taking money from Khalidor. The Khalidorans paid him in Ceuran gold, probably in case he was found, and also so he wouldn't start spending the money immediately and bring attention to himself.

"Now that Corbin is dead, his things have been searched, and unfortunately, there hasn't been any clear answer. If he was Khalidoran, he was far more dangerous than we had thought, and the Sa'kagé should have brought him in and had him tortured until they knew for sure, but at the time, they thought it was more important to set a graphic example of what happens to those who mismanage Sa'kagé endeavors. The problem now is bigger.

"We don't think Corbin was in place long enough to cultivate any loyalty to Khalidor among the guilds—street rats don't care much where their meals come from—but the fact Khalidor would work on taking over the guilds tells us that they are thinking long term."

"How do you know he wasn't just the easiest person they could get in the Sa'kagé?"

Momma K smiled. "We don't. Khalidor is putting down some rebellions right now, and it's not going well for them. But the Godking has earned a reputation as a man who plans for victory, and my guess is that he thinks it may be years before he's ready to march south, but he wants Cenaria to fall at the slightest blow when he does. If he controls the Sa'kagé, taking the city will be easy. Our problem is that if he was able to get a man as highly placed as Corbin, then there may be dozens of others. The other heads of the snake may show up at any time. Anyone we trust may be working for Khalidor."

"Why's that your problem?" Azoth asked.

"It's my problem because I'm one of the Nine, too, Kylar. I'm the Mistress of Pleasures."

Azoth's mouth formed a little O. Always before, the Sa'kagé had been something dangerous, huge, and distant. He supposed it fit—everyone knew Momma K had been a whore and that she was wealthy—but he'd never even thought of it. Being the Mistress of Pleasures meant that Momma K controlled all of the prostitution in Cenaria. Everyone who plied the pleasure trade ultimately answered to her.

She smiled. "Aside from my girls' more . . . strenuous duties, they also keep their ears open. You'd be amazed at how talkative men can be in front of what they think is just a dumb whore. I'm in charge of the Sa'kagé's spies. I need to know what Khalidor is doing. If I don't know, the Sa'kagé doesn't know, and if we don't know, the country may fall. Believe me, we do not want Garoth Ursuul as our king."

"Why are you telling me all this?" Azoth said. "I'm nobody."

"Azoth was nobody. You are about to become Kylar Stern," she said, "And I think you're smarter than Durzo gives you credit for. I'm telling you because we need you on our side. Azoth was stupid to go wandering the other day, and it may cost you or Durzo your lives. But if you had known what was happening, you wouldn't have gone there. You did the wrong thing, but Durzo shouldn't have beaten you for showing initiative. In fact, I'm sure he's sorry for beating you, though he'll never apologize. It isn't in the man to admit he's wrong. We need you to be more than an apprentice, Kylar. We need you to be an ally. Are you ready for that?"

Azoth—Kylar—nodded slowly. "What do you want me to do?"

17

Kylar tried to gawk at the right things as he was ushered through the Gyre estate. Azoth, Momma K had told him, would gawk at anything big or gold. Baronet Kylar Stern would gawk only at things that were both—and the art. Logan had invited him to visit to make amends for hitting him, and Kylar's first job for the Sa'kagé was to make sure they became friends.

The porter escorted him to another, better-dressed man—Kylar almost greeted him as Duke Gyre before realizing he must be the Gyre's chamberlain. The chamberlain took him through a vast entry hall with dual stairs that climbed three stories flanking an enormous marble statue of two men, twins, facing each other in battle, each seeing the same opening in the other's defense, each lunging. It was one of the most famous statues in the world, Momma K had told Kylar: The Grasq Twins' Doom. In history, Momma K said, the Grasq twins had been heavily armored and during a long battle each had lost the thin tabards that at the time were all men wore over plate mail and all that identified them if they were separated from their standard bearers. They had indeed killed each other, though each had avoided the other in earlier battles. Here, the men were naked except for a shield and sword. Because of the shields' placement, each was seeing his twin's face for the first time even as he struck the death blow.

The chamberlain took Kylar up the stairs and down one long wing of the estate. The hallway was wider than most of the alleys in the Warrens. Both sides were crowded with marble busts and paintings of men speaking, men fighting, men seizing women, families moving, women mourning, the aftermath of battles, and horrible monsters boiling out of gaps in the ground. Every picture was framed with heavy gold leaf. Most were big. Walking behind the chamberlain, Kylar could gawk as much as he wanted, and he did. Then they stopped at a huge door. The chamberlain rapped on it with the staff he carried and opened the door to a library with dozens of shelves in orderly rows and the walls lined with books and scrolls to a height of two stories.

"My lord, Baronet Kylar Stern."

Logan Gyre rose from a table with an open scroll laid across it. "Kylar! I was just finishing—I borrowed this scroll from—oh, never mind. Welcome!"

"Thank you for inviting me, Duke Gyre; your estate is beautiful. The statue of the Grasq twins is breathtaking." He was reciting it the way Momma K had taught him, but now he meant it.

"Please, call me Logan. You're most kind. You really like it?" Logan asked.

The "you're most kind" gave him away. Logan was

trying as hard to be an adult as Kylar was. Kylar was nervous because he was a fraud, but "Duke" Logan felt like a fraud, too. The title was too big and too new for him to feign comfort convincingly. So Kylar answered honestly, "Actually, I think it's amazing. I just wish they weren't naked."

Logan burst out laughing. "I know! Most the time I don't notice it anymore, but every once in a while I come in the door and—there's two huge naked men in my house. Because of my new duties I'm meeting all of my father's retainers and friends, again. Really it's a chance for ladies to introduce their daughters and hope I fall madly in love. I was greeting a lady and her daughter, I won't name names, but they are beautiful women and very prim, very modest. So I'm pretty tall, right? and they both have to really look up to look me in the eye, and as I'm talking and I'm in the middle of a story and the mom is tittering and the daughter looks utterly captivated, and I start to wonder if I've got something in my hair or on my ear or something, because they both keep glancing just a bit to the side."

"Oh no," Kylar said, laughing.

"I glance over my shoulder, and there's . . . well, there, three times life size, is marble . . . genitalia. And there's this moment where they realize that I've noticed that they've been looking over my shoulder the whole time, and I realize this is the first time that the daughter has ever seen a naked man—and I totally forget what story I was telling them."

They laughed together, Kylar desperately thankful that Logan had given enough context so he could figure out what "genitalia" meant. Did all nobles talk like this?

What if next time Logan gave the punch line without the context? Logan pointed to a portrait on the library wall of a square-jawed bald man dressed in an unfamiliar style. "I have him to thank for that. My great-great-great grandfather, the art lover."

Kylar smirked, but he felt he'd been slapped. Logan knew things about his great-great-great grandfather. Kylar didn't even know who his father was. There was a silence, and Kylar knew it was his turn to fill it. "I, uh, heard that the Grasq twins actually led like six battles against each other."

"You know their story?" Logan asked. "Not many people our age do."

Belatedly, Kylar realized the risk of posing as a story lover to this man who loved books—and could actually read them. "I really like old stories," Kylar said. "But my parents don't really have any use for me 'wasting my time filling my head with stories.'"

"You really do like stories? Aleine always starts pretending to snore when I talk about history." *Aleine? Oh, Aleine Gunder, Prince Aleine Gunder X.* Logan's world really was different. "Look at this," he beckoned Kylar to the table. "Here, read this part."

Be happy to, if I could read. Kylar's heart seized up. His disguise was still so fragile. "You're making me feel like my tutors," he said, waving it off. "I don't want to read for an hour while you're twiddling your thumbs. Why don't you tell me the good parts?"

"I feel like I'm doing all the talking," Logan said, suddenly awkward. "It's kind of rude."

Kylar shrugged. "I don't think you're being rude. Is it a new story, or what?"

Logan's eyes lit up and Kylar knew he was safe. "No, it's the end of the Alkestia Cycle, right before the Seven Kingdoms fall. My father's having me study the great leaders of the past. In this case, Jorsin Alkestes, of course. When they were under siege at Black Barrow, his right hand man, Ezra the Mad—well, it wasn't Black Barrow yet, and Ezra didn't go hide out in Ezra's Wood for another fifty years or something—anyway, Ezra's maybe the best magus ever, behind Emperor Jorsin Alkestes himself. They're under siege at what's now Black Barrow and Ezra starts making the most amazing stuff: the war hammers of Oren Razin; fire and lightning traps even un-Talented soldiers can use; Curoch, the sword of power; Iures, the staff of law; and then these six magic artifacts, *ka'kari*. They each look like a glowing ball, but the Six Champions can squeeze one and it melts and covers their whole bodies like a second skin and gives them power over their element. Arikus Daadrul gets this skin of silver liquid metal that makes him impervious to blades. Corvaer Blackwell becomes Corvaer the Red, the master of fire. Trace Arvagulania goes from grossly ugly to the most beautiful woman of the era. Oren Razin gets earth, weighs a thousand pounds and turns his skin to stone. Irenaea Blochwei gets the power of everything green and growing. Shrad Marden gets water and can suck the very liquid from a man's blood.

"The thing that has always made me curious is that Jorsin Alkestes was a great leader. He brought together so many talented people, and lots of them were difficult and egotistical, and he put them in harness together, and they *worked*. But at the end, he insults one of his best friends, Acaelus Thorne, and gives a ka'kari to Shrad Marden instead, whom he doesn't even like. Do you know Acaelus Thorne?"

"I've heard the name," Kylar offered. That much was true. Sometimes the guild rats would huddle around a window to one of the taverns when a bard visited, but they could only hear bits and pieces of the stories.

"Acaelus was this amazing fighter but a noble fool. No subtlety. He hated lies, politics, and magic, but put a sword in his hand, and he'd go charging an enemy force solo if he had to. He was so crazy and so good that his men would follow him anywhere. But he was all about honor, and seeing lesser men honored before him was a huge insult. It was that insult that led Acaelus to betray Jorsin. How could Jorsin have missed it? He had to have known he was insulting him."

"What do you think?" Kylar asked.

Logan scrubbed a hand through his hair. "It's probably something boring, like that there was a war going on, and everyone was exhausted and starving and not thinking clearly and Jorsin just made a mistake."

"So what does that teach you about being a leader?" Kylar asked.

Logan looked perplexed. "Eat your vegetables and get enough sleep?"

"How about 'be nice to your inferiors, or they might kick your ass'?" Kylar suggested.

"Are you asking me to spar, Baronet Stern?"

"Your exalted dukeliness, it will be my pleasure to take you down."

18

$\mathcal{K}$ylar stepped into the safe house, flushed from his victory. He'd got three touches to Logan's two. Logan fought better, but as Momma K had told Kylar, he'd also grown a foot in the last year and hadn't adjusted to his new height yet. "Not only did I just make Logan Gyre my friend," Kylar said, "I also beat him in sparring."

Durzo didn't even look up from the calcinator. He turned the flame up higher beneath the copper dish. "Good. Now never spar with him again. Hand me that."

Hurt, Kylar took a flask from under the whirling tubes of the alembic and gave it to him. Durzo poured the thick blue mixture onto the calcinator. For the moment, it sat there, still. Small bubbles began forming and within moments the mixture was boiling rapidly.

"Why not?" Kylar asked.

"Get the slops, boy." Kylar grabbed the pig's slop bowl and brought it to the table.

"We fight differently from what any of this city's sword masters teach. If you spar with Logan, you will adopt his by-the-book style and become a worthless fighter, or you'll give away that you're being taught something utterly different, or both."

Kylar scowled at the calcinator. His master was right, of course, and even if he weren't, his word was law. The blue mixture was now a dark blue powder. Durzo lifted the copper plate from the flames with a thick wool pad and scraped the powder into the slop bowl. He grabbed another copper plate and poured more of the blue mixture into it and put it above the flames, setting the first aside to cool with a heavy mitt. "Master, do you know why Jorsin Alkestes would insult his best friend by not giving him a ka'kari?"

"Maybe he asked too many questions."

"Logan said Acaelus Thorne was the most honorable of Jorsin's friends, but he betrayed Jorsin and that led to the fall of the Seven Kingdoms," Kylar said.

"Most people aren't strong enough for our creed, Kylar, so they believe comforting illusions, like the gods, or Justice, or the basic goodness of man. Those illusions fail in war. It breaks men. That's probably what happened to Acaelus."

"Are you sure?" Kylar asked. Logan's reading of it had been so different.

"Sure?" Blint asked, scornfully. "I'm not sure about what the nobles here did seven years ago when they ended slavery. How would anyone be sure about what happened hundreds of years ago far away? Take that to the pig." Kylar picked up the slops and took them to the pig they'd recently acquired for Master Blint's experiments.

As he was returning, he saw Blint staring at him as if about to say something. Then there was a small whoosh as flame leaped from the copper plate behind Master Blint. Before Kylar could flinch, Blint whirled around. A phantom hand stretched out from his hands and grabbed the metal plate directly from the fire and set it down on the table. Then the hand was gone. It happened so fast, Kylar wasn't sure he hadn't imagined it.

The plate was smoking and what should have been blue powder was now a black crust. A black crust that Kylar had no doubt he would soon be scraping off until the copper shone.

Blint swore. "See, you get caught up in the past and you become useless to the present. Come on, let's see if that stinking pig's still alive. Then we need to do something with your hair."

The pig wasn't still alive, and after the amount of poison it had ingested, it wasn't safe to eat, so Kylar spent half the day cutting it into pieces and burying it. After that, Master Blint made him strip to the waist and rubbed a pungent paste through his hair. It burned his scalp and Blint made him keep it in for an hour. But when he finally rinsed the hair clean, Blint showed him his own reflection in the glass and he barely recognized himself. His hair was white blond.

"Just be thankful you're young, or I would have had to smear it on your eyebrows, too," Blint said. "Now get dressed. The Azoth clothes. The Azoth persona."

"I get to go with you? On a job?"

"Get dressed."

"I understand why 'Apparent Consumption' is nine hundred gunders. I'm sure you have to do multiple poison-ings to mimic the disease," the noble said. "But fifteen hundred for apparent self-murder? Ridiculous. Stab your man and put the knife in his hand."

"How about we start again," Master Blint said quietly. "You speak as if I'm the best wetboy in the city, and I'll speak as if there's a chance this side of hell that I'll take the job."

The tension sat thick in the upstairs room of the inn. Lord General Brant Agon wasn't pleased, but he took a breath, ran a hand through his gray hair, and said, "Why does faking a suicide cost fifteen hundred gold?"

"A properly staged suicide takes months," Master Blint said. "Depending upon the deader's history. If I'm after a known melancholic, that can be shortened to six weeks. If he's tried to suicide before, it can be as little as a week. I gain access in one way or another and administer special concoctions."

Azoth was trying to pay attention, but there was something about being back in his old clothes that made the illusions of the last weeks come crashing down. Kylar was gone—and not because Azoth was following orders and pretending to be Azoth. Kylar had been a mask of confidence. It had fooled Logan, and it had fooled Azoth for a little while, but the mask had fallen away. He was Azoth. He was weak. He didn't understand what he was doing here, or why, and he was scared.

Blint continued, not so much as glancing at him, "The deader becomes depressed, withdrawn, suspicious. Symptoms gradually worsen. Then maybe a favorite pet dies. The target is already peevish and paranoid, and soon he lashes out at his friends. The friends who visit—at least those who take refreshment—grow irritable while they are with the deader. They quarrel. They stop visiting. Sometimes the target writes the note himself. Sometimes he even commits the suicide himself, though I monitor that closely to make sure he chooses an appropriate method for the effect desired. When given proper time, no one suspects anything but self-murder. The family itself will often hush up the details, and scatter what little evidence there is."

"By the High King's beard, is such a thing possible?" the lord general asked.

"Possible? Yes. Difficult? Very. It takes a considerable number of carefully mixed poisons—do you know that everyone reacts differently to poisons?—and a huge amount of my time. If a forged note is required, the target's correspondence and journals are analyzed so that not only the handwriting, but also the writing style and even certain choices of wording are identical." Durzo smiled wolfishly. "Assassination is an art, milord, and I am the city's most accomplished artist."

"How many men have you killed?" the lord general asked.

"Suffice it to say I'm never idle."

The man fiddled with his beard and continued looking through the handbill Master Blint had given him, obviously unsettled. "May I ask about others, Master Blint?" he said, suddenly respectful.

"I prefer that you only inquire about those deaths you're seriously considering," Master Blint said.

"Why is that?"

"I value secrets very highly, as I must. So I don't like to discuss my methodology. And, to be honest, knowing too much tends to frighten those who employ me. I had a client some time ago who was very proud of his defenses. He asked me how I'd fulfill a contract on him. He irritated me, so I told him.

"Afterward, he tried to hire another wetboy to kill me. He was turned down by every professional in Cenaria. He ended up hiring an amateur."

"You give yourself the status of a legend," the lord general said, his thin face pinching.

Of course Durzo Blint was a legend! Who would hire him if they didn't know that? At the same time, hearing Master Blint speak of his trade to a noble—to someone like Count Drake—was eerie. It was like Azoth's two worlds were being pressed uncomfortably close to each other, and he could feel the noble's awe in himself.

In the guild, Durzo Blint had been a legend because he had power, because people were afraid of him, and he never had to be afraid of anyone. That was what had drawn Azoth to him. But this noble was awed for different reasons. To him, Durzo Blint was a creature of the night. He was a man who could come violate those things he held dear. He undermined all of what the lord general had thought safe. The man didn't look afraid; he looked disgusted.

"I'm not suggesting that I terrify every wetboy in the city." Master Blint smiled. "The fact is that we professionals are, if not a close group, at least a small one. We're colleagues, some of us even friends. The second wetboy he went to was Scarred Wrable—"

"I've heard of him," Brant Agon said. "Apparently the second best assassin in the city."

"Wetboy," Blint corrected. "And a friend of mine. He told me what this client was doing. After that—well, if a military metaphor works better for you—it would be like trying a small raid on a city that was expecting it instead of an unsuspecting city. In the second case it might work, in the first it's suicide."

"I see," the lord general said. He paused for a moment, apparently surprised Master Blint knew who he was, then suddenly grinned, "And you're a tactician, too."

"How so?"

"You haven't had many contracts taken out on you since you started telling that story, have you?"

Master Blint smiled broadly. These were two men, Azoth saw, who understood each other. "Not a one. After all, diplomacy is an extension of warfare," Blint said.

"We usually say that warfare is an extension of diplomacy," Brant Agon said. "But I think I agree with you. I once found myself outnumbered and forced to hold a position against the Lae'knaught for two days to wait for reinforcements. I had some captives, so I put them in a vulnerable position and told their guards we would receive reinforcements at dawn. During the fighting, the prisoners were allowed to get free and promptly told their superiors the news. The Lae'knaught army was so disheartened that they held back until we *had* been reinforced. That diplomacy saved our lives. Which brings us back to the matter at hand," the lord general said. "I need some diplomacy that's not on this list of yours. I'm afraid I've not been completely forthright with you, Master Blint," the lord general said. "I'm here for the king."

Master Blint's face went suddenly devoid of emotion.

"I understand that by telling you that, we might lose the man who provided me with your name. But the king deems this to be worth risking the lives of both a contact and one of his ministers—namely, myself."

"You haven't done anything foolish like surround the building with soldiers, have you?" Master Blint asked.

"Nothing of the kind. I'm here alone."

"Then you've made one wise choice today."

"More than one. We've chosen you, Master Blint. And I've chosen to be honest with you, which I hope you appreciate.

"As you know, the king's wealthy, but not politically or militarily strong. That's a bitter pill, but it's not news. Our kings haven't been strong for a hundred years. Aleine Gunder wishes to change that. But in addition to internal struggles of which you no doubt know more than I'd care to learn, the king has recently learned of some rather devious plots to steal vast sums of money not only from the treasury, but—in a multitude of schemes—also from almost every nobleman in the country. The idea being, we think, that Cenaria becomes so impoverished that we'll be unable to maintain an army."

"Sounds like a lot of money to steal without anybody noticing," Master Blint said.

"The Chancellor of the Exchequer has noticed—he's the one arranging it. But no one else has noticed, yet. The schemes are little short of brilliant. The plot won't even ripen for six or ten years. Men are being placed in key positions and have as yet have done nothing wrong. There's more, much more, but you don't need to know it."

"What do I need to know?" Blint asked, his eyes heavy-lidded.

"I've made a study of you, Master Blint," the lord general said. "Though information about you is difficult to find. Everyone knows that the Sa'kagé holds an enormous amount of power here. People outside the country know it. Khalidor knows it.

"The king needs you for more than a dozen jobs, spanning years. Some will involve simple assassination, some will involve information planting, and some will not involve killing at all, but simply being seen. Godking Ursuul must believe the Sa'kagé and its assets have an alliance with us."

"You want me to become a government agent."

"Not . . . exactly."

"And I suppose you'd give me a pardon for all I've done?" Master Blint asked.

"I've been authorized to offer that."

Master Blint stood, laughing. "No, Lord General. Good day."

"I'm afraid I can't take no for an answer. The king has forbidden it."

"I do hope you're not planning on threatening my life," Master Blint said.

"First," the lord general said, looking at Azoth for the first time, "we'll kill the boy."

19

Master Blint shrugged. "So?"

"And we'll kill your lover. I believe her name's Vonda?"

"You can kill the bitch. But that might give you some trouble, considering she's four months dead."

The lord general didn't even pause. "And we'll kill this 'Momma' Kirena who seems to be your only friend. Then we'll come after you. I don't want it to be this way, but this is what the king offers."

"You're making two mistakes," Master Blint said. "First, you're assuming that I value other people's lives more than my own. How can you know what I do and believe such a thing? Second, you're assuming that I value my own life."

"Please understand. I'm under orders. Personally, I'd rather have nothing to do with you," the lord general said. "I think it's beneath the dignity of a king to hire criminals. I think it's immoral and foolish for him to put money in your purse rather than chains on your wrists. I find you abhorrent. A wreck of a human being barely resembling what once must have been a man. But the king has decided we need a sellsword like you. I'm a soldier. I've been sent to get you, and I won't fail."

"And you're making a tactical blunder," Master Blint said. "The king might kill my apprentice, my friend, and even me, but at the least, he will have lost his lord general. A poor trade."

"I don't think he would find my death to be such a very great loss," the lord general said.

"Ah, figured that out, have you?" Blint asked. "This may be the first time you've seen me, Brant Agon, but it isn't the first time I've seen you."

The lord general looked puzzled. "So you've seen me. So have half the people in the city."

"Does your wife still crowd your side of the bed? Sweet, isn't it? Does she still wear that drab nightgown with the daisies embroidered on the hem? You really love her, don't you?"

Lord General Agon froze.

"You call me abhorrent?" Durzo asked. "You owe me your life!"

"What?"

"Didn't you ever wonder why you got a promotion instead of a knife in the back?"

From his eyes, even Azoth could tell that the lord general had.

"I was in your house the night King Davin died, when you and Regnus Gyre met. I was to kill your wife as a warning to you. Later, the prince would offer you a better marriage to a young noblewoman who would be able to give you sons. And I was authorized to kill both you and Regnus if you were plotting treason. I spared you—and I don't get paid unless I leave corpses. I don't expect your gratitude, lord general, but I demand your respect!"

Lord General Agon's face went gray. "You . . . you told Aleine that my price was the promotion. He thought he bought me off with a promotion rather than a wife." Azoth could see him mentally reviewing comments he must have heard over the last four months, and getting sicker and sicker. "Why?"

"You're the illustrious general, the old war hero. You tell me." Durzo sneered.

"Putting me in charge of the army divided the Sa'kagé's enemies. It kept the king from putting someone he could trust in charge of the military. You bastards have got people everywhere, don't you?"

"Me? I'm just a sellsword. I'm just a wreck of a human being."

The general's face was still gray, but his back never bent an inch. "You've . . . you've given me much to think about, Master Blint. Though I still believe the murders you've committed merit hanging, I dishonored you and myself with my hasty words. I apologize. My apology, however, has no effect on the king's determination that you serve him. I—"

"Get out," Master Blint said. "Get out. If you reconsider your threats, I'll be here for a few minutes."

The general rose, and watching Master Blint carefully, walked to the door. He opened it, and kept his eyes on Master Blint until he closed the door behind himself. Azoth heard his steps echo down the hall.

Master Blint stared at the door and scooted back from the table. Instead of relaxing now that the general was gone, he tensed. Everything about him spoke of potential action. He looked like a mongoose waiting for a serpent to strike.

"Step away from the door, Azoth," he said. "Stand by the window."

There was no hesitation. Azoth had learned that lesson. He didn't have to understand; he just had to obey.

He heard a crash on the stairs and loud cursing. Azoth stood by the window and looked at Master Blint, but the man's pockmarked face betrayed nothing.

Moments later, the door banged open. The lord general lurched in, sword drawn. "What have you done?" he roared. His knees bowed and he leaned heavily against the doorframe to keep from falling.

Master Blint didn't say anything.

The general blinked and tried to straighten, but a spasm passed through his body as his stomach cramped. It passed, and he said, "How?"

"I put a contact poison on the door latch," Master Blint said. "It seeps right through the skin."

"But if we'd reached a deal . . ." the lord general said.

"I'd have opened the door for you. If you'd worn gloves, I had other plans. Now I want you to listen very closely. The king is an incompetent, treacherous, foul-mouthed child, so I'm going to make this very clear. I'm a first-rate wetboy. He's a second-rate king. I won't work for him. If you want, you can hire me yourself: I'll kill the king, but I won't kill for him. And there's no way you or he can pressure me.

"I know he won't believe that, because Aleine Gunder is the kind of man who believes he can get whatever he wants. So here's why he's going to believe." Master Blint stood. "First, I'm going to leave a message for him tonight in the castle. Second, you're going to investigate what happened to Count Yosar Glin. He was the client who betrayed me. Third, there's what has already happened to you. And fourth—do sit, Agon, and put away the sword. It's insulting."

Lord General Agon crashed into a chair. The long sword fell from his fingers. He didn't appear to have the strength to pick it up. Regardless, his eyes were still clear, and he was hearing every word Master Blint said.

"Lord General, I don't care who he kills. I know you have this inn surrounded, that there are crossbowmen covering the windows of this room. They don't matter. More importantly, the king's threats don't matter. I will be no man's lapdog. I serve who I will, when I will, and I will never serve Aleine Gunder. Azoth, come here."

Azoth went to his master, wondering why Blint had used his name. He stood in front of Master Blint, who rested his hands on Azoth's shoulders and turned him to face General Agon.

"Azoth here is my best apprentice. He's agile. He's smart. He learns things after being told once. He works tirelessly. Azoth, tell the general what you've learned about life."

Without hesitation, Azoth said, "Life is empty. Life is meaningless. When we take a life, we aren't taking anything of value. Wetboys are killers. That's all we do. That's all we are. There are no poets in the bitter business."

"Lord General," Blint said, "are you with me?"

"I'm with you," the general said, fire raging in his eyes.

Master Blint's voice was ice. "Then know this: I'd kill my own apprentice before I'd let you use him against me."

The general jerked sharply in his chair as if shocked. He was staring at Azoth. Azoth followed his gaze to his own chest.

Several inches of bloodied steel were protruding from him. Azoth saw them and felt an uncomfortable pushing, spreading sensation from his back all the way through his center. It seemed cool, then warm, then painful. He blinked his eyes slowly and looked back to the general, whose eyes were full of horror. Azoth looked at the steel.

He recognized that blade. He'd cleaned it that day he went looking for Doll Girl. He hoped Master Blint would at least wipe it down before he brought it back for Azoth to clean. It had filigree on the blade that held blood if you let it dry there. Azoth had had to use the point of a stiletto to pick it out. It took hours.

Then Azoth was drawn to the location of the dagger. At that angle on a child's chest, it would have clipped the fat vessel above the heart. If so, the deader would go down as soon as the dagger was drawn out. There would be a lot of blood. The deader would die within seconds.

Azoth's body jerked as the dagger disappeared. He was vaguely aware of his knees folding. He slumped over sideways and felt something warm spilling over his chest.

The wood planks of the floor jostled him unmercifully as he sprawled over them. He lay facing up. Master Blint was holding a bloody dagger in his hand and saying something.

Did Master Blint just stab me? Azoth couldn't believe it. What had he done? He thought Master Blint had been pleased with him. It must have been Doll Girl. He must have still been mad about it. It had seemed things were going so well. There was white-gold light everywhere. And he was warm. So warm.

20

"Your Majesty, please!"

King Aleine Gunder IX threw himself down into his throne. "Brant, it's one man. One!" He swore a stream of curses. "You'd have me send my family to the country for fear of one man?"

"Your Majesty," Lord General Brant Agon said, "the definition of 'man' might not cover Durzo Blint. I understand the implications—"

"Indeed! Do you know the talk it will cause if I send my family away on a moment's notice?" The king cursed again, unconsciously. "I know what they say about me. I know! I'll not give them this to drool on, Brant."

"Your Majesty, this assassin is not given to idle threats. For the sake of all that's holy, he murdered his own apprentice just to make a point!"

"A sham. Come on, general. You were drugged. You didn't know what was going on."

"My body was afflicted, not my mind. I know what I saw."

The king sniffed, then curled his lip as he caught the faint odor of brimstone in the air. "Dammit! Can't those idiots make anything work?"

One of the ducts that carried hot air from the Vos Island Crack just north of the castle had broken again. *He doesn't appreciate how much the engineers save us every year by heating the entire castle with pipes embedded in the very stones. He doesn't care that the turbines spinning in the wind rising from the Crack give him the power of two hundred windmills. That he smells brimstone once a fortnight infuriates him.* Agon wondered what god Cenaria had offended to deserve such a king.

He should have pushed Regnus Gyre. He should have spelled it out to him more clearly. He should have lied to him about what would happen to Nalia's children by Aleine. He could have served Regnus proudly. Proudly and honorably.

"Maybe you saw him kill a boy," the king said. "Who cares?" *You should. Regnus would have.* "It was obviously some street rat he picked up for the purpose of impressing you."

"With all due respect, sire, you're mistaken. I've dealt with formidable men. I faced Dorgan Dunwal in single combat. I fought Underlord Graeblan's Lae'knaught lancers. I—"

"Yes, yes. A thousand goddam battles from my goddam father's time. Very impressive," the king said. "But you never learned anything about ruling, did you?"

General Agon stiffened. "Not like you have, Your Majesty."

"Well, if you had, *general,* you'd know that you can't damage your own reputation." He cursed long and unfluently again. "Flee my own castle in the night!"

There was no working with him. The man shamed Agon and should have shamed himself. Yet Agon was sworn to him, and he'd decided long ago that an oath measured the man who gave it. It was like his marriage; he wouldn't take back his vows simply because his wife couldn't give him children.

But did vows hold when your own king had plotted to take your life? And not in honorable battle, but with an assassin's blade in the night?

That had been before Agon had sworn his allegiance to the man, however. Now that he had sworn, it didn't matter that—had he known then what he knew now—he would have chosen to die rather than serve Aleine Gunder IX.

"Your Majesty, may I at least have permission to hold an exercise tonight for my guards and include your mage? The Captain is in the habit of doing such things unannounced to keep the men at the ready." *Though I wonder why I preserve your empty head.*

"Oh, to hell with you, general. You and your goddam paranoia. Fine. Do as you please."

General Agon turned to leave the throne room. The king's predecessor, Davin, had been empty-headed too. But he'd known it, and he'd deferred to his counselors.

Aleine X, this king's son, was only fourteen years old, but he showed promise. He seemed to have gotten some of his mother's intelligence, at least. *If X were old enough to take power, maybe I'd provoke this assassin. Dear God, maybe I'd hire him.* General Agon shook his head. That was treason, and it had no place in a general's mind.

* * *

Fergund Sa'fasti had been appointed to serve in Cenaria more for his political acuity than his Talent. The truth was, he'd barely earned his blue robe. But his talents, if not his Talent, had served him well in Cenaria. The king was both stupid and foolish, but he could be worked with, if one didn't mind petulance and showers of curses.

But tonight Fergund was wandering the castle as if he were a guard. He'd appealed to the king, but Aleine IX—they called him Niner, short for "the nine-year-old" and not "the ninth," only when drinking with friends—had cursed him and ordered him to do whatever the lord general said.

As far as Fergund was concerned, Lord General Agon was a relic. It was too bad that he hadn't been able to adapt to Niner. The old man had things to offer. Then again, the fewer counselors the king had, the more important Fergund became.

Disgusted with his night's assignment—what was he looking for, anyway?—Fergund continued his lonely circuit of the castle yard. He'd considered asking for an escort, but mages were supposed to be more deadly than any hundred men. If that wasn't exactly true in his case, it didn't do him any good to advertise the fact.

The castle yard was an irregular diamond three hundred paces wide and almost four hundred long. It was bordered on the northwest and southeast by the river as the Plith—split for half a mile by Vos Island—came rushing back together south of the castle.

The yard was animated with the sounds of men, horses, and dogs settling down for the night. It was early enough that men were still up gambling in the barracks, and the sounds of a lyre and good-natured cursing floated a short way into the dense fog.

Fergund pulled his cloak tighter around his shoulders. The sliver of moon wasn't doing much to penetrate the cold fog pouring off the rivers and through the gates. The wet air kissed Fergund's neck and he regretted his recent haircut. The king had mocked his long hair, but Fergund's lover had adored it.

And, now that his hair was short, the king mocked him for that.

The fog billowed strangely at the iron gate and Fergund froze. He embraced the power—*embrace?* he'd always thought it felt more like a wrestling match—and peered through the fog. Once he held it, the power calmed him. He could see nothing threatening, and his hearing and sight were sharper.

Breathing deeply, Fergund made himself continue past the gate. He didn't know if it was his imagination, but it felt like the fog pressed against the whole wall of the castle like an invading army and poured in through the breach of the iron gate. Fog pooled almost to his shoulders, and the torches mounted over the heads of the two guards did little to cut the mist.

Nodding to them, Fergund turned and started walking back to the castle. He felt a weight between his shoulder blades as of eyes boring into him and repressed the urge to look over his shoulder. But as he walked toward the stables, the feeling only grew. The air felt heavy, so thick it was like walking through soup. The fog seemed to curl around him in his passing and lick at the back of his bare neck, taunting him.

With the rising of the fog, the moon and stars totally disappeared. The world was enveloped in cloud.

Fergund stumbled as he passed by the corner of the

stables. He threw a hand out to steady himself against the wood, but felt something yielding for a moment before it disappeared. Something like he'd touched a man standing there.

Staggering back in fear, Fergund clawed for the embrace. He could see nothing. There was no one there. Finally his Talent came to him. He caught a brief flicker of movement into the stables—but it might have been his imagination.

Had he smelled garlic? Surely that could only be his imagination. But why would he imagine such a thing? He hesitated for a long moment. But he was a weak mage, not a weak man. He readied a fireball and drew his knife. He came wide around the corner, straining every sense magical and mundane.

He jumped through the door and looked around frantically. Nothing. The horses were in their stalls, their odors mingling with the heavy fog. He could hear only the stamping of hooves and the even breathing of sleeping animals. Fergund probed the darkness for any sign of movement, but saw nothing.

The longer he looked, the more foolish he felt. Part of him thought he should go deeper into the stables, and part of him wanted to leave now. No one would know that he'd left. He could go to the other side of the castle and wander there. On the other hand, if he single-handedly caught an intruder, the king would doubtless reward him well. If Niner was good for anything, it was rewarding his friends.

Slowly, Fergund drew the fire he'd prepared into visible form. It flickered a little and then held, burning in his palm. A horse in the first stall snorted, suddenly shying back, and Fergund moved to shush the beast. But with fire in one hand and a gleaming knife in the other, the horse was hardly calmed.

It whinnied loudly and stomped on the ground, waking its neighbors.

"Shh!" Fergund said. "Relax, it's only me."

But an unfamiliar man with magefire was too much for the animals. They started neighing loudly. The stallion in the second stall started kicking.

"Wooja stop skearin' 'orses?" a loud voice said behind him. Fergund was so startled he dropped his knife and lost the fire in his hand. He wheeled around. It was just the stable master, a squat, bearded man from the isle of Planga. Dorg Gamet came in behind Fergund, holding a lantern. He gave Fergund a look of pure disdain while the mage picked his knife gingerly out of a pile of horse droppings.

Dorg moved down the row quickly, and at his touch and his voice, the horses calmed instantly. Fergund watched, feeling awkward. Finally Dorg came back past him.

"I was just patrol—"

"Use a lantern, ya lut," Dorg said. He stuck his lantern into Fergund's hand. He walked away, saying to himself, "Skearin' ma damn 'orses with wytchfire."

"It's magefire. There's a difference!" Fergund said to his back.

Dorg stormed out of the stables, and Fergund had barely turned around when he heard a thump.

Fergund ran outside. Dorg was lying on the ground, unconscious. Before he could shout anything, Fergund felt something hot in his neck. He reached a hand up and felt someone take the lantern gently out of his other hand. His muscles went rigid.

The light went out.

21

"What the hell have you done?" Momma K asked, looking up as Durzo crashed through the door.

"Good work," Durzo said. "And with time left for a night out." He grinned sloppily. He reeked of alcohol and garlic.

"I don't care about your binges. What have you done to Azoth?" She looked at the still form lying on the bed in her home's guest room.

"Nothin'," Durzo said, grinning foolishly. "Check. Ain't nothin' wrong with him."

"What do you mean? He's unconscious! I came back here and the servants were all in a flutter because you'd appeared here with—they said it was a corpse. I came up and Azoth was here. I can't wake him. He's dead to the world."

For some reason, that set Durzo off. He started laughing.

Momma K slapped him, hard.

"Tell me what you've done. Have you poisoned him?"

That brought Durzo back. He shook his head, trying to clear it. "He's dead. Has to be dead."

"Whatever do you mean?"

"Gwinvere gorgeous," Durzo said. "I can't say. Someone threatened me. Someone who can do what they said. Said they'd come after Azo first, then you—and they knew about Vonda!"

Momma K drew back. Who had the power to threaten Durzo? Who or what could scare Durzo Blint?

Durzo sank onto a chair and put his face in his hands. "They have to think he's dead. 'Specially after tonight."

"You faked killing Azoth?"

Durzo nodded. "To show I didn't care. To show they couldn't push me."

But you do, Momma K thought, and they can. She knew Durzo was thinking it, too. The wetboy had never been as invincible as he seemed. And when his control cracked, it burst wide open. The best Momma K could do was make sure that Durzo went to one of her brothels and have someone keep an eye on him. He might be there for two or three days straight, but she could make sure he was safe. Relatively.

"I'll take care of the boy," Momma K heard herself saying. "Do you have any idea what to do with him once he wakes up?"

"He'll stay with the Drakes like we were planning. He's dead to this world."

"What did you use?"

Durzo looked at her, confused.

"What poison—never mind, just tell me, how long will he be unconscious?"

"I dunno."

Momma K's eyes narrowed. She wanted to slap him again. The man was insane. Even for a poisoner as gifted as Durzo, it was too easy to misjudge with a child. A child wasn't simply a scaled-down adult. Durzo could have killed him. Durzo might have killed him. Azoth might never recover. Or he might wake and be an idiot, or not have the function of his limbs.

"You knew he might die," she said.

"Sometimes you have to gamble." Durzo patted his pockets, looking for garlic.

"You're starting to love that boy, and it scares the hell out of you. Part of you wants him dead, doesn't it, Durzo?"

"If I have to listen to your chitchat, can't you at least give me a drink?"

"Tell me."

"Life's empty. Love is failure. Better he dies now than gets us both killed later." With that, Blint seemed to deflate. Momma K knew he would say no more.

"How long will you be whoring?" she asked.

"I dunno," Blint said, barely stirring.

"Damn you! Longer or shorter than usual?"

"Longer," Durzo said after a minute. "Definitely longer."

The stream of curses preceded the king into the throne room by a good ten seconds. Lord General Agon could hear servants scurrying out of the way, see the guards at the entrances of the throne room shifting uncomfortably, and note that whatever staff members didn't absolutely need to be there were fleeing.

King Aleine IX barged in. "Brant! You pile of—" the lord general mentally erased the long list of repulsive things he resembled and refocused his attention when Niner got to the point. "What happened last night?"

"Your Majesty," the lord general said, "we don't know."

Another stream of curses, some of them more creative than usual, but Niner wasn't terribly creative, and no one dared to swear in his presence, so his arsenal was limited to variations on the word *shit.*

"What we do know is this," Brant Agon said. "Someone broke into the castle. I suppose we can assume it was the man we've spoken about." No need for listening spies to learn everything.

"Durzo Blint," the king said, nodding.

The lord general sighed. "Yes, Your Majesty. He apparently rendered unconscious one guard in the castle itself, and Fergund Sa'fasti, and your stable master in the stables."

More curses, then "What do you mean, 'rendered unconscious'?" The king paced back and forth.

"They didn't have any marks on them, and they couldn't remember anything, though the guard had a small puncture wound on his neck, as if from a needle."

The king cursed more and then cursed the abashed mage. As usual, Agon found himself getting more bored than offended. The king's curses didn't mean anything except "Look at me, I'm a spoiled child." Niner finally stumbled across another point: "There was nothing else?"

"We haven't found anything yet, sire. None of the guards outside your rooms, your wife's, your daughters', or your son's reported seeing anything unusual."

"It isn't fair," the king said, stomping over to his throne. "What have I done to deserve this?" he threw himself down in his throne—and squealed.

He practically flew out of the throne. He clutched Lord General Agon. "Oh gods! I'm feeling faint. I'm dying! Damn you all! I'm dying! Guards! Help! Guards!" The king's voice pitched higher and higher and he started crying as the guards blew whistles and rang bells and the throne room roared to life.

General Agon plucked the king's hands free and put the weak-kneed man in the arms of his sycophant, Fergund Sa'fasti, who didn't know enough to hold on. The king collapsed to the ground and wept like a child. General Agon ignored him and strode to the throne.

In a moment, he saw what he was looking for: a fat, long needle, pointing up from a well-worn cushion on the throne. He tried to pull it out with his fingers, but the needle stuck. It was supported so that it wouldn't just fold over if the king sat on it wrong.

General Agon drew his knife and slit the cushion open. He pulled out the needle, ignoring the bells, ignoring the guards pouring into the room, surrounding the king and herding everyone else into a side room where they could be held and questioned.

Lord General Agon pulled out the needle. A note tied to it said, "I could have been poisoned."

"Move aside!" a little man from the back was calling out, pushing soldiers out of his way. It was the king's physician.

"Let him through," the lord general ordered. The soldiers moved back from the king, who was whimpering on the floor.

Brant motioned to the physician, showed him the note, and whispered, "The king will need some poppy wine, maybe a lot. But he isn't poisoned."

"Thank you," the man said. Behind him, the king had pulled down his pants and was arching his neck trying to see the wound on his buttock. "But believe me, I know how to deal with him."

The general suppressed a smile. "Escort the king to his apartments," he told the guards. "Set a watch on the door, with two captains inside the room. The rest of you return to your duties."

"Brant!" the king yelled as the guards picked him up. "Brant! I want him dead! Dammit, I want him dead!"

Brant Agon didn't move until the throne room was empty once more. The king wanted to wage war against a shadow, a shadow with no corporeal parts except the steel of its blades. That was what it would be to assassinate a wetboy. Or worse. How many men would die before the king's pride was salved?

"Milord?" a woman asked tentatively. It was one of the housekeepers. She had a wrapped bundle in her hands. "I was . . . chosen to report for the housekeepers, sir. But with the king gone and all . . . Could I . . . ?"

The general looked at her closely. She was an old woman, obviously afraid for her life. He bet she was "chosen" by having pulled a short straw. "What is it?"

"Us housekeepers found these. Someone left them in each of the royal bedchambers, sir."

The housekeeper handed him the bundle. Six black daggers were inside it.

"Where?" Brant asked, choking the word out.

"Under—under the royal family's pillows, sir."

22

Little feet pattered into Azoth's consciousness. It was a strange sound to hear when you were dead, but Azoth couldn't sort it out any other way. Bare little feet on stone. He must be outside, because the sound didn't reverberate against any walls. He tried to open his eyes and failed. Maybe this is what it was to be dead. Maybe you never left your body. Maybe you laid inside your corpse and had to just *feel* as you slowly decomposed. He hoped dogs didn't get to him. Or wolves. He'd had terrifying dreams of a wolf grinning at him, yellow eyes ablaze. If he were stuck in his dead body, what would happen if they started tearing pieces of him off? Would he find oblivion like he'd finally fallen asleep or would he just split into pieces of consciousness, and slowly dissipate into the soil after passing through the bellies of a dozen beasts?

Something touched his face and his eyes leapt open. He heard the startled gasp before his eyes could focus on who had made it. It was a little girl, maybe five years old, her eyes so wide they covered half of her face.

"Never seen a corpse?" he asked.

"Father! Father!" she shrieked with all the surprising volume small children can muster.

He groaned as the sound jammed knives in his head and he fell back on the pillows. *Pillows?* So he wasn't dead. That was probably supposed to be a good thing.

When he woke again, time must have passed, because the room was light and airy. Wide windows had been thrown open, and cherrywood furnishings and marble flooring gleamed in the sunlight. Azoth recognized the molded ceiling; he'd stared at it before. He was in Count Drake's guest room.

"Back from the dead, are you?" Count Drake asked. He was smiling. Seeing the look on Azoth's face, he added, "Here, now, sorry. Don't think about that. Don't think at all. Eat."

He set a plate full of steaming eggs and ham in front of Azoth, along with a glass of well-watered wine. The food spoke directly with Azoth's stomach, completely bypassing higher cognitive functions. It was several minutes later when he realized the plate and the glass were both empty.

"Better," the count said. He sat on the edge of the bed and absently polished his pince nez. "Do you know who I am and where you are? Good. Do you remember who you are?"

Azoth nodded slowly. *Kylar.*

"I've been given some messages for you, but if you're not feeling well enough . . ."

"No, please," Kylar said.

"Master *Tulii* says that your work now is to get ready

for your new life, and to get well. To wit, 'Keep your arse in bed. I expect you to be ready when I come get you.'"

Kylar laughed. That was Master Blint all right. "When is he coming, then?"

A troubled look passed over the count's face. "Not for a while. But you don't need to worry about that. You'll be living here now. Permanently. You'll continue your lessons with your master, of course, but we'll be doing all we can to get the look of the street off of you. Your master said to tell you that you aren't going to be well as soon as you expect. There's something else I want to tell you, though. About your little friend."

"You mean . . . ?"

"She's doing well, Kylar."

"She is?"

"Her new family has named her Elene. She has good clothes, three meals a day. They're good people. They'll love her. She'll have a real life now. But if you're to be of any use to her, you need to get well."

Kylar felt as if he were floating. The sunlight streaming through the windows seemed brighter, sharper. An arrangement of orange roses and lavender glowed on the sill. He felt good in a way he hadn't since before Rat had become Black Dragon's Fist.

"They even took her to a mage and she said she'll be fine, but she couldn't do anything for the scars."

Someone had just outlined all his happiness with tar.

"I'm sorry, son," Count Drake said. "But you've done the best you can, and I promise you, she'll have a better life than she ever could have on the street."

Kylar barely heard him. He stared out the window,

away from the count. "I can't pay you yet. Not until I start getting my wages again from Master . . . my master."

"There's no rush. Pay me when you can. Oh, and one last thing your master asked me to pass along. He said, 'Learn from these people those things that will make you strong, forget the rest. Listen much, speak little, get well, and enjoy this. It may be the only happy time of your life.'"

Kylar was bedridden for weeks. He tried to sleep as much as the Drakes told him to, but he had far too much time. He'd never had time before; he didn't like it. When he'd been on the street, every moment had been spent worrying about his next meal, or worrying about Rat or any of the older boys or girls terrorizing him. With Master Blint, he'd been kept so busy training that he didn't have time to think.

Sitting in bed all day and all night, he had nothing but time. Training was impossible. Reading was possible, but still excruciating. For a while, Azoth spent his time becoming Kylar. With the guidelines Master Blint had given him, and the facts that anyone checking would find, he had made up more stories about his family, the area he was from, and the adventures he'd had, keeping them harmless, the way people liked to think eleven-year-olds' lives were.

He soon mastered that, though, and most of the time thought of himself as Kylar. He was getting to know Count Drake's daughters, too. Ilena was the pretty five-year-old he'd scared half to death when he first woke; Mags was a gangly eight, and Serah an alternately awkward and aloof twelve. They provided some diversion, but the countess kept them from "bothering" Kylar so he could "get his rest."

The count and countess were fascinating, but Count Drake was working most of the time and the countess had definite ideas about eleven-year-old boys—which didn't coincide at all with what Kylar knew about eleven-year-old boys. He could never decide if she knew what he was and pretended not to so she could reform him, or if Count Drake had kept her in the dark.

She was willowy, fair-skinned, and blue-eyed, an earthly vision of the heavenly beings the Drakes believed in. Like the count, she had beliefs about serving Kylar herself, as if to prove that she didn't think herself above it. But it wasn't a false humility: when Kylar had gotten terribly ill the first week and vomited all over the floor, she'd come in and held him until he was done shaking, and then she'd rolled up her sleeves and cleaned up the vomit herself. He'd been too sick to even be properly horrified until long afterward.

He couldn't count the times she came in to stuff him with food or check on how he was feeling or to read him stupid kid books. The books were full of valiant heroes who killed evil wytches. Children never had to dig through heaps of garbage and vomit outside an inn looking for scraps of edible food. Older boys never tried to bugger them. They never abandoned their friends. The princesses they saved never had their faces battered beyond recognition. No one was ever so badly scarred that a mage couldn't fix it.

Kylar hated the stories, but he knew the countess only

wanted the best for him, so he nodded and smiled and cheered when the heroes won—as they did every time.

No wonder all the little nobles want to lead armies. If it were like the books their mothers read, it would be fun. It would be fun if you felt satisfied when the bad guy died rather than wanting to puke because you saw raw cartilage and gushing blood where you cut off an ear. Blood wafting in a million beautiful swirls with water as he bled to death, held under the water by the rope you'd tied around his ankle.

The countess always interpreted his shaking and nausea after she was done with the stories as a need for more rest, so after raising memories to haunt Kylar's room, she'd leave him with their angry ghosts.

Every night Kylar became Azoth. Every night Azoth turned from the repair bay and saw Rat walking toward him, naked, hairy, massive, eyes glowing with lust. Every night Azoth watched Rat splashing into the water, straining against the weight tied to his ankle. Every night he watched Rat carve Doll Girl's face.

The nightmares woke him, and he lay in bed fighting the memories. Azoth had been weak, but Azoth was no more. Kylar was strong. Kylar had acted. Kylar would be like Master Blint. He would never be afraid. It was better now. It was better to lie in a bed having nightmares than it was to listen to Jarl getting buggered, weeping.

Sleeping again only moved him from one nightmare to another. Day brought little relief, and only slowly did the memories fade. Every morning, he told himself that he'd done what he had to, that he'd had to kill Rat, that he'd had to abandon Doll Girl, that he'd had to leave Jarl, that it was best that he never see them again, that he couldn't have known what would happen to Doll Girl. He told himself that life was empty, that he wasn't taking away anything of value when he took a life.

He wouldn't have made it without Logan Gyre's visits. Every other day, Logan would come to see him, inevitably with Serah Drake. At first, Kylar thought he came because he still felt guilty, but that soon passed. They enjoyed each other's company, and they became fast friends. Logan was strange: he was as smart as Jarl, and he'd read hundreds of books. Kylar didn't think he would survive for a week in the Warrens, but at the same time, he spoke about court politics as if it were all so easy. He knew the names, histories, friends, and enemies of scores of courtiers, and knew the major life events and important motivations of every highly ranked noble in the kingdom. Half the time, Kylar didn't know if he didn't understand what Logan was talking about because it was all part of the courtly life he'd never known, or just because Logan liked to use big words. A *sesquipedalian,* he called himself. Whatever that meant.

Nonetheless, the friendship worked, and Serah Drake helped it work by happening to stop by often so she could be with Logan. She filled in the gaps. Kylar couldn't count the times he sat silent because he hadn't understood some reference Logan had made. The silence would begin to stretch, but before Logan could ever ask him why he didn't understand, Serah would get uncomfortable and launch into something else entirely. The chatter might have driven Kylar mad if he hadn't been so thankful for it. Anyway, maybe this was how noble girls were.

Kylar was sitting in bed one morning after having spent another night cowering under the covers. He'd dreamed that he had been the one beating Doll Girl, that it had been *his* feet kicking her, and exultation writhed in *his* eyes as her beauty melted in the heat of his fury.

Count Drake came in. His fingers were ink-stained and he looked tired. He pulled a chair close to the bed.

"We think the danger's passed," he said.

"Excuse me?" Kylar said.

"I'm sorry we've had to keep you in the dark, Kylar, but we had to make sure you didn't do anything rash. In the past few weeks, there have been a number of attempts on your master's life. And consequently, there are now four fewer wetboys in the city. After three attempts, your master let the king know that if there were any more attempts, the king would die next."

"Master Blint killed the king?" Kylar asked.

"Shhh! Don't say that name. Not even here," Count Drake said. "One of the Nine, Dabin Vosha, the man in charge of the Sa'kagé's smuggling, heard about your master's threat to the king. He decided it would be a good time to make his own play for power and sent a wetboy after Durzo, thinking Durzo would either be killed or would kill the king in retaliation. Durzo found out and killed both the wetboy and Vosha."

"You mean all this has been happening while I've been lying in bed."

"There was no way you could help," Count Drake said.

"But what did Dabin Vosha have against Master—my master?" Kylar had never even heard the name.

"I don't know. Maybe nothing. That's the way the Sa'kagé works, Kylar. There are plots within plots, and most of them go nowhere. Most of them take one step and then die, like this one. If you worry about what everyone is trying to do, you become a spectator and not a player.

"Anyway, the king's learned of the last attempt on your master's life and has become very frightened. Usually, this would be good news, but he's rather clumsily consolidating his power. Logan is going to have to spend a while out of the city."

"He was just starting to be my friend," Kylar said.

"Believe me, son, a man like Logan Gyre will be your friend for life."

23

Someone slapped Kylar. Not gently.

"Wake up, boy."

Kylar clawed his way out of a nightmare and saw the face of Master Blint, a foot away, about to slap him again. "Master—" he stopped. "Master Tulii?"

"Good to see you remember me, Kylar," Master Blint said.

Master Blint got up and shut the door. "I don't have much time. Are you well yet? Don't lie to please me."

"I'm still a little weak, sir, but I'm getting better." Kylar's heart was pounding. He'd been desperate to see Master Blint for weeks, but now that he was here, Kylar was inexplicably angry.

"You'll probably feel terrible for a few more weeks. Either the kinderperil and avorida paste interacted in a way I didn't expect, or it might have something to do with your Talent."

"What's that mean? The Talent?" Kylar asked. His

words were sharper than he'd intended, but Blint didn't seem to notice.

"Well, if it was that." Master Blint shrugged. "Sometimes a body doesn't react well to magic at first."

"I mean, what does it mean? Will I be able to—"

"Fly? Become invisible? Scale walls? Throw fire? Walk as a god among mortals?" Blint smirked. "Doubtful."

"I was going to ask if I'll be able to move as fast as you do." Again, that edge came into his voice.

"I don't know yet, Kylar. You'll be able to move faster than most men without the Talent, but there aren't many who are as gifted as I am."

"What will I be able to do, then?"

"You're weak, Kylar. We'll talk about this later."

"I don't have anything to do! I can't even get out of bed. No one tells me anything."

"Fine. It means everything and nothing," Master Blint said. "In Waeddryn or Alitaera, they'd call you a mage and six different schools would fight over where and what you should study and what color robes you should wear. In Lodricar or Khalidor, they'd call you a meister and you'd grow the vir on your arms like tattoos and worship your king as a god while you plotted how to stab his royal back. In Ymmur, you'd be a stalker, an honored and honorable hunter of animals and sometimes men. In Friaku, you'd be *gorathi,* a Furied warrior invincible in your clan and one day a king versed in the arts of subjugation and slavery. In the west, well, you'd be in the ocean." He grinned.

Kylar didn't.

"The mages guess—they'd say *hypothesize* to make it more respectable—that different countries produce different Talents and that's why men with pale skin and blue eyes become wytches while swarthy men are warrior *gorathi*. They say that's why the only mages they get from Gandu are Healers. They see men with yellow skin who can heal and proclaim that yellow skin means healing. But they're wrong. Our world is divided, but the Talent is one. Every people recognizes some form of magic—except for the Lae'knaught who hate magic and simultaneously don't believe in it, but that's a different subject—but every people has its own expectations about magic. Gandu once produced some of the most destructive archmagi the world has known. They saw horrors you couldn't imagine, and because of that, they turned away from magic as weaponry. The only magic they value is healing magic. So as centuries have passed, they've added greatly to their knowledge of healing magics, and lost most others. A Gandian who is greatly Talented with fire is a shame to himself and his family."

"So we'd never hear about him," Kylar said.

"Right. There's an intersection between what the people around you know well enough to teach, what you're naturally good at, and what it is possible for you to learn. So the Talent both is what it is and it is what it has to be. Like your mind."

Kylar just looked at him.

"Take it this way: some people can add long lists of numbers in their heads, right? And some can speak a dozen languages. To do that, they have to be smart, right?"

"Right."

"But just because you can learn to add lists of numbers doesn't mean you will. But a woman who handles account books and has a gift for numbers can. Or a diplomat might have a gift for languages, but if he never learns another language, he'll still only know one."

Kylar nodded.

"The woman with a head for numbers could probably learn another language if she worked hard enough, but she'll never be fluent in a dozen, and the man will never be able to add columns of numbers mentally. Do you see where this is going?"

Kylar thought, and Master Blint waited. "We know that I'm Talented but not how or how much, so you can't tell what I'll be able to do."

"Right," Master Blint said. "From having me teach you, you'll definitely learn some things. You need to hide? Your Talent will bend some light away. You need to walk quietly? It will muffle your steps. But like any talent, it has limits. If you walk in the noonday sun, you'll be seen. If you step on dry leaves, you'll be heard. You're Talented; you're not a god. You might have the smoothest tongue in the world, but if you swear at the king, you'll meet the headsman."

"If I know twelve languages, and you speak to me in a thirteenth, I won't know what you're saying."

"Sometimes you do listen," Master Blint said. "I have to go now. Count Drake will take care of you. He's a good man, Kylar. Too good. You can trust him with your life; just don't get him started on your soul. And think of yourself as Kylar always. Azoth is dead."

"Dead?" That released all the memories and fear and anger that had been building up in Kylar like pressing the trigger plate of a crossbow. Just like that his mask fell away, and he was Azoth once more.

Azoth grabbed Master Blint's arm. "I—I really d—"

"No! No you didn't. Does this look like hell?" Blint gestured. "Ha. And they wouldn't let me visit heaven."

But Azoth could remember looking down at a knife sticking out of his chest—it had seemed so real. *How could such a thing be?*

"I couldn't work for them," Master Blint said. "I'd be a bloody sword to them. They wouldn't be able to clean me, and they wouldn't be able to sheathe me. They'd have killed me eventually. It's easier to keep your eye on your enemies than on your friends."

"So you've been killing wetboys?" Azoth asked, trying to get a hold of himself. For weeks, he'd been keeping himself from thinking about that afternoon, but now he couldn't hold it back. He remembered the look in the lord general's eyes, the utter shock. He remembered following those eyes to his own chest. . . .

"Nobody good would take the job on me. Men like Wrable and Gibbet and Severing get paid too well doing regular jobs to risk their lives taking on a real wetboy. Now remember, you're a Stern. You're proud of that, even if you are poor. The Sterns are barons, so they're upper nobility, but at the lowest level—"

"I know," Azoth said, cutting him off. "I know."

Was it just his imagination, or had Master Blint just looked guilty? The wetboy fished in a pocket and popped a garlic clove in his mouth. If it were anyone else, Azoth would have sworn he was trying to distract him, rushing to get out of the room before Azoth could pin him down. *Why was I so eager to please a man who was willing to murder me?*

I thought he cared. In the weeks that he'd been here in bed, Kylar had been alone. He'd left everything of his old life. He'd had real friends in Jarl and Doll Girl. They had cared about him. Now he was pretending to be friends with Logan Gyre—and even he had left. Not even Momma K came to visit.

It almost physically hurt when the count and countess came in at the same time. They so obviously loved each other; they were safe and happy and real together. Even Logan and Serah sometimes traded looks that made it obvious they liked each other. Those looks, that love, filled Kylar with a yearning so deep he thought his chest was going to cave in. It wasn't just hunger; a guild rat knew hunger like he knew the sewers where he huddled for warmth in the winter. Hunger wasn't comfortable, but it was familiar and it was nothing to fear. This was a thirst, like his whole body was parched, drying up, about to crumple. He was dying of thirst on the shores of the world's biggest lake.

None of it was for him. To him, that lake was an ocean. It was a salt sea that if he drank would make him thirstier and thirstier until he went mad and died. Love was death for a wetboy. Madness and weakness and vulnerability and death, not just for the wetboy himself, but also for anyone he loved. Everything about Azoth's life was dead. He'd sworn that he would never love, but he'd never seen anything like what the count and countess shared when he'd promised that. It would be tolerable if anyone cared about him at all.

In the time he'd been with Master Blint, he'd started to think that the wetboy liked him, cared about him. He'd believed that sometimes Master Blint was even proud of him. Even though everything about the gray-haired lord general was foreign to Azoth, there was something right in the outrage and disbelief that had been in his eyes when Master Blint stabbed Azoth. He shouldn't have done it.

Azoth burst into tears. "How could you do it? What's wrong with you? It wasn't right."

Blint was caught off-guard for a moment, then he was suddenly furious. He grabbed Azoth's tunic and shook him. "Damn you! Use your head! If you aren't smarter than this, I *should* have killed you. Did he believe me when I said I didn't care if they killed you?"

Azoth looked away, admitting it. "You planned it all along."

"Of course I did! Why do you think we bleached your hair? It was the only way to save you. Azoth had to die so Kylar could live. Otherwise they had a hold. Any attachment you make in this life will be used against you. That's why we're strong. That's why four wetboys couldn't kill me. Because I have no attachments. That's why you can't fall in love. It makes you weak. As soon as you find something you can't walk away from, you're trapped, doomed. If anyone thinks I give the hair on a rat's arse what happens to you, you become a target. For everyone."

How does he do it? How is he so strong?

"Now look. Look at my damn hands!" Blint held them up. Both were empty. He made a fist and smacked it down on one arm. A bloody dagger sprouted from the opposite side. He jerked his hand away and the knife pulled back through his flesh. Then it frayed apart like smoke and disappeared.

"I have a small Talent with illusions, Kylar. I did a better job with yours because I had to sell it. But all I did was hit you in the back with a knockout needle, then hold the illusion until it took effect."

"But I felt it," Kylar said. He was regaining his balance. The tears were gone. He was thinking of himself as Kylar again.

"Sure you felt it. You felt me hit you and you saw a dagger coming out of your chest. At the same time your body was trying to fight off a dozen minor poisons. You made what sense of it you could. It was a gamble. That illusion used up almost all the power I can use in a day. If Agon's men had stormed the place, we would have been finished. The poisons I used wreaked havoc with your body. They could have killed you. Again, a gamble I had to make."

Master Blint does care what happens to me. It hit him like lightning. Master Blint had risked using up his power to save Azoth. Even if it were just the affection a master might have for a talented apprentice, Blint's approval washed over Azoth—*Kylar!*—as if the wetboy had given him a hug.

No adult had ever cared what happened to him. The only other person who'd ever risked anything for him was Jarl, and Jarl was part of another life.

The truth was, Azoth hated Azoth. Azoth was a coward, passive, weak, afraid, disloyal. Azoth had hesitated. Master Blint didn't know it, but the poisons on the needle *had* killed Azoth. He was Kylar now, and Kylar would be everything Azoth hadn't dared to be.

In that moment, Azoth became Kylar and Kylar became Blint's. If he had ever obeyed his master halfheartedly before, or out of fear, if he had ever fantasized about one day coming back and killing him for how hard the training was, it all dried up and blew away now. Master Blint was being hard on Kylar because life was hard.

Life was hard, but Blint was harder, stronger, tougher than anything the Warrens could throw at him. He forbade love because love would destroy Kylar. Master Blint knew better than Kylar did. He was strong and he would make Kylar strong. He was fierce and Kylar would be fierce. But it was all for Kylar. It was all to protect him, to make him the best wetboy he could be.

So it wasn't love. So what? It was something. Maybe nobles got to live on the shores of that lake and drink at their pleasure. That life hadn't been decreed for a guild rat. Kylar's life was a desert life. But there is life in the desert, and a small oasis had Kylar's name on it. There was no room for Azoth. The oasis was too small and Azoth was too thirsty. But Kylar could do it. Kylar would do it. He'd make Master Blint proud.

"Good," Master Blint said. Of course, he couldn't see what Kylar was thinking, but Kylar knew the eagerness in his eyes was unmistakable. "Now, boy, are you ready to become a sword in the shadows?"

24

$g$et up, boy. It's time to kill."

Kylar was awake instantly. He was fourteen years old, and the training had sunk in enough that he went through his survival checklist instantly. For each question, there was only a terse answer. Each sensation got only the briefest moment of his attention. *What woke you?* Voice. *What do you see?* Darkness, dust, afternoon light, shack. *What do you smell?* Blint, sewage, the Plith. *What do you feel?* Warm blanket, fresh straw, my bed, no warning tingles. *Can you move?* Yes. *Where are you?* Safe house. *Is there danger?* The last question, of course, was the culmination. He could move, his weapons were in their sheaths, all was well.

That wasn't guaranteed, not even here, in this dingy safe house in the shadow of one of the few sections of the ancient aqueduct that was still standing. More than once, Durzo had tied a sword to the ceiling over Kylar's bed, and the damn thing was nearly invisible when you had to look at it point first. Durzo had woken Kylar, and when he didn't recognize the danger within three seconds, Durzo had cut the rope. Fortunately, he'd capped the point that first time, and the second time. The third time, he didn't.

Another time, Durzo had had Scarred Wrable—only Durzo called him Ben—wake Kylar. Scarred Wrable had even worn Durzo's clothes and mimicked his voice perfectly—that was part of Scarred Wrable's Talent. That time, Kylar hadn't been caught. Even a garlicky meal didn't give a man the same smell as chewing the cloves straight.

Decoding Durzo's words came last. Time to kill.

"You think I'm ready?" Kylar asked, his heart pounding.

"You were ready a year ago. I just needed the right job for your first solo."

"What is it?" *I was ready a year ago?* Blint's compliments came like that, when they came at all. And usually, even a grudging compliment would be followed by some criticism.

"It's at the castle, and it's got to be finished today. Your deader is twenty-six years old, no military training, shouldn't be armed. But he's well-liked, a busy little bee. Very busy. An *assassin* would incur . . . ancillary fatalities." He said *assassin* with a sneer, as would any wetboy. "But it doesn't matter for the contract. The deader just has to die. Just finish the job."

Kylar's heart pounded. So this was how it was going to be. This wasn't a simple test. It wasn't, Can Kylar kill solo? It was, Can Kylar do what a wetboy does? Can Kylar decide a suitable entry strategy (to the castle itself, no less), can he kill solo, can he do it without killing innocents, can he get out after the hit? Oh, and can he use his Talent, the true measure of what separates a wetboy from a common assassin.

How the hell does Blint come up with these things? The man had a brilliance for ferreting out and exploiting Kylar's weaknesses, especially his biggest weakness of all: Kylar hadn't been able to use the Talent. Not yet. Not even once. It should have quickened by now, Blint said. He was forever pushing Kylar in new ways, hoping that some new extreme of stress, of need, might bring it out of him. Nothing had worked yet.

Durzo had wondered aloud if he should just kill Kylar. Instead, he'd decided that as long as Kylar could do everything a wetboy could do, Durzo would keep training him. He promised that it would ultimately fail. It was impossible. A wetboy wasn't a wetboy without the Talent.

"Who took out the contract?" Kylar asked.

"The Shinga."

"You're trusting me with that?"

"You're going in this afternoon. If you fuck it up, I go in tonight, and I bring the Shinga two heads." Kylar didn't have to ask who the other head would belong to.

"What did the deader do?"

"You don't need to know."

"Does it matter?"

A knife appeared in Durzo's hand, but his eyes weren't violent. He was thinking. He flipped the knife from finger to finger. Finger, finger, finger, stop. Finger, finger, finger, roll. Kylar had seen a bard do that once with a coin, but only Durzo used a knife.

"No," Durzo said. "It doesn't. Name's Devon Corgi and let's just say that when most people try to turn away from the darkness, they want to take a few bags packed with goodies with them. It slows them down. They never make it. I've only known one man in all my life who was willing to pay the full price of leaving the Sa'kagé."

"Who was it?"

"Boy, in two hours, you've got a date with a deader. You've got better questions to ask."

"Devon Corgi?" The guard furrowed his brow. "Nah, don't know him. Hey, Gamble, you know a Devon Corgi?" he asked another guard walking through the castle's enormous west gate.

It was almost too easy. Kylar had long ago stolen the tunic and bag that was the uniform of the city's most widely used courier service. People who didn't have their own servants employed boys—east side boys, never guild rats—to take their messages. Whenever guards had looked like they might ask questions, Kylar walked up to them and asked for directions.

Don't they know? Can't they see? These men were guards, they were supposed to be protecting Devon Corgi and everyone else in here, and they were going to direct a killer right to him? How could they be so dumb? It was an uneasy feeling of power. It was gratifying that all the hours with Blint were definitely doing something. Kylar was becoming dangerous. And yet—how could they not see what he was?

"Sure, he's the one came in this all week with his eye twitchin', jumping at shadows. I think he's up in the north tower. If you want me to take your message, I could. I'm on duty in ten minutes, it's the first stop on my rounds."

"No thanks. I'm hoping for a good tip. Which way is it?"

As the guard gave Kylar directions, he tried to formulate his plan. The kill itself shouldn't be hard. A kid could get much closer than a grown-up before he roused suspicion, and then it would be too late. The hard part was finding the man. Devon didn't just have an office somewhere. He moved around. That added all sorts of risk, especially because Kylar needed to get the kill done today. The north tower sounded good. Isolated. The guard coming sounded bad. Kylar had just talked to the man, and told him who he was looking for.

With the makeup Blint had used on him, Kylar looked totally different and younger by years. But it was best to let every death be a mystery. *A wetboy leaves corpses, not evidence.* So Kylar would find Corgi and hide until the guard came and left, then he'd kill him.

In and out, no problem, even without the Talent.

The castle was awe-inspiring. Though Blint always spoke of it with scorn, it was the most magnificent building Kylar had ever seen. It was the same black granite as the old aqueducts in the Warrens, quarried in the mountains on the Ceuran border. The entire quarrying industry was owned by the Sa'kagé, so now only the wealthy could afford to build with stone. It was one of the reasons most of the aqueduct pillars were gone now. The non-Sa'kagé poor in the Warrens scavenged the rock for their own use, or their own black-black market sale (bilking the Sa'kagé entailed distinct dangers) to the middle class.

The castle had been built four hundred years ago, when for the thirty years of King Abinazae's rule Cenaria was a major power. He had barely finished the castle when he decided to push further east and take the Chantry, and several thousand magae had ended his ambitions permanently. The castle had first been constructed on the motte-and-bailey design at least a hundred years earlier. Surrounded by the natural moat of the Plith River, Vos Island had been built up into a larger hill, on top of which sat the fortress. What was now the north side of the Warrens had been the original bailey. The Warrens were on a narrow peninsula that dropped off sharply into the sea except for the last half mile, which flattened out before the shoreline. The design was so defensible that neither the wood fortress nor the wood-walled Warrens had ever been taken. But the city had expanded along with King Abinazae's pride, so Castle Cenaria had been built of stone and the city jumped to the east shore of the Plith. The aqueducts, however, were a mystery. They had been there long before King Abinazae and seemed to serve no purpose, as the Plith was freshwater—if not terribly clean.

Leaving the diamond-shaped castle yard, Kylar walked up stone stairs that had been climbed by so many feet over the centuries that the middle of each step dipped several inches lower than the sides. The guards ignored him, and he assumed the attitude of a servant. It was one of his most frequent guises. Blint liked to say that a good disguise cloaked a wetboy better than the shadows. Kylar could walk right past almost anyone he knew with the exception of Count Drake. Not much escaped him.

Soon he passed through most of the buzz of activity that filled the inner yard and the great hall. He went past the lines of people waiting for an audience in the throne room, past the open double doors of the gardens, and made his way to the north tower. The halls were busy everywhere until he stepped into the north tower's antechamber.

Devon Corgi wasn't there. For the first time taking pains to be silent, Kylar opened the door that led to the stairs and climbed them quietly. The stairway was blank. Nothing decorative, no niches, no statues, no ornamental curtains or anything that would afford Kylar a place to hide.

He made his way to the top of the tower. It was, it seemed, just a large bedchamber, currently not being used. A young man balancing a large ledger book was going through the drawers of a bureau, apparently taking an inventory of the neatly folded sheets for the enormous featherbed and the alternate curtains for the large shuttered window. Kylar waited. Devon was turned sideways to the door, and without the Talent to shadow Kylar's approach, there was a good chance the man would see him enter.

The waiting was always the worst. Keyed up with no place to go, Kylar began to entertain fantasies that the guard was going to come up the stairs at any minute. Seeing him here, this late, he'd search him. Searching him, he'd find the slit in Kylar's trousers. Finding that handsized slit, he'd find the long knife strapped to Kylar's inner thigh. But there was nothing for it. Kylar waited just out of sight, listening, willing his ears to hear even the scritch of the quill on the ledger.

Finally, he checked and saw Devon disappearing into the closet on the far side of the nearly circular chamber. Kylar crept into chamber and looked for places to hide. His feet made no sound, not even the sound of leather scuffing against stone. Master Blint had taught Kylar how to boil the sap of the rubber tree to make a shoe sole that was soft and silent. It was expensive to import, and only a little quieter than properly worked leather, but to Master Blint, even the smallest margin mattered. It was why he was the best.

There were no good places to hide. A *great* place to hide was one where Kylar would be able to see the entire room, keep his weapons at ready, and be able to move quickly either to strike or to escape. A *good* place to hide gave a decent view and the ability to strike or escape with only a little difficulty. This room had no dark corners. It was practically a circle. There were rice paper screens, but they'd been folded and were leaning against the wall. Pitifully, the only place to hide was under the bed. If Kylar were a wetboy, perhaps he could have vaulted up a wall and dangled off the chains of the chandelier, but that wasn't an option.

Under the bed? Master Blint will never let me live this down.

But there was no other option. Kylar dropped flat onto his toes and fingertips crawled under the bed. It was good he was still slight, because there wasn't much space. He was uncomfortably in place when he heard someone coming up the stairs.

The guard. Finally. Now take a quick look and get the hell out.

He'd chosen the side of the bed with a view of the closet, and that meant that he didn't have a view of the stairs, but from the sound of the footsteps, he became certain that it wasn't a guard. Devon stepped out of the closet holding a chest, and guilt flashed across his face.

"You can't be here, Bev," he said.

"You're leaving," the unseen woman said. It was an accusation.

"No," he said. His eye started twitching.

"You stole from them, and now you're stealing from the king, and for some reason I'm surprised you'd lie to me. You asshole." Kylar heard her turn, and then Devon was stepping close to the bed, putting the chest down on it, his legs just inches away from Kylar.

"Bev, I'm sorry." He was moving toward the door, and Kylar was stricken with panic. What if Devon went after her, and she went down the steps? Kylar would have to kill both of them on the stairs, knowing that the guard would be coming along any minute. "Bev, please—"

"Go to hell!" she said, and slammed the door.

Wish granted. It was the blackest kind of humor, Durzo's kind of humor. He liked to say that the irony of overheard conversations was one of the best perks of the bitter business, though he said that the wisdom of last words was highly overrated. *Wish granted?* Kylar didn't like that he'd even thought that. Everything this man had planned was about to end, and Kylar was smirking about it.

Devon swore to himself, but he didn't follow the woman. "Where's that guard anyway? He was supposed to be here by now."

This was what it was like, Durzo had told Kylar. You come in at the end of a drama—whether it's just started or has been going on for years, your arrival signals the end—and you rarely get to know what the story was about. Who was Bev to Devon? His lover? His partner in crime? Just a friend? His sister?

Kylar didn't know. He'd never know.

There was jingling on the stairs, muffled behind the door. Devon picked up his ledger. The door opened.

"'Lo, Dev," the guard said.

"Oh, hello, Gamble." Devon sounded nervous.

"That courier find you?"

"Courier?"

"Little shite musta got lost. Everything fine up here?"

"Sure, just fine."

"See ya round."

Devon waited until the guard had been gone thirty seconds, and then he stepped close to the bed and started stuffing his pockets. Kylar couldn't see with what.

Here it is. The guard would be far enough away now that even if Devon managed to cry out, he wouldn't be heard. Devon stepped away from the bed toward the bureau and Kylar crawled out from beneath the bed like a bug. He stood and drew the knife. Devon was mere paces away. Kylar's heart was pounding. He thought he could hear the rush of blood in his ears.

Kylar did everything right. Low ready stance, advancing quietly but quickly, balanced so that if at any moment the deader reacted, Kylar wouldn't be caught flat-footed. He brought the knife up to eye level, preparing to grab Devon and give him what Durzo called the red grin—a slash across the jugular and deep through the windpipe.

Then he imagined Doll Girl giving him the look she'd given him when he took the biggest piece of bread for himself. *What are you doing, Azoth? You know this is wrong.*

He recovered late, and it was as if his training abandoned him. Kylar was inches away from Devon, and Devon still hadn't heard him, but the very nearness panicked Kylar. He stabbed for Devon's neck and must have made some sound, because Devon was turning. The knife bit into the back of Devon's neck, hit spine, and bounced out. Because of his convulsively tight grip that Durzo would have beaten Kylar for, the knife bounced right out of his hand, too.

Devon turned and yelped. It seemed he was more surprised by Kylar's sudden appearance than by the sting in his neck. He stepped back at the same time Kylar did. He put a hand to his neck, looked at his fingers and saw the blood. Then they both looked down to the knife.

Devon didn't go for it. Kylar scooped up the knife and as he stood, Devon dropped to his knees.

"Please," he said. "Please don't."

It seemed incredible. The man's eyes were big with fear—looking at little Kylar, whose disguise made him look even smaller and younger. There was nothing frightening about him, was there? But Devon looked like a man who's seen his judgment come. His face was white, eyes round, pitiful, helpless.

"Please," he said again.

Kylar slashed his throat in a fury. Why didn't he protect himself? Why didn't he even try? He was bigger than Kylar. He had a chance. Why must he act like a sheep? A big stupid human lamb, too dumb to even move. The cut was through the windpipe, but barely clipped one jugular. It was deep enough to kill, but not fast. Kylar grabbed Devon's hair and slashed again, twice, slightly up, so the blood shot down rather than up. Not a drop got on Kylar. He'd done it just like Durzo had taught.

There was a sound on the stairs. "Devon, I'm sorry," Bev said before she even got into the room. "I just had to come back. I didn't mean—" She stepped into the room and saw Kylar.

She saw his face, she saw the dagger in his hand, she saw him holding the dying Devon by his hair. She was a plain young woman wearing a white serving dress. Wide hips, wide-spaced eyes, mouth open in a little O and beautiful raven hair.

Finish the job.

The training took hold. Kylar was across the room in an instant. He yanked the woman forward, swept a foot in, pivoted, and she flipped over onto the ground. He was as inexorable as Durzo Blint. The woman was beneath him, face down on the carpet that covered this section of floor. The next move was to slide the knife between her ribs. She'd hardly feel it. He wouldn't have to see her face.

He hesitated. It was his life against hers. She'd seen him. His disguise was good only as long as no one knew there was a fourteen-year-old murderer about. She'd seen his face. She had intruded on a deader. She was just collateral damage. An ancillary fatality, Blint said. A wetboy would do what needed to be done. It was less professional but sometimes unavoidable. It doesn't matter, Blint had said. Just finish the job.

Blint only allowed him to live so long as he proved he could do everything a wetboy did, even without the Talent.

Yet here she was, face down, Kylar straddling her on the floor, the point of his dagger pricking her neck, his left hand twisting her hair, trying not to imagine the red blood blooming on her white servant's dress. She'd done nothing.

Life is empty. Life is meaningless. When we take a

life, we aren't taking anything of value. I believe it. I believe it.

There had to be another way. Could he tell her to run? To tell no one? To leave the country and never come back? Would she do it? No, of course not. She'd run to the nearest guard. As soon as she was in the presence of some burly castle guard, any fear Kylar might inspire in her would look as small and weak as a guild rat with a knife.

"I told him what would happen if he stole from the Sa'kagé," she said, her voice oddly calm. "That bastard. With everything else he took from me, he didn't even have the decency to die alone. I was coming to apologize, and now you're going to kill me, aren't you?"

"Yes," Kylar said, but he was lying. He had moved the knife to the correct place on her back, but it refused to move.

Out of the corner of his eye, he saw a shadow shift on the stairs. He didn't move, didn't acknowledge that he'd seen it, but he felt a chill. It was the middle of the afternoon; there were no torches burning now, no candles. That shadow could only be Master Blint. He'd followed Kylar. He'd watched everything. The job was for the Shinga, and it wouldn't be botched.

Kylar slid the knife between her ribs, pulled it sideways, felt the shudder and the sigh of the woman dying beneath him.

He stood and pulled the knife from her flesh, his mind suddenly detached, pulling away from him as it had the day in the boat shop with Rat. He wiped the red blade on her white dress, sheathed it along his thigh, and checked himself in the room's mirror for blood, just like he'd been taught.

It was all the sorrow in the world to him that he was clean. There wasn't any blood on his hands.

When he turned, Blint stood in the open doorway, arms folded. Kylar just looked at him, still hovering somewhere behind his own body, glad for the numbness.

"Not great," Durzo said, "but acceptable. The Shinga will be pleased." He pursed his lips, seeing the distance in Kylar's eyes. "Life is meaningless," Durzo said, rolling a garlic clove between his fingers. "Life is empty. When we take a life, we take nothing of value."

Kylar stared at him blankly.

"Repeat it, damn you!" Durzo's hand moved and a knife blurred through the air, thunking into the bureau behind Kylar.

He didn't even flinch. He repeated the words mechanically, fingers atingle, feeling again and again that easy slip of meat parting around the knife. Was it so easy? Was it so simple? You just pushed, and death came? Nothing spiritual about it. Nothing happened. No one was whisked to Count Drake's heaven or hell. They just stopped. They stopped talking, stopped breathing, stopped moving, finally stopped twitching. Stopped.

"That pain you feel," Master Blint said almost gently, "is the pain of abandoning a delusion. The delusion is meaning, Kylar. There is no higher purpose. There are no gods. No arbiters of right and wrong. I don't ask you to like reality. I only ask you to be strong enough to face it. There is nothing beyond this. There is only the perfection we attain by becoming weapons, as strong and merciless as a sword. There is no essential good in living. Life is nothing in itself. It's a place marker that proves who's winning, and we are the winners. We are always the winners. There is nothing but the winning. Even winning means nothing. We win because it's an insult to lose. The ends don't justify the means. The means don't justify the ends. There is no one to justify to. There is no justification. There is no justice. Do you know how many people I've killed?"

Kylar shook his head.

"Me neither. I used to. I remembered the name of every person I killed outside of battle. Then it was too many. I just remembered the number. Then I remembered only the innocents. Then I forgot even that. Do you know what punishments I've endured for my crimes, my *sins?* None. I am proof of the absurdity of men's most treasured abstractions. A just universe wouldn't tolerate my existence."

He took Kylar's hands. "On your knees," he said. Kylar knelt at the edge of a pool of the blood seeping from the woman's body.

"This is your baptism," Master Blint said, putting both of Kylar's hands in the blood. It was warm. "This is your new religion. If you must worship, worship as the other wetboys do. Worship Nysos, god of blood, semen, and wine. At least those have power. Nysos is a lie like all the gods, but at least he won't make you weak. Today, you've become an assassin. Now get out, and don't wash your hands. And one more thing: when you've got to kill an innocent, don't let them talk."

Kylar staggered through the streets like a drunk. Something was wrong with him. He should feel something, but instead, there was only emptiness. It was like the blood on his hands had burst from some soul wound.

The blood was drying now, getting sticky, the bright red fading to brown everywhere but inside his clenched fists. He hid his hands, hid the blood, hid himself, and his mind—less numb than his heart—knew that there was a point in this, too. He would be a wetboy, and he would always be hiding. Kylar himself was a mask, an identity assumed for convenience. That mask and every other would fit because before his training was done, every distinguishing feature of the Azoth who had been would be obliterated. Every mask would fit, every mask would fool every inspector, because there would be nothing underneath those masks.

Kylar couldn't wear his courier disguise into the Warrens—couriers never went to the Warrens—so he headed to an east side safe house on a block crowded with the tiny homes of artisans and those servants not housed at their lords' estates. He rounded a corner and ran straight into a girl. She would have gone sprawling if he hadn't grabbed her arms to catch her.

"Sorry," he said. His eyes took in the simple servant's white dress, hair bound back, and a basket full of fresh herbs. Last, he saw the gory red smears he'd just left on each of her sleeves. Before he could disappear, start running down the street before she saw how he'd stained her, the arcs and crosses of scars on her face clicked into place like the pieces of a puzzle.

They were white now, scars now, where he had branded them into his mind as deep, red, inflamed cuts, burst tissue, dribbling blood, the rough scrape and muted gurgle of blood being swallowed, blood bursting in little bubbles around a destroyed nose. He only had time to see unmistakable scars and unmistakable big brown eyes.

Doll Girl looked down demurely, not recognizing this murderer as her Azoth. The downward glance showed her the gore on her sleeves, and she looked up, horror etched every feature not already etched with scars.

"My God," she said, "you're bleeding. Are you all right?"

He was already running, sprinting heedlessly through the market. But no matter how fast he ran, he couldn't outrun the concern and the horror in those beautiful eyes. Those big brown eyes followed him. Somehow, he knew they always would.

25

γou ready to be a champion?" Master Blint asked.

"What are you talking about?" Kylar asked. They'd finished the morning's sparring and he'd done better than usual. He didn't even think he'd be sore tomorrow. He was sixteen years old now, and it seemed like the training was finally starting to pay off. Of course, he still hadn't won a single fight with Master Blint, but he was starting to have hope. On the other hand, Blint had been in a foul mood all week.

"The king's tourney," Master Blint said.

Kylar grabbed a rag and mopped his face. This safe house was small and it got stiflingly hot. King Aleine Gunder IX had convinced the Blademasters to certify a tourney in Cenaria. Of course, they might watch and decide that not even the winner was good enough to be a Blademaster, but on the other hand, they might decide that three or four contestants were. Even a first echelon Blademaster could find great work at any royal court in Midcyru. But, typically, Blint had sneered about the whole affair. Kylar said, "You said the king's tourney was for the desperate, the rich, and the foolish."

"Mm-hmm," Blint said.

"But you want me to fight anyway," Kylar said. He guessed that made him "desperate." Most children's Talent quickened by their early teens. His still hadn't, and Blint was losing his patience.

"The king's holding the tourney so he can hire the winners to be bodyguards. He wants to make sure he isn't hiring any wetboys, so this tourney has a special rule: no one Talented allowed. There will be a maja at the tourney to check all the contestants, a Chantry-trained healer. She's also there to ward the swords so the contestants don't kill each other and to heal anyone who gets hurt. The Nine have decided to flex their muscle. They want one of their own to win, to remind everyone who's who in this city. So it's a situation that fits you like a peg leg fits a cripple. Not that that's a coincidence. This tourney wouldn't even be happening if they hadn't suggested it. The Nine knows all about you and your little problem."

"What?" Kylar was incredulous. He hadn't even known they knew who he was. What if he lost?

"Hu Gibbet showed off his apprentice Viridiana to the Nine this week. A girl, Kylar. I watched her fight. She's Talented, of course. She'd take you, no problem."

Kylar felt a wave of shame. Hu Gibbet was a murderer of the vilest sort. Hu loved murder, loved cruelty for its own sake. Hu never failed, but he also always killed more than just the target. Blint despised him. Kylar was making his master look second-best to a butcher.

"Wait," Kylar said. "Isn't the tourney today?"

*   *   *

It was noon when Kylar arrived at the stadium on the north side of the Warrens. It had only been used for horse races for the last twelve years. Before that, it had been the home of the Death Games. As Kylar approached, he could hear the crowds within. The stadium could hold fifteen thousand people, and it sounded full.

He walked in a cocky glide. It was meant not only to suggest an arrogant young swordsman, but also to disguise his own natural stride. Count Drake wouldn't attend an event that he saw as reminiscent of the Death Games, but Logan Gyre might, as would any number of the young nobles Kylar had to interact with on a fairly regular basis. Usually, Kylar felt no anxiety when he was disguised. First, he was good enough with disguises now that he didn't feel much danger. Second, anxiety drew attention like a lodestone. But now his stomach was in an uproar because his disguise was no disguise at all.

Master Blint had given him the clothes without comment. They were wetboy grays as fine as anything Master Blint owned himself. These were the mottled gray and black that made a better camouflage in darkness than pure black did, the mottling breaking up the human shape. They were fitted perfectly, thin and tight on his limbs, but not impeding his movement. He suspected that the slender cut had another purpose: the Nine wanted him to look as young as possible. *We sent an un-Talented child as our champion. He thrashed you. What happens when we send a wetboy?*

His clothes were completed with a black silk—silk!—cloak, a black silk mask that left only holes for his eyes, a slit for his mouth, and a shock of his dark hair uncovered. He'd rubbed a paste into his hair to make it look utterly black and pulled it into short, disheveled points. In place of his black weapons harness, Blint had given him one of gold, with gold sheaths for each of his daggers, throwing knives, and sword. They stood out starkly against the drab wetboy grays. Blint had rolled his eyes as he gave it to Kylar. "If you've got to go for melodrama, you might as well do it right," he said.

Like this is my *fault?*

Few people lingered on the streets, but when Kylar strode to the side entrance of stadium, spectators and vendors gawked at him. He walked inside and found the fighters' chamber. There were over two hundred men and a couple dozen women inside. They ranged from huge bashers Kylar recognized to mercenaries and soldiers to indolent young noblemen to peasants from the Warrens who had no business holding a sword. The desperate, the rich, and the foolish indeed.

He was noticed immediately and a silence spread through the men joking too loudly, soldiers stretching, and women checking and double-checking their blades.

"Is that everyone?" a bookish woman asked, coming in from a side room. She almost bumped into the huge man who was walking in with her as he stopped abruptly. Kylar's breath caught. It was Logan. Logan wasn't going to watch—he was going to compete. Then the maja saw Kylar. She covered her surprise better than most. "I—I see. Well, young man, come with me."

Acutely aware of maintaining his cocky glide, Kylar walked right past Logan and the others. It was oddly satisfying to hear whispers erupt behind him.

The examination room had once been used to treat injured slave fighters. It had the feel of a room that had seen a lot of death. There were even gutters around at the base of each wall so blood could be washed away easily. "I'm Sister Drissa Nile," the woman said. "And though Blade-masters learn to use all edged weapons, for this tourney you can only use your sword. I'm going to have to ask you to remove your other weapons."

Kylar gave her his best Durzo Blint stare.

She cleared her throat. "I suppose I could bind them magically to their sheaths. You won't be able to draw them for perhaps six hours, when the weaves dissipate."

Kylar nodded acquiescence. As she muttered under her breath, wrapping weaves around each of his sheaths, he studied the brackets that had been posted on the wall. He found Logan quickly, then actually looked for a few moments for his own name. *Like the Nine entered me under my real name.* "What am I listed as?" Kylar asked.

She paused and pointed. "I'm going to go out on a limb and guess that's you." The name was listed as "Kage." Drissa muttered, and an accent appeared out of nowhere over the E. "Kagé, the Shadow. If the Sa'kagé didn't send you, young man, you'd better find yourself a fast horse."

No pressure. Kylar was just glad to see that he was in the opposite bracket from Logan. His friend had grown into his height. Logan Gyre was no longer clumsy; he had a huge reach, and he was strong, but training for an hour every other day wasn't the same as training for hours every day under Master Blint's tutelage. Logan was a good fighter, but there was no way he'd make it to the top of his own bracket, which meant Kylar wouldn't have to face him.

Kylar drew his sword and Sister Nile warded it. He tested the edge and it was not just flat but blunted in a small circle around each edge, which showed she knew what she was doing. Even a practice sword could cut if you sliced someone hard enough. At the same time, the weaves didn't appear to add any weight to the blade, or to change how it traveled through the air. "Nice," Kylar said. He was trying to be as laconic as Durzo so he didn't give away his voice. Most of Kylar's voice disguises still made him sound like a child trying to sound like a man. It was more embarrassing than effective.

"The rules of the tourney are the first swordsman to touch his opponent three times wins. I've bonded a ward to each fighter's body that makes opponents' swords react. The first time you touch your opponent, your sword will glow yellow. Second, orange. Third, red. Now, the last thing," she said. "Making sure you have no Talent. I'll have to touch you for this."

"I thought you could See."

"I can, but I've heard rumors of people being able to disguise their Talent, and I won't break my oath to make sure this fight is fair, not even here, not even for the Sa'kagé." Drissa put her hand on his hand. She mumbled to herself the whole time. As Blint had explained it, women needed to speak to use their Talent, but apparently it didn't need to be comprehensible.

She stopped abruptly and looked him in the eye. She chewed her lip and then put her hand back on his. "That's no disguise," she said. "I've never seen . . . Do they know? They must, I suppose, or they wouldn't have sent him, but . . ."

"What are you talking about?" Kylar asked.

Sister Nile stepped back reluctantly, as if she didn't appreciate having to deal with a human being when she had something far more interesting on her hands. "You're broken," she said.

"Go to hell."

She blinked. "I'm sorry, I meant . . . People colloquially speak about 'having the Talent' as if it's simple. But it's not simple. There are three things that must all work together for a man or woman to become a mage. First, there's your *glore vyrden,* roughly your life-magic. It's magic gleaned perhaps from your living processes, like we get energy from food, or maybe it's from your soul— we don't know, but it's internal. Half of all people have a glore vyrden. Maybe everyone, just in most it's too small to detect. Second, some people have a conduit or a process that translates that power into magic or into action. It's usually very thin. Sometimes it's blocked. But say a man's brother has a loaded hay wagon fall on him—in that extremity, the man might tap his glore vyrden for the only time in his life and be able to lift the wagon. On the other hand, men who have a glore vyrden and a wide-open conduit tend to be athletes or soldiers. They sometimes perform far better than the men around them, but then, like all others, it takes them time to recuperate. The amount of magic they can use is small and quickly exhausted. If you told them they were using magic, they wouldn't believe you. For a man to be a mage, he needs a third component as well: he must be able to absorb magic from sunlight or fire so that he can refill his glore vyrden again and again. Most of us absorb light through the eyes, but some do it through the skin. That is why, we think, Friaku's gorathi go into battle naked, not to intimidate their foes, but to give themselves access to as much magic as possible."

"So what's that got to do with me?" Kylar asked.

"Young man, you can absorb magic, either through your eyes like a magus, or through your skin. Your skin is practically glowing with it. I'd guess you would have a natural bent toward body magics. And your glore vyrden? I've never seen one like it. You could use magic for half the night and not empty it. It's perfect for a wetboy. But. . . " She grimaced. "I'm sorry. Your conduit."

"What, it's blocked? Is it bad?" He already knew it was blocked. Blint had been trying to break the block for years. That also made sense of why Blint had made him lie out in the sun, or sit uncomfortably close to forge fires—he'd been trying to force an overflow of magic, so that Kylar couldn't help but use it.

"You have no conduit."

"Will you fix it? Money's no object," Kylar said, his chest tight.

"It's not a matter of drilling a hole. It's more like making new lungs. This is not something any healer in the Chantry has even seen, much less tried to fix, and with a Talent of your Talent's magnitude, my guess is that the attempt would be lethal to you and the healer both. Do you know any magi who would risk their life for you?"

Kylar shook his head.

"Then I'm sorry."

"Could the Gandians help me? They have the best healers, don't they?"

"I'm going to choose not to take offense at that, though most Sisters would. I've heard wild stories from the men's green school. Not that I believe it, but I heard of a magus who saved a dying woman's unborn child by putting it in her sister's womb. Even if that's true, that's dealing with pregnancy, and we healers work with difficult pregnancies all the time. What you've got we never see. People come to us because they're sick. They bring their children to the Chantry or one of the men's schools because they've set a barn on fire, or healed a playmate, or thrown a chair at someone's head using only their minds. People like you don't come to us; they just feel frustrated by life, like they're supposed to be something more than they are, but they can never break through."

"Thanks," Kylar said.

"Sorry."

"So that's it. There's nothing for me?"

"I'm sure the ancients could have helped you. Maybe there's some forgotten old manuscript in a Gandian library that could help. Or maybe there's someone at the Chantry who is studying Talent disorders and I simply don't know about it. I don't know. You could try. But if I were you, I wouldn't throw my life away looking for something you're never going to find. Make your peace with it."

This time, Kylar didn't have to try. The Durzo Blint glare came to his eyes no problem.

26

*K*ylar walked onto the sands of the stadium ready to hurt someone. The stands were full to overflowing. Kylar had never seen so many people. Vendors walked the aisles hawking rice, fish, and skins of ale. Noblemen and women had servants fanning them in the rising heat, and the king sat in a throne, drinking and laughing with his retinue. Kylar thought he even spied a sour-faced Lord General Agon to one side. The crowd buzzed at the sight of Kagé.

Then the gate opened opposite him and a big peasant stepped in. There was a smattering of disinterested cheering. No one really cared who won, they were just happy that another fight was about to start. A horn blew and the big peasant drew a big rusty bastard sword. Kylar drew his own blade and waited. The peasant charged Kylar and lifted his blade for an overhead chop.

Kylar jumped in, jabbed his blade hard into the man's stomach, then as the peasant tripped past, Kylar slashed his kidney and hamstring. His sword glowed yellow-orange-red.

Everyone seemed taken off guard except for the Blademasters, sitting in a special section in their red and iron-gray cloaks. They pealed a bell immediately.

There were a few cheers and a few boos, but most of the audience seemed more startled than anything. Kylar sheathed his sword and walked back into the fighters' chamber as the peasant dusted himself off, cursing.

He waited alone, sitting still, not talking to anyone. Just before his next turn, a huge basher with a tattoo of a lightning bolt on his forehead sat next to him. Kylar thought his name was Bernerd. Maybe it was Lefty—no, Lefty was the twin with the broken nose.

"You've got Nine fans out there who'd love it if you'd make a bit of a show next time," the big basher said, then he moved on.

Kylar's second opponent was Ymmuri. The horse lords didn't often come to the city, so the audience was excited. He was a small man, covered with layers of brown horsehide, even his face masked behind leather. He too had kept the knives at his belt, big forward-curving gurkas. His blade was a scimitar, excellent for slashing from horseback, but not as good for a swordfight. Further, the Ymmuri was drunk.

As ordered, Kylar played with him, dodging heavy slashes at the last moment, mixing in spin kicks and acrobatics, basically violating everything Durzo had taught him. Against a competent opponent, Durzo said, you never aim a kick higher than your opponent's knee. It's simply too slow. And you don't leave your feet. Jumping commits you to a trajectory you can't change. The only time to use a flying kick was what the Ceurans had developed it for: to unseat cavalry when you yourself were on foot and had no other option. This time when Kylar won, the crowd roared.

As Kylar came in from his fight, he saw Logan going out. Logan's opponent was either Bernerd or Lefty. Kylar hoped the twin wouldn't be too hard on him. A few minutes later, though, Logan came in, flushed and triumphant. Bernerd (or Lefty) must have gotten overconfident.

Kylar's third fight was against a local sword master who made his living tutoring young noblemen. The man looked at Kylar as if he were the vilest snake in Midcyru, but he was overeager on his ripostes. After scoring a single touch on Kylar, he lost and stormed off.

It was only when Logan won his third fight against another sword master that Kylar smelled a rat. Then Kylar won his fourth fight against a veteran soldier—oddly enough, a low-ranking one and not from a good family, but against whom Kylar should have had a tough match. The soldier wasn't a good pretender. Kylar almost didn't attack the openings the man left; they were so blatant that Kylar was sure they were traps.

Then he understood. The peasant had been real. The Ymmuri had been drugged. The sword master had been intimidated. The soldier had been bought. It was a single-elimination tourney, so now there were only sixteen men left. Kylar recognized four of them as Sa'kagé, which meant there were probably another four Sa'kagé he didn't recognize. The Nine had stacked the brackets. It infuriated him. But he sailed through his last fights as if they mattered, doing jumping spin kicks, arm bars, leg sweeps, elaborate disarming combos, and everything else ridiculous he could think of.

He'd thought that the Nine believed in him, that they were giving a real chance, do or die. But this was just another scam. There were great fighters here, but they'd been bought off. No doubt the bookies were making money hand over fist as Kylar rose through one bracket and none other than Logan Gyre rose through the other. Logan, tall, handsome Logan, the scion of a leading family, was hugely popular. So Logan's first fights had been staged to be very close so the Sa'kagé could depress the odds against him. Then Logan had sailed through the more recent rounds. Great fighters took their dives at unlikely times, padding the Sa'kagé coffers further.

In most cases, it was done convincingly. When a semicompetent swordsman was trying to stab you, it didn't take much pretence to miss a block. But Kylar could tell, and he could tell that the Blademasters could tell. They looked furious, and Kylar imagined it would be a long time before they could be convinced to hold a tourney in Cenaria again. The process must be so obviously corrupt to them that Kylar doubted they would grant him Blademaster status even if he earned it twice over.

Just as obvious was that the king couldn't tell, at least not until one of the Blademasters went over and talked to him. Aleine jumped to his feet and it took his counselors some time before they could calm him enough to make him sit. So the Nine had made their point with the king, but there was still money to be made, and if Kylar guessed correctly, the Nine wanted to make their point with the whole city.

Kylar was disgusted as he walked out onto the sand to

face Logan. It was the last fight. This was for the championship. There was no good way out. He had half a mind to toss his sword at Logan's feet and surrender—but the king would think that the Sa'kagé was declaring its support for Logan. Then it would only be so long before he hired a wetboy to go visit the Gyre estate—or a simple assassin, if the Sa'kagé wouldn't take the job. Nor could Kylar let him win after a close fight. Now that the king knew the Sa'kagé had stacked the whole event, he would think they were trying to make Logan look good. So what was Kylar supposed to do? Humiliate his best friend?

The earlier elation had faded completely from Logan's face. He was dressed in fine, light chain mail with black links in the shape of a gyrfalcon on front and back, and the crowd roared as the two came together, but neither of the young men paid the crowd any attention.

"I'm not good enough to make it this far. You've set me up," Logan said. "I've been trying to decide what to do about it. I was thinking of throwing my sword down and capitulating to spoil it for you. But you're Sa'kagé, and I'm a Gyre. I'll never surrender to darkness and corruption. So what's it going to be? Do you have another blade hidden that isn't warded? Are you going to kill me publicly, just to remind Cenaria whose boot is on her throat?"

"I'm just a sword," Kylar said, his voice as gruff as Blint's.

Logan scoffed. "A sword? You can't excuse what you are so easily. You're a man who's betrayed every part of his better nature, who at every junction has decided to walk deeper into the darkness, and for what? Money." Logan spat. "Kill me if that's what you've been paid for,

Shadow, because I tell you this: I will do my best to kill you."

Money? What did Logan know about money? He'd had money every day of his life. One of his worn-out gloves could be sold to feed a guild rat for months. Kylar felt hot rage wash through his blood. Logan didn't know anything—and yet he couldn't be more right.

Kylar leapt forward at the exact moment the horn blew, not that he cared whether he was following the rules. Logan began to draw his sword, but Kylar didn't bother. He launched himself forward with a lunging kick at Logan's sword hand.

The kick connected before Logan had the sword halfway out of the sheath. It smacked the hilt from his fingers and twisted him to the side. Kylar ran into Logan, twined a foot around the bigger man's legs, and carried them both to the ground.

Kylar landed on top of him and heard the breath whoosh from Logan's lungs. He grabbed each of Logan's arms and yanked them up behind his back, trapping them in one hand. He grabbed a fistful of Logan's hair with the other hand and slammed his face into the sand as hard as he could, again and again, but the sand was too yielding to knock him out.

Standing, Kylar drew his sword. The sounds of Logan moaning and his own heavy breathing seemed to be the only sounds in all the world. The stadium was silent. There wasn't even any wind. It was hot, so damned hot. Kylar slashed viciously across Logan's left kidney and then his right. The sword was warded, so it didn't cut of course, but it was still like getting smacked with a cudgel.

Logan cried out in pain. He sounded suddenly so young.

Despite his huge body, Logan was barely eighteen, but the sound embarrassed Kylar. It was weakness. It was humiliating, infuriating. Kylar looked around the stadium. Somewhere, the Nine were here watching, each dressed as an ordinary man, pretending to share his neighbors' horror. Pretending to be friends with men they despised, men they would betray for nothing more than money.

There was a noise behind Kylar, and he saw Logan had fought to his hands and knees. He was struggling to stand. His face was bleeding from a hundred tiny cuts from the sand, and his eyes were unfocused.

Kylar lofted his glowing orange sword to the crowd. Then he spun and smashed the flat of the blade into the back of Logan's head. His friend crumpled, unconscious, and the crowd gasped.

Humiliating Logan had been the only way to save him, but humiliation served in such a dishonorable manner would not draw attention to Logan's defeat, but instead to the Sa'kagé. They were vile, and shameless, and omnipotent, and today Kylar was their avatar. He tossed the red sword down and raised his hands to the crowd once more, this time in dual one-fingered salutes. *To hell with all of you. To hell with me.*

Then he ran.

27

The Modaini Smoking Club's windows were Plangan plate glass cut into wedges and fanciful zoomorphic shapes. If you looked at the shapes in the glass, you could ignore the outside world completely, which was the point. If you looked at the shapes, you wouldn't notice the bars on the other side of the window. Kylar stood at that window, staring through those bars at a girl down in the Sidlin Market.

She was bargaining with a vendor for produce. Doll Girl—Elene—was growing up, perhaps fifteen years old now that Kylar was eighteen. She was beautiful—at least from this safe distance. From here he could see her body, supple curves clad in a simple serving dress, her hair pulled back and shining gold in the sun, and the flash of an easy smile. Though he couldn't make out her scars from this distance, through the colored glass, her white dress was blood red. The leaded zoomorphic whorls reminded him of the whorls of her scars.

"She'll destroy you," Momma K said behind him.

"She's part of a different world from any you'll ever know."

"I know," he said quietly, barely glancing over his shoulder. Momma K had come into the room with a new girl, an east side girl, young and pretty. Momma K was combing the girl's blonde hair out. The Modaini Smoking Club was very different from most of the brothels in the city. The courtesans here were trained in the arts of conversation and music as much as the arts of the bedchamber. There was no scandalous dress, no nudity, no groping in the public areas, and no commoners allowed.

Momma K had found out about Kylar's excursions long ago, of course. You couldn't keep anything secret from Momma K. She'd argued with him about it, and still made her comments whenever she happened to be here, but once she'd found out that he wouldn't stop coming, she'd made him swear that he come into the smoking club and watch from inside. If he was going to be stupid, she said, he might as well be safe. If he went outside, sooner or later he'd bump into the girl and talk to her and bed her and fall in love with her and get himself killed for his defiance.

"Don't be shy," Momma K said to the girl. "You're soon going to be doing a lot more while a man's in the room than changing your clothes."

Kylar didn't turn as he heard the sounds of clothes being shed. Just what he needed. He was depressed already.

"I know it's scary your first time, Daydra," Momma K said gently. "It's a hard business. Isn't that right, Kylar?"

"It had better be. It doesn't do much when it's soft."

Daydra giggled, more from her nerves than Kylar's cleverness, no doubt. He didn't turn from the barred window. He was soaking his eyes in Elene. What would her clear brown eyes say as she looked at the girl behind him, preparing for her first client?

"You're going to feel guilty at first, Daydra," Momma K said. "Expect it. Ignore it. You're not a slut, you're not a liar. You're an entertainer. Men don't buy a fine Sethi wine because they're thirsty. They buy it because it makes them feel good and buying it makes them feel good about themselves. That's why they come here, too. Men will always pay for their vices, whether it's wine or lifting your skirt—"

"Or murder," Kylar said, touching the full coin purse and the dagger at his belt.

He could almost feel a chill in the air, but Momma K ignored him and continued on. "The secret is to decide what you won't sell. Never sell your heart. Some girls won't kiss. Some won't be kept by one man. Some won't perform certain services. I did it all, but I kept my heart."

"Did you?" Kylar said. "Really?" He turned, and his heart jumped into his throat. Through Momma K's art, Daydra now looked identical to Elene. Similar build, similar glorious curves, the same gleaming gold hair, the same simple servant's dress, similar to everything but that she was on this side of the bars, close enough to touch, and Elene was out there. Daydra had an uncertain smile, like she couldn't believe how he was talking to Momma K.

Momma K was furious. She swept across the room and grabbed Kylar's ear like he was a naughty little boy. She hauled him out of the room by his ear onto the second-story landing. It was full of overstuffed chairs and fine rugs, with a bodyguard sitting in one corner and doors leading to four different courtesans' rooms. Stairs led down to a parlor lined with suggestive but not explicit paintings and leather-bound books. Momma K finally released his ear and closed the door behind her quietly.

"Damn you, Kylar. Daydra is terrified already. What the hell are you doing?"

"Telling an ugly truth." He shrugged. "Telling lies. Whatever."

"If I wanted truth I'd look in the goddam mirror. This life isn't about truth, it's about making the best of what you've got. This is about that girl, isn't it? That madness. You saved her, Kylar. Now let her go. She owes you everything."

"She owes me her scars."

"You're a damned fool. Have you ever looked at what's happened to all the other girls in your guild? Not even ten years out, they're drunks and riot weed smokers, cutpurses and cripples, beggars and cheap whores, fifteen-year-old mothers with starving children, or unable to bear children at all because they've used tansy tea so many times. I promise you Elene's not the only girl from your guild with scars given to her by some twist. But she is the only one with a hope and a future. You gave her that, Kylar."

"I should have—"

"The only thing you could have done better was murder that boy earlier—before he did anything to you. If you'd been the kind of child capable of murder, you wouldn't have been the kind of boy who cared what happened to some little girl. The truth is that even if they were your fault, Elene's scars are a small price for the life you've given her."

Kylar turned away. The landing had a window overlooking the market, too. It was simple glass, clear, neither cut nor colored like the glass in the courtesan's room. It too was barred, though with simple straight iron, the bars' edges as sharp as one of Blint's knives. Elene had come closer and he could see her scars, but then she smiled and her scars seemed to disappear.

How often did girls in the Warrens smile like that? Kylar found himself smiling in response. He felt lighter than he could ever remember. He turned and smiled at Momma K. "I wouldn't have expected to find absolution from you."

She didn't smile back. "It's not absolution, it's reality. And I'm the perfect person to give you that. Besides, you carry guilt as badly as Durzo."

"Durzo? Durzo never feels guilty about anything," Kylar said.

A flicker of disgust passed over her face. She turned to look at Elene. "End this farce, Kylar."

"What are you talking about?"

"Durzo told you the rules: you can fuck but you can never love. He doesn't see what you're doing, but I do. You believe you love Elene, so you won't fuck at all. Why don't you get this out of your system?" Her voice got gentle. "Kylar. You can't have that girl out there. Why don't you take what you can have?"

"What are you talking about?"

"Go in to Daydra. She'll thank you for it. It's on the house. If you're worried because you're inexperienced, she's a virgin, too." *"Too"? Gods, did Momma K have to know everything?*

"No," Kylar said. "No thanks, I'm not interested."

"Kylar, what are you waiting for? Some glorious soul

union with that girl out there? It's just fucking, and that's all you get. That's the deal, Kylar, and you knew it when you started. We all make our deals. I did, Durzo did, and you did too."

Giving up, Momma K gestured to one of her bashers downstairs to let a client through.

A hairy-knuckled slob wheezed his way up the stairs. Though richly dressed, he was fat and ugly and foul smelling and grinning broadly with black teeth. He paused on the landing, licking his lips, a slack-jawed picture of lust. He nodded to Momma K, winked conspiratorially at Kylar, and went into the virgin courtesan's room.

"Maybe they were bad deals," Kylar said.

"It doesn't matter. There's no going back."

28

$\mathcal{F}$eir Cousat knocked on a door high inside the great pyramid of Sho'cendi. Two knocks, pause, two, pause, one. When he and Dorian and Solon had been students at the magi's school of fire, they hadn't rated such prestigious rooms. But he and Dorian hadn't been given the rooms now so much to thank them for their historic services as to keep an eye on them.

The door cracked open, and Dorian's eye appeared on the other side. Feir always thought it was funny: Dorian was a prophet. He could foretell the fall of a kingdom or the winner of a horserace—a lucrative trick when Feir could convince him to do it—but he couldn't tell who was at his own door. He said that prophesying concerning himself involved spiraling uncomfortably close to madness.

Dorian ushered Feir inside and barred the door behind him. Feir felt himself passing through an improbably high number of wards. He looked at them. A ward against eavesdropping he'd expected. A ward against entry was unusual to maintain when you were in the room yourself.

But the truly strange one was a ward to keep magic in. Feir fingered the threads of the weave, shaking his head in astonishment. Dorian was the kind of magus born once a generation. After studying at Hoth'salar, the Healers' School on Gandu, and mastering all they had to teach him by the time he was sixteen, Dorian had come to the school of fire and mastered fire magics while not even pretending to be interested in them. He'd only stayed because he'd become friends with Feir and Solon. Solon's talents were almost solely in Fire, but he was the strongest of the three. Feir wasn't sure why the two had become friends with him. Maybe because he wasn't threatened by their excellence. They were so obviously the kind of men who'd been touched by the gods that Feir didn't even think to be jealous for a long time. Maybe it helped that he'd been born a peasant. It probably also helped that whenever he was struggling with his studies and started to be jealous, one or the other of his friends would suggest sparring with him.

Feir looked fat, but he could move and he trained daily with the Blademasters, who kept their central training facility mere minutes from Sho'cendi. For Solon or Dorian to volunteer to spar with him was to volunteer for bruises. Dorian could heal bruises later, but they still hurt.

Dorian had half-packed saddlebags open on the bed.

Feir sighed. "You know the Assembly's forbidden you to leave. They don't care about Cenaria. Honestly, if Solon weren't there, I wouldn't either. We could send him a message to leave." The school's leaders hadn't phrased it that way, of course. They were more worried about delivering the continent of Midcyru's only—perhaps the world's only—prophet into the Godking's hands.

"You don't even know the best part yet," Dorian said, grinning like they were children.

Feir felt the blood draining from his face. The wards to keep magic in the room suddenly made sense. "You aren't planning to steal it."

"I could make the argument that it's ours. The three of us were the ones who tracked it, found it, and brought it back. They stole it from us first, Feir."

"You agreed it would be safer here. We let them take it from us."

"So I'm taking it back," Dorian said, shrugging.

"So it's you against all the world again."

"It's me *for* all the world, Feir. Will you come with me?"

"Come with you? Is this the madness?" When Dorian's gift for prophecy had surfaced, one of the first things he'd tried was to tell his own future. He'd learned that no matter what he did, he would go mad one day. Delving into his own future would only hasten that day's arrival. "I thought you said you had still had a decade or so."

"Not so long, now," Dorian said. He shrugged like it didn't matter, as if it didn't break his heart, exactly the way he'd shrugged when he'd asked Solon to go to Cenaria, knowing it would cost Solon Kaede's love. "Before you answer, Feir, know this: if you come with me, you will regret it many times, and you will never again walk the halls of Sho'cendi."

"You make such a convincing plea," Feir said, rolling his eyes.

"You will also save my life at least twice, own a forge, be known throughout the world as the greatest living weaponsmith, have a small part in saving the world, and die satisfied, if not nearly so old as you or I hoped."

"Oh, that's better," Feir said sarcastically, but his stomach was doing flips. Dorian rarely told what he knew, but when he did, he never lied. "Just a small part in saving the world?"

"Feir, your purpose in life isn't your happiness. We're part of a much bigger story. Everyone is. If your part is unsung, does that make it worthless? Our purpose on this trip isn't to save Solon. It's to see a boy. We will face many dangers to get there. Death is a very real possibility. And do you know what that boy needs from us? Three words. Maybe two if the name counts as only one. Do you want to know what they are?"

"Sure."

"'Ask Momma K.'"

"That's it? What's it mean?" Feir asked.

"I have no idea."

Sometimes a seer could be a pain in the ass. "You ask for a lot from me," Feir said.

Dorian nodded.

"I'll regret it if I say yes?"

"Many times. But not in the end."

"It might be easier if you told me less."

"Believe me," Dorian said, "I wish I didn't have such a clear view of what lies before you down each possible choice here. If I told you less, you would hate me for holding back. If I told you more, you might not have the heart to carry on."

"Enough!" Gods, was it going to be that bad?

Feir looked at his hands. He'd have a forge. He'd be known throughout the world for his work. It had been one of his dreams. Maybe he could even marry, have sons. He thought of asking Dorian, but didn't dare. He sighed and rubbed his temples.

Dorian broke into a big smile. "Good! Now help me figure out how we're going to get Curoch out of here."

Feir was sure he had misunderstood. Then he felt the blood draining from his face. There were wards on the door to keep magic *in*. "When you say 'here' you mean 'here, in the school.' Like I still have a chance to convince you *not* to try to steal the most guarded artifact in Midcyru. Right?"

Dorian threw back the covers on the bed. There was a plain sheathed sword on it. It looked entirely normal, except that the sheath was made entirely of lead, and it covered the sword entirely, even the hilt, damping the magic. But this wasn't just a magic sword. It was more like The Magic Sword. This was Curoch, Emperor Jorsin Alkestes' sword. The Sword of Power. Most magi weren't even strong enough to use it. If Feir (or most others) tried, it would kill him in a second. Dorian had said even Solon couldn't use it safely. But after Jorsin Alkestes' death, there had been quite a few magi who had been able to— and they'd destroyed more than one civilization. "At first, I thought I was going to have to prophesy my own future to get it, but instead, I prophesied the guards'. Everything worked perfect except one guard came down a hallway that he only had maybe a one in a thousand chance of taking. I had to knock him out. The good news is, he's going to be nursed back to health by a lovely girl whom he'll later marry."

"You're telling me there's some guard unconscious upstairs right now, just waiting to be found? While we're talking? Why are you even doing this?"

"Because he needs it."

"He? You're stealing Curoch for 'ask Momma K' boy?" Feir asked.

"Oh no, well, not directly. The boy who needs to hold Curoch—the one the whole world needs to hold Curoch—isn't even born yet. But this is our only chance to take it."

"Gods, you're serious," Feir said.

"Stop pretending this changes anything. You've already decided. We're going to Cenaria."

Sometimes a seer could be a pain in the ass? Try always.

29

*W*hat is your problem!" Master Blint screamed.

"I don't—" Kylar said.

"Again!" Blint roared.

Kylar stopped the practice knife with an X block, crossing his wrists in front of him. He tried to grab Durzo's hand and twist, but the wetboy slipped aside.

They ranged around the practice building of Blint's newest safe house, vaulting off walls, maneuvering each other into beams, attempting to use every uneven edge of the floor against each other. But the match was even.

The nine years Kylar had spent under Blint's tutelage had seen him harden and grow. He was maybe twenty now. He was still not as tall as Blint and never would be, but his body was lean and taut, and his eyes were the same light light blue. As he sweated and fought, every muscle in his arms, chest, and stomach was distinct and moving precisely to its task, but he couldn't make himself really engage.

Durzo Blint saw it, and it infuriated him. Swearing long

and eloquently, Master Blint compared his attitude unfavorably with a lackadaisical prostitute's, his face with unlikely and unhealthy body parts, and his intelligence with several species of farm animals. When he attacked again, Kylar could see him mentally ratcheting up the level.

One of the many dangerous things about Master Blint was that even when he was furious, it never showed in his fighting. His fury would only be allowed expression after you were lying on the ground, usually bleeding.

He moved Kylar across the open room slowly, hand clenched in fist or extending in knife hand, the practice knife glittering in quick arcs and jabs. For a fraction of a second, he overextended a stab and Kylar managed to slip around it and hit Master Blint's wrist.

But Master Blint held onto the knife, and as he drew it back, the dull blade caught Kylar's thumb.

"That impatience cost you a thumb, boy."

With his chest heaving, Kylar stopped, but he didn't take his eyes off of Master Blint. They'd already practiced with swords of several kinds, with knives of varying lengths. Sometimes they fought with the same weapon, and sometimes they'd mismatch—Master Blint taking a double-edged broadsword against a Gandian blade, or Kylar taking a stiletto against a gurka. "Anyone else would have lost the knife," Kylar said.

"You're not fighting anyone else."

"I wouldn't fight you if you were armed and I wasn't."

Master Blint drew back the knife and threw it past Kylar's ear. Kylar didn't flinch. It wasn't that he didn't still wonder sometimes if Master Blint was going to kill him. It was that he knew he couldn't stop him.

When Blint attacked again, it was full speed. Kick met stop kick, punches were diverted, jabs dodged, blows absorbed against arms, legs, and hips. There were no tricks, nothing showy. Just speed.

In the midst of the flashing limbs, as usual, Kylar realized that Master Blint would win. The man was simply better than Kylar. It was usually about now that Kylar would try something desperate. Master Blint would be waiting for it.

Kylar unleashed a storm of blows, fast and light as a mountain breeze. None of them alone would hurt Master Blint even if they connected, but any would cause him to miss the next. Kylar fought faster and faster, each blow being brushed aside or only connecting with flesh tensed for the impact.

One low spear hand got through, jabbing Master Blint's abdomen. As he hunched over involuntarily, Kylar went for the full strike on Blint's chin—then stopped. Blint lashed up fast enough that he would have blocked the strike, but with no contact where he'd expected it, he brought the block too far and couldn't bring his hand back before Kylar lashed his still-cocked fist at his nose.

But Kylar's strike didn't catch Master Blint. It was brushed aside by an unseen force like an invisible hand. Stumbling, Kylar tried to recover and block Durzo's kick, but it blew through his hands with superhuman force. Kylar smashed into the beam behind him so hard that he heard it crack. He dropped to the ground.

"Your turn," Blint said. "If you can't touch me, I'll have a special punishment for you."

"Special punishment"? Beautiful.

Hunched on the ground with both arms throbbing,

Kylar didn't answer. He stood, but when he turned, in
Blint's place stood Logan. But the sneer on Logan's face
was all Durzo Blint. It was an illusion, an illusion seven
feet tall, matching Blint's moves precisely. Kylar kicked
viciously at his knee—but his foot went right through the
figure, shattering the illusion and touching nothing at all.
Blint stood two feet behind it. As Kylar staggered off balance, Blint raised a hand. With a whoosh, a phantom fist
shot from his hand and knocked Kylar off his feet.

Kylar bounced back to his feet in time to see Blint leap.
The ceiling was twelve feet high, but Blint's entire back
hit it—and stuck to it. He started crawling, and then disappeared as shadows writhed over him and merged with
the greater darkness of the ceiling. First Kylar could hear
Blint moving to a spot above him, then the sound cut off
abruptly. Blint's Talent was covering even the scuffing
sound of brushing against wood.

Moving constantly, Kylar searched the ceiling for any
shadow out of place.

"Scarred Wrable can even throw his voice, or any other
sound," Blint said, from the far corner of the ceiling. "I
wonder if you could."

Kylar saw, or thought he saw, the shadow moving back
toward him. He flung a throwing knife at the shadow—
and it burst apart, leaving his knife quivering in the wood.
It was another illusion. Kylar turned slowly, trying to hear
the slightest sound out of place over the pounding of his
heart.

The slight brush of cloth hitting the floor behind him
made him spin and lash out. But there was nothing there
except Blint's tunic in a pile on the floor. A thump announced Blint himself landing behind Kylar. Kylar spun

once more, but something caught his left hand, then his right.

Master Blint stood bare-chested, a dead look in his eyes, his real hands at his sides. Kylar's wrists were held in the air by magic. Slowly, his arms were pulled apart until he was spread-eagled, then further. Kylar held his silence for as long as he could, then screamed as he felt his joints on the verge of dislocating.

The bonds dropped and Kylar crumpled, defeated.

Durzo shook his head in disappointment—and Kylar attacked. His kick slowed as it approached Durzo's knee as if it were sinking into a spring, then bounced back, spinning him hard and throwing him in a tangle to the floor.

"Do you see what just happened?" Durzo asked.

"You kicked my ass again," Kylar said.

"Before that."

"I almost hit you," Kylar said.

"You fooled me and you would have destroyed me, but I used my Talent and you still refuse to use yours. Why?"

Because I'm broken. Since meeting Drissa Nile four years ago, Kylar had thought a hundred times about telling Durzo Blint what she'd told him: he didn't have a conduit, and it couldn't be fixed. But the rules had always been clear. Kylar became a wetboy, or he died. And as Blint had just proved again, Kylar wouldn't be a wetboy without the Talent. Telling Blint the truth had always seemed like a quick way to die. Kylar had tried everything to get his Talent to work or to learn about anything that might help, but had found nothing.

Blint breathed deeply. When he spoke again, his voice

was calm. "It's time for some truth, Kylar. You're a good fighter. Deficient still with pole arms and clubs and cross-bows and—" He was starting to lecture but noticed it. "Regardless, you're as good at hand-to-hand fighting and with those Ceuran hand-and-a-half swords you like as any fighter I've seen. Today you would've had me. You won't win next time, but you'll start winning. Your body knows what to do, and your mind has got it mostly figured out, too. In the next few years, your body will get a bit faster, a bit stronger, and you'll get cleverer by half. But your weapons training is finished, Kylar. The rest is practice."

"And?" Kylar asked.

"Follow me. I've got something that may help you."

Kylar followed Blint to his workroom. This one was smaller than the one Azoth had first seen in Blint's old safe house, but at least this house had doors between the animals' pens and the work area. It smelled much better. It was also familiar now. The books lining the shelves were like old friends. He and Blint had even added dozens of recipes to them. In the past nine years, he had come to appreciate Blint's mastery of poisons.

Every wetboy used poisons, of course. Hemlock, and blood flower, and mandrake root, and ariamu were all local and fairly deadly. But Blint knew hundreds of poisons. There were entire pages of his books crossed out, notes scrawled in Durzo's tight angular hand, "Fool. Dilutes the poison." Other entries were amended, from how long it took for the poison to take effect to what the best methods for delivery were, to how to keep the plants alive in foreign climes.

Master Blint picked up a box. "Sit."

Kylar sat at the high table, propping an elbow on the

wood and holding his chin. Blint upended the box in front of him.

A white snake slid onto the table with a thump. Kylar barely had time to register what it was before it struck at his face. He saw its mouth open, huge, fangs glittering. He was moving back, but too slowly.

Then the snake disappeared and Kylar was falling backward off the stool. He landed flat on his back but bounced up to his feet in an instant.

Blint was holding the snake behind the head. He had grabbed it out of the air while it was striking. "Do you know what this is, Kylar?"

"It's a white asp." It was one of the most deadly snakes in the world. They were small, rarely growing longer than a man's forearm, but those they bit died within seconds.

"No, it's the price of failure. Kylar, you fight as well as any non-Talented man I've ever seen. But you're no wetboy. You've mastered the poisons; you know the techniques of killing. Your reaction speed is peerless; your instincts are good. You hide well, disguise well, fight well. But doing those things *well* is shit, it's nothing. An *assassin* does those things well. That's why assassins have targets. Wetboys have deaders. Why do we call them deaders? Because when we take a contract, the rest of their short lives is a formality. You have the Talent, Kylar, but you aren't using it. Won't use it. You've seen a little of what I have to teach you, but I can't teach it to you until you tap your Talent."

"I know. I know," Kylar said, refusing to meet his master's gaze.

"The truth is, Kylar, I didn't need an apprentice when you came along. Never did. But I heard a rumor that an ancient artifact was hidden in Cenaria: the silver ka'kari. They say Ezra the Mad himself made it. It's a small silver ball, but when you bond it, it makes you impervious to any blade and it extends your life indefinitely. You can still be killed any way that doesn't involve metal, but immortality, Kylar! And then you came along. Do you know what you are? Did that maja Drissa Nile tell you?"

Durzo knew about Drissa Nile? "She said I was broken."

"The ka'kari were made for people 'broken' like you are. There's supposed to be an attraction between people who are vastly Talented but don't have a conduit and the ka'kari. You were supposed to call it, Kylar. You don't know how to bond it, so you'd call it, hand it over, and I'd be immortal."

"And I'd still be broken," Kylar said bitterly.

"Once I had it, we could have Drissa study it. She's a great healer. Even if it took her a few years, it would have been fine. But we're running out of time," Durzo said. "Do you know why I can't just let you be an *assassin?*" Even now he sneered.

Kylar had wondered a hundred times, of course, but he'd always figured it was because Blint's pride wouldn't let him have a failed apprentice.

"Our Talent allows us to swear a magically binding oath of service to the Shinga. It keeps the Shinga safe, and it keeps us above suspicion. It's a weak compulsion, but to break it a wetboy would have to submit himself to a mage or a meister, and all the mages in this city work for the Sa'kagé and only an idiot would submit to a meister. You've become a skilled assassin, Kylar, and it's making the Shinga nervous. He doesn't like being nervous."

"Why would I ever do anything against the Shinga? It would be signing my own death warrant."

"That's not the point. Shingas who aren't paranoid don't live long."

"How could you never tell me all this?" Kylar demanded. "All the times you've beaten me for not using my Talent—it's like beating a blind man because he can't read!"

"Your desperation to use your Talent is what calls the ka'kari. I was helping you. And I'm going to help you some more." He gestured to the snake in his hand. "This is motivation. It's also the kindest poison I know." Master Blint held Kylar with his eyes. "Getting that ka'kari has always been your final test, boy. Get it. Or else."

The air took on a chill. There it was. Kylar's last warning.

Master Blint put away the snake, collected a few of his weapons, grabbed the bag he already had packed, and picked Retribution off its pegs on the wall. He checked the big black blade, then slid it back into its scabbard. "I'm going to be gone for a while," he said.

"I'm not coming with you?"

"You'd get in the way."

Get in the way? The casual way Blint said it hurt almost as much as the fact that it was true.

30

I don't like it," Solon said.

Regnus Gyre stared into the winds that blew his silver hair almost straight back. The Twins were quiet today, so there was only the sound of the wind rushing over the wall. He listened to the wind as if it were trying to tell him something.

"After ten years, a summons," Solon said. "Why would the king do such a thing on the eve of your son's majority?"

"What's the best reason to gather all your enemies in one place?" Regnus asked, barely raising his voice enough to be heard over the wind. It was still cold even in late spring. Screaming Winds was never warm. The north wind cut through wool, made a mock of the beards and long hair the men grew to hold some extra iota of heat in.

"To smash them," Solon said.

"Better to smash them before they can gather," Regnus said. "The king knows that I'll do everything in my power to be home for my son's ascendance. That means traveling fast. That means a small escort."

"Clever of him not to command a small escort," Solon said. "I'd have put such subtlety beyond him."

"He's had ten years to think about this, my friend, and the help of his weasel." His weasel was Fergund Sa'fasti, a magus who was not exactly Sho'cendi's finest moralist. Fergund also knew Solon by sight and would gladly tell the world Solon was a magus if he thought it would cause mischief. Fergund was why Solon had been staying with Regnus year-round as Logan took more responsibilities at court.

It was, he was beginning to think, a serious mistake.

"So you think they'll attack us on the way?" Solon asked.

Regnus nodded into the wind.

"I don't suppose I'll be able to convince you not to go?" Solon asked.

Regnus smiled, and Solon couldn't help but love the man. For all that it had crippled his house and destroyed any ambitions Regnus might have had for the throne, taking command of Screaming Winds had given Regnus life.

There was fire in Regnus Gyre, something fierce and proud like a warrior king of old. His command had clear authority, and the power of his presence made him father, king, and brother to his men. In the simple fight against evil, he excelled, even reveled. The highlanders of Khalidor, some of whom had never bowed the knee to any man, were warriors. They lived for war, thought it a disgrace to die in bed, believed the only immortality was immortality through deeds of arms sung by their minstrels.

They called Regnus the *Rurstahk Slaagen,* the Devil of the Walls, and in the last ten years, their young men had smashed themselves against those walls, tried to climb them, tried to sneak past them, tried to bribe their way through them, climbed over the Twins and tried to descend on Screaming Winds from behind. Every time, Regnus had crushed them. Frequently, he did it without losing a man.

Screaming Winds was made of three walls at the three narrowest points in the only pass between Cenaria and Khalidor. Between the walls were killing fields sown thick by Regnus's engineers with caltrops, pits, snares, and deadfalls of rock from the surrounding mountains. Twice clans had made it past the first wall. The traps had reaped such a harvest of death that none had survived to tell what they found beyond it.

"It could be genuine, I suppose," Solon said. "Logan says he has become close friends with the prince. Maybe this is the prince's influence at work."

"I don't think much of the prince," Regnus said.

"But he thinks a lot of Logan. We can hope that the prince takes after his mother. This may even be her work."

Regnus said nothing. He wouldn't say Nalia's name, not even now.

"Hope for the best, plan for the worst?" Solon asked. "Ten of our best men, extra horses for all of us, and go down the coast road instead of the main road?"

"No," Regnus said. "If they've set one ambush, they'll have set two. We might as well make them play their gambit on open ground."

"Yessir." Solon only wished he knew who the other players were.

"You still write letters to that Kaede woman?"

Solon nodded, but his body went rigid. His chest felt hollow. Of course the commander would know. A letter sent every week, and never a one received.

"Well, if you don't get a letter after this one, at least you'll know it's not because yours are boring." Regnus clapped a hand on Solon's shoulder.

Solon couldn't help but smile ruefully. He didn't know how Regnus did it, but somehow in his company it was as easy to face heartbreak as it was to face death.

Momma K sat on the balcony of an estate that had no business being where it was. Against all tradition and sanity, Roth Grimson's opulent estate had been built in the middle of the Warrens.

She didn't like Roth and never had, but she met few people in her work that she did like. The fact was, she had to deal with Roth because she couldn't afford to ignore him. He was one of the Sa'kagé's rising stars. Not only was he intelligent, but everything he touched seemed to turn to gold. After the guild wars, he had emerged as the guild head of the Red Bashers, and had promptly taken over half of the Warrens.

Of course, the Sa'kagé had stepped in, only beginning with Durzo's assassination of Corbin Fishill, but it had taken years to get things truly settled. There had been, of course, curiosity among the Nine at how Roth had managed his guild so well that they'd claimed so much territory. And Roth obviously hadn't liked her questions, but he'd accepted them. A word from her and he'd never be on the Nine. Another word, and he'd be dead. He was smart enough to know that.

Roth was in his late twenties. A tall, formidable young man who carried himself like a prince among dogs. Close-set blue eyes, dark hair, a penchant for fine clothing: today he wore a gray tunic decorated with the Plangan knotwork that was just coming into fashion, matching breeches, and high boots worked in silver. He wore his black hair lightly oiled, a wavy lock sometimes drooping into his eyes.

"If you ever tire of working for our Master of Coin, you'd do well in one of my brothels. The men would adore you." She threw that out just to see how he'd take it.

He laughed. "I'll keep that in mind."

With a wave, he signaled the servants to bring their breakfast. Their little table graced the edge of the balcony, and they sat beside each other. Apparently, Roth wanted her to admire his estate. Probably he was hoping she'd ask him why he'd built here.

She didn't want to give him the satisfaction. Besides, she'd already looked into it. The reasons were good enough, she knew. He had some waterfront, which would allow him to do some smuggling, though the dock was too small for high profitability and royal attention. He'd also been able to purchase the land for a pittance, though he'd had to hire so many bashers during the construction he'd lost the savings. When the poor had been displaced, both the honest and the thieves among them had been eager to steal whatever they could from the fool who would build a manse on their side of the river. The bashers had probably beaten hundreds. Momma K knew that they had killed at least half a dozen. It was death to be found on Grimson's grounds without permission.

The walls were high, lined with crushed glass and metal spikes that stood as pointed shadows in the dawn light. Bashers manned those walls, men who were both efficient and enjoyed their work. None of the locals tried to intrude anymore. The amateurs had either already tried and paid the price or knew of others who had. The professionals knew they could cross Vanden Bridge and find easier pickings.

His gardens were beautiful, if given to flowers and plants that kept low to the ground so that his archers didn't have their killing angles obscured. The splashes of vermilion, green, yellow, and orange of his gardens were a stark contrast against the grays and dingy browns of the Warrens.

The servants brought the first course, halved blood oranges with a caramelized sugar crust. Roth opened with a comment on the weather. Not a particularly inspired choice, but Momma K didn't expect more.

He moved on to commenting on his gardens as the servants brought hot sweetbread. He had the newly rich's irritating propensity for revealing how much things had cost. He should have known that she would be able to tell from the quality of the service and the meal exactly how much he was spending on this estate of his. When would he get to the point?

"So there's going to be an opening on the Nine," Roth said. Abruptly done. He should have divulged an amusing anecdote from his work and used that to lead here. Momma K was starting to doubt this one.

"Yes," she said. She let it sit. She wasn't going to make this easy. The sun was just rising above the horizon and the sky was turning a glorious orange. It was going to be a scorching day; even at this hour she barely needed the shawl around her shoulders.

"I've been working with Phineas Seratsin for six years. I know the job better than anyone."

"You've been working *for* the Trematir, not with him."

His eyes flashed, but he said nothing. A dangerous temper, then. Master Grimson didn't like to be corrected.

"I think your spies must not be smart enough to have seen the amount of work I do versus what that old man does."

She lifted an eyebrow. "Spies?"

"Everyone knows you have spies everywhere."

"Well. Everyone knows. It must be so, then."

"Oh, I see," Roth said. "It's one of those things everyone knows but I'm not supposed to mention because it's rude."

"There are people within this organization with whom it is dangerous to be rude, boy. If you're asking for my vote, you'd do well to make a friend of me."

He motioned to the servants, who took their plates and replaced them with cuts of spiced meats and a lightly broiled egg dish with cheese.

"I'm not asking," he said quietly.

Momma K finished her eggs and began on the braised meat. Delightful. The man must have brought a chef from Gandu. She ate and looked at the lightening sky, the sun rising slowly over the great iron gate to Grimson's estate. If he took that comment back, she'd let him live.

"I don't know how you have such influence on the Nine, but I know I need your vote, and I will have it," Roth said. "I will take your vote, or I will take your niece."

The meat that a moment ago had seemed so delightfully spiced, that seemed to melt in Momma K's mouth, suddenly tasted like a mouthful of sand.

"Pretty girl, isn't she? Adorable little braids. It's so sad about her mother dying, but wonderful that she had a rich aunt to find her a place to live, and in the castle itself, no less! Still, a rich old whore ought to have done better than have her niece raised by a serving woman."

She was frozen. *How did he find out?*

The ledgers. Her ledgers were done all in code, but Phineas Seratsin was the Sa'kagé's Master of Coin. He had access to more financial records than the next five people in the kingdom combined. Roth must have followed the records and found payments made to a serving woman in the castle. She was a frightened woman. A single threat from Roth and she'd have folded.

Roth stood, his plate already empty. "No, do sit. Finish your breakfast."

She did, mechanically, using the time to think. Could she spirit the girl away? She couldn't use Durzo for this, but he wasn't the only wetboy she knew.

"I am a cruel man, Gwinvere. Taking a life is . . ." Roth shivered with remembered ecstasy. "Better. Better than any of the pleasures you sell. But I control my appetites. And that's what makes us human rather than slaves, isn't it?"

He was pulling on a thick leather glove. The portcullis of his gate was rising as he spoke. Outside, Momma K saw dozens of ragged peasants gathered. Obviously, this was a daily ritual.

Below, four servants were carrying a table laden with food into the garden. They set it down and walked back inside.

"These wretches are slaves to their appetites. Slaves, not men."

The starving peasants behind pushed forward and those in front were pushed inside. They looked at the spiked portcullis above them and then at Roth and Momma K. But their eyes were mostly on the food. They looked like animals, hunger driving them wild.

A young woman made a break for it. She sprinted

forward. After she had only taken a few steps, others followed her. There were old men and young, women, children, the only thing they seemed to have in common was desperation.

But Momma K couldn't see the reason for their frenzy. They reached the food and tore into it, stuffing pockets full of sausages, stuffing their mouths full of delicacies so rich they'd probably be sick later.

A servant handed an arbalest to Roth. It was already drawn and loaded.

"What are you doing?" Momma K asked.

The peasants saw him and scattered.

"I kill by a very simple pattern," Roth said, lifting the weapon. He pressed the trigger plate and a young man dropped with a bolt in his spine.

Roth set the point of the arbalest down, but instead of cranking the winch to draw back the string, he grabbed the string with his glove and drew it back by hand. For the barest moment, black tattoo-like markings rose up as if from beneath the surface of his skin and writhed with power. It was impossible.

He shot again and the young woman who had been the first to run for the table fell gracelessly.

"I feed my little herd every day. The first week of the month, I kill on the first day. The second week, the second day." He paused as the arbalest drew level again. He shot and another woman dropped as a bolt blew through her head. "And so on. But I never kill more than four."

Most of the peasants were gone now, except for one old man moving at a crawl toward the gate that was still thirty paces distant. The bolt clipped the old man's knee. He fell with a scream and started crawling.

"The slaves never figure it out. They're ruled by their bellies, not their brains." Roth waited until the old man reached the gate, missed a shot, then tried again, killing him. "See that one?"

Momma K saw a peasant come in through the portcullis. All the others had scattered.

"He's my favorite," Roth said. "He figured out the pattern." The man walked inside, unafraid, nodded to Roth, and then went to the table and started to eat without haste.

"Of course, he could tell the others and save a few lives. But then I might change the pattern, and he'd lose his edge. He's a survivor, Gwinvere. Survivors are willing to make sacrifices." Roth handed the arbalest and the glove to a servant and regarded Momma K. "So, the question is, are you a survivor?"

"I've survived more than you'll ever know. You have your vote." She'd kill him later. There was no showing weakness now. No matter how she felt. He was an animal, and he would sense her fear.

"Oh, I want more than a vote. I want Durzo Blint. I want the silver ka'kari. I want . . . much more. And I'll get it, with your help." He smiled. "How'd you like the braised peasant?"

She shook her head, distracted, looking blankly at her empty plate. Then she froze. In the garden, servants were collecting the bodies and bringing them inside.

"You did say 'pheasant,'" she said.

Roth just smiled.

31

"Well, if you don't look like the south end of a north-bound horse," Logan said as he intercepted Kylar in the middle of the Drake's yard.

"Thanks," Kylar said. He stepped past Logan, but his friend didn't move. "What do you want, Logan?"

"Hmm?" Logan asked. He was a picture of innocence, at least, if a picture of innocence could be so tall. Nor was he able to get by with the big-oaf routine. For one thing, Logan was far too intelligent for anyone to take a dumb act seriously. For another, he was too damn handsome. If there were a model of perfect masculinity in the realm, it was Logan. He was like a heroic statue made flesh. Six months a year with his father had lined his big frame with muscle and given him a hard edge that had more than just the young women of Cenaria swooning. Perfect teeth, perfect hair, and of course, ridiculous amounts of money that would be his when he reached twenty-one—in three days—filled out the picture. He drew almost as much attention as his friend Prince Aleine—and even more from the girls who weren't interested in being bedded and then dropped the next day. His saving grace was that he had absolutely no idea how attractive he was or how much people admired and envied him. It was why Kylar had nicknamed him Ogre.

"Logan, unless you were just standing in the yard, you came out here when you saw me come in the gate, which means you were waiting for me. Now you're standing there rather than walking with me, which means you don't want anyone to overhear what you're about to say. Serah *isn't* in her regular place two steps behind you, which means she's with your mother shopping for dresses or something."

"Embroidery," Logan admitted.

"So what is it?" Kylar asked.

Logan shifted from one foot to the other. "I hate it when you do that. You could've let me get to it in my own time. I was going to—hey, where do you think you're going?"

Kylar kept walking. "You're stalling."

"All right. Just stop. I was just thinking that sometime we ought to pull out the old fisticuffs," Logan said.

Fisticuffs. And people expected that someone so big to be dumb.

"You'd beat me black and blue," Kylar said, smiling the lie. If they fought, Logan would ask questions. He'd wonder. It was unlikely, but he might even guess that it hadn't truly been nine years since they'd last fought.

"You don't think I'd win, do you?" Logan asked. Ever since Logan had been humiliated in the fight at the stadium, he'd gotten serious about training. He put in hours every day with the best non-Sa'kagé sword masters in the city.

"Every time we've fought you slaughtered me. I'm—"

"Every—? Once! And that was ten years ago!"

"Nine."

"Regardless," Logan said.

"If you caught me with one of those anvils you pass off as your fists, I'd never get up," Kylar said. That was true enough.

"I'd be careful."

"I'm no match for an ogre." Something was wrong. Logan asked him to fight about once a year, but never so strenuously. Logan's honor wouldn't allow him to push a friend who'd made a decision clear, even if he didn't understand why. "What's this about, Logan? Why do you want to fight?"

Lord Gyre looked down and scratched his head. "Serah's asked why we don't spar with each other. She thinks it would be a good match. Not that she wants to see us get hurt, but . . ." Logan trailed off awkwardly.

But you can't help but want to show off a little, Kylar thought. He said, "Speaking of good matches, when are you going to march to the headsman's block and finally marry her?"

Ogre breathed a big sigh. All of his sighs were big, but this was a proportionally big sigh. It took a while. He grabbed a stable boy's stool and sat on it, oblivious of his fine cloak dragging in the dirt.

"Actually, I spoke with Count Drake about that a couple days ago."

"You did?" Kylar asked. "And?"

"He approves—"

"Congratulations! When'll it be, you big about-to-be-un-bachelored bastard?"

Ogre stared at nothing. "But he's worried."

"Are you joking?"

Logan shook his head.

"But he's known you since you were born. Your families are best friends. She's marrying up in terms of title. Way up. You've got great prospects and you two have been practically betrothed for years. What can he possibly be worried about?"

Logan fixed his eyes on Kylar's. "He said you'd know. Is she in love with you?"

Oof. "No," Kylar said after too long a pause.

Logan noticed. "Is she?"

Kylar hesitated. "I think she doesn't know who she loves herself." It was a lie of omission. Logan was on the wrong track. Serah didn't love Kylar, and he didn't even like her.

"I've loved her for my whole life, Kylar."

Kylar didn't have anything to say.

"Kylar?" Ogre stared at him intently.

"Yes?"

"Do you love her?"

"No." Kylar felt sick and furious, but his face showed nothing. He'd told Serah she had to confess to Logan, demanded it. She'd promised she would.

Logan looked at him, but his face didn't clear the way Kylar expected it to.

"Sir," a voice said behind Kylar. Kylar hadn't even heard the porter approaching.

"Yes?" he asked the old man.

"A messenger just came with this for you."

Kylar opened the unsealed message to avoid looking at Logan. It read: "You must see me. Tonight at the tenth hour. Blue Boar. —Jarl"

A chill shot through Kylar. *Jarl.* He hadn't heard from Jarl since he'd left the streets. Jarl was supposed to think he was dead. That meant Jarl was either seeking him because he needed Kylar Stern or because he knew that Kylar was Azoth. Kylar couldn't imagine any reason that Jarl would need to see Kylar Stern.

If Jarl knew who he was, who else knew, too?

Master Blint was already gone. Kylar would have to see him. He'd have to take care of this on his own.

"I have to go," he said. He turned and strode toward the gate.

"Kylar!" Logan said.

Kylar turned. "Do you trust me?" he asked.

Logan raised his hands helplessly. "Yes."

"Then trust me."

The Blue Boar was one of Momma K's nicest brothels. It was off Sidlin Way on the east side, not far from the Tomoi Bridge. It had a reputation for having some of the best wines in the city, a fact not a few merchants mentioned when their wives asked awkward questions. "A friend told me she saw you go into the Blue Boar today." "Yes, of course, dear. Business meeting. Wonderful wine selection."

It was Kylar's first visit. The brothel had three stories. The first, where food and wine were served, resembled a nice inn. A sign denoted the second floor as the "lounge" and the third as "guest rooms."

"Hello, my lord," a breathy voice said next to Kylar as he stood awkwardly just inside the entrance.

He turned and felt his cheeks growing hot. The woman stood very close to him, close enough that the spicy scent of her perfume wafted over him. Her voice was pitched low and inviting, too, like they shared secrets or soon could. But that was nothing compared with what she was wearing. He had no idea if it would be called a dress, for though it covered her from neck to ankles, it was made entirely of white lace, it wasn't a tight pattern, and she wasn't wearing anything underneath it.

"Excuse me?" he said, pulling his gaze back up to her eyes, and blushing even deeper.

"Is there any way I can help you? Would you like me to bring you a glass of Sethi red and explain our range of services?" She seemed amused at his difficulties.

"No thank you, milady," he said.

"Perhaps you'd prefer to come to the lounge and speak with me more . . . privately," she said, running a finger along his jawline.

"Actually, I'd, um, prefer not to. Thank you all the same."

She arched an eyebrow at him as if he had suggested something devilish. "Normally I like a man to warm me up a little, but if you want to go straight to my room, I'd be—"

"No!" Kylar said, then realized he'd raised his voice and people were turning to look at him. "I mean, no thank you. I'm here to see Jarl."

"Oh, you're one of those," she said, her voice abruptly normal. The switch was total, jarring. Kylar noticed for the first time that she wasn't even his age. She couldn't be more than seventeen. Involuntarily, he thought of Mags. "Jarl's in the office. That way," she said.

Now that she'd abandoned seducing him, Kylar saw her differently. She looked hard, brittle. As he walked away, he heard her say, "Seems the good-looking ones always hoe the other row."

He didn't know what she meant, but he kept walking, worried she was laughing at him. He was halfway through the tables on his way to the office when he looked back. She was plying her trade with an older merchant, whispering something in his ear. The man beamed.

Kylar knocked on the door of the office.

The door opened. "Come in, quickly," Jarl said.

Kylar stepped inside, his mind a whirl. Jarl—for it was undoubtedly his old friend—had grown into a handsome man. He was impeccably dressed in the newest fashion, his tunic indigo silk, his pants tight fawnskin adorned with a belt of worked silver. Jarl's dark hair had been woven into a multitude of small long braids, each oiled and drawn back. He had an appraising look in his eyes.

There was a slight sound of cloth on cloth from the corner. Someone moving toward Kylar from behind his field of vision. Kylar kicked instinctively.

His foot caught the bodyguard in the chest. Though the guard was a big man, Kylar could feel ribs cracking. The man flew backward into the wall. He slid down and lay on the floor, unmoving.

Scanning the rest of the room in an instant, Kylar saw no other threats. Jarl had his hands spread to show he had no weapons.

"He wasn't going to attack you. He was just making sure you didn't have weapons. I swear it." Jarl looked at the man on the floor. "By the High King's balls, you've killed him."

Scowling, Kylar looked at the man, sprawled unconscious in the corner. He knelt by him and put fingers against the man's neck. Nothing. He ran his hands across the man's chest to feel if one of the broken ribs might have penetrated his heart. Then he slammed his fist down the man's chest. And again.

"What the hell are you—" Jarl cut off as the man's chest suddenly rose.

The bodyguard coughed and moaned. Kylar knew that every breath would be agony for the man. But he'd live.

"Get someone to take care of him," Kylar said. "His ribs are broken."

Eyes wide, Jarl went into the main room and came back a few moments later with two more bodyguards. Like the first, they were big and brawny, and looked like they might be able to use the short swords at their sides. They merely glared at Kylar and picked up the big man between them.

They carried him out of the room and Jarl closed the door behind them. "You've learned a thing or two, haven't you?" Jarl said. "I wasn't testing you. He insisted on being here. I didn't think . . . never mind."

After a moment of staring at his friend, Kylar said, "You look well."

"Don't you mean, 'How in the nine hells did you find me, Jarl?'" Jarl laughed.

"How in the nine hells did you find me, Jarl?"

Jarl smiled. "I never lost you. I never believed you were dead."

"No?"

"You never could get anything past me, Azoth."

"Don't say that name. That boy's dead."

"Is he?" Jarl asked. "That's a shame."

Silence sat in the room as the men looked at each other. Kylar didn't know what to do. Jarl had been his friend, Azoth's friend anyway. But was he Kylar's friend? That he knew who Kylar was, maybe had known for years, told Kylar that he wasn't an enemy. At least not yet. Part of Kylar wanted to believe that Jarl just wanted to see him, wanted a chance to say goodbye that they'd never been afforded on the street. But he'd spent too many years with Master Blint to take such a naive view. If Jarl had called him in now, it was because Jarl wanted something.

"We've both come a long way, haven't we?" Jarl asked.

"Is that what you brought me here to talk about?"

"A long way," Jarl said, disappointed. "Part of me was hoping you hadn't changed as much as I have, Kylar. I've been wanting to see you for years. Ever since you left, really. I wanted to apologize."

"Apologize?"

"I didn't mean to let her die, Kylar. I just couldn't get away much. I tried, but even sometimes when I did get away I couldn't find her. She had to move around a lot. But then she just disappeared. I never even found out what happened. I'm so sorry." Tears gleamed in Jarl's eyes and he looked away, his jaw clenched tight.

He thinks Elene is dead. He blames himself. He's been living with that guilt for all these years. Kylar opened his mouth to tell him that she was alive, that she was doing well from all the reports he got, that sometimes he watched her from afar on the days she went out shopping, but no sound came. Two can keep a secret, Blint used to say, if one of them is dead. Kylar didn't know Jarl now. He was managing one of Momma K's brothels, so Jarl certainly reported to her, but maybe he reported to others as well.

It was too dangerous. Kylar couldn't tell him. *Relationships are ropes that bind. Love is a noose.* The only thing that kept Kylar safe was that no one knew there was a noose with his name on it. Even he didn't know where Elene was. She was safe somewhere on the east side. Maybe married by now. She would be seventeen, after all. Maybe even happy. She looked happy, but he didn't even sneak close. Master Blint was right. The only thing keeping Elene safe was Kylar's distance.

Jarl's guilt wasn't enough to outweigh Elene's safety. Nothing was. *Dammit, Master Blint, how do you live like this? How can you be so strong, so hard?*

"I never held it against you," Kylar said. It was pathetic. He knew it wouldn't help, but there was nothing more he could offer.

Jarl blinked and when he met Kylar's eyes, his dark eyes were dry. "If that were all, I never would have asked you to come. Durzo Blint has enemies, and so do you."

"That's not exactly news," Kylar said. No matter that he and Blint never spoke about the jobs they did, and that anyone who knew of their work firsthand was dead. Word got out. Word always gets out. Another wetboy would attribute a job to them. A client would brag about who he'd hired. They had enemies they'd wronged, and more enemies who only thought that Durzo had wronged them. It was one of the costs of being the best. The families of deaders never attributed a successful hit to a second-rate wetboy.

"Do you remember Roth?"

"One of Rat's bigs?" Kylar asked.

"Yes. Apparently, he's smarter than we ever realized. After Rat died . . . well, everyone left like the guild was burning down. The other guilds moved in and took our territory. Everyone had to scramble to survive. Roth didn't make any friends when he was Rat's right hand. He nearly got killed half a dozen times. Apparently he always blamed you."

"Me?"

"For killing Rat. If you hadn't killed him, no one would have dared come after Roth. He never believed you were dead, either, but he hasn't been in a position to find out who you became. That's changing."

Kylar's chest was tight. "Does he know I'm alive?"

"No, but he'll sit with the Nine within the year, maybe sooner. There's a spot open right now that he's trying for. From a position of that kind of power, he'll find you. I haven't even met him, but the stories I hear . . . He's a real twist. Cruel. Vengeful. He frightens me, Kylar. He frightens me like no one since you know who."

"So that's why you invited me here? So you could tell me that Roth is coming after me?" Kylar asked.

"Yes, but there's more to it," Jarl said. "There's going to be a war."

"War? Hold on. What's your part, Jarl? How do you know all this?"

Jarl paused. "You've spent the last ten years under Master Blint's tutelage. I've spent the last ten years under Momma K's. And just as you've learned more than fighting, I've learned more than . . . fornicating. This city's secrets flow through its bedchambers." That was Momma K speaking, sure enough.

"But why are you helping me? A lot's changed since we were guild rats stealing bread."

Jarl shrugged, looked away again. "You're my only friend."

"Sure, when we were children—"

"Not 'you were.' You are. You're the only friend I've ever had, Kylar."

Trying to beat back his sudden guilt—how long had it been since he'd thought of Jarl?—Kylar said, "What about everyone here? The people you work with?"

"Coworkers, employees, and clients. I've even got something like a lover. But no friends."

"You've got a lover and she's not your friend?"

"Her name's Stephan. She's a fifty-three-year-old cloth merchant with a wife and eight children. He gives me protection and beautiful clothes, and I give him sex."

"Oh." Suddenly the whore's muttering about hoeing the other row made a lot more sense. "Are you happy here, Jarl?"

"Happy? What the hell kind of question is that? Happy doesn't have anything to do with it."

"I'm sorry."

Jarl laughed bitterly. "Where'd you get your innocence back, Kylar? You said Azoth was dead."

"What are you talking about?"

"Are you going to leave now that you know I'm a bugger?"

"No," Kylar said. "You're my friend."

"And you're mine. But if I hadn't seen you nearly kill Gerk just now, I'd wonder if you really were a wetboy.

How do you kill people and keep your soul intact, *Kylar?*"
He gave the name a little twist.

"How do you keep your soul intact and whore?"

"I don't."

"Me neither," Kylar said.

Jarl went quiet. He studied Kylar intently. "What happened that day?"

Kylar knew what Jarl was asking. A tremor passed through him. "Durzo told me if I wanted to be his apprentice, I had to kill Rat. After what he did to Doll Girl . . . I did it."

"Easy as that, huh?"

Kylar debated lying, but if anyone deserved the truth, it was Jarl. He'd suffered more at Rat's hands than anyone. After holding back about Doll Girl, he couldn't do it again.

Kylar told him the whole story, like he hadn't told anyone since Master Blint.

The description of the gore and how pathetic Rat had been didn't move Jarl. His face remained passive. "He deserved it. He deserved it and then some," Jarl said. "I only wish I'd had the nerve to do it. I wish I could have watched." He dismissed it with an effeminate wave of his hand. "I've got a client coming, so listen," Jarl said. "Khalidor is going to invade. Different parts of the Sa'kagé have been mobilized, but they're mostly smoke screens. Probably only the Nine know what's really happening, maybe only the Shinga. I can't even tell which side we're going to take.

"The thing is, we can't afford for Cenaria to lose this war. I don't know if the Nine realize that. The Ursuuls have put forward claims on Cenaria for generations, but several months ago Godking Ursuul demanded a tribute of some special gem and free passage, claiming to be more interested in taking war to Modai than here. King Gunder told him where he could go—and it wasn't across the king's highways.

"A source told me the Godking vowed to make us an example. He's got more than fifty wytches, maybe many more. I don't think King Gunder can field ten mages to stand against them."

"But the Sa'kagé will survive," Kylar said. Not that he gave a damn about them. He was thinking about the Drakes and Logan. The Khalidorans would kill them.

"The Sa'kagé will survive, Kylar, but if all the businesses are burned down, there's no money to extort. If all the merchants are broke, they can't gamble or go whoring. Some wars we could profit from. This one will ruin us."

"So why tell me?"

"Durzo's in the middle of it."

"Of course he is," Kylar said. "Probably half the nobles in the army's chain of command are trying to off their superiors so they can take their places. But Master Blint wouldn't take a job that would seriously endanger the city. Not if things are as bad as you say."

Jarl shook his head. "I think he's working for the king."

"Master Blint would never work for the king," Kylar said.

"He would if they had his daughter."

"His what?"

32

$\mathcal{L}$ord General Agon stood in the middle of the brushed white gravel of the castle's statue garden and tried not to look as uneasy as he felt. *Damn fine place to meet an assassin.*

Ordinarily, he would think it was fine place to meet an assassin. Though Blint had ordered him not to bring soldiers, if he had been of a mind to do so, there were any number of places for them to hide. Of course, that this meeting was happening within the castle grounds should also have made Agon feel better. It might have, if Blint hadn't been the one who suggested it.

The night wind blew a cloud across the moon and Agon strained to hear the slight crunch of gravel that would herald Blint's arrival. He had no doubt that Blint could make it into the castle. His memory was as sharp as the daggers that they'd once found under the royal pillows. Still, he had his orders.

He looked at the statues around him. They were heroes, every one of them, and he wondered what he was doing in their company. Usually this garden was a haven. He would walk on the serene white and black rock and stare at these marble heroes, wondering how they might act if they were in his shoes. Tonight, their shadows loomed and lingered. Of course it was his imagination, but he still remembered that Blint had been in his bedroom ten years ago, ready to do murder. Nothing was safe with a man like that.

There was the slightest crunch of gravel under one of the statues. Agon turned and without thinking gripped his sword.

"Don't bother," Durzo Blint said.

Agon whipped back around. Durzo was standing not two feet away. Agon stepped back.

"The noisy one was one of yours. Not me." Blint smiled wolfishly. "But wait, didn't I tell you not to bring men?"

"I didn't," Agon said.

"Mm-hmm."

"You're late," Agon said. He had his equilibrium back now. It was unsettling dealing with a man who didn't value life. He believed that Blint really didn't, now. There was a rationale behind it, too. The only way he himself could deal with Blint was to realize that he could be killed but that that wasn't important; his life or death wasn't why he had summoned Blint; his life or death wasn't vital to what they would talk about. Still, a part of him asked, how can wetboys live like this?

"Just making sure I knew where all your soldiers were hidden," Blint said. He was wearing a killing outfit, Agon realized queasily. A tunic of mottled dark gray cotton, thin but cut for easy movement, pants of the same material, a harness with a score of throwing weapons, some of which the general didn't even recognize. What he did recognize was that the points of some of those weapons bore more than steel. Poison.

Is he bluffing? Agon hadn't brought soldiers. Even if his life wasn't vital to this discussion, he wasn't going to throw it away. "I keep my word, even to a Sa'kagé thug," he said.

"The funny thing is, I believe you, Lord General. You're many things, but I don't think you're either dishonorable or stupid enough to betray me. Are you sure you don't want me to kill the king? You have the army. If you're smart and lucky, you might be king yourself."

"No," Agon said. "I keep my vows." *If only those words didn't burn as I spoke them.*

"I'd give you a discount." Blint laughed.

"Are you ready to hear the job?" Agon asked.

"It seems we've had this conversation before," Blint said. "My answer remains the same. I only showed up because I miss your smiling face, Lord General. And to show that your—let's be honest—rather pathetic defenses still can't keep me out should you choose to try to make my life difficult."

"You haven't even heard what the job is. The king respects your talents now. He will pay better than anyone has ever paid you. He wishes you—"

"To protect his life. I know. Hu Gibbet took a contract on him." Durzo ignored the stricken look on Agon's face. "Sorry. I won't take the job. I'd never take a job for that foul sack of wind. Let's be honest. Aleine Gunder, who ridiculously fashions himself 'the Ninth' as if he had any connection to the previous eight kings who bore the name Aleine, is a waste of skin."

Someone burst out from under the tall statue of Duke Gunder behind Agon. Agon's heart sank as he recognized the man's gait.

Aleine Gunder IX threw back his hood. "Guards! Guards!"

Archers and crossbowmen sprang up from every balcony, bush, and shadow in sight. Others came running from the perimeter of the garden.

"My liege. What a surprise," Blint said, sweeping into a perfect court bow. "Who would have expected to find you hiding in your father's shadow?"

"You shitting . . . shitting! . . . shit!" the king yelled. "What are you doing?" he yelled at the guards. "Surround him!" The guards surrounded Durzo, Agon, and the king in a tight circle. They looked nervous to have the king standing so close to a wetboy, but none of them dared invoke the king's ire by forcibly separating them.

"Your Majesty," Agon said, stepping in front of the king before the man tried to hit Durzo Blint. Tried to hit Durzo Blint!

"You will work for me, assassin," the king said.

"No. I've said it before, but maybe you need to hear it yourself. I'm willing to kill you, but I won't kill for you."

The guards were less than pleased by this, of course, but Agon held up a hand. With the guards pressed so close, the archers were useless. *Brilliant, Your Majesty.* If it came to bloodshed, both he and the king would die, and he'd give even odds that Blint wouldn't.

"Fine, then," the king said.

"Fine, then." Blint smiled joylessly.

The king smiled back. "We'll kill your daughter."

"My what?"

The king's smile grew. "Look into it." He laughed.

A dangerous second stretched out and Agon wondered if he was about to be holding a dead king in his arms. Then there was a blur of motion. Even though he was looking right at him, Durzo Blint moved faster than his eye could follow. He flipped up over the circle of soldiers, caught a statue and changed his trajectory.

A moment later, there was a scuttling sound up the side of the castle wall, akin to a cat's claws scraping as it climbed a tree.

Startled, one of the soldiers discharged his crossbow—mercifully, it was pointed into the air. Agon shot a look at the man.

The man swallowed. "Sorry, sir."

The king walked inside, and it was only two minutes later that Agon realized how close Durzo had brought him to speaking treason in front of the king.

Kylar felt the air stir as someone opened the front door of the safe house. He lifted his eyes from the book in front of him and reached for the short sword unsheathed on the table.

He had a perfect view of the door from his chair, of course. Master Blint wouldn't set up his workroom any other way. But he would have known it was Master Blint just by the sound: click-CLICK-click. Click-CLICK-click. Click-CLICK-click. Master Blint always locked, unlocked, and then relocked every lock. It was just another of his superstitions.

He didn't ask his master about the job. Blint never liked

to talk about a job right after it. The Night Angels didn't like it, he said. Kylar interpreted that, *Let my memories fade.*

The vial of white asp venom was sitting on the table with the rest of Blint's collection, but to distract himself as much as Blint, Kylar said, "I don't think it'll work. I've been looking over your books. They haven't got anything about this."

"They'll write a new book," Blint said. He started putting the poisoned blades in special cases, and wiping off the ones bearing poison that spoiled over time.

"I know animals can eat some poisons and it doesn't make them sick. And I know their meat will make you sick if you eat it. Our experiments have proved that. But then your deader's just sick. That's fine as far as it goes, but this dual poison thing—I don't get it."

Blint hung up his weapons harness. "Your deader eats the pork, he feels nothing. Maybe a little tipsy. He eats the quail, he gets dizzy. He eats both, he gets dead. It's called *potentiation*. The poisons work together to reach their fullest potential."

"But you've still got to get an entire pig and a flock of quail past the food tester."

"Big places use multiple tasters. By the time they suspect anything, the deader's dead," Blint said.

"But then you poison everyone in the room. You can't control—"

"I control everything!" Blint shouted. He threw a knife down and walked out, slamming the door so hard it set every weapon on the wall jingling.

*   *   *

Elene stared at the blank page and dipped the drying quill back into the ink pot. Further down the table in the Drakes' dining room, Mags and Ilena Drake were playing a game of tiles. Mags, the older sister, was concentrating intently, but Ilena kept glancing at Elene.

"Why," Elene said, "do I always get crushes on unattainable men?" Elene Cromwyll had been friends with Mags and Ilena Drake for years. The gap between a servant and a count's daughters should have precluded friendship, but the Drakes counted all as equal before the One God. As they'd grown older, the girls had become more aware of how odd their friendship was, so it had become more private, but no less real.

"That groundskeeper Jaen was attainable," Ilena said, moving a tile. Mags scowled at the move and then at her fifteen-year-old sister.

"That lasted two hours," Elene said. "Until he opened his fat mouth."

"You must have had a crush on Pol at some point," Mags said.

"Not really. He just loved me so much I thought I should love him back," Elene said.

"At least Pol was real," Ilena said.

"Ilena, don't be a brat," Mags said.

"You're just mad because you're losing again."

"I am not!" Mags said.

"I'll win in three moves."

"You will?" Mags looked at the tiles. "You little snot. I, at least, am so glad you turned Pol down, Elene," Mags said. "But it does leave you without an escort to our party."

Elene had abandoned the quill and buried her face

in her hands. She sighed. "Do you have any idea what I wrote to him last year?" She stared at the blank paper in front of her.

"I didn't know Pol could read," Ilena said.

"Not Pol. My benefactor."

"Whatever you wrote, he didn't stop sending money, did he?" Ilena asked, ignoring her sister's murderous glance. Ilena Drake was only fifteen, but most of the time, she seemed in pretty good control of Mags, if not her oldest sister Serah.

"He's never stopped. Not even when I told him that we had more than enough money. But it's not about the money, Lena," Elene said. "Last year I told him that I was in love with him." She couldn't quite bear to confess that she'd smudged the ink with her own tears. "I told him I was going to call him Kylar, because Kylar's nice and I never found out my benefactor's name."

"And now you do like Kylar . . . who you've also never talked to."

"I'm totally hopeless. Why do I let you talk to me about boys?" Elene asked.

"Ilena can't help but talk about Kylar," Mags said with the air of a big sister about to pull rank. "Because she has a crush on him herself."

"I do not!" Ilena shrieked.

"Then why'd you say so in your journal?" Mags said. Mags's voice lilted, mimicking Ilena's, "'Why won't Kylar talk more to me?' 'Kylar talked to me today at breakfast. He said I'm sweet. Is that good or does he still just see me as a little girl?' It's gross, Ilena. He's practically our brother."

"You wytch!" Ilena yelled. She leaped over the table

and attacked Mags. Mags screamed, and Elene watched, frozen between horror and laughter.

The girls were screaming, Ilena pulling Mags's hair and Mags starting to fight back. Elene got to her feet, figuring she'd better stop them before someone got hurt.

The door crashed open, almost blowing off its hinges, and Kylar stood there, sword in hand. The entire atmosphere of the room changed in the blink of an eye. Kylar exuded a palpable aura of danger and power. He was primal masculinity. It washed over Elene like a wave that threatened to yank her from her feet and pull her out to sea. She could hardly breathe.

Kylar flowed into the room in a low stance, the naked sword held in both hands. His eyes took in everything at once, flicked to every exit, to the windows, the shadows, even to the corners of the ceiling. The girls on the floor stopped, a handful of Mags's hair still clenched in Ilena's hand, guilt written all over their faces.

His pale, pale blue eyes seemed so familiar. Was it just Elene's fantasies that put that flicker of recognition in them? Those eyes touched hers and she felt a tingle all the way up her spine. He was looking at her—her, not her scars. Men always looked at her scars. Kylar was seeing *Elene*. She wanted to speak, but there were no words.

His mouth parted as if he, too, was on the edge of words, but then he turned white as a sheet. His sword flashed back into a sheath and he turned. "Ladies, your pardon," he said, ducking his head. Then he was gone.

"Good God," Mags said. "Did you see that?"

"It was scary," Ilena said, "and . . ."

"Intoxicating," Elene said. Her face felt hot. She turned

away as the girls stood. She sat and picked up the quill. As if she could write now.

"Elene, what's going on?" Mags asked.

"When he saw my face, he looked like death warmed over," Elene said. *Why?* He'd barely even looked at her scars. That was what scared away most of the boys.

"He'll come around. You're an angel. Give him a chance. We'll ask him to the party for you and everything," Ilena said.

"No. No, I forbid it. He's a baronet, Lena."

"A poor baronet whose lands have been taken by the Lae'knaught."

"He's just another unattainable man. I'll get over it."

"He doesn't have to be unattainable. If he joins the faith . . . In the eyes of the God, all men are created equal."

"Oh, Lena, don't dangle that in front of me. I'm a serving girl. A scarred serving girl. It doesn't matter what the God sees."

"It doesn't matter what the God sees?" Mags asked gently.

"You know what I mean."

"Logan might marry Serah, and that's as big a gap as there is between a poor baronet and you."

"A noble marrying a lower noble is frowned on, but a noble marrying a commoner?"

"We're not saying you should marry him. Just let us ask him to the party."

"No," Elene said. "I forbid it."

"Elene—"

"That's final." Elene looked at the girls until each grudgingly gave their assent. "But," she said, "you could tell me a little more about him."

*   *   *

"Kylar," Count Drake called out as Kylar tried to sneak past his office to get up the stairs. "Would you come in for a moment?"

There was nothing for it but to obey, of course. Kylar cursed inwardly. Today was turning into a long day. He'd been hoping to get a few hours of sleep before doing his predawn chores for Master Blint. He had a good idea what this was about, so when he stepped into the count's office, he had to try not to feel like a boy about to have his father explain sex to him.

The count hadn't been touched by the years. He would look forty if he lived to be a hundred. His desk was in the same place, his clothes were the same cut and color, and when he was warming up to a difficult conversation he still rubbed the bridge of his nose where his pince nez sat.

"Have you made love to my daughter?" the count asked.

Kylar's chin dropped. So much for warming up. The count watched him expressionlessly.

"I haven't laid a hand on her, sir."

"I wasn't asking about your hands."

Kylar goggled. This was the man who talked about the God as often as most farmers talked about the weather?

"No, don't worry, son. I believe you. Though I suspect it hasn't been for any lack of effort on Serah's part."

The blood rushing to Kylar's entire face was answer enough.

"Is she in love with you, Kylar?"

He shook his head, almost relieved to be asked a question he could answer. "I think Serah wants what she thinks she can't have, sir."

"Does that include making love to numerous young men, none of whom is Logan?"

Kylar spluttered, "I hardly think it's right or honorable for me to—"

The count raised a hand, pained. "Which is not the answer you would have given if you thought the charge was false. You'd have said absolutely not, and then that you didn't think it was right or honorable for me to ask. And you'd have been right." He rubbed the bridge of his nose and blinked. "I'm sorry, Kylar. That wasn't fair of me. Sometimes I still use the wits the God gave me in dishonorable ways. I'm trying to do what's right, whether or not that measures up with what men call honorable. There's a gap between those, you know?"

Kylar shrugged, but no answer was required.

"I'm not interested in condemning my baby girl, Kylar," the count said. "I've done far worse in my life than she'll ever dream of. But more than her happiness is at stake. Is Logan aware of her . . . indiscretions?"

"I asked her to tell him, but I don't believe she has, sir."

"You know that Logan has asked for my permission to marry Serah?"

"Yes, sir."

"Should I give him my blessing?"

"You couldn't hope to gain a better son."

"For my family, it would be wonderful. Is it right for Logan?"

Kylar hesitated. "I think he loves her," he said finally.

"He wants to know within two days," the count said.

"When he turns twenty-one he takes possession of the Gyre household and becomes one of the richest and most powerful men in the realm, even given how the king has interfered with his house in the last decade. Sixth in the line of succession. First behind the royals. People will say he's marrying beneath himself. They'll say she isn't worthy of him." The count looked away. "I don't usually give a damn what they think, Kylar, because they think it for all the wrong reasons. This time, I'm afraid they'll be right."

Kylar couldn't say anything.

"I've prayed for years that my daughters would find the right men to be their husbands. And I've prayed that Logan would marry the right woman. Why doesn't this feel like the answer?" He shook his head again and squeezed the bridge of his nose. "Forgive me, I've asked you a dozen questions you can't possibly answer, and haven't asked the one you can."

"What's that, sir?"

"Do you love Serah?"

"No, sir."

"And that girl? The one you've been sending money to for almost a decade?"

Kylar flushed. "I've sworn not to love, sir."

"But do you?"

Kylar walked out the door.

As Kylar stepped into the hall, the count said, "You know, I pray for you, too, Kylar."

33

The whorehouse had closed hours ago. Upstairs, the girls slept on fouled sheets amid the brothel smells of stale alcohol, stale sweat, old sex, wood smoke, and cheap perfume. The doors were locked. All but two of the plain copper lamps downstairs had been extinguished. Momma K didn't allow her brothels to waste money.

There were only two people downstairs, both of them at the bar. Around the man's seat were the remains of a dozen smashed glasses.

He finished the thirteenth beer, lifted the glass, and threw it onto the floor. It shattered.

Momma K poured Durzo another beer from the tap, not even blinking. She didn't say a word. Durzo would speak when he was ready. Still, she wondered why he'd chosen this brothel. It was a hole. She sent her attractive girls elsewhere. Other brothels she'd bought had been worth fixing, but this one huddled deep in the Warrens, far from main roads in the maze of shacks and hovels. This was where she'd lost her maidenhead. She'd been paid ten silvers, and had counted herself lucky.

It wasn't high on her list of places to visit.

"I should kill you," Durzo said finally. They were the first words he'd spoken in six hours. He finished his beer and shoved it along the bar. It slid several feet, fell over, rolled off the bar, and cracked.

"Oh, so you do have the power of speech?" Momma K said. She grabbed another glass and opened the tap.

"Do I have a daughter too?"

Momma K froze. She closed the tap too late and beer spilled all over.

"Vonda made me swear not to tell you. She was too scared to tell you and then when she died. . . . You can hate Vonda for what she did, Durzo, but she did it because she loved you."

Durzo gave her a look of such disbelief and disgust that Gwinvere wanted to hit his ugly face.

"What do you know about love, you whore?"

She had thought that no one could hurt her with words. She'd heard every whore comment in the book, and had added a few besides. But something in how Durzo said it, something about that comment—coming from him!—struck her to the core. She couldn't move. She couldn't even breathe.

Finally, she said, "I know if I'd had the chance for love that you had, I would have quit whoring. I would have done anything to hold onto that. I was *born* into this chamber pot of a life; you're the one who chose it."

"What's my daughter's name?"

"So that's it? You bring me here to remind me how many times I got fucked in this stinking hole? I remember. I remember! I whored so my baby sister wouldn't have to. And then you came along. You fucked me five times a week and told Vonda you loved her. Got her pregnant. Left. I could have told her that much was a given. That part of the story's so predictable it's not even worth repeating, is it? But you weren't just any john. No, you got her kidnapped too. And then what? Did you go after her? No, you showed exactly how much you loved her. Called their bluff, didn't you? You always were willing to gamble with other people's lives, weren't you, Durzo? You coward."

Durzo's glass exploded against the keg behind her. He was trembling violently. He pointed a finger in her face. "You! You don't have any right. You would have given it all up for love? Horseshit. Where's the man in your life now, Gwin? You don't whore anymore, so there's nothing for a man to be jealous of, right? But there's still no man, is there? Do you want to know why you're the perfect whore? For the same reason there's no man. Because you don't have the capacity for love. You're all cunt. You suck everyone dry and make them pay you for the pleasure. So don't give me that bleeding heart, I-did-it-to-save-my-sister horseshit. It's always been power for you. Oh sure, there are women who whore for money or for fame or because they don't have any other options. But then there are *whores*. You might not fuck anymore, Gwin, but you will *always* be a whore. Now. What. Is. Her. Name?" He bit off each word like moldy bread.

"Uly," Gwinvere said quietly. "Ulyssandra. She lives with a nurse in the castle."

She looked at the beer she was holding in her hand. She didn't even remember filling it. *Was this what Durzo*

reduced her to? A submissive little. . . . She didn't even
know. She felt like she'd been eviscerated, that if she
looked down, she'd see ropes of her own intestines coiled
around her feet.

It took all of her strength to spit in the beer and set it on
the counter with even a shadow of nonchalance.

"Well, it's tough to be a victim of circumstance," Durzo
said. His voice had that killing edge on it.

"You aren't. . . . You wouldn't kill your own child."
Not even Durzo could do that, could he?

"I won't have to," Durzo said. "They'll kill her
for me."

He picked up the beer, smiled at Gwinvere over the
spit, and drank. He finished half the beer at a gulp and
said, "I'm leaving. It smells like old whore in here." He
poured the rest of his beer onto the floor and set the glass
carefully on the bar.

Kylar woke two hours before dawn and briefly wondered
if death would be too high a price to pay for a full night's
sleep. The correct answer, however, was unavoidable, so
after a few minutes, he dragged himself out of bed. He
dressed quietly in the dark, reaching into his third drawer
where his wetboy grays were folded as always and reaching into his ash jar to smear his features black.

In the past nine years, he'd learned to compensate for
not having the Talent. When Blint was in an optimistic
mood, which was increasingly rare, he praised Kylar for
it. He said that too many wetboys relied on their Talent
for everything and that he kept his mundane talents honed
for unpredictable situations. In the bitter business, unpre-

dictable situations were the norm. Besides, Blint said, if there's almost no noise of a footstep to cover in the first place, you don't have to use as much of your Talent to muffle it.

Sometimes Kylar's adaptability showed itself in more spectacular ways, but mostly it was in these little things, like putting his grays in the same dresser, the same way every time he washed them. At least, he hoped it was his adaptability and not Blint's mania for organization infecting him. Seriously, what was it with the man's locking locks three times and spinning knives and the garlic and the Night Angel this and Night Angel that?

The window opened silently and Kylar crept across the roof. Years of practice taught him where he could walk and where he had to crawl to be unheard by those below. He slipped over the edge of the house, dropped onto the flagstones in the courtyard, and vaulted off a rock to grab the edge of the wall. He raised himself to peek over the edge, saw no one, pulled himself over the wall, and then moved stealthily up the street.

He probably could have just walked; sneaking wasn't really necessary once he got out of sight of the Drake's home and until he got within sight of the herbiary, but it was a bad habit to get into. *A job is a job, it isn't done till it's done.* Another of Blint's pearls, there. Thanks.

Tonight, it wasn't just Blint's ingrained discipline that kept him creeping from shadows to shadow, making the two-mile walk to the herbiary take almost an hour. To-night, Jarl's words kept going through his head. "You have enemies. You have enemies."

Maybe it was time he moved out of the Drakes' house. For their safety. He was twenty years old, and though of

course he didn't have the income of a noble, Blint was
more than generous with his wages. In fact, Blint didn't
really care about money. He didn't spend much on himself, aside from the infrequent binges on alcohol and rent
girls. He did buy the best equipment and ingredients for
poisons, but what he bought he kept forever. With what he
made for each kill and the frequency with which he took
jobs, Blint had to be wealthy. Probably obscenely wealthy.
Not that Kylar cared. He'd adopted much of Blint's attitude. He gave Count Drake a portion of his wages for
Elene and still had plenty left over. He kept some in coins
and jewels and split the rest between investments Momma
K and Logan made for him. It meant nothing to him because money couldn't buy him anything. His cover as a
poor country noble and his real work as a journeyman
wetboy kept him from living a lifestyle that would attract
attention. So even if he had wanted to spend his money,
he couldn't afford to.

He could move out, though. Rent a small home further south on the east side, at the edges of one of the less
fashionable neighborhoods. Blint had told him that if you
bought the cheapest house in a neighborhood, no matter how expensive the neighborhood, you were invisible.
Even if your neighbors noticed you, they'd take pains not
to notice you.

Then Kylar was at the shop. The Sa'kagé had long had
an arrangement with herbalists in the city. The herbalists
made sure they kept certain plants on hand that weren't
strictly legal, and the Sa'kagé made sure that the herbalists' shops were never burglarized. The crown knew about
it but was powerless to stop it.

Goodman Aalyep's Herbiary was frequented by rich

merchants and the nobility, so he had refused to keep il-
licit herbs openly in his shop, fearing that such defiance
in the very face of authority might not be ignored. He'd
been able to refuse the Sa'kagé, but no one refused Master Blint. Goodman Aalyep supplied Durzo with the rarest
herbs. In return, Master Blint made sure no one else in the
Sa'kagé so much as went near his shop.

It fell to Kylar to gather the necessaries and drop off
the money, which he was doing tonight. The benefit to
running these errands wasn't only that he learned the
trade, or that he established relationships with the people
who would supply him in the future, it was also that he
could build his own collection. An elaborate collection
like Master Blint's took years and thousands or even tens
of thousands of gunders to build.

The bad part was losing sleep. It didn't do for a young
noble to sleep until noon unless he'd been out carous-
ing with his friends. So even though he wouldn't get
home until almost dawn, Kylar would have to wake with
the sun.

He grumbled silently, remembering a time when sneaking through the streets of Cenaria at night had been fun.

The back door of the shop, as always, was locked.
Goodman Aalyep kept good locks on his doors, too.
Though he'd never met him—they only wrote notes—
Kylar felt he knew Goodman Aalyep, and the man was a
strange one. With Durzo Blint's protection in the Sa'kagé,
the man could have safely left his doors wide open. No
one in the city would dare steal from him.

But as Blint said, a man's greatest treasures are his illusions. For all the man claimed to hate teaching, he seemed
to have an aphorism for every occasion. Kylar selected

the proper pick and anchor from the kit on the inside of his belt, and he knelt in front of the door and started working. He sighed. It was a new lock, and from Master Procl's, the best locksmith in the city. New locks, even if they weren't high quality, always tended to be tighter, and if losing an anchor wasn't the end of the world, it was still irritating to break one.

Kylar raked the pick over the pins. Four pins, two of them a little loose. That meant it was the work of one of Procl's journeymen and not the master himself. In ten seconds, he turned the anchor, bending it, and the door opened. Kylar cursed silently—he'd have to get another new anchor—then tucked his tools away. Someday, he was going to have to commission a set of mistarille picks and anchors like Master Blint had. Or at least one anchor. Mistarille would flex but never break, but it was more expensive by weight than diamonds.

Goodman Aalyep's claim that his business was an herbiary wasn't an idle boast. It had three rooms: the large comfortable shop with labeled glass jars for the display of herbs, a tiny office, and the herbiary in which Kylar stood. The little room was humid, and the wet, fecund odors were almost overwhelming.

Checking on the progress of some fungi, Kylar was pleased. Several lethal mushrooms would be ready within a week. Mushrooms were one kind of plant Goodman Aalyep could grow with impunity in his shop—lethal varieties were indistinguishable from edible mushrooms to anyone except trained herbalists and, of course, trained poisoners.

Treading carefully so he didn't step on any of the boards that creaked, Kylar moved through the rest of the herbiary, judging the plants with a practiced eye. Kylar lifted the third plant box in the second row and saw six bundles carefully packed in individual lambskin pouches. He lifted them out and checked that each was what he had ordered. Four bundles for Master Blint, and two for himself. Kylar put the herbs in the pack secured flush against his back under his cloak, and put the purse with Aalyep's money into the little space. He set the planter back in position.

Then something felt wrong. In the blink of an eye Kylar drew two short swords.

But he didn't move a step. The feeling of wrongness continued, not something wrong of itself, but just something here and now and close. There was no sound. There was no attack, just a slight pressure, as of the softest possible touch of a finger.

Kylar focused on the sensation even as his eyes scanned the shop and his ears strained to hear the slightest sound. It was like a touch, but it was pressing past him, toward—

The lock on the back door clicked home. He was trapped.

34

Restraining an impulse to run to the door and fling it open, Kylar stayed utterly still. No one was in the room with him. Of that he was certain. But he thought—yes, he could hear someone breathing in the shop.

Then he realized that it was more than one person. One was breathing quickly, shallowly, excited. The other was breathing lightly but slowly. Not tense, not excited. That scared Kylar.

Who could ambush a wetboy and not even be nervous?

Afraid of losing all initiative, Kylar moved slowly toward the wall that separated the herbiary from the shop. If he was right, one of the men was standing just on the other side of it. Sheathing a short sword—to be silent he had to do it so slowly that it was painful—Kylar then drew out the Ceuran hand-and-a-half sword he carried in a back scabbard.

He brought the tip of the blade close to the wall and waited for the slightest sound.

There was nothing. Now he couldn't even hear the excited man breathing. That meant the excited one must be on the other side of this wall, while the calm man was further.

Kylar waited. He trembled with anticipation. One of the men on the other side of the entry was a wytch. Were they with the Khalidorans Jarl had warned him about? Kylar pushed the thought out of his head. He could worry about that later. Whoever they were, they had trapped him. Whether they thought he was Master Blint or just a common thief didn't matter.

But which one was the wytch? The nervous one? He wouldn't have thought so, but the feeling that had pressed past him and had locked the door had seemed to come from that side.

A board creaked. "Feir! Back!" the man further away from Kylar shouted. Kylar rammed his sword through the finger-thick pine.

He yanked the sword back as he charged through the entry. He burst through the curtain and launched himself off the doorpost and over the sales counter, toward the man he'd tried to stab.

The man was on the ground, rolling over as Kylar took a slice at his head. He was huge. Bigger even than Logan, but proportioned like a tree trunk, thick everywhere, with no definable waist or neck. For all that, even on his back, he was bringing up a sword to block Kylar's blow.

He would have blocked it, too, if Kylar's sword had been whole. But half of Kylar's Ceuran blade was lying on the ground by the man, sheared off with magic a moment after he had rammed it through the wall.

Finding no sword where he expected it, the big man's parry went wide as Kylar attacked from his knees. Without the full weight of the blade, Kylar brought his half-sword down faster than the big man could react and stabbed for his stomach.

Then Kylar felt as if his head were inside the sound-bow of a temple bell. There was a concussion, pitched low but focused, as if a cornerstone had fallen two stories and landed an inch from Kylar's head.

The force blew him sideways through one shelf of herb jars and into a second, sending them crashing down underneath him.

Then there was nothing but the light flashing in front of Kylar's eyes. His sword was gone. He blinked, vision slowly returning. He was face down on the floor with a shattered shelf, lying amid the remnants of broken jars and scattered herbs.

He heard a grunt from the big man, and then footsteps. Kylar kept still, not having to fake much to appear incapacitated. A few inches from his nose, he was slowly able to make out some of the plants. Pronwi seed, Ubdal bud, Yarrow root. This shelf should have—and there it was, near his hand, delicate Tuntun seed, ground to powder. If you breathed it, it would make your lungs hemorrhage.

The footsteps came closer and Kylar lurched, spinning to one side and flinging Tuntun powder in an arc. He came to his feet and drew a pair of long knives.

"Enough, Shadowstrider."

Air congealed around Kylar like a jelly. He tried to dive away, but the jelly became as hard as rock.

The two men regarded Kylar through the cloud of Tuntun seed hanging frozen in the air.

The blond mountain folded meat-slab arms across

his chest. "Don't tell me you expected this, Dorian," he growled at the other man.

His friend grinned.

"Not much to look at, is he?" the Mountain asked.

The smaller man, Dorian, wore a short black beard under intense blue eyes, had a sharp nose and straight white teeth. He reached forward and took some of the floating Tuntun powder between two fingers. Black hair lightly oiled, blue eyes, pale skin. Definitely Khalidoran. He was the wytch. "Don't be a sore loser, Feir. Things would gone badly for you if I hadn't broken his sword."

Feir scowled. "I think I could hold my own."

"Actually, if I hadn't intervened, right now he'd be wondering how he was going to move such a large corpse. And that was without his Talent."

That got an unhappy grunt. The smaller man waved a hand and the Tuntun powder fell to the ground in a tidy pile. He looked at Kylar and the bonds holding him shifted, forcing him to stand upright, with his hands down at his sides, though still holding the knives. "Is that more comfortable?" he asked, but didn't seem to expect a reply. He touched Kylar's hand with a single finger and stared into him as if his eyes were cutting him open. He frowned. "Look at this," he said to Feir.

Feir accepted the hand Dorian put on his shoulder and stared at Kylar the same way. Kylar stood there, not knowing what to say or do, his mind filled with questions that he wasn't sure he should give voice to.

After a long moment, Feir said, "Where's his conduit? It almost seems shaped, like there's a niche for . . . " He exhaled sharply. "By the Light, he ought to be . . . "

"Terrifying. Yes," Dorian said. "He's a born ka'karifer.

But that's not what worries me. Look at this." Kylar felt something twist in him. He felt as if he were being turned inside out.

Whatever he was seeing, it scared Feir. His face was still, but Kylar could almost feel the sudden tension in his muscles, the slight tang of fear in the air.

"There's something here that resists me," Eyes said. "The stream's winning. The Shadowcloaked makes it worse."

"Let it go," Feir said. "Stay with me."

Kylar felt whatever had been pulling him open drop away, though his body was still bound in place. Dorian rocked back on his heels, and Feir grabbed his shoulders in meaty hands and held him up.

"What'd you call me? Who are you?" Kylar demanded.

Dorian smirked, regaining his balance as if by the force of good humor alone. "You ask who *we* are, Wearer of Names? It's Kylar now, isn't it? Old Jaeran punning. I like that. Was that your sense of humor, or Blint's?" At the startled look on Kylar's face, he said, "Blint's apparently."

Dorian looked through Kylar again, as if there were a list inside him that he was reading. "The Nameless. Marati. Cwellar. Spex. Kylar. Even Kagé, not terribly original, that."

"What?" Kylar asked. This was ridiculous. Who were these men?

"Sa'kagé means Lords of the Shadow," Dorian said. "Thus Kagé means 'Shadow,' but I don't suppose that one's your fault. In any case, you ought to be more curious. Did it never occur to you to wonder why your peers had common names like Jarl, or Bim, or slave names like Doll Girl or Rat, and you were burdened with Azoth?"

Kylar went cold. He'd heard that wytches could read minds, but he'd never believed it. And those names. That wasn't a random list. "You're wytches. Both of you."

Feir and Dorian looked at each other.

"Half right," Dorian said.

"A little less than half, really," Feir said.

"But I was a wytch," Dorian said. "Or, more properly, a meister. If you ever have the misfortune of meeting one, you may not want to use a slur."

"What are you?" Kylar asked.

"Friends," Dorian said. "We've made a long journey to help you. Well, not only to help you, but to help you and—"

"And we've come at great personal cost and greater risk," Feir interrupted, looking at Dorian sharply.

"We hope you have no doubt that we could kill you. That if we wished you harm, we could have already done it," Dorian said.

"There are more types of harm than just killing. A wetboy knows that," Kylar said.

Dorian smiled, but Feir still looked wary. Kylar felt the bonds release him. That unnerved him. They'd seen how fast he could move and yet they released him, armed.

"Allow me to introduce us," Dorian said. "This is Feir Cousat, one day to be the most renowned swordsmith in all Midcyru. He is Vy'sana and a Blademaster of the Second Echelon."

Great. "And you?" Kylar asked.

"You won't believe me." Dorian was enjoying this.

"Try me."

"I am Sa'seuran and Hoth'salar, and once a Vürdmeister of the twelfth *shu'ra.*"

"Impressive." Kylar had no idea what those were.

"What should be important to you is that I'm a prophet. My name is Dorian," Dorian said with a native Khalidoran accent. "Dorian Ursuul."

"You were right," Feir said. "He doesn't believe you."

Aside from carelessness, the only things that could kill wetboys were other wetboys, mages, and wytches. In Blint's estimation, wytches were the worst. He hadn't neglected Kylar's education. "Let me see your arms," Kylar said.

"Ah, so you know about the vir," Dorian said. "How much do you know about them?" Dorian bared his arms to the elbows. There were no marks on them.

"I know that all wytches have them, that they grow in proportion to the wytch's power and their intricacy shows the wytch's level of mastery," Kylar said.

"Don't do it, Dorian," Feir said. "I'm not going to lose you over this. Let's tell him the words and get the hell out of here."

Dorian ignored him. "Only men and women who are Talented can use the vir. It's easier to manipulate than the Talent and more powerful. It's also terribly addictive and, if one dare speak in moral absolutes—which I do—it's evil," Dorian said, his eyes bright, holding Kylar. "Unlike the Talent, which can be good or bad like any talent, it is in itself evil, and it corrupts those who use it. It has proven useful to my family to have all meisters marked, so they are. My ancestors never saw any reasons to be marked ourselves unless we so chose. The Ursuuls can make their vir disappear at will, so long as they aren't using it."

"Blint must have skipped that lesson," Kylar said.

"A pity it is, too. We're the most dangerous Vürdmeisters you could possibly imagine."

"Dorian, just tell him the words. Let's—"

"Feir!" Dorian said. "Silence. You know what do."

The big man obeyed, glowering at Kylar.

"Kylar," Dorian said. "You're asking a drunkard who's quit drinking to take just one glass of wine. I'll live in misery for weeks for this. Feir will have to watch me constantly to see that I don't slip away to that madness. But you're worth it."

Feir's mouth tightened, but he didn't say a word.

Dorian held his arms out and a shimmer passed over them. As Kylar stared at them, it looked as if veins deep in the man's arms were wriggling, struggling to get to the surface of his skin. Then, rapidly, they rose all together. Dorian's arms turned black like a million fresh tattoos were being inked over each other. Layer knotted on layer, each distinct, interlocking with those below and above, darker over lighter with darker still coming in above. It was beautiful and terrible. The vir swelled with power and moved, not just with Dorian's arms, but independently. It seemed that they wanted to burst free of the confines of his skin. The darkness of the vir spread to the room, and Kylar was sure it wasn't his imagination: the vir were sucking the light from the room.

Dorian's eyes dilated until the cool blue irises were tiny rims. A fierce joy rose in his face and he looked ten years younger. The vir started to swell, crackling audibly.

Feir picked up Dorian like most men might pick up a doll and shook him violently. He shook and didn't stop shaking. It would have been comical if Kylar weren't too scared to move. Feir just shook and shook until the room was no longer dark with power. Then he set Dorian down in a chair.

The man groaned and abruptly looked frail and older once more. He spoke without raising his head. "I'm glad you're convinced, Shadowstrider."

It had convinced him, but Dorian couldn't know that. "How do I know it wasn't an illusion?" Kylar asked.

"Illusions don't suck light. Illusions—" Feir said.

"He's just being stubborn, Feir. He believes." Dorian glanced at Kylar and quickly looked away. He groaned. "Ah, I can't even look at you now. All your futures. . . ." He squeezed his eyes shut.

"What do you want from me?" Kylar asked.

"I can see the future, Nameless One, but I am only human, so I pray that I can be wrong. I pray that I am wrong. By everything I've seen, if you don't kill Durzo Blint tomorrow, Khalidor will take Cenaria. If you don't kill him by the day after that, everyone you love will die. Your Sa'kagé count, the Shinga, your friends old and new, all of them. If you do the right thing once, it will cost you a year of guilt. If you do the right thing twice, it will cost you your life."

"So that's what this is? All this is just a setup so I'll betray Master Blint? Did your masters think I would buy it?" Kylar said. "Oh, you learned a lot about me, must have cost a fortune to buy all that information."

Dorian held up a weary hand. "I don't ask you to believe it all now. It's too much all at once. I'm sorry for that. You think now that we're Khalidorans and we want you to betray Blint so that he can't stop us. Maybe this will convince you that you're wrong: What I beg of you above all else is that you kill my brother. Don't let him get the ka'kari."

Kylar felt as if he'd just been stung. "The what?"

"Feir," Dorian said. "Say the words we came to say."

"Ask Momma K," Feir said.

He shook his head. "Wait! What? Ask her about the ka'kari?"

"Ask Momma K," Feir said.

"What about your brother, who is he?"

"If I tell you now, you'll lose when you fight him." Dorian shook his head, but still didn't look at Kylar. "Damn this power. What good is it if I can't tell you in a way you'll understand? Kylar, if time is a river, most people live submerged. Some rise to the surface and can guess what's going to happen next, or can understand the past. I'm different. When I don't concentrate, I detach from the flow of time. My consciousness floats above the river. I see a thousand thousand paths. Ask me where a leaf will fall, and I couldn't tell you. There are too many possibilities. There's so much noise, like I'm trying to follow a drop of rain from the clouds to a lake, then over a waterfall and pick it out in the river two leagues downstream. If I can touch someone or chant rhymes, it gives me focus. Sometimes." Dorian seemed to be looking through the wall, lost in reverie.

"Sometimes," he said, "sometimes when I transcend the river, I start to see a pattern. Then it isn't like water, it's a fabric made up of every insignificant decision of every peasant as much as it is of great decisions by kings. As I begin to comprehend the vastness and intricacy of that skein, my mind starts to pull apart." He blinked, and

he turned his eyes to Kylar. He squinted, as if even looking at him caused him pain.

"Sometimes it's merely images, totally unbidden. I can
see the anguish on the young man's face who will watch
me die, but I don't know who he is or when that will be or
why he'll care. I know that tomorrow, a square vase will
give you hope. I see a little girl crying over your body.
She's trying to pull you away but you're too heavy. Away
from what? I don't know."

Kylar felt a chill. "A girl? When?" Was it Ilena
Drake?

"I can't tell. Wait." Dorian blinked and his face went
rigid. "Go, go now. Ask Momma K!"

Feir threw open the front door. Kylar stared from
one mage to the other, stunned at the abruptness of his
dismissal.

"Go," Feir said. "Go!"

Kylar ran into the night.

For a long moment, Feir stared after him. He spat. Still
staring into the depths of the night, he said, "What didn't
you tell him?"

Dorian let out a shaky breath. "He's going to die. No
matter what."

"How does that fit?"

"I don't know. Maybe he's not what we hoped."

35

$\mathcal{K}$ylar ran, but Doubt ran faster. The sky was lightening in the east, and the city was showing its first signs of life. The odds of running into a patrol were small, especially because Kylar knew better than to run on the roads past the rich shops that somehow saw patrols more frequently than roads with poor shops, but if he did run into guards, what would he say? I was just out for a morning walk with dark gray clothes, illegal plants, a small arsenal, and my face smudged with ash. Right.

He slowed to a walk. Momma K's wasn't far now, anyway. What was he doing? Obeying a madman and a giant? He could almost see the vir rising from Dorian's arms, and it turned his stomach. Maybe not a madman. But what was their piece? The only people Kylar knew who did things just because they should were the Drakes, and he figured that they were the exception to the rule. In the Sa'kagé, in the court, in the real world, people did what was best for themselves.

Feir and Dorian hadn't denied that they had other

motives for coming to Cenaria, but they certainly acted like he was the most important thing. They'd acted like they really believed he would change the course of the kingdom! It was madness. But he had believed them.

If they were just liars, wouldn't they try to tell him how great things would be if he killed Blint? Or were they just that much cleverer than most liars? It seemed that by what Dorian had said that Kylar was going lose everything no matter what he did. What kind of fortune-teller told you that?

Still, Kylar found himself jogging again, and then running, startling a laundress filling her buckets with water. He stopped at Momma K's door and suddenly felt uneasy again. Momma K stayed up late and woke early every day, but if there was one time of the day that he could be sure she'd be in bed, it was right now. It was the only time of day that the door would be locked. *Dammit, would you just make a decision?*

Kylar rapped on the door quietly, berating himself for being a coward, yet deciding all the same that he would leave if no one answered it.

The door opened almost immediately. Momma K's maid looked almost as surprised as Kylar was. She was an old woman, wearing a shift, with a shawl around her shoulders. "Well, good morning, my lord. If you aren't a sight. I couldn't sleep, I just kept on thinking that we'd run out of flour for some reason, though I checked it just last night, for some reason I couldn't get it out of my mind that it was all gone. I was just walking past the door to check it when you knocked—oh by the twelve nipples of Arixula, I'm chattering like a daft old ninny."

Kylar opened his mouth, but a word wouldn't fit in the

cracks of the ex-prostitute's rambling, edgewise or any other way.

"'Time for a swift blow to the head, and a heave into the river, mistress,' I tell her, and she just laughs at me. I do wish I were young, if only so I could see the look on your face like I used to get. Once these old sacks would make men stand up and take notice. You'd walk right into a wall because you couldn't take your eyes off. It used to be that the sight of me in my night clothes—of course, I didn't wear old lady's rags like this, neither, but if I wore the kind of stuff I used to, I'm afraid I'd scare the children. It does make me miss the—"

"Is Momma K awake?"

"What? Oh, actually, I think so. She hasn't been sleeping well, poor girl. Maybe a visit will do her good. Though I think it was a visit from that Durzo that's got her knickers in such a bunch. It's hard at her age, going from what she's been to being like me. Almost fifty years old she is. It reminds me—"

Kylar edged past her and walked up the stairs. He wasn't even sure the old woman noticed.

He knocked and waited. No response. A sliver of light peeked through the crack along the sill, though, so he opened the door.

Momma K sat with her back to him. Two candles burned almost to nubs provided the only illumination in the room. She barely stirred when Kylar came in. Finally, she turned slowly toward him. Her eyes were swollen and red as if she'd been up all night crying. *Crying? Momma K?*

"Momma K? Momma K, you look like hell."

"You always did know just the thing to say to the ladies."

Kylar stepped into the room and closed the door. It was then he noticed the mirrors. Momma K's bedside mirror where she put on makeup, her hand mirror, even her full-length mirror, every one of them was smashed. Shards twinkled feebly from the floor in the candlelight.

"Momma K? What's going on here?"

"Don't call me that. Don't ever call me that again."

"What's going on?"

"Lies, Kylar," she said, looking down at her lap, her face half concealed in the shadows. "Beautiful lies. Lies I've worn so long I don't remember what's beneath them."

She turned. In a line down the middle of her face, she'd wiped off all her makeup. The left half of her face was free of cosmetics for the first time Kylar had ever seen. It made her look old and haggard. Fine wrinkles danced across the once delicate—now merely small and hard—planes of Gwinvere Kirena's face. Dark circles under her eyes gave her a ghostly vulnerability. The effect of half of her face being perfectly presented and the other stripped was ludicrous, ugly, almost comic.

Kylar covered his shock too slowly, not that he could ever hide much from her, but Momma K seemed satisfied to be wounded.

"I'll assume you're not here just to stare at the sideshow freak, so what do you want, Kylar?"

"You're not a sideshow—"

"Answer the question. I know what a man with a mission looks like. You're here for my help. What do you need?"

"Momma K, dammit, quit—"

"No, damn you!" Momma K's voice cracked like a whip. Then her mismatched eyes softened and looked beyond Kylar. "It's too late. I chose this. Damn him, but he was right. I chose this life, Kylar. I've chosen every step. It's no good switching whores in the middle of a tumble. You're here about Durzo, aren't you."

Kylar knuckled his forehead, put off track. He could read the look in her face, though. It said, "Discussion over." Kylar surrendered. Was he here about Durzo? Well, it was as good of a place to start as any.

"He said he's going to kill me if I don't find the silver ka'kari. I don't really even know what it is."

She took a deep breath. "I've been trying to get him to tell you for years," she said. "Six ka'kari were made for Jorsin Alkestes' six champions. The people who used the ka'kari weren't mages, but the ka'kari gave them mage-like powers. Not like the feeble mages of today, either, the mages of seven centuries ago. You are what they were. You're a ka'karifer. You were born with a hole in your Talent that only a ka'kari can bridge."

Momma K and Durzo had both known all of this, and they were only telling him now? "Oh, well, thanks. Can you direct me to the nearest magical artifact store? Perhaps one with a discount for wetboys?" Kylar asked. "Even if there were such things, they've either been collected by the mages or they're at the bottom of the ocean or something."

"Or something."

"Are you saying you know where the silver is?"

"Consider this," Momma K said. "You're a king. You manage to get a ka'kari, but you can't use it. Maybe you don't have anyone you trust who can. What do you do? You keep it for a rainy day, or for your heirs. Maybe you never write down what it is because you know that people will go through your things when you die and steal your most valuable possession, so you plan to tell your son someday before he takes the throne. In some way or another, though, as kings so often do, you get yourself killed before you can have that talk. What happens to the ka'kari?"

"The son gets it."

"Right, and doesn't know what it is. Maybe even knows it's important, that it's magical, but like you said, if he ever tells the mages, they'll take it from him or from his heirs sooner or later. So he keeps it, and he keeps it secret. After enough generations pass, it becomes just another jewel in the royal treasury. By the time seven hundred years go by, it's switched hands dozens of times, but no one has a clue what it is. Until one day, Khalidor's God-king demands a tribute that includes one particular jewel, and a remarkably stupid king gives the very same jewel to his mistress."

"You mean—" Kylar said.

"I just found out today that Niner gave Lady Jadwin the silver ka'kari, the Globe of Edges. It looks like a small, oddly metallic jewel, like a diamond with a silver tint to it. It also happens to be one of Queen Nalia's favorite jewels. She thinks it's lost, and she's furious, so tomorrow night, someone the king trusts—I don't know who—will be sent to get it back. The Jadwins are having a party that night. So tomorrow, the ka'kari will be exposed. No royal guards, no mages, no magically warded treasury. Lady Jadwin will either be carrying it or it will be in her room. Kylar, you need to understand what's at stake. The ka'kari supposedly choose their own masters, but the Khalidorans believe they can magically force a bond. If the Godking succeeds . . . imagine the havoc a Godking would wreak if he could live forever."

It made prickles go up the back of Kylar's scalp. "You really mean this, don't you? Have you told Durzo?"

"Durzo and I . . . I'm not too inclined to help Durzo just now. But there's more, Kylar. I'm not the only one who knows this." Anguish twisted her features and she looked away.

"What do you mean?"

"Khalidor has hired someone to get it. That's how my spies found out in the first place. Supposedly the job is a smash-and-dash."

"Supposedly?"

"They've hired Hu Gibbet."

"Nobody would hire Hu for a smash-and-dash. The man's a butcher."

"I know," Momma K said.

"Then who's his deader?"

"Take your pick. Half the nobles in the realm will be there. Your friend Logan has accepted his invitation, perhaps even the prince will be there. Those two do seem to be inseparable; for all that they are night and day to each other."

"Momma, who's your spy? Can you get me an invitation?"

She smiled mysteriously. "My spy can't help you, but I know someone who can. In fact, despite my best efforts, you know her too."

36

Kylar had walked up to men in broad daylight within paces of the city guard to kill them. He'd crawled under tables while a cat clawed him as guards searched the room for intruders. He'd had to break into a vat of wine and hide inside it as a noble's wine taster had picked out an appropriate bottle for dinner. He'd waited a yard from a fully stoked oven after he'd poisoned a stew while a cook debated with himself on what spice he'd added too much of to make it taste so strange.

But he'd never been this nervous.

He stared at the door, a narrow servants' entrance, in dismay. He was a beggar today, come to beg a crust. His hair was lank and greasy, smeared with ash and tallow. His skin was tough and brown, hands gnarled and arthritic. To get to that door, he had to make it through the guards at the estate's tall gate.

"Oy, old man," a stumpy guard with a halberd said. "Whatcha be wanting?"

"I heard my little girl is here. Miss Cromwyll. I hoped she might find me a crust, is all."

That woke up the other guard, who had only given Kylar a cursory glance. "What'd you say? You're related to Miss Cromwyll?" The protective air around the man, who must have been nearly forty, was palpable.

"No, no, she's not mine," Kylar protested, scraping a laugh across his lungs. "Just an old friend."

The guards looked at each other. "You gwyna go find 'er and bring 'er out here at this time of day with the goin's on tonight?" Stumpy asked.

The other shook his head, and with a grumble, started patting Kylar down gingerly. "Swear I'll get lice off of one of Miss Cromwyll's strays one of these days."

"Ah know it, but she's worth it, inn't she?"

"You're not so magnamorous when you're the one patting the beggars, Birt."

"Ah, stuff it."

"Go on. Kitchen's that way," the older guard told Kylar. "Birt, I'm lenient with ya, but if you tell me to stuff it one more time, I'll show you the business end o' my boot—"

Kylar shuffled to the kitchen favoring a stiff knee. The guards, for all their talk, were professionals. They held their weapons like they knew what to do with them, and though they hadn't seen through his disguise, they hadn't neglected their duty to search him. Such discipline boded ill for him.

Though he took his time walking and memorizing the layout of the estate grounds, the walk wasn't nearly long enough. The Jadwins had been dukes for five generations, and the manse was one of the most beautiful in the city. The Jadwin estate overlooked the Plith River, and directly faced Cenaria Castle. Just north of the estate was

East Kingsbridge, which was ostensibly for military use, but it was rumored to be used more often for the king's nocturnal liaisons. If Lady Jadwin really was the king's mistress, the Jadwin estate was perfectly placed for easy access. The king also kept the duke running all over Midcyru on diplomatic missions that everyone but the duke knew were pure pretense.

The manse itself was set on a small central hill that allowed it to look over the river, despite twelve-foot spiked walls that bordered the entire property.

With a trembling hand he masked as a palsy, Kylar knocked at the servants' entrance.

"Yes?" The door opened and a young woman wiping her hands on an apron looked at Kylar expectantly.

She was a beautiful woman, maybe seventeen, with an hourglass figure that even through a servant's woolens obviously would have been the envy of any of Momma K's rent girls. The scars were still there, an X on her cheek, an X across her full lips, and a loop from the corner of her mouth to the outside of her eye. The scar gave her a permanent little grin, but the kindness of her mouth eased the cruelty of the scar.

Kylar remembered how her eye had looked, swollen grossly. He'd been afraid she would never see out of it. But her eyes, both of them, were clear and bright brown, sparkling with goodness and happiness. Doll Girl's nose had been broken to mush, and Elene's wasn't completely straight, but it didn't look bad. And she had all her teeth— of course, he realized, she'd been young enough that she'd only lost small teeth in the beating.

"Come in, grandfather," she said quietly. "I'll find you something to eat." She offered her arm, and didn't seem offended by his staring. She took him to a small side room with a narrow table for the servants who needed to be within earshot of the kitchen. Calmly, she told a woman ten years older than she was that she needed her to take over while Elene took care of her guest. From her tone and the older woman's reaction, Kylar could see that Elene was adored here, and that she took care of beggars all the time.

"How are you, grandfather? Can I get a salve for your hands? I know it's painful on these chilly mornings."

What had he done to deserve this? He'd come as the most foul sort of beggar, and she showered him with kindness. He had nothing to give her, yet she treated him like a human being. This was the woman who had almost died because of his arrogance and stupidity, his failure. The only ugliness in her life was because of Kylar.

He'd thought he'd set aside his guilt two years ago when Momma K had told him the simple truth that he'd saved Elene from worse than scars. But looking at those scars up close threatened to throw him right back to that hell.

She put a crust covered with fresh hot gravy down on the table, and started to cut it into smaller pieces. "Would you like to sit here? We'll just make this a little easier to chew, yes?" she said, speaking loudly the way people who work with old people learn to. She smiled and the scars tugged at her full lips.

No. He'd put her here, with these people who adored her, where she could afford to share a crust. Elene had made her own choices to become who she was, but he had made those choices possible. If there was one good thing he'd done, it was this. He closed his eyes and breathed deeply. When he opened his eyes and looked at her without guilt darkening his vision, she was stunning. Elene's hair was lustrous gold, aside from the scars her skin was flawless, eyes large and bright, cheekbones high, lips full, teeth white, neck slender, figure entrancing. She was leaning forward to cut the crust for him, her bodice gapping in front—

Kylar tore his eyes away, trying to slow his pulse. She noticed his sharp move and looked at him. He met her eyes. Her look was quizzical, open. He was going to ask this woman to betray her employer?

A tangled snarl of emotions that he'd kept shoved into some dark corner closet of his soul surged and burst through the doors. Kylar choked on a sob. He blinked his eyes hard. *Get a hold of yourself.*

Elene put her arm around him, heedless of his filthy clothing and stench. She didn't say anything, didn't ask anything, just touched him. Tingles shot through him, and his emotions surged again.

"Do you know who I am?" Kylar asked. He didn't use the beggar voice.

Elene Cromwyll looked at him strangely, uncomprehending. He wanted to stay hunched, to hide from those gentle eyes, but he couldn't. He straightened his back and stood up, and stretched his fingers.

"Kylar?" she asked. "It is you! What are you doing here? Did Mags and Ilena send you? Oh my God, what did they tell you?" Her cheeks flushed and her eyes lit with hope and embarrassment. It wasn't fair that a woman could be so beautiful. Did she know what she was doing to him?

Her face was the face of a girl surprised by a boy in the best way. Oh, gods. She thought he was here to ask her to Mags's party. Elene's expectations were about to meet reality like a toddler charging the Alitaeran cavalry.

"Forget Kylar," he said, though it pained him. "Look at me and tell me who you see."

"An old man?" she said. "It's a very good costume, but it isn't a costume party." She flushed again as if she were presuming too much.

"Look at me, Doll Girl." His voice was strangled.

She stopped, transfixed, peering into his eyes. She touched his face. Her eyes went wide. "Azoth," she whispered. She put a hand on the table to steady herself. "Azoth!" She flung herself at him so fast, he almost tried to block her attack. Then she was squeezing him. He stood stock still, his mind refusing to understand for a long moment: she was hugging him.

He couldn't make himself move, couldn't think; he simply felt. The smooth skin of her cheek brushed his scruffy, unshaven one. Her hair filled his nostrils with the clean scent of youth and promise. She hugged him fiercely, the notes of strong hard arms joining with supple firm stomach and back joining with the pure feminine softness of her chest pressed against his making a chord of perfect acceptance.

Tentatively, he lifted his hands from his sides and touched her back. He tasted salt on his lips. A tear, his tear. His chest convulsed uncontrollably, and suddenly he was sobbing. He grabbed her, and she squeezed him harder still. He felt her crying, staccato breaths shaking her slender frame. And for a moment, the world was reduced to a single hug, reunion, joy, acceptance.

"Azoth, I heard you were dead," Elene said, all too soon.

You will always be alone. Kylar froze up. If tears could stop halfway down a cheek, his would have.

He released Elene deliberately, stepped back. Her eyes were red, but still shining as she dabbed her tears away with a handkerchief. A sudden desire to sweep her into his arms and kiss her crashed over him in a wave. He blinked, held himself still until reality could reassert itself. He opened his mouth, couldn't say a thing, couldn't ruin it. He tried again, ready to lay out his lies, couldn't. *Relationships are ropes. Love is a noose.* Durzo told me. He gave me a chance. I could have been a fletcher, an herbalist. I chose this.

"I was ordered never to see you. By my master." His tongue was leaden. "Durzo Blint."

He could tell even Elene had heard of Durzo Blint. Her eyes tightened in confusion. He could see her working through it: if Durzo was his master, that meant . . . He saw a quick little disbelieving smile, as if she were about to say, "But wetboys are monsters, and you're not a monster." But then the smile faded. Why else would her Azoth never contact her? How else would a guild rat disappear so completely?

Her eyes grew distant. "When I was hurt, I remember you arguing with someone, demanding that he save me. I thought it was a dream. That was Durzo Blint, wasn't it?"

"Yes."

"And you . . . now you're what he is?" Elene asked.

"Close enough." Actually, I'm not even full-fledged horror, I'm just an assassin, a hack.

"You apprenticed with him so he would save me?" she asked, her voice barely above a whisper. "You became what you are because of me?"

"Yes. No. I don't know. He gave me a chance to leave after I killed Rat, but I didn't want to be afraid anymore, and Durzo was never afraid, and even as an apprentice, he paid me so well that I could—" he stopped.

Her eyes narrowed as she puzzled it out. "That you could support me," she finished. She put her hands over her mouth.

He nodded. *Your beautiful life is built on blood money.* What was he doing? He should be lying to her, the truth could only destroy. "I'm sorry. I shouldn't have told you. I—"

"You're sorry?!" Elene interrupted him. He knew what the next words out of her mouth would be: *You're a failure. Look at what you've done to me.* "What are you talking about?" she asked. "You've given me everything! You fed me on the streets when I was too young to find food for myself. You saved me from Rat. You saved me when your master was going to let me die. You put me with a good family who loved me."

"But—aren't you mad at me?"

She was taken aback. "Why would I be mad at you?"

"If I hadn't been so arrogant, that bastard wouldn't have come after you. I humiliated him! I should have been watching. I should have protected you better."

"You were eleven years old!" Elene said.

"Every scar on your face is my fault. Gods, look at you! You would have been the most beautiful woman in the city! Instead, you're here, giving crusts to beggars."

"Instead of where?" she asked quietly. "Do you know any girls who've been prostitutes since they were children? I do. I've seen what you saved me from. And I'm grateful for it every day. I'm grateful for these scars!"

"But your face!" Kylar was on the edge of tears again.

"If this is the worst ugliness in my life, Azoth, I think

I'm pretty lucky." She smiled, and despite the scars, the room lit up. She was breathtaking.

"You're beautiful," he said.

She actually blushed. The Drake sisters were the only girls Kylar knew who blushed, and Serah didn't blush anymore. "Thank you," she said, and touched his arm. At her touch, shivers went through him.

He looked into her eyes, and then he blushed, too. He'd never been so mortified in his life. *Blushing!* That only made it worse. She laughed, not a laugh at him in his discomfort, but a laugh of such innocent joy it pained him. Her laugh, like her voice, was low, and it brushed over him like a cool wind on a hot day.

Then her laughter passed and a look of profound sorrow stole over her face. "I'm so sorry, Azoth—Kylar. I'm sorry for what you've had to pay to put me here. I don't even know what to think. Sometimes it seems the God's hand doesn't reach very far into the Warrens. I'm sorry." She looked at him for a long time and another tear tracked down her cheek. She ignored it, just absorbing him. "Are you a bad man, Kylar?"

He hesitated. Then said, "Yes."

"I don't believe you," she said. "A bad man would have lied."

"Maybe I'm an honest villain." He turned away.

"I think you're still the boy who shared his bread with his friends when he was starving."

"I always took the biggest piece," he whispered.

"Then we remember differently," Elene said. She heaved a deep breath and brushed her tears away. "Are you . . . are you here for work?"

It was a shot in the solar plexus. "There's a wetboy

coming to kill someone at the party tonight and steal something. I need an invitation to get in."

"What are you going to do?" she asked.

In truth, Kylar had barely thought about it. "I'm going to kill him," he said. And it was the truth. Hu Gibbet was the kind of twist who started killing beggars when he had to go too long between jobs. He needed murder like a drunkard needs wine. If Kylar came and stole the silver ka'kari first, Hu Gibbet would come after him. Hu was a full wetboy, and reputed to be as strong of a fighter as Durzo. Kylar's only chance to kill him would be to catch him off-guard. Tonight.

Elene still didn't look at him. "If you're a wetboy, you've got other ways to get in. You must know forgers. Kylar Stern must have contacts. Maybe an invitation from me would be the easiest way in, but that's not why you came. You came here to case the place, didn't you?"

His silence was answer enough.

"All these years," Elene said, turning her back, "I thought Azoth was dead. And maybe he is. Maybe I helped kill him. I'm sorry, Kylar. I'd give my life to help you. But I can't give you what's not mine to give. My loyalty, my honor, belongs to the God. I can't betray my lady's trust. I'm afraid I'm going to have to ask you to leave."

It was a gentler banishment than he deserved, but banishment all the same. Kylar hunched and curled his fingers into arthritic claws and left. He turned once he reached the gate, but Elene wasn't even watching him go.

37

Like all good ambushes, this one came at a time and place where they least expected it. Solon and Regnus and his men had made it down the mountains, over the central plains, and had come within two miles of Cenaria's sprawling northern edge.

Duke Gyre and his men were between two wide rice paddies on the raised road when they came upon a man leading a cart horse. Several peasants were working in the paddies, but they were dressed simply, trouser legs rolled up to their knees, obviously devoid of armor or weapons. The carter pulled his old horse to the side, looking at the men in armor intently.

Solon should have noticed it earlier, of course. Peasants didn't wear long sleeves in the paddies. But it wasn't until he was within twenty paces of the carter that he saw it. The Vürdmeister dropped the horse's reins and brought his wrists together, green fire roaring down his vir and filling each hand. He clapped his wrists together and wytchfire spurted forward.

The wytchfire hit the guard to Solon's left and went right through him. The magic was designed to melt off in layers like an icicle as it punched through each man. It was the size of a man's head as it went through the first man, then the size of a man's fist as it hit the second, then the size of a man's thumb as it hit the third. In an instant, all three were dead, flames roaring off their flesh, burning on the blood that spilled out of the men as if it were oil.

A second later, wytchfire hit the guards from each side as a Vürdmeister on either side of the road hurled death into their midst. Another three men dropped.

That left Solon, Duke Gyre, and two guards. It was a tribute to the men's discipline that they did anything at all, but Solon knew they were doomed. One guard rode right. Duke Gyre and the other guard rode left, leaving Solon to take care of the Vürdmeister on the road.

Solon didn't move. The Vürdmeister had set their ambush so they'd have ample time to get off two or three balls of wytchfire. Twelve swordsmen were no match for three wytches.

There was no time to weigh the consequences. Not even time to draw the sunlight streaming onto the paddies into magic. Solon drew directly on his *glore vyrden* and threw three tiny sparks through the air. They flew as fast as arrows and somehow avoided hitting the duke or his guards. Both Vürdmeister were gathering green fire again as the sparks, each hardly as big as a fingertip, touched their skin.

They weren't even close to lethal. Solon didn't have enough magic to face even one Vürdmeister alone, much less all of them together. But the sparks shocked them. A small shock, but enough to tense their muscles for a second and totally break their concentration. Before they could gather their wits, three swords descended with all the force of three galloping horses and three battle-hardened arms, and the two wytches to either side of the road died.

Solon threw the spark at the wytch on the road last, and the man blocked it. Indeed, it wasn't so much blocking as merely snuffing. The spark flew toward him and then died as if it were a fiery twig being dropped in the ocean. His counterattack was a gush of fire that roared toward Solon with the sound and rage of a dragon's breath.

There was no blocking it. Solon flung himself from the saddle and threw another spark as he fell to the ground and rolled off the road.

The wytch didn't even bother to quench the spark as it flew a good ten feet wide of him. He turned, bridling almost fifty feet of fire as if it were a living thing and turning it in his hands to follow Solon.

The spark hit the cart horse's flank. The old beast was already terrified by the blood, the sounds, and the flash of unnatural fire. It jerked against the cart and then reared and lashed out with its hooves.

The Vürdmeister never even heard the horse's whinny beneath the roar of the flames. One second, he was reining the stream of fire down the bank of the road onto Solon, and the next, a hoof caught him in the back. He dropped on all fours, not knowing anything but that something was terribly wrong. He gasped and turned to see the horse regain its balance. Then horse and cart ran right over the man, crushing him into the road.

Solon pulled himself out of the water and mud of the rice paddy as the cart horse ran as it must not have run in ten years. His own horse was dead, of course, its skull a smoking ruin and the smell of burnt hair and cooked meat mingling over its half-ruined corpse.

The wytchfire was barely smoldering on the bodies of the dead guards now. Even as he watched, it guttered out. Wytchfire spread horribly fast, but only lasted about ten seconds.

Ten seconds? Has it only been that long?

The sound of hooves brought Solon back into reality. He looked up at Duke Gyre, whose face was still and hard.

"You're a mage," the duke said.

"Yes, my lord," Solon said heavily. The lines were written now, by Solon's silence. The duke had no choice. Confronted with such a surprise, a more clever man would have pretended to have known Solon was a mage all along. Then he could have decided what to do with him later. Duke Gyre was too straightforward for that. It was his strength and his weakness.

"And you've been reporting on me to other mages."

"Only, only to friends, my lord." It was weak, and it made him sound weak to say it, Solon knew, but he couldn't imagine that it could all disappear like this. Surely his friendship with Regnus, surely ten years of service were worth more than this.

"No, Solon," Duke Gyre said. "Loyal vassals don't spy on their lords. You've saved my life this day, but you've been betraying me for years. How could you?"

"It wasn't—"

"For my life, I give you yours. Begone. Take one of the horses and go. If I ever see your face again, I'll kill you."

"Stay with him," Dorian had said. "His life depends on

it. A kingdom depends on it. 'By your word—or silence—a brother king lies dead.'" But he'd never said how long Solon had to serve his Lord Gyre, had he? Solon bowed low in front of his friend and took a bridle from Gurden, who looked too stunned for emotion. Solon mounted and turned his back on Lord Gyre.

Did I save Cenaria today, or doom it?

38

Kylar's afternoon had been frantic. He'd had to get Logan to get someone else to get him an invitation, and then when he'd tried to find Durzo, the wetboy was gone, leaving a typically terse note: "On a job." Durzo didn't often give Kylar a lot of detail on his jobs, but lately Kylar felt that he was being more and more excluded, as if Durzo were trying to create space between them so that it would be easier to kill Kylar when the time came.

Durzo's absence had meant that Kylar didn't have to confess to talking with Elene, botching it, and probably tightening security at the Jadwin estate all at once, so it wasn't altogether a bad thing. Now, because he'd told Logan he was coming to the party, he had to come without a disguise, but because he'd told Elene he was coming, if she saw him, she'd report him immediately.

That was why he'd come in a carriage, even though it would seem odd for a young noble alone not to ride. The carriage stopped at the gate and he handed his invitation to Birt. The man didn't recognize him, of course. He just looked over the invitation carefully and waved him in. Kylar was glad to see the man. If he was still guarding the door, it meant that the Jadwins didn't have enough guards to replace all the ones who'd worked earlier in the day and still guard the party. Maybe they hadn't believed Elene. After all, how would a serving girl know about the plots of wetboys?

Kylar took one step out of his carriage and froze. The carriage directly in front of his was open and a whip-thin man was stepping out of it. It was Hu Gibbet, all in chocolate leather and silks like a lord, long blond hair combed and gleaming, smiling with the disdain of a man superior to those around him. Kylar ducked back into his carriage. So it was true. He counted to ten and then, afraid that his driver would wonder what he was doing and maybe call attention to him, he stepped out of the carriage himself. He saw Hu disappearing inside. Kylar followed, producing the invitation again for the guards in front of the monstrous white oak door.

"So have you gotten the old goat's permission?" Prince Aleine asked.

Logan looked at his friend on the other side of the long table heaped high with every delicacy the Jadwins thought would impress their guests. The table was near one of the walls of the vast great hall of white marble and white oak. Against the monochrome background, the nobles were a riot of color. Several of the realm's most influential hecatonarchs, priests of the hundred gods, mingled in their myriad-colored robes. A band of minstrels in flamboyant cloaks and makeup fought for attention with lords and ladies high and low. Terah Graesin had shown up to the last big party two weeks ago in a scandalously low-cut red gown with a soaring hem. Terah was eighth in line for the throne, after the prince, the Gunder daughters, Logan, and her father Duke Graesin, and she adored the attention her position gave her. Her daring had touched off a new fashion, so this week all the gowns were either red or dared to expose more leg or breast or both than most prostitutes did. This was fine for Terah Graesin, who was somehow able to look glamorous instead of cheap. Most women weren't so fortunate.

"I spoke with the count this morn—" Logan said when he was suddenly silenced as breasts went past. No, not just breasts. The breasts. They were perfect. Not precipitously exposed, but perfectly shaped, these floated past him, held in a gossamer embrace of fabric rejoicing to cling to such nubile curves. Logan didn't even see the woman's face. Then, as she walked past, the sweet curves of swaying hips and a flash of lean, muscular calves.

"And?" the prince asked. He looked at Logan expectantly, holding a plate with little samples of every delicacy on the table. "What'd he say?"

Logan face flamed. Too much time in the wilds. Except that that wasn't really true. His eyes seemed unattached to his mind at all, controlled directly from elsewhere. He moved further down the line, trying to remember what he'd been saying, his plate still empty as he rejected a few delicacies fricasseed, flambéed, or frosted. "He said—ah, my favorite!" Logan started heaping strawberries on his plate, grabbed a bowl, and filled it with chocolate fondue.

"Somehow I'm sure whatever Count Drake said, it

wasn't 'ah, my favorite,'" Prince Aleine said, arching an eyebrow. "If he said no, you don't have to be embarrassed. Everyone knows Count Drake is a little off. Their family mixes with commoners."

"He said yes."

"Like I said," the prince said. "He's a little off." He smiled and Logan laughed. "When are you going to propose?"

"Tomorrow. It'll be my birthday. Then no one can stop me."

"Does Serah know?" the prince asked.

"She suspects that I might do it soon, but she thinks that I need some time to consolidate my household and speak with my parents about it first."

"Good."

"What do you mean?" Logan asked.

They had reached the end of the long table. The prince stepped close to him. "I wanted to give you a birthday present myself. I know you've got feelings for Serah and I respect that, but Logan, you're a duke's son. Tomorrow you'll become one of the most powerful men in the realm, behind only the other dukes and my family. My father would love for you to marry Serah, and we both know why. If you marry her, you'll set your family back from the throne for two generations."

"Your Highness," Logan said, awkward.

"No, it's true. My father fears you, Logan. You are admired, respected, even held in awe here. That you've been gone half of every year hasn't alienated you like my father hoped. Instead, it's made you romantic. The hero off fighting for us on the borders, keeping the Khalidorans at bay. The king fears you, but I don't, Logan. His spies look at you and they can't believe that you are what you appear to be: a scholar, a fighter, and a loyal friend of the prince. They're schemers, so they see schemes. I see a friend. There are those who would destroy your family, Logan, by any means, and they won't tell me what they're planning—but I won't allow it. In fact, I'll do all I can to stop it." He looked down, grabbed a bit of fried plantain off a plate. "I'm here tonight to do a favor for my father. In return, he promised to give me whatever I ask. *Whatever* I ask."

"That's some favor," Logan said.

The prince waved a hand. "King Stupid gave my mother's favorite jewel to his mistress. I'm here to get it back. It doesn't matter. You know my sister?"

"Of course." Jenine was here somewhere. She was usually described as "sunny": very pretty, and very fifteen.

"She's smitten with you, Logan. She's been in love with you for two years. Talks about you all the time."

"You're joking. I've barely exchanged two words with her."

"So what," the prince said. "She's a great kid. She's pretty, only getting prettier, and she has my mother's intelligence—I know how important to you that is to you, my vituperative friend."

"I'm not vituperative," Logan said.

"See? I don't even know if you are or not. I just grabbed the biggest word I know. But Jeni would."

"What are you saying, Your Highness?"

"Jenine's your birthday present, Logan. If you want her. Marry her. Just give me the word."

Logan was stunned. "That's, that's quite the birthday present."

"Your family will be restored. Our children will grow up together. One of your grandchildren could share the throne with one of mine. You've been the best friend a man could ask for, Logan, and friends are something most princes don't get. I want to do well by you. You'll be happy, I promise it. Jenine is turning into an amazing woman. As I think you've noticed." The prince nodded.

Logan saw her then, looking at him across the room, and he realized he'd already seen her tonight. Or at least her breasts.

His face flamed. He tried to summon words, but they abandoned him. Jenine stood there across the room, with the elegance of a woman far older, at least until one of her friends said something to her and she started giggling.

The prince laughed. "Say yes, and you can do all the things you were imagining a minute ago. Legitimately."

"I, I . . ." Logan's jaw worked. "I'm in love with Serah, Your Highness. Thank you for your offer, but—"

"Logan! Do everyone a favor. Say yes. Your parents will be overjoyed. Your family will be saved. Jenine will be ecstatic."

"You didn't tell her, did you?"

"Of course not. But think about it. Serah's great. But let's be honest, she's kind of pretty, but she's not as smart as you like, and you know what the rumors say about her getting around—"

"She's the opposite of a loose woman, Aleine. She hasn't even more than kissed *me*."

"But the rumors—"

"The rumors are because people hate her father. I love her. I'm going to marry her."

"Excuse me," a young blonde said. She slid between

them and brushed past the prince to reach for a sweet roll. She was a scandal in red. The friction between her chest and the prince's nearly pulled her breasts free of her dress, which had something more like a navel-line than a neck-line. The prince noticed, Logan saw. But then, he usually did. And so did Logan.

"I'm Viridiana," the girl said, catching the prince's eyes as they came back up. "I'm so sorry, excuse me." Not that it was an apology. Not that it was an accident.

Viridiana slipped back into the crowd, her dancer's body carrying the prince's eyes and his thoughts away from Logan. "Well, uh, think about it. Let's talk tomor-row, before you ask," the prince said, watching Viridiana head out to the back porch. She looked over her shoulder, and seeing him looking, smiled.

The prince looked down at his plate, piled high with a little bit of each delicacy on the table. Then he looked at Logan's, piled high with just one thing. "This, my friend," the prince said, "is the difference between us. If you'll excuse me, I've seen a dish I simply must sample."

Logan sighed. His eyes fell on Jenine again, who was still looking at him. It looked like her friends were urging her to go talk to him.

Damnation. Where's Serah?

39

There were guards on every stair. This wasn't good news. Kylar had made his way surreptitiously through the party, trying to look so ordinary that no one gave him a second glance, but it wasn't easy. Especially doing it while keeping an eye out for Hu Gibbet, who most likely was doing the same thing. If Hu saw him, Kylar would lose the only advantage he had.

He made his way onto the back porch. Normally, he would have avoided it, because it was liberally strewn with couples. If one thing was guaranteed to make you feel lonely, it was seeing other people kissing passionately in an alcove in the moonlight.

Now, though, Kylar was looking for a way to the second floor. A balcony hung just above the porch, and if he could figure out a route, he could climb to it quickly enough that no one would even notice. Of course, once he was upstairs, he'd still have to find the ka'kari, but he bet it was in the duchess's room. People liked to keep their favorite jewels close.

The wall had no trellises. Maybe he could jump off the rail and vault off the wall high enough to grab the edge of the balcony, a good fifteen feet above. He could probably do it, but he'd have to get it on the first try. If he fell, no one would be able to ignore the noise he made when he crashed through the rose bushes below.

Still, it's better than standing here. Kylar breathed deeply.

"Kylar?" It was a woman's voice. "Kylar, hello. What are you doing here?"

Kylar turned guiltily. "Serah! Hello." She looked like she'd spent all day getting ready for the night. Her dress was modestly cut, but classic, beautiful, and obviously far more expensive than anything Count Drake could afford. "Wow, Serah. That dress . . ."

She smiled and glowed, but only for a moment. "Logan's mother gave it to me."

He turned and grabbed the rail. Across the river, behind high walls, the castle towers gleamed in the moonlight, as near and unreachable as Serah herself.

She came and stood beside him. She said, "You know Logan is going to—"

"I know."

She put her hand on his. He turned and they looked into each other's eyes. "I'm so confused, Kylar. I want to say yes to him. I think I love him. But I also—"

He swept her into his arms roughly, throwing an arm around her back and a hand behind her neck. He pulled her to him and kissed her. For a moment, she gasped. And then she was kissing him back.

In the distance, as if all the way across the river, somewhere in the castle, he heard a door slam. But it was so far away, surely it didn't matter. Then he felt Serah stiffen in his arms and pull back.

A hand clapped on Kylar's shoulder, not gently.

"What the hell are you doing!" Logan shouted, spinning Kylar around.

Heads popped out of nooks and the porch went still. Kylar saw the prince's head among them.

"Something I should have done a long time ago," Kylar said. "You mind?"

"Oh shit," the prince said. He started trying to disentangle himself from the young blonde who was wrapped around him in an alcove.

Kylar turned away from Logan as if to kiss Serah again, but Logan hauled him back around. Kylar's fist came first and caught Logan on the jaw. The big man stumbled back and blinked his eyes.

Serah shrank away, horrified, but she was already forgotten. Logan came forward, his hands up like a proper boxer. Kylar dropped into an unarmed fighting stance, Wind Through Aspens.

Logan came in and fought as Kylar knew he would: honorably. His punches came in above the belt. Textbook jabs and hooks. He was fast, far faster than he appeared, but fighting in such a rule-bound style, he might as well have been a cripple. Kylar wove in among his punches, brushing them aside, falling back slowly.

A crowd gathered in moments. Someone shouted that there was a fight and people started pouring outside.

The guards, admirably enough, were the first ones out. They moved forward to stop them.

"No," the prince said. "Let them fight."

The guards stopped. Kylar was so surprised he didn't

dodge and the next punch knocked the wind out of him. He staggered back as Logan came in, his weight on his toes, crowding Kylar back against the railing.

Kylar gasped a few breaths, blocking his friend's punches with difficulty. As his wind returned, rage swept over him. He blocked a punch up, ducked beneath it, and rained four quick punches on Logan's ribs, sliding away from the railing.

Logan turned and swept a gale through the air with a huge roundhouse, stepping forward at the same time. Kylar dropped beneath the blow and flicked a foot into Logan's pelvis. Instead of taking a step, Logan found that his foot wasn't where he'd told it to be. He fell. Then Kylar's fist caught him across the face and he crashed to the ground.

"Don't get up," Kylar said.

There was a stunned silence from the crowd, followed by murmurs. They'd never seen anything like what Kylar was doing, but however effective it was, it wasn't noble to kick a man while boxing. Kylar didn't care. He had to finish this immediately.

Logan got up on his hands and knees, then on his knees, obviously about to stand. Gods, it was just like in the arena. Logan didn't know when to stay down. Kylar kicked him in the side of the head and he went down hard.

Serah rushed forward to Logan's side. "Well, Serah, you always wanted us to spar. Looks like I win." Kylar smiled triumphantly at her. The murmurs started immediately, all of them disapproving.

Serah slapped him with a crack that rattled his teeth. "You aren't half the man Logan is." She knelt by Logan, and Kylar could see that he'd suddenly ceased to be part of her world.

He straightened his tunic and cloak and pushed through the crowd. The first rows stepped back for him, as if even touching him would bring them shame, but as he pushed his way inside, people were still pushing outside, desperate to see the fight that they didn't know was already finished. Within a few feet of the door, he became just another noble in the crowd. He followed a wall to the servants' staircase, which was now unguarded, and went upstairs.

Well, that hadn't exactly been a roaring success. It had cost him his reputation and had quite possibly revealed his presence to Hu Gibbet. But it had gotten him up the stairs, and for now, that was all that mattered. He could worry about the consequences tomorrow. The rest of the job would be easier. It had to be, right?

Hu Gibbet had been tempted to head up the stairs as soon as the guards abandoned them to go break up some fool nobles' fight. The unguarded stairs were a temptation, but he was confident of his skills. Besides, his plan would still work, and it would give him information he couldn't get if he walked upstairs now.

Lady Jadwin was standing near the doors to the porch, either distraught or pretending to be. It was one of those little mysteries of life that the king had chosen her as his mistress. Surely there were more attractive women who would sleep with a king, even this king. Lady Jadwin was living proof of the hazards of inbreeding. She was a tall woman with a horse's face, large enough and old enough that she certainly didn't belong in the dress she was wearing tonight, and known to be sexually voracious by everyone in the kingdom—except her husband.

He figured that the distress was an act. Lady Jadwin was a passionate woman, but generally unflappable. This would probably be her excuse to go upstairs.

There. She spoke briefly to one of her guards, then went back to apologizing to the guests streaming back in from outside, most of them disappointed at having missed the fun.

The guard, having the subtlety of most guards, walked directly to the guard just now resuming his post at the servants' stair. He leaned close and whispered an order. The man nodded. Meanwhile, the duchess waited until the prince came through the door. She spoke a few words to him, then began feigning more distress as he disengaged himself from a young blonde hanging on his arm.

After a few more seconds, the duchess excused herself, told her husband that she wasn't feeling well, turned down what must have been an offer to send someone with her, and went up the grand stair by herself. Doubtless, she'd told him she just needed to lie down for a little while. "Enjoy the party, dear," she'd said, or something.

The prince was more circumspect, but not difficult to follow. He made his way to the sweet meats, chatted with a few ladies politely, excused himself and walked to the washroom, which was just down the hall from the servants' stair. He emerged from the dark hallway a minute later, looked quickly to see that no one was looking at him, and walked past the guard, who pretended not to see him.

Hu followed hard on the prince's heels, wrapping himself in shadows. The guard was so busy not seeing the prince, the wetboy probably could have slipped past him even without them.

*　*　*

The servants' stair opened on the grand hallway by the duke's chambers. The floors were the same white marble, with the middle of the hall covered by a red carpet for its entire length, all the way from this wing to the opposite one, where the duchess's chambers were. The lights were dimmed as a visual redirection for the guests who might have been at past parties where both floors were open to guests.

Kylar had no idea how long he had to get the Globe of Edges, but he was sure faster was better. It occurred to him that he wasn't the only person who might have seized the opportunity of the stairs being unguarded. Hu Gibbet might already be upstairs.

The only advantage Kylar had—he hoped—was that Hu probably wasn't coming just for a smash-and-dash. He was probably coming to kill someone. If that had been Kylar's goal, the simplest way would be to wait until the duchess gave the ka'kari to the king's agent, whoever it was, and then kill both of them. That way, Hu would get to satisfy his bloodlust and he would kill the two people who knew for sure what had happened. The king wouldn't know if the jewel had been stolen or not, and would have no way to ask without publicly acknowledging that Lady Jadwin was his mistress.

If that guess was right, Kylar had until Lady Jadwin came upstairs to get the Globe of Edges. It might be another hour, or it might be two minutes.

Halfway down the hallway, a guard was walking toward him. Kylar stepped backward into the corner, where the shadows were deeper. But then the guard turned and walked down the grand staircase. It was Kylar's chance.

He walked forward quickly, with no attempt at stealth. His chest tightened as he stepped past the one area of the hallway that was well-lit. The landing at the top of the stairs was bathed in light, but with six steps, eyes locked straight forward, he made it across.

The corridor was lined with disturbing sculptures and excellent paintings. Unless Kylar missed his guess, the duke was something of an artist. The brilliant and diverse paintings were obviously selected by a man with a keen eye and a deep purse. Though similarly striking, the sculptures were unmistakably the product of one vision.

Pained figures appeared to be tearing themselves from the rock. One stumbling woman looked over her shoulder with terror writ in every feature. A man raged at the cloud of black marble that enveloped his hands. A nude woman lay back erotically into the cloud devouring her, rapture on her face.

Even in the hurry Kylar was in, the sculpture stopped him in his tracks. It was beautiful. Devastating. It mixed sensuality with something unsettling that Kylar couldn't identify. And it was unmistakably Elene.

So that's how it is. Kylar felt as if something were tearing the lining of his stomach. It felt empty, raw. *Of course she sleeps with him. He's a duke; she's a servant, and it's hard to say no. Even if she wanted to. Maybe she didn't. It happens all the time.*

He looked at the statue closely, giving a cursory glance to the supple limbs, narrow waist, and high breasts—and found what he was looking for. Though he'd given her a perfect nose, with the lightest of scratches, the duke had hinted at the scars on her face. So the man didn't just see them as imperfections. He was interested in the mysteries beneath.

This isn't the time for art appreciation, damn you.

With a lump in his throat, Kylar jogged down the hall on the balls of his feet. He grabbed the pouch from his back and had his picks out by the time he reached the door. No light or sound came from the room, so he picked the lock quickly. It had only three pins, so it opened in three seconds. Kylar stepped inside and locked the door after himself. If Hu came to the door, he'd have three seconds' warning before the wetboy came.

Kylar drew the bollock dagger he'd strapped to the small of his back. The blade was a foot long, and he'd prefer something ten times its size if he had to fight Hu, but it was the best he'd been able to smuggle in.

He cased the room quickly. Most people, aware of the number of difficulties already present in a thief's life, were kind enough to use the same few hiding places. Kylar checked the mattress, behind the paintings, even the floor under the bureau and several of the chairs for trapdoors. Nothing. He checked the writing desk's drawers for false bottoms. Still nothing.

Most people who kept items of great value wanted to be able to check on them without much hassle, so Kylar didn't even go into the enormous closet. Unless Duchess Jadwin was comfortable handing her most prized possession to a servant, the Globe would be somewhere easily reached.

It didn't help that the duchess seemed to be quite the collector. There were knickknacks everywhere. And flowers, probably brought in for the duke's homecoming, sprouted from every flat surface in the room, obscuring Kylar's view.

So the duke bought his wife some flowers. And, from the

musky smell in the air and the rumpled covers on the bed, apparently had been welcomed home enthusiastically.

Then one of the vases caught Kylar's eye. It was ornately carven jade, but more importantly, it had a square base. Kylar picked it up from the writing desk. Roses, spray roses, stargazer lilies, and snapserpents splayed every which way. Ignoring the flowers, he took it to the mantel and pushed aside a hardwood jewel box.

There was an indentation in the stone of the mantelpiece. A square indentation. Kylar felt a surge of hope.

The prophet was right.

The base fit the indentation and Kylar turned it; there was a muffled click. Kylar pulled all the knickknacks off the mantel and put them on the ground. On hidden hinges the entire mantelpiece opened up.

Ignoring the documents and gold bullion, Kylar grabbed the jewelry box. It was large, large enough to hold the Globe of Edges. Kylar opened it.

Empty.

Gritting his teeth, Kylar replaced the case and closed the mantel. So there was his lesson in prophecy. "A square vase will give you hope," Dorian had said. He hadn't said that it would turn out to be a false hope. *Damn!* Kylar paused long enough to fit a knockout needle into a small trap, just in case Hu came in here instead of following the duchess.

Replacing the knickknacks and putting the vase back on the desk, Kylar tried to think. Where could it be? Everything that could have gone wrong tonight had. The only point of light was that he hadn't seen Elene.

Elene! The leaden feeling in his stomach told Kylar that he knew exactly where the ka'kari was.

40

The prince felt hands grab him as soon as he stepped out of the staircase. An instant later, Lady Jadwin was pressing hot lips against his mouth. She pressed him back as he retreated until he bumped into the door of the duke's chambers.

He tried to hold her back, but she just reached past him and pulled the latch. He almost fell as the door opened behind him. She closed the door behind herself and locked it.

"My lady," he said. "Stop. Please."

"Oh yes, I'll stop," she said. "When it pleases me. Or should I say, after *you* please me?"

"I told you, we're finished. If my father finds out—"

"Oh, bugger your father. He's as much of a bumbler out of bed as he is in it. He'll never know."

"Your husband is just downstairs—anyway, it doesn't matter, Trudana. You know what I'm here for."

"If your father wants his globe back, he can come get

it himself," she said. She put her hand on the front of his breeches.

"You know he couldn't come see you here," the prince said. "It'd be a slap in my mother's face."

"He gave it to me. It was a present."

"It's magic. My father thought it was just a stone, but Khalidor demanded it. Why would they do that if it weren't—no!" he slapped her hand away as she tugged open the laces.

"I know you like it," the duchess said.

"I do like it. But we're finished. It was a mistake, and it will never happen again. Besides, Logan is waiting for me downstairs. I told him what I was doing." The lie came out easily. Anything to get away from this woman. The worst of it was how much he had enjoyed her. The woman might be ugly, but she was more skilled than almost any of the women he'd bedded. Still, waking up and seeing her the first thing in the morning was more than he wanted to think about ever again.

"Logan's your friend," she said. "He'll understand."

"He's a great friend," the prince said. "But he sees things in black and white. Do you know how uncomfortable he was with me leaving him downstairs while I came upstairs with my father's mistress? I need you to get the gem. Now." Sometimes, he could just thank the gods that Logan was a known prig.

"Fine," she said peevishly.

"Where is it? Your husband could come in any second."

"My husband just came home today."

"So?"

"So whatever else he is, the pig's faithful, so he's

practically burning with passion whenever he gets back from a diplomatic assignment. He's recuperating downstairs. The poor dear, I think I exhausted him." She laughed, and it was a harsh, callous sound. "I kept imagining it was you—" With what she must have imagined was a seductive look, she shrugged her shoulders and the front of her dress fell open. She rubbed up against his body and tugged at the laces of his breeches again.

"Trudana, please. Please keep that on. Where is it?" He didn't even look at her body, and he could tell it infuriated her.

"As I was saying," she said finally, "I knew you'd be here tonight, so I gave the globe to my maid. She's just two doors down. Are you satisfied?" She hitched up her dress and walked to her dresser. She looked at herself in the mirror.

The prince turned without saying anything. He'd thought this was going to be easy, that he was going to make his father owe him a huge favor for doing practically nothing. Now he saw that Trudana Jadwin was going to be a lifelong enemy. Never again, he promised himself. I will never sleep with a married woman again.

He didn't even pay any attention to the sound of a drawer sliding open. He didn't even want to look at Trudana. He wasn't even going to stay long enough to lace up his breeches. One second more was one second too many.

His hand was on the latch when he heard the rapid shuffle of her feet. Then something hot lanced into his back. It felt like a wasp sting. Then Trudana's body crushed into him, and he felt the stinger sink deeper. His head smacked against the door in front of him, and he felt the sting again.

It wasn't a sting. It was too deep. He gasped as roaring filled his ears. There was something wrong with one of his lungs. He wasn't breathing right. The stabbing continued and the roaring receded. The world took on a startling clarity.

He was being stabbed to death. By a woman. It was embarrassing, really. He was the prince. He was one of the top swordsmen in the realm, and this fat-assed old woman with saggy, uneven breasts was killing him.

She was breathing, practically gasping in his ear, the same way that she had when they made love. And she was speaking, crying as if every stab were somehow hurting her. The self-pitying bitch. "I'm sorry, oh, oh, I'm sorry. You don't know what he's like. I have to I have to I have to."

The stabbing continued, and it irritated him. He was already dying, his lungs filling with blood. Coughing, he tried to clear them, which succeeded in spraying blood on the door, but his lungs were mincemeat and blood just rushed back into the gaps.

He slumped, hit his knees in front of the door, and she finally stopped. His vision was going dark, and his face slumped forward into the door.

The last thing he saw, through the keyhole, was an eye on the opposite side of the keyhole, emotionlessly watching him die.

He found the door with no problem. It was locked, but he picked it in seconds. *Let her be asleep. Please.*

Easing open the door of the cramped room, Kylar found himself staring at an oversized meat cleaver. It was being held by Elene. She was very much awake.

In the darkness, Elene obviously didn't recognize him. She looked torn between screaming and hacking at him. Her eyes locked on the sword in his hand. She decided to do both.

Slapping her hand with the flat of his bollock dagger, Kylar launched the knife out of her grip. He dodged a grasping hand and got behind her in a moment, clapping a hand over her mouth.

"It's me. It's me!" he said as he had to twist this way and that to dodge flying elbows. He couldn't hold a hand over her mouth and pin both arms and stop the kicks she was aiming at his groin. "Be quiet or your mistress dies!"

As she seemed to regain her sanity, Kylar finally let Elene go. "I knew it!" she said, furiously but quietly. "I knew I couldn't trust you. I knew it was just going to be you."

"I meant your mistress will die because your noise will bring the wetboy here."

Silence, then, "Oh."

"Yes." In the dim moonlit room, he couldn't be sure, but Kylar thought he saw her blushing.

"You could have knocked," she said.

"Sorry. Old habit."

Suddenly awkward, she picked up the cleaver off the bed and put it under her pillow. Looking down at her night-gown, which was disappointingly chaste, she seemed embarrassed. She grabbed a robe and turned her back while she pulled it on.

"Relax," Kylar said as she turned back to face him. "It's a little late for modesty. I saw your statue. You look good naked." Why had he twisted that last bit to make her sound like a whore? Even if she was sleeping with the duke, what choice did she have? She was a servant in the man's house. It wasn't fair, but Kylar still felt betrayed.

Elene folded as if he'd hit her in the stomach.

"I begged her not to display it," Elene said. "But she was so proud of it. She said I should be proud too."

"She?"

"The duchess," Elene said.

"The duchess?" Kylar repeated stupidly. Not the duke. Not the duke?

He felt at once vastly relieved and more confused than ever. Why should he feel relieved?

"Did you think I'd model naked for the duke?" she asked. "What do you think, that I'm his mistress?" Her eyes widened as she saw the expression on his face.

"Well . . ." Kylar felt like he'd unjustly accused her, then felt mad that she was making him feel embarrassed for drawing a perfectly good conclusion, then felt mad that he was wasting time talking to a girl when a wetboy was probably waiting out in the hall. *This is madness.* "It happens," he said defensively.

Why am I doing this?

For the same reason I've watched her from afar. Because I'm intoxicated by her.

"Not with me," Elene said.

"You mean you're a . . ." he was trying to sound snide, but he trailed off. Why was he trying to sound snide?

"A virgin? Yes," she said, unembarrassed. "Are you?"

Kylar clenched his jaw. "I—look, there's a killer here."

Elene seemed about to comment about Kylar avoiding her question, then her look darkened as the joy leached out of it. "Two," she said quietly.

"What?"

"Two killers."

She meant him. Kylar nodded, again feeling a lump in his throat, and suddenly he was ashamed of what he was. "Yes, two. I saw Hu coming in, Elene. Is the Globe safe?"

He was watching her eyes. As expected, they darted to where she'd hidden it: the bottom of her closet.

"Yes," she said. "It's . . ." her voice died. "You're going to steal it."

"I'm sorry," Kylar said.

"And now you know where I hid it. You set me up."

She was naive, but she wasn't stupid. "Yes."

Anger built in her brown eyes. "Is there even an assassin, or was it all a lie?"

"There is one. I give you my word," Kylar said, looking away.

"For all that's worth."

Ouch. "I am sorry, Elene, but I have to."

"Why?"

"It's hard to explain," he said.

"I spent all day being embarrassed about everything I'd ever written to you. I spent all day feeling terrible how much you'd given for me. I didn't even tell the guards you were coming because I thought—I thought . . . You're a real piece of work, *Kylar,*" she said. "I guess Azoth really did die."

Not like this. Not like this.

"I really do have to take it," he said.

"I can't let you do that," she said.

"Elene, if you stay here, they'll think you helped me. If Hu doesn't kill you, the Jadwins might. They could throw you in the Maw. Elene, come with me. I couldn't live with myself if they did that."

"You'll manage. Just take a new name. Throw money at whatever makes you feel guilty."

"They'll kill you!"

"I won't repay good with evil."

He was running out of time. He had to get out of here.

Kylar exhaled. So everything was going to go the worst possible way tonight. "Then I'm sorry for this," he said, "but it's to save you."

"What is?" she asked.

Kylar punched her, twice. Once in the mouth, hard enough to draw blood. And once in her beautiful, piercing eyes, hard enough that they would blacken and swell shut, so they wouldn't see what he did. As she staggered backward, he spun her around and clamped her in a chokehold. She flailed vainly against his grip, doubtless thinking he was killing her. But he merely held her and jabbed a needle in her neck. In seconds, she was unconscious.

She'll never forgive me for this. I'll never forgive me for this. Kylar laid her on the floor and pulled out a knife. He cut his hand and dripped blood onto Elene's face to make it look like she'd been beaten. It was gross, and the contrast of her beauty with the ugliness of what he was doing made him uncharacteristically squeamish, but it had to be done. She had to look like a victim. Looking at her there, unconscious, was like eating his own little slice of the bitter business. The bitterness of the business was the truth of the business. Even here, when he hadn't killed, when he didn't have to bathe in the all-permeating odors of death, Kylar had closed the eyes that saw the truth of him, blackened the eyes of light that illuminated the darkness in him, had bloodied and blinded the eyes that pierced him. *Who says there are no poets in the bitter business?*

Finished, Kylar arranged Elene's limbs in a suitably graceless pattern.

The silver ka'kari was tucked in a slipper in the bottom of the closet. Kylar held it up to examine it in the moonlight. It was a plain, metallic sphere, utterly featureless. In truth, it was a little disappointing. Despite the metallic sheen, it was translucent, which was novel. Kylar had never seen anything like that, but he'd been hoping the ka'kari would do something spectacular.

He tucked the ball into a pouch and moved to the door. So far, so good. Well, actually, so far tonight had been pretty much an unmitigated disaster. But getting out should be relatively easy. If he couldn't sneak past the guard at the bottom of the servants' stairs, he could walk right up to the man and pretend that he'd been looking for the toilet and had needed to go so badly that he'd gone for the first available one. The guard would give him a warning that the upstairs was off limits, Kylar would say they should have guards at the bottom of the steps if they didn't want anyone to go up them, the guard would be chagrined, and Kylar would go home. Not foolproof, but then, tonight Kylar would have distrusted anything that was foolproof.

Looking through the keyhole, he watched the hallway

and listened closely for thirty seconds. There was nothing out there.

The moment he cracked the door, someone kicked the other side with more than mortal strength. The door blew into him, hitting his face first, then his shoulder. It launched him back into the room.

He almost kept his feet, but as he flew back, he tripped over Elene's unconscious body and went down hard. He slid across the stone floor until his head collided with the wall.

Barely holding onto consciousness, black spots exploding in front of his eyes, Kylar must have drawn the pair of daggers on pure instinct because his hands protested in pain as the daggers were knocked out of them.

"Boy?"

Kylar had to blink several times before he could see again. When his vision cleared, the first thing he saw was the knifepoint an inch from his eye. He followed that up the gray-clad arm and hooded body.

Woozy, Kylar wondered why he wasn't dead. But even before Hu pulled back his hood, Kylar knew.

Momma K had betrayed them. She'd sent him to kill the wrong man.

"Master Blint?" he asked.

41

What are you doing!" Master Blint backhanded Kylar soundly. He stood, furious, the illusory features of Hu Gibbet melting away like smoke.

Kylar staggered to his feet, his head still spinning and his ears ringing. "I had to—you were gone—"

"Gone planning this!" Blint whispered hoarsely. "Gone planning this! Never mind now. We've got three minutes until the guard's next round." He nudged Elene's limp form with a toe.

"That one's still alive," Durzo Blint said. "Kill her. Then go find the ka'kari while I fix the deader. We'll discuss your punishment later."

I'm too late. "You killed the duchess?" Kylar asked, rubbing his shoulder where the door had hit him when Durzo burst in.

"The deader was the prince. Someone else got there first." Boots were clomping up the steps. Durzo unsheathed Retribution and checked the hallway.

Gods, the prince? Kylar looked at the unconscious

girl. Her innocence was irrelevant. Even if he didn't kill her, they'd think she helped steal the ka'kari and kill the prince.

"Kylar!"

Kylar looked up, dazed. It was all like a bad dream. It couldn't be happening. "I already . . ." He held out the pouch limply.

Scowling, Durzo snatched it away from him and turned it over. The Globe of Edges fell into his hand. "Damn. Just what I thought," he said.

"What?" Kylar asked.

But Durzo wasn't in any mood to answer questions. "Did the girl see your face?"

Kylar's silence was enough.

"Take care of it. Kylar, that's not a request. It's an order. Kill her."

Thick white scars crisscrossed what had once been a beautiful face. Her eyes were swelling, blackening—and that was as much Kylar's fault as the ten-year-old scars were.

"Love is a noose," Blint had told him when he began his apprenticeship a decade ago.

"No," Kylar said.

Durzo looked back. "What did you say?" Black blood dribbled down Retribution, pooling on the floor.

There was still time to stop. Time to obey, and live. But if he let Elene die, Kylar would be lost in shadow forever.

"I won't kill her. And I won't let you. I'm sorry, master."

"Do you have any idea what that means?" Durzo snapped. "Who is this girl that she's worth being hunted for the rest of your short—" he stopped. "She's Doll Girl."

"Yes, master. I'm sorry."

"By the Night Angels! I don't want apologies! I want obedien—" Durzo held up a finger for silence. The footfalls were close now. Durzo threw open the door and blurred into the hall, inhumanly fast, Retribution flashing silver in the low light.

The guard fell in two thumps. It was Stumpy, the older guard who'd frisked Kylar so gingerly when he'd cased the estate this morning.

The hall lantern behind Durzo swaddled darkness's favorite child in shadow, casting his form over Kylar and making his face invisible. Silhouetted, black blood dripped from the tip of Retribution. Drip, drip. Durzo's voice strained like bending steel. "Kylar, this is your last chance."

"Yes," Kylar said, his bollock dagger hissing against its scabbard as he turned to face the man who'd raised him, who'd been more than a father to him. "It is."

There was the sound of something metallic rolling across marble. It came toward Kylar. He raised a hand and felt the ka'kari slap into his outstretched palm.

He turned his hand over and saw the ka'kari burning a brilliant, incandescent blue. It was stuck to his palm. As he looked, runes began burning on the surface of globe. They shifted, changed, as if trying to speak to him. Blue light bathed his face and he could see through the ka'kari. It was sucking blood from the cut on his palm. He looked up and saw dismay on Master Blint's face.

"No! No, it's mine!" Blint yelled.

The ka'kari pooled like black oil in an instant.

Blue light exploded like a supernova. Then the pain came. The cold in Kylar's hand became pressure. It felt like his hand was splitting apart. Staring at the now uniformly burning puddle in his hand with horror, Kylar saw that it was shrinking. It was pushing itself *into* his hand. Kylar felt the ka'kari enter his blood. Every vein bulged and contorted, freezing as the ka'kari passed through him.

He didn't know how long it lasted. He sweated and shivered and sweated coldly. Gradually the cold faded from his limbs. More gradually still, warmth replaced it. Perhaps seconds, perhaps half an hour later, Kylar found himself on the floor.

Oddly, he felt good. Even face down on stone, he felt good. Complete. Like a gap had been bridged, a hole had been filled. *I'm a ka'karifer. I was born for this.*

Then he remembered. He looked up. From the look of frozen horror on Durzo's face, it all must have taken only seconds. Kylar jumped to his feet, feeling stronger, healthier, more full of energy than he could ever remember.

The look on Durzo's face wasn't anger. It was grief. Bereavement.

Kylar slowly turned his hand over. The skin was still cut on his palm, but it wasn't bleeding anymore. The ka'kari had seemed to push into—

No. It couldn't have.

From every pore in his hand, black poured out like sweat. It congealed. In a moment, the ka'kari rested in his palm.

A strange glee filled Kylar. Fear followed. He wasn't sure the glee was all his own. It was as if the ka'kari were happy to have found him. He looked back to

Durzo, feeling stupid, so far out of his depth he didn't know how to act.

It was then he realized how clearly he could see Durzo's face. The man still stood in the hallway, the lantern behind him. A moment before—before the ka'kari—his face had been all but invisible. Kylar could still see the shadows falling on the floor where Durzo blocked the light, but he could see *through* them. It was like looking through glass. You could tell the glass was there, but it didn't impede your vision. Kylar glanced around Elene's little room and saw that the same applied to everything he looked at. The darkness welcomed his eyes now. His eyes were sharper, clearer—he could see further, could see the castle across the river as if it were high noon.

"I have to have the ka'kari," Durzo said. "If he doesn't get it, he'll kill my daughter. Night Angels have mercy, Kylar, what have you done?"

"I didn't! I didn't do anything!" Kylar said. He held the ka'kari out. "Take it. You can have it. Get your daughter back."

Durzo took it from him. He stared into Kylar's eyes, his voice sorrowful, "You bonded it. It bonds for life, Kylar. Your Talent will work now, whether you're holding it or not, but its other powers won't work for anyone else until you're dead."

There was sound of feet running up the steps. Someone must have heard Durzo's yell. Kylar had to go now. The import of Durzo's words was barely beginning to register.

Durzo turned to face whoever was coming up the steps, and the prophet's words echoed in Kylar's ears: "If you don't kill Durzo Blint tomorrow, Khalidor will take Cenaria. If you don't kill him by the day after that, everyone you love will die. If you do the right thing once, it will cost you years of guilt. If you do the right thing twice, it will cost you your life."

The bollock dagger was in his hand. Durzo's back was turned. Kylar could end it now. Not even Durzo's reflexes could stop him when Kylar was this close. It would mean stopping an invasion, saving everyone he loved—surely that meant he held Elene's life in his hands right now. Logan's. Maybe the Drakes'. Maybe the whole invasion hinged on this. Maybe hundreds or thousands of lives were balanced now on the point of his dagger. A quick, painless cut, and Durzo would die. Hadn't he said that life was empty, worthless, meaningless, cheap? He wouldn't be losing anything of value when he lost his life, he'd sworn that.

Durzo had said it, and more, but Kylar had never really believed him. Momma K had already stabbed Durzo in the back with her lies; Kylar couldn't do it with his hands.

The moment took on a startling clarity. It froze like a diamond and rotated before his eyes, every facet gleaming, futures shearing off and sparkling. Kylar looked from Elene on his right hand to Durzo on his left, from Durzo to Elene, Elene to Durzo. There was his choice, and their futures. He could kill Elene, the woman he loved, or he could kill Durzo, who had raised him as his son. In every facet, this truth glared pitilessly: If one lived, the other must die.

"No," Kylar said. "Master, do it. Kill me."

Durzo looked at him as if he couldn't believe his ears.

"She's only seen me. She won't be a threat to anyone if I'm dead. You can take the ka'kari and save your daughter."

Blint's eyes filled with a look Kylar had never seen before. The hard, jagged cast of his master's face seemed to ease and it made him seem a different man, not old and tired and worn, but younger, a man more like Kylar than Kylar had ever imagined Blint could look. Durzo blinked as bottomless wells of grief threatened to spill over in tears. He shook his head. "Just go, son."

Kylar wanted to go. He wanted to run away, but he was right. It was the only way. He stood there, frozen, but not with indecision. He was just praying that Durzo would act before he lost his courage. *What am I saying? I don't want to die. I want to live. I want to take Elene out of here. I want to—*

The door to the duke's chambers opened and the blood-spattered duchess stumbled out, screaming, "Assassin! Assassin! He's killed the prince!"

Durzo acted instantly. He slammed into Kylar, driving them both into Elene's room. It took all of Kylar's presence of mind to not trample Elene, but Durzo was still moving. He had a hold of Kylar's cloak and was swinging him with the surprising speed and force of his Talent. Kylar exploded through the window and out into the night.

By the grace of the God, or His cruelty, or sheer dumb luck, or Durzo's preternatural skills, Kylar landed squarely in the center of a hedge. He crashed through it, rolling out of control, and popped out onto the ground. It was ridiculous; nothing was broken, nothing was sprained, he didn't even get scratched. He looked up and saw guests craning their heads on the balcony where so recently he'd kissed Serah, but they were on the other side of lamps and couldn't make him out.

Then the screaming from inside was taken up by others, women's voices and men's. Orders were being shouted and armed men were running, clanking and ringing in their chain mail. Kylar looked up at the second story with his heart in his throat. He didn't know whether to curse or laugh. The decision was out of his hands for now. He was alive, and it felt good.

There was nothing else to do. Kylar jogged to the estate's garden gate, broke the lock, and disappeared into the night.

42

The Godking Garoth Ursuul was awake before the functionary knocked on his bedchamber door. No one could approach this room without waking him. It meant less sleep than he might like, but he was an old man now; he didn't need much sleep. Besides, it kept the slaves on their toes.

The room wasn't what one might expect of a Godking. It was open, light and airy, filled with beautiful Plangan stained glass and ivory mirrors and Sethi lace on the bed and dire bear rugs from the Freeze on the floors and freshly cut flowers on the desk and the mantel, all chosen and arranged by a slave with aesthetic sensibilities. Garoth cared for none of it but the paintings. Portraits of his wives lined the walls. His wives had come from almost every nation in Midcyru, and with few exceptions, all were beautiful. Petite or willowy, buxom or boyish, pale or dark, the images all pleased Garoth Ursuul. He was a connoisseur of feminine beauty, and he spared no expense in indulging this vice. It was, after all, a service to his family and the world that he breed the best sons possible. That was where the unattractive women came in. He'd experimented with kidnapping women from royal families in hopes that they might produce more acceptable sons. Two of his current nine aethelings had been born of such women, so Garoth supposed that nobles might produce acceptable sons at a slightly better rate than the rabble, but it was ever so much more tedious to breed with an ugly woman.

Partly for his sons' sake and partly for his own amusement, he'd even indulged in making some of the women love him. It had been surprisingly easy; he hadn't had to lie as much as he'd expected. Women were so willing to do that to themselves. He'd heard that love made the sex better, but he wasn't impressed. With magic, he could make a woman's body respond to him however he pleased, and there was a joy in watching a woman try to hold her fury and hatred while his magic pleased her in ways she'd never felt before. Unfortunately, such pleasures did have their price: those wives had to be watched closely; he'd lost two to suicide.

The functionary's hand banged on the door and Garoth gestured it open. The functionary came in on his knees, scooting forward, crossing his arms on his chest. "My god, my majestic king—"

Garoth sat up. "Out with it. You have a message from the Jadwin slut."

"She reports that she has killed the prince, but has lost possession of the ka'kari. So sorry, Your Holiness."

"Doubtless it's another counterfeit," Garoth said, addressing himself, not the functionary. "Have the ships arrived for the Modaini invasion?"

Cenaria he could deal with whenever he pleased, but a straight march south would tie up his armies for weeks or months. That damned Duke Gyre had turned the defenses at Screaming Winds into a serious obstacle. He could take it, of course. He could probably defeat any army in the world now except the Alitaerans', but a Godking didn't waste men or meisters on frontal assaults. Not when he had other options.

Besides, what conqueror would really want a hive like Cenaria, anyway? He'd almost do better to exterminate everyone there and send his own subjects to colonize the city.

Garoth Ursuul's interest wasn't in temporal power. The bid for Cenaria was just an amusement. He had far more reliable intelligence that the red ka'kari was in Modai. Once there, he would have Cenaria surrounded. He could probably take the country without even fighting for it. Then, Ceura, and a strike right into the mages' heart, Sho'cendi. He wouldn't have to face Alitaera until he was sure of victory.

"Two ships are still passing through Cenarian waters."

"Good, then—"

"Your Holiness—" the man squeaked as he realized whom he had just interrupted.

"Hopper?"

"Yes, Your Holiness?" Hopper's voice was barely a whisper.

"Don't ever interrupt me again."

Hopper nodded, wide-eyed.

"Now what did you have to say?"

"Lady Jadwin claims to have seen someone bond the

ka'kari in the hallway outside her room. Her description was . . . accurate."

"By Khali's blood." Garoth breathed. A ka'kari, after all this time. A ka'kari someone had bonded. That almost made it easier. A ka'kari alone was small enough it could be hidden or lost anywhere, but a ka'kari that was bonded would be kept close by whomever bonded it.

"Reroute those ships. And order Roth to go ahead with the assassinations. The Gyres, the Shinga, all of them. Tell Roth he's got twenty-four hours."

Something was terribly wrong. Regnus Gyre knew that as soon as he reached the gates of his home. No guards were standing outside. Even with how many of his servants and guards the king had managed to have fired or driven off in the last decade, that was disturbing. The lamps were still burning inside the manse, which was odd, an hour past midnight.

"Should I call out, my lord?" Gurden Fray, his guard, asked.

"No." Regnus dismounted and looked through his saddlebags until he found the key. He opened the gate and drew his sword.

On either side of the gate, out of the lamplight, was a body. Each had his throat cut.

"No," Regnus said. "No." He started running for the manse.

He burst through the front door and saw red everywhere. At first his mind refused to accept it. In every room, he found the dead. All looked like they had been caught unawares. Nothing was broken. There were no signs of violent conflict at all, except the bodies. Not even the guards had fought. Almost everyone had had his throat slashed. Then the bodies had been turned so they would bleed as much as possible. Here, old Dunnel was seated upside down in a chair. There Marianne, who had been Logan's wet nurse, was laid down the stairs with her head on the bottom step. It was as if Death himself had strolled through the house, and no one had even tried to stop him. Everywhere, Regnus saw trusted servants, friends, dead.

He found himself running up the stairs, past the statue of the Grasq Twins, toward Catrinna's room. In the hall, he saw the first signs of a struggle. An errant sword had smashed a display case. A portrait of his grandfather had a chunk of frame missing. The guards here had died fighting, the killing wounds on their chests or faces. But the winner was clear, because each body had had its throat cut, and its legs propped up on the walls. The puddles from a dozen men met, coating the floor as if it were a lake of blood.

Gurden knelt, his fingers touching a friend's neck. "They're still warm," he said.

Regnus kicked open the door of his room. It banged noisily; if it had been closed and locked earlier in the night, it wasn't now.

Four men and two women were there, stripped, lying face down in an open circle. Above them, naked, hanging upside down from one foot tied to the chandelier high above while the other leg flopped grotesquely, was Catrinna. Cut into the backs of the corpses, one word to each, were the words: LOVE AND KISSES, HU GIBBET. The knife standing straight out of his steward Wendel North's back served as the period.

Regnus ran. He ran from room to room, checking the dead, calling out their names, turning them over to look at their faces. He became dimly aware of Gurden shaking him.

"Sir! Sir! He's not here. Logan's not here. We have to leave. Come with me."

He let Gurden drag him outside, and the smell of air without blood in it was sweet. Someone was repeating over and over, "Oh my God. Oh my God. Oh my God." It was him. He was babbling. Gurden paid no attention to him, just pulled him along, stumbling.

They got to the front door just as six of the king's elite lancers rode up to it with lances leveled.

"Hold!" their lieutenant called. His men fanned out around Regnus and Gurden. "Hold! Are you Regnus Gyre?"

Something about the bared steel and the sound of his own name wakened him. "Yes," he said, looking at his bloody clothes. Then, stronger, "Yes, I am he."

"Lord Gyre, I've been ordered to arrest you. I'm sorry, sir." He was young, this lieutenant. His eyes were wide, as if he couldn't believe whom he was arresting.

"Arrest me?" His mind was slowly coming back under his power, like a horse that had taken the bit in its teeth and galloped its own way, and was now willing to submit once more.

"Yes, my lord. For the murder of Catrinna Gyre."

A wave of cold washed through Regnus. He could brace, or he could break. He clenched his jaw, and the tears that sprang from his eyes seemed oddly out of place with the command in his voice. "When did you get your orders, son?"

"An hour ago, sir," the lieutenant said, then looked peeved that he'd so automatically obeyed a man he was supposed to be arresting.

"She hasn't been dead fifteen minutes. So tell me, what does that say about your orders?"

The lieutenant's face blanched. A moment later, the lances were wavering. "Our captain said you'd been seen killing—doing it, sir. An hour ago he said that." The lieutenant looked at Gurden. "Is it true?"

"Go see for yourself," Gurden said.

The lieutenant went inside, leaving the men nervously guarding them. Some of the men peeked through the windows and quickly looked away. Regnus felt impatient, as though, if he were given time, he might think again, might detach from his mind. Tears were running down his cheeks again, and he didn't know why. He had to think. He could find out the captain's name, but the man was also just obeying orders. Whether from the Sa'kagé, or the king.

Several minutes later, the lieutenant emerged. He had vomit in his beard and was shaking violently. "You may go, Lord Gyre. And I'm sorry. . . . Let him go."

The men withdrew and Regnus mounted, but he didn't leave. "Will you serve the men who massacred my whole family?" Regnus asked. "I intend to find my son, and I intend to find who—" His voice betrayed him, and he had to clear his throat. "Come with me, and I swear you will serve with honor." His voice cracked on the last word, and he knew he could say no more.

The lieutenant nodded. "We're with you, sir." The men nodded, and Regnus had his first squad. "My lord," the lieutenant said. "I, I cut her down, sir. I couldn't leave her like that."

Regnus couldn't speak. He sawed at his reins viciously and galloped for the gates. *Why didn't I do that? She was my wife. What kind of man am I?*

Lord General Agon was one of the few nobles who hadn't been at the Jadwins' party last night. He hadn't been invited. Not that he felt left out.

The sun was just creeping over the horizon, and the situation didn't look any better in the light of day. Usually, of course, the city guard would handle a murder. But usually the victims of murder weren't heirs to the throne. Agon needed to oversee this one personally.

"Why don't you tell me what really happened, milady," Agon said. No matter what he did here, he was going to be the loser.

Lady Jadwin sniffled. She was genuinely distraught. Agon was sure of that. What he wasn't sure of was whether it was because she had been caught, or because she was sorry the prince was dead. "I have told you," she said. "A wetboy—"

"A what?"

She stopped.

"How do you know what a wetboy is, Trudana?"

She shook her head. "Why are you trying to confuse me? I'm telling you, an assassin was here, standing in this hallway. Do you think I beheaded my own guard? Do you think I'm strong enough for that? Why won't you listen to Elene? She'll tell you."

Blast. He had thought about that. Not only did he

doubt that Lady Jadwin was strong enough to behead a man, but she had no weapon to do it with. And if she'd just murdered the prince without saying a word, why would she cry out and draw people upstairs before she had a chance to clean the blood off her hands and face?

"Explain this," he said. He lifted the red dress she'd worn the night before. His men had discovered it wadded up in the closet. It was still damp with hardening blood. A lot of blood.

"After—after the assassin stabbed the prince, he fell, and I—I caught him. And he died in my arms. I tried to go get help, but the assassin was still in the hall. I was terrified. I panicked. I couldn't stand to have his blood all over me."

"What were the two of you doing alone in the bedchamber?"

The duchess stared at him as if her eyes were hot coals. "How dare you!"

"How dare you, Trudana?" Agon said. "How dare you cheat on your husband not just with the king but also with the king's son? What kind of perverse pleasure did you take out of that? Did you like making the prince betray his father?"

She tried to slap him, but he moved.

"You can't slap everyone in the kingdom, Trudana. We found the bloody knife in your room. Your servants vouch that it's yours. I'd say the odds are that you're going to be beheaded. Unless, that is, the king decides you deserve a common traitor's death on the wheel."

At those words, Trudana Jadwin paled and turned green, but she didn't say another word. Agon gestured angrily, and his men took her away.

"That was unworthy of you," a woman said.

Agon turned and saw Elene Cromwyll, the Jadwins' maidservant who'd been found beaten up and unconscious in her room. She was curvaceous, pretty except for the scars and bruises on her face. But Lady Jadwin fancied herself an artist, so she liked to surround herself with pretty things.

"Yes," Agon said. "I suppose it was. But seeing what she's done . . . what a waste."

"My mistress has made many poor choices," Elene said. "She's hurt many people, destroyed marriages, but she isn't a murderer, Lord General. My lord, I know what happened here last night."

"Really? So you're the one." His voice was more cutting than he intended. He was still trying to put the pieces together himself. How had that guard, Stumpy, who now resembled his nickname more than ever, been killed? Why would the duchess kill the prince silently and change her clothes but not finish washing her hands and face before screaming for help?

Surely, if she'd been cold-blooded enough to murder the prince, maybe in a cold rage as he left her, and been self-possessed enough to start hiding the evidence, she would have done a better job of it before calling people to her.

But then, some of the guests had claimed it was a man's voice they had heard yell upstairs. The guard? Had he stumbled upon the murder, yelled wordlessly, and then been beheaded? Beheading someone wasn't easy. Agon knew that. Even if you cut between the vertebrae, it took substantial strength. Agon had examined Stumpy, and the blade had cut *through* the vertebra.

He turned his eyes back to Elene. "Sorry," he said. "This has been a difficult night. Any way you can help would be welcome."

She looked up, and there were tears in her eyes. "I know who killed the prince. He's a wetboy masquerading as a lord. I knew what he was, and I knew that he was coming, but I didn't think he'd hurt anybody. His name is Kylar. Kylar Stern."

"What?" Agon said.

"It's true. I swear it."

"Look, young lady, your loyalty to your mistress is admirable, but you don't need to do this. If you hold to that story, you'll go to jail. At the least. If you're found to be an accomplice, or even an unwitting accessory to the murder of the prince, you may be hanged. Are you sure you want to do that, just to save Trudana Jadwin?"

"It isn't for her." Tears coursed down her cheeks.

"Then it's for this Kylar Stern? He was the young man who had the fight with Logan Gyre? You must hate him fiercely."

She just looked away. In the rising sunlight, the tears on her cheeks glowed like jewels. "No, sir. Not at all."

"Lord General," a soldier said quietly from the doorway. He looked shaken. "I just came from the Gyre estate, sir. It's chaos there. There are hundreds of people going through the house, wailing, sir. They're dead, sir."

"Get a hold of yourself. What do you mean dead? You mean murdered?"

"More like butchered, sir."

"Who's been murdered, soldier?"

"Sir. All of them."

43

The king fidgeted in his throne. It was a vast piece of ivory and horn inlaid with gold tracery, and it made him look a boy. The audience chamber was empty today except for the regular guards, several guards hidden in the room's secret exits, and Durzo Blint. The emptiness made the chamber seem cavernous. Banners and tapestries adorned the walls, but did nothing to stave off the perpetual chill of such a large stone room. Seven pairs of pillars held the high ceiling and two sets of seven steps each led to the throne.

Durzo stood quietly, waiting for the king to initiate the conversation. He already had a battle plan, if it came to that. It was second nature to him. The meister standing by the king would have to die first, then the two guards flanking the throne, then the king himself. With his Talent, he could probably jump from the throne up to the passage above it, currently obscured by a banner. He'd kill the archer within, and from there he'd be uncatchable.

Like all battle plans, it would last only until the first

move, but it was always useful to have a general plan, especially when you had no idea what your enemies knew. Durzo felt himself reaching into his garlic pouch, but he forced his hand to be still. Now was no time to show nerves. It was harder to stop his hand than he would have guessed, something about the bite of garlic was comforting when he was stressed.

"You let my boy die," the king said, rising. "They killed my boy last night and you did nothing!"

"I'm not a bodyguard."

The king grabbed a spear from the guard standing beside him and threw it. Durzo was surprised at how good a throw it was. Had he stood still, the spear would have caught him in the sternum.

But of course he didn't stand still. He swayed to the side, not even moving his feet, with careless—and he hoped infuriating—ease.

The spear bounced off the floor and then hissed as wood and steel slid across stone. There was a rattle of armor and the whisper of arrows being drawn back all around the room, but the guards didn't attack.

"You're not shit unless I say so!" the king said. He strode forward, coming down his double flight of seven steps to stand in front of Durzo. Tactically, a poor move. He was now blocking at least three of the archers' shots. "You're . . . you're shit! You shitting, shitting shit!"

"Your Majesty," Durzo said gravely. "A man of your stature's cursing vocabulary ought to extend beyond a tedious reiteration of the excreta that fills the void between his ears."

The king looked momentarily confused. The guards looked at each other, aghast. The king saw the look, and realized from their expressions that he'd been insulted. He backhanded Durzo, and Durzo let the blow fall. Any quick motion now, and a nervous archer might loose his arrow.

The king wore rings on all of his fingers, and two of them carved furrows in Durzo's cheek.

Durzo clenched his jaw to quell the rising black fury. He breathed once, twice. He said, "The only reason you're alive right now isn't that I'm not willing to trade my life for yours, Aleine. I'd hate to be killed by amateurs. But know this: if you ever lay a hand on me again, you'll be dead less than a second later. Your Majesty."

King Aleine Gunder IX lifted his hand, seriously contemplating becoming the late King Aleine Gunder IX. He lowered his hand, but a triumphant gleam filled his eyes. "I won't have you killed yet, Durzo. I won't have you killed because I have something better than death for you. You see, I know about you, Durzo Blint. I know. You have a secret, and I know it."

"Forgive my quaking."

"You have an apprentice. A young man styling himself as a noble. Kyle something or other. A young man staying with those holier-than-thou Drakes, quite a student of the sword, isn't he, Master Tulii?"

A chill shot down Durzo's spine. *Night Angels have mercy.* They knew. It was bad. Worse than bad. If they knew Kylar was his apprentice, it couldn't be long before they pinned the prince's death on him. Especially with the spectacle Kylar had made of himself by fighting with Logan Gyre. If Durzo's apprentice had been involved with killing the prince, the king would assume he had done it with Durzo's approval, if not under his orders.

Roth would not be pleased.

The garlic crunched in his mouth, giving a soothing jolt to his senses. He took a breath and willed himself to relax. *How had they done it?*

Master Tulii. Dammit. Anything can go wrong, and something will. Durzo hadn't been betrayed. There was no grand scheme. That name meant that one of the king's spies had been watching the Drakes. Probably just routine spying on a formerly powerful man. The spy had seen Durzo enter and had recognized him. Probably the spy had been one of the guards the king had tried to awe him with in the statue garden. It didn't matter.

"Oh, I wish Brant were here right now to see that look on your face, Durzo Blint. In fact, where is Brant?" the king asked a chamberlain.

"Sire, he's in the castle now, on his way here to report. He went to the Gyre estate after investigating . . . matters at the Jadwin estate."

Durzo's throat tightened. Agon would have put the pieces together about Kylar. If he came in while Durzo was still here, Durzo would die.

The king shrugged. "His loss." At the word, grief and fury rippled through the little king, and he seemed abruptly a different man. "You let them kill my boy, you shit, so I'm going to kill yours. His death will come from the last hand he'd expect, and it will be arriving—oh!— any moment now."

"I heard you had a little tussle with Logan last night," Count Drake said.

Kylar blinked through bleary eyes and went from dead

tired to wide-awake in the space of a second. He'd only slept for a few hours, and he'd had the nightmare again. Every death he saw made him dream of Rat's.

They were seated at the breakfast table and Kylar had a forkful of egg poised in front of his mouth. He stuffed it in to give himself a little time. "Mit wuv nuffin," he said.

This was a disaster. If Count Drake knew about the fight, he might know about the prince's death. Kylar had thought that he'd have time to pack his things and leave this morning before the Drakes got word. That he needed to leave was undeniable. He just thought he'd have a little more time.

"Serah was quite upset," the count said. "She took Logan to her aunt's house near the Jadwins' to have his wounds tended. She just got back a few minutes ago."

"Oh." Kylar chewed more eggs mechanically. If Serah had left right after the fight, she and Count Drake didn't know about the prince yet. Apparently Kylar's perfect streak of bad luck was breaking. But now that he knew that matters of life and death weren't threatening him, he realized that Serah coming home and telling Count Drake what had happened last night would have other implications.

"I gave Logan my permission to propose to her yesterday. You knew that, didn't you?"

That would be the count's gentle way of saying *why the hell did you kiss my Serah and beat up my future son-in-law and your best friend after you told me you had no feelings for her?*

"Um . . ." Out of the corner of his eye, Kylar saw someone pass the window quickly, and a moment later, the old porter toddled after, looking upset.

The front door banged open. A moment later, the door to the dining room slammed open with such force that the dishes on the table rattled.

"Milord," the porter protested.

Logan stormed into the room, red-eyed but regal. He held a claymore the size of Alitaera in his hand.

Kylar jumped to his feet, sending his chair crashing into the wall. He was pinned in a corner. Count Drake was rising, shouting something, but he was too slow. Nothing could stop Logan now.

Logan hefted the claymore. Kylar hefted a butter knife.

"I'm engaged!" Logan shouted. He swept Kylar into a massive hug.

By the time Logan released him, Kylar's heart had started beating again. Count Drake collapsed into his chair in relief.

"You big bastard!" Kylar said. "Congratulations! I told you it would work, didn't I?"

"Work?" Count Drake asked, recovering his voice.

Logan plowed forward, ignoring the count. "Well, you didn't have to hit me so hard."

"I had to convince her," Kylar said.

"You nearly widowed her! I haven't been beaten so badly since that fight in the arena."

"Excuse me," the count said. "Work? Convince her?"

They stopped and looked at the count guiltily. "Well," Logan said, "Kylar said Serah really did love me and she only needed to be reminded, and . . ." he trailed off.

"Kylar, are you telling me your fight was staged? You made a fool of yourself in public, deceived my daughter, and traded her affections like a cheap trinket?"

"That's not exactly . . ." He couldn't match the count's stare. "Yes, sir."

"And you dragged Logan into this? Logan, who ought to know better?" the count asked.

"Yes, sir," Kylar said. At least Logan was looking as pained as he felt.

The count looked from one of them to the other, then broke into a grin. "God bless you!" he said, sweeping Kylar into a hug.

After he released Kylar, Count Drake turned. There were tears in his eyes as he gripped Logan's forearms, "And God bless you. Son."

Lord General Agon stormed into the castle, flanked by his bodyguards. The day had already been long, and the sun had only been up three hours.

Seeing the look on his face, the men guarding doors in the castle made sure he didn't have to wait for them to open. Servants quickly disappeared out of the halls.

Walking into the audience chamber, he passed a cloaked man coming out who seemed vaguely familiar, but the man had his hood up and his face was invisible. One of the king's spies, no doubt. Agon didn't have time for him.

None of the news was good. The Gyres were the foremost family in the realm. To have their murder come on the same night the prince was killed was too much to bear. Agon had liked the prince, but the Gyres had been his friends. And what he'd seen at their estate, he wouldn't wish on his worst enemy. The pieces weren't fitting.

This had all the marks of a move, a big move, a play

for the throne. But why this way? Killing the prince shook everything, of course, but killing the Gyres' servants and Lady Gyre did nothing politically. Did it? As of today, his birthday, Logan Gyre became the Gyre in his father's absence. If you wanted to wipe out a family, you started with the heirs, not everyone else, and unless the news was still en route, both Gyre heirs were still alive.

The prince's death wasn't only a terrible blow to the Gunder line, it was an enormous scandal. The king's affairs had been ignored, but finding the prince dead after apparently having had relations with the king's mistress would shed all sorts of unflattering light on the entire Gunder line. The assassination, if it were such, wasn't just a tragedy. It was a horror and an embarrassment.

The lord general wondered whether the horror or the embarrassment would be foremost on the king's mind. What would the queen do?

He approached the throne and climbed the stairs. The usual men were there, talking with the king. Agon trusted none of them.

"Out," he roared. "All of you, out!"

"Excuse me," Fergund Sa'fasti said. "But as the king's chief—"

"OUT!" Agon bellowed in his face.

The mage shrank and joined the men streaming out of the room. Agon motioned to his bodyguards to step outside, too.

The king didn't even look up. At length, he said, "I'm ruined, Brant. What will history say about me?"

That you were weak, ineffectual, selfish, and immoral. "Sire, we have more pressing matters."

"Everyone's talking about it, Brant. My son—she murdered my boy—" the king started weeping.

So the man is capable of thinking of others. If only he'd show his humanity more often.

"Your Highness, the duchess didn't kill your son."

"What?" the king looked up at Agon through bleary eyes.

"Sire, it was a wetboy."

"I don't care who actually did it, Brant! Trudana was behind it. Trudana and Logan Gyre."

"Logan Gyre? What are you talking about?"

"You think you're the only person I have working on this, Brant? My spies have already told me. Logan was behind it all. That bitch Trudana just cooperated. I've already sent men to arrest him."

Agon reeled. It couldn't be. In fact, he was sure it wasn't. "Why would Logan do such a thing?" he asked. "Logan was one of your son's best friends. He's isn't ambitious in the least. By the gods, he just got engaged to Serah Drake. A count's daughter!"

"It didn't have anything to do with power or ambition, Brant. It was jealousy. Logan felt that my son had totally humiliated him over some trivial matter. You know how boys get. It's just like the Gyres to covet our every success. Besides, I have witnesses who heard Logan threaten him."

It was all rattling together, the pieces spinning and falling into place. Kylar Stern, the false noble, the wetboy, was a close friend of Logan's. In a fit of rage, Logan hired Kylar to kill the prince. It all fit—except that it was Logan. Agon knew him, and he didn't believe it.

"Which wetboy did they hire, Brant?" the king asked.

"It was Kylar Stern," Agon said.

The king snorted. "Huh. The gods must be with me for once."

"Sire?"

"I just hired Hu Gibbet's apprentice to go kill him, a girl wetboy, if you can believe it. Kylar is Blint's apprentice. Or was. He's probably dead by now."

Kylar is Blint's apprentice? The picture that had been slowly spinning together burst apart. The king had hired Blint! Blint's apprentice wouldn't have killed his employer's son. Would he?

The name Hu Gibbet had been carved into the bodies at the Gyre estate. Of course, only a fool would carve his own name onto such a massacre. But from his hours at the estate, Agon was sure that all the murders had been the work of a single man. He could think of no one who could kill so many people except a wetboy, and the style certainly fit what he had heard of Hu Gibbet. He couldn't imagine Durzo Blint mutilating bodies. Blint would consider it unprofessional.

Hu Gibbet would only sign his name if he thought the authorities would never have a chance to come after him. The king said the prince's murder didn't have anything to do with power, but this was Cenaria. Everything had to do with power.

If Durzo Blint's apprentice really had killed the prince, why would he have left a witness? Blint's apprentice would be as professional as Blint himself. A witness was a loose end that was easy to tie up.

It was all about power.

Agon scowled. "Has there been any word from our garrison at Screaming Winds?"

"No."

"So the Khalidoran army is at least four days away. What are you planning to do about the festival tonight?"

"I'm not going to celebrate Midsummer's on the day after my son's death."

The lord general had a sinking feeling. "My king, I think perhaps you should."

"I will not host a party for my boy's murderers." The king's eyes flashed, and he looked less like a petulant child and more like a king than Agon had ever seen. "I have to do something!" the king said. "Everyone will think . . ." He went on, but Agon ignored him.

Everyone will think. That was the key. *What will everyone think?*

The prince was dead, killed in a shameful way either by the king's mistress or by a wetboy. The beloved Gyres were dead or imprisoned. Agon suspected now that an assassin had probably made his way into Screaming Winds and killed Regnus as well. It wouldn't make sense to leave him alive. Not when someone was going to such pains to set plans in motion.

Everyone will think that the king ordered his own son killed in a jealous rage, and that to get back at his unfaithful mistress he framed her.

With the right rumors, everyone's bewilderment over why the Gyres had been murdered could be turned, too. People would connect all the murders, but how?

The Gyres were next in line for the throne after the Gunders, though the family had never challenged the king. The king, weak and jealous, could be portrayed as paranoid all too easily. And the Gyres were far more respected than the Gunders. Lord Gyre's faithful service would be seen as being rewarded with treachery and murder.

Logan—the new Lord Gyre—had been seized by the king, and the king's natural inclination would be to keep him in prison. But Logan was known to be absolutely moral, without ambitions. For the gods' sakes, he was betrothed to a lowly Drake!

So if the king were to die, who would succeed him?

The vastly popular Logan Gyre would be in prison, where he could easily be killed. The king's son was dead. His eldest daughter was fifteen, the others even younger, too young to hold the throne in a nation at war. His wife Nalia might try to take the throne, but the king had feared her and marginalized her as much as he could, and she seemed content to stay out of politics. The Jadwins were finished after their part in the scandal. That left the kingdom's two other duchies. Either Duke Graesin or Duke Wesseros, the queen's father, could make a grab for power. But the queen's brother, Havrin, was out of the country, so he seemed an unlikely usurper. Duke Graesin was feeble. Any of a dozen lesser families might try for the throne.

But no one could hold it. It would be a civil war in which the four main parties were equally matched. Civil war of a kind far worse than the civil war that Regnus had feared ten years ago when he allowed Aleine to take the throne.

Where did that leave the other players he'd been worried about so much recently? Where did the Sa'kagé and Khalidor fit? If the price were right, Khalidor could buy the Sa'kagé's help.

And then all the pieces snapped together for him at once.

Lord General Agon swore loudly. He cursed so rarely that the king stopped in midsentence. Aleine looked at Agon's face, and whatever he read there made him afraid.

"What is it? What is it, Brant?"

All these years, he and the king had been so focused on Khalidor that they'd never thought of a threat coming from within. Khalidor was taking out the entire line of succession, and manipulating the king into helping. Once all the heirs who were both legitimate and powerful were eliminated, Khalidor would kill the king. They would act quickly, before he could establish a new line of succession, before he could consolidate power or mend the relationships he was about break. Then they could watch the chaos, and march when they pleased.

"Your Highness, you must listen. This is the prelude to a coup. We may only have days. If it starts, all our preparations against Khalidor will be useless. And you'll be the first to die."

The king's face was painted with fear. "I'm listening," he said.

44

After congratulating Logan a few more times, Kylar had excused himself to let the young duke speak with his father-in-law-to-be. Serah was in the back of the house getting changed, and they had agreed that she probably shouldn't see Logan and Kylar being friendly until after the wedding.

"I'll understand if I'm not invited," Kylar had said. "But if you ever do tell her, I'll expect an apology. Congratulations."

He climbed up the stairs to his room, pitched his tunic in a corner, and stared into the looking glass. "And congratulations to you. Your master is going to kill you and all the women in your life hate you."

Next to the mirror, he noticed a bundle of letters bound together with a ribbon. He picked it up. Scrawled on a scrap of paper in Blint's hand was a note: "Since you've crossed the line, I guess there's no reason to hide these from you anymore."

What? Kylar untied the ribbon and read the first letter. It had been written by a child, all big letters and disconnected thoughts: "Thank you so ~~mutch~~. much. I love it here. You are great. It is my birthday today. I love you. -Elene" An adult had written below that. "Sorry, Count Drake, she overheard us talking about her lord benefactor. She's been wanting to write this letter since we started teaching her how to write. She wouldn't let go of the idea once she got aholt of it. Tell us if we shouldn't let her write no more. -Humbly Yours, Gare Cromwyll."

Kylar was spellbound. There was a letter for each year, each getting longer, the handwriting better. He felt like he was watching Elene grow up before his eyes. She, too, had changed her name, but there was no denial in her of what she had been, no divorce from her previous weakness and vulnerability.

When she was fifteen, she wrote, "Pol asked if I get mad because my face got cut up. He said it's not fair. I said it's not fair that I got out of the Warrens while so many others never did. Look at everything I've got! And it's all because of you. . . ."

Kylar had to flip through the letters, just skimming them. He was living on borrowed time. Sooner or later word would arrive about the prince's death. And damn! the girl could write a lot. He flipped to the last letter. It was dated just a few days ago.

"You don't know what you've done for me. I've told you about all the ways your money has saved my family, especially when my adoptive father died, but you've done more than that. Just knowing that somewhere out there, there's a young lord who cares about me (me! a slaveborn girl with a scarred face!) has made all the difference. You've made me feel special. Pol proposed to me last week." Kylar had a sudden impulse to find this Pol and kick his ass. "I would have said yes, even though I hate his temper and . . . other things, too. The point is, just that you're out there caring about me makes me believe that I'm worth more than a lousy marriage to the first man who will propose to a scarred girl. It gives me faith that the God has something better for me." *Oh, she's a God person. Great.* So that was how she knew the Drakes. "Thank you. And sorry about my last letter, I'm totally mortified by what I wrote. Please ignore everything I said."

Huh? Kylar turned back to the last letter and couldn't help grinning. Elene had been deep in the throes of full-blown sixteen-year-old–girl romanticism. "I think I'm in love with you. In fact, I'm sure of it. Last year when I went to Count Drake's to drop off my letter—mother *finally* lets me do a few things by myself—I think I saw you. Maybe it wasn't you. But it could have been you. There's this boy there, a young lord like you. He's so handsome and they totally love him. I mean, you can just tell how much everyone thinks of him, even Count Drake. I mean, I know he's not really you because he's not rich like you are. Because his family is poor, he lives with the Drakes . . . " Kylar's breath caught. Elene had seen him. She had seen him a year ago and she thought he was handsome. She thought he was handsome? " . . . but what does money matter when you have love?"

There were . . . *no* . . . yes, there were tear splotches on the page.

Well, Kylar had grown up around three girls. It didn't totally surprise him. He just wondered when Elene had started crying. "So since you're the strong silent type, and you never write back to my letters, I've decided I'm going to call you Kylar. ~~I suppose you might be fat and ugly and have a big nose and . . .~~ I am SO sorry. I should start over, but mother says I already use too much paper as it is. I'm sorry. I am a total brat. But can't you write back to me even once? Have Count Drake give it to me next year when I drop off my letter? Pol says I'm not infatuated with a man, I'm infatuated with a bag of money." Elene didn't know anything about him, but hey, she'd been barely sixteen, and Kylar still wanted to kick Pol's ass. "But I'm not. And it's not infatuation. I love you, Kylar."

A chill washed through him at those words. How he wanted to hear those words! How he wanted to hear them from *her.* And here they were. Here they were in knots and knots of his duplicity. She said those words to him, not thinking he was he, not knowing Count Drake gave her letters to Durzo, not knowing Kylar really was her young benefactor, not knowing Kylar was really Azoth, not knowing Kylar was a killer, not knowing that for that one time she'd seen him that he had seen her hundreds of times: twice every week, whenever he could make it, in the market off Sidlin Way. He'd watched her grow up in that market, told himself a thousand times that next week he wouldn't go and try to catch a glimpse of her, and always succumbed. He'd watched from afar and come to have his own infatuation, hadn't he? He'd told himself that she was just forbidden fruit, that that was all that appealed to him about her. He'd told himself he just wanted to see that she was well. When that didn't work, he told himself that it would pass.

He was twenty years old now, and he was still waiting for it to pass. His sudden hope—she'd been infatuated with him!—hit reality like Gandian porcelain hitting the floor. The delicate tracery of thin possibilities smashed. Now the stricken look on her face yesterday made more sense. The revelations that could have been so poignant for her—I am Kylar and Azoth and your young lord and I love you, too!—had hit her like a sledge hammer instead. I am Kylar and Azoth and your young lord . . . and a murderer. Help me. Give me your trust so I can betray it.

There wasn't time for self-pity, and Kylar had already indulged in too much of it. He'd left behind a witness who knew he was a wetboy and who knew he was Kylar Stern, and who believed him guilty of stealing the Globe of Edges, if not worse. So he'd quite possibly thrown away an identity he'd spent ten years building for a little ball that he hadn't even kept.

The buckets of hot water that the maid usually put in his room in the morning were empty. For some reason, that set him off. He felt his eyes getting hot, and tears threatening. It was so ridiculous, he almost laughed. Those empty buckets were the smallest inconvenience, but it was like the gods or Drake's One God wanted to crush him. Everything that could go wrong had.

Master Blint was going to kill him. The woman he was trading his life to save hated him. Even Serah Drake, who had been unsure about whether she loved him or Logan just last night now hated him. The worst part of it was that it was all his fault. Everything that had gone wrong had gone wrong because of decisions he had made.

Well, at least the empty buckets weren't his fault. Kylar grabbed the buckets and walked down the hall. He ran into the maid coming up the stairs with two buckets full of steaming water.

"Hello," he said. He didn't recognize her, but she was prettier than most of the girls Mistress Bronwyn hired.

"Hello I'm so sorry I'm late it's my first day and I don't know where to find everything I'm really sorry," she said. She squeezed past him and Kylar couldn't help but notice her large breasts gliding across his bare chest. She disappeared into his room and he followed.

"I can take those if you—"

"You aren't mad, are you?" she asked. "Please don't tell Count Drake or Mistress Bronwyn that I was late I don't think she likes me and if I mess up on my first day I'm sure she'll throw me out and I need this job ever so bad sir." She had set down the buckets, and she was wringing her hands.

"Whoa," Kylar said. "Relax. I'm not mad. I'm Kylar." He extended a hand and a smile.

She seemed to warm instantly. She smiled and took his hand. Her eyes flicked briefly over his bare chest and stomach. Briefly, but appreciatively. "Hello. I'm Viridiana."

The porter showed a handsome Ladeshian man into the den. Logan had stepped out to grab something to eat from the kitchen, so Count Drake was alone. "Sir," the porter said, "he insisted that he must deliver a message in person."

"Very well. Thank you," Count Drake said.

The Ladeshian had such presence that it seemed odd for him to be acting as a messenger. He looked rather like a courtier or a bard. He was holding something in his hand that took all Count Drake's attention away from the man. It was an arrow; its entire length, including steel head and feathers, had been painted a glossy red the color of fresh blood.

As soon as the porter stepped out, the man said, "Good morning, my lord. I wish our meeting could be under different circumstances, but I'm afraid my message is quite important. This comes from Durzo Blint. He said, 'If he's still alive, give this to the boy and tell him to meet me for dinner at the Tipsy Tart.'" The man bowed and presented the red arrow to the count.

From the doorway, Logan laughed. "'If he's still alive'? I guess one of Kylar's friends saw me coming here this morning, huh?"

Count Drake chuckled. "I'm sure you scared *everyone* who saw you." He turned to the messenger. "I'll give it to him, thank you."

"My lord," the Ladeshian said, turning to Logan. "We mourn your loss." He bowed again and walked out.

Logan shook his head. "Was that a bachelor joke?"

"I don't know. I visited Ladesh once, and I never did understand their humor. Maybe I should take this upstairs."

"Here I thought we were about to have the big father-son dialectic about marital intimacies."

Count Drake smiled. "You put it so primly."

"Serah's pretty prim," Logan said.

"Believe me, there's nothing prim about marital intimacies, Logan." Count Drake looked at the arrow in his hand and put it aside. "Well, the first thing you have to understand about lovemaking is . . ."

Viridiana rubbed her shoulder and said, "It's so nice to see someone nice I thought this place was going to be awful to work at after how mean Mistress Bronwyn was you don't mind do you?"

"No, not at all," Kylar said, not really sure what he was not minding, but sure that he wasn't supposed to.

As if it were the most natural thing in the world, Viridiana untied the laces of her bodice, which Kylar had already noticed was unusually tight. "Oh, that's better," she said, drawing a deep breath. She closed and locked the door and then walked over to the buckets, peeling off her bodice and dropping it.

"Um," Kylar said. Then Viridiana bent over to pick up the water buckets again.

She must have had six feet of cleavage, because Kylar was totally lost in it. His mouth opened, but no words came out. It was with an unseemly amount of effort that he pulled his eyes up. Viridiana was watching him, and even as his face got hot, he saw that she was anything but displeased. With a deft twist, she released her tightly bound hair, and it cascaded around her face in long curls. "Are you ready for your bath, my lord?"

"No! I mean—I mean—"

"You want to bathe *after*," she said, walking forward. She reached behind her back and started opening buttons.

After? Kylar stepped back, but his resistance was crumbling. *Why not? What the hell have I been waiting for? For Elene?* Viridiana filled his vision, full lips, gorgeous hair that he could practically feel already in his fingertips, on his chest. Those breasts. Those hips. And she wanted him. It would be sex, just sex, not lovemaking. Not some grand expression of romance and commitment. Just passion. Simpler. More like Momma K's version of things.

Less like Count Drake's version. But damn. Her body was more persuasive than a room full of scholars.

His calves hit his bed and he almost fell. "I, I don't really feel very comf—"

Her hand came up to his chest, and then she slammed it into him. He was falling back as her other hand came up from behind her dress in a glimmering metallic arc.

By the time his back hit the bed, she was straddling him, her knees pinning his arms to his sides, one hand grabbing his hair, the other pressing the knife to his neck.

"Comfortable?" she asked, finishing his sentence. She wasn't kidding with the knife; it was pressed against the side of his neck just at the point where a little pressure would break the skin, and it was poised over an artery. As his lungs filled with gasps of air, he had to try not to move his neck.

"Ah, shit," he said. "You're Hu Gibbet's apprentice, Vi. Viridiana, Vi, how'd I miss it?"

She smiled joylessly. "Who're you working for? The prince was my deader."

"Seriously. How embarrassing. To be taken in by another wetboy. Hmm. Or are you a wetgirl?"

"Not the way you're hoping." She ground her hips against him and he blushed.

She pinched his cheek. "You aren't too ugly, you know. It'll be a shame to kill you."

"The shame's all mine, I assure you."

"Don't feel bad," she said. "Part of my Talent is a glamour. It's to your credit you weren't actually drooling."

"You mean those are an illus—"

"Move your hands and die," she said. "The body's real, thanks."

"I should say thank you, but this knife at my throat is muting my appreciation some."

"If you're trying to charm your way out of this, you need practice. Who're you working for?"

"You're working for the king," Kylar said. "Aren't you?"

"Backbone," she said. "I like that."

"Wetting myself would be awfully messy for both of us," Kylar said. She chuckled and he smiled as charmingly as he could. "Was that better?"

"Better. I'll give you one for effort. I took this job from the king. He was a little peeved that you killed his son. So I take his money, but I take my orders from Roth. Last chance now," she pressed the knife a little further into his skin and he had to lean his head as far to the side as he could to keep it from cutting him.

"Maybe you can appreciate my dilemma," Kylar said, straining his neck. "If I don't answer, you'll kill me painfully but it will take a while. If I do answer, you'll kill me quickly but soon."

"Or you can try to string this out for as long as you can and hope someone saves you. You're smart. I suppose you'd have to be. We've all been curious why Blint would choose an apprentice without the Talent. I guess smart wins it."

"You all? You've been taking bets on me? Wait, they say I don't have the Talent?"

"Like they say, there are no secrets worth knowing in the Sa'kagé," Vi said. "So you aren't going to tell me who you were working for, are you? Probably just another one sent by Roth. When he wants a job done, he makes sure it gets done. There's even a rumor he got Lady Jadwin to do it, but I know a wetboy's work when I see it."

"You're kind of chatty, aren't you?" Kylar said.

If he had a hand free, he would have slapped himself. *Note: when attempting to buy time, do not criticize the prolixity of your captor.*

Her beautiful face turned ugly for half a second, and Kylar saw the Hu Gibbet in her. Then she smiled, but Hu didn't leave her eyes. "In the next life," she said. "Work on that charm."

The next feeling would be the glide of a knife, the flesh of his neck parting, warmth. Kylar's muscles bunched with need and desperation.

There was a knock on the door. "Kylar?" the count said. Vi flinched and turned her head.

Kylar threw his head to the side and bucked, trying to throw her off. Or that's what he told his body to do. Instead, he felt energy pouring through him like lightning on a leash. A brief euphoria, power swelling through him, well-being as if he'd been sick his entire life and now felt health for the first time. It was the Talent that Durzo had always said he had, and now it was his.

Vi flew into the air, but she held onto Kylar's hair and one of her legs got tangled with one of his. So instead of flying off him, she flew up and then crashed back down on top him. She tried to slash him, but both of his hands were up now, and he caught both of her arms and rolled.

They fell off the bed and he landed on her. She grunted and raised a knee between his legs. It was like the sun exploding in his pants. He groaned and it was all he could do not to let go of her hands as she rolled on top of him.

"Kylar?" the count shouted through the door. "Do you have a lady in there?"

I wouldn't call her a lady. Kylar's stones hurt so bad, he could barely move, much less fight. "Help!"

"You're pathetic," she said.

He could only grunt.

She launched herself off of him. He struggled to his feet as the door burst open, but he was too slow. She was already throwing her knife at Count Drake.

The count threw himself to the side, and the knife sailed past him harmlessly. Instantly, he had a throwing knife in his own hand, but he hesitated. Vi saw his hand raised and leaped for the window.

Kylar grabbed the knife from the count's hand and threw it as Vi disappeared through the window. He thought he saw it sink into her shoulder. He grabbed the sword that was secreted under his bed, but when he looked out the window, she was gone.

The count looked shaken. He was holding a red arrow in his other hand. "I hesitated," he said. From anyone else, it would have been a concession of defeat, but Count Drake sounded victorious. "After all these years, I wondered, but it's true. I really have changed. Thank you, God."

Kylar looked at him strangely. "What are you talking about?"

"Kylar, we have to talk."

45

I'll be dead in a day or two, so please pay attention, Jarl," Momma K said.

Jarl hesitated for a moment, and then sipped the ootai she'd poured him.

Damn, but the boy can be cold. But then, that was why she was having this talk with him, rather than with anyone else. "Tomorrow or the next day, Kylar or Durzo will come here and kill me," she said. "Because I sent Kylar to kill a man he thought was Hu Gibbet, but actually was Durzo, disguised as Hu. Whichever one lived through their fight now knows that I lied, and that I betrayed them both. I know that you were once friends with Kylar, Jarl—"

"I still am."

"Fine. I wasn't going to ask you to avenge me. I'm ready for justice. Life from here is just a series of disappointments anyway." Was that pity in the boy's eyes? She thought it was, but she didn't care. He'd understand if he lived to be this old.

"What can I do to help you, Momma K?"

"I don't want you to help me. Things are happening fast, Jarl. Maybe too fast. Roth's making a play at becoming Shinga. I suspect we'll be hearing the sad news that Pon Dradin is dead any time now."

"You're not going to warn him? You're just going to let Roth kill him?"

"Two reasons, Jarl. Knowing either of them could cost you your life. Are you ready to be a player on this stage?"

He scowled, actually thought about it, and then nodded.

"First, I'm going to let Pon Dradin die because I've been compromised. Roth blackmailed me into betraying Durzo and Kylar. I won't share how. I've been humiliated enough. All that matters is that Roth owns me. I can't oppose him in any way that he might detect or suspect or it will cost me something I value more than my life. So I'm going to die. I want you to replace me."

"You want me to take your seat on the Nine?"

She smiled into her *ootai*. "I was never just the Mistress of Pleasures, Jarl. I've been the Shinga for nineteen years." She had some satisfaction in the way her unflappable protégé's eyes widened. He sank back in his chair.

"Gods," he said. "That explains a few things."

She laughed, and for what felt like the first time in years, she really felt like laughing. If exposing your throat always felt like this, she thought she understood for the first time why Durzo had loved the danger in his work. It made you appreciate being alive, standing this close to death.

"Tell me how it works," he said.

It was what she would have said in his place. She

would have accepted what the Shinga had said about her death and immediately started looking for how it would affect her, rather than expressing any sorrow that the Shinga would be dead. Or perhaps, in Jarl's place, she would have given some moue of sorrow that her mistress would die, but it would have been a lie. Jarl gave no such pretense, and maybe she could respect him for that. He'd learned her lessons well. But it still hurt.

"I'm sorry," he said. He sounded like he really meant it. Maybe he did. Or maybe he was just sorry that she was sinking into such softness that at the approach of her death she who had taught him how to manipulate his own pities and loves should want him to do that toward her. She couldn't tell. Jarl was what she had made him to be. It was worse than looking in a mirror.

"Everyone in the Sa'kagé knows who their boss is. The smarter ones know who their representative on the Nine is. Of course, the Shinga's identity is an open secret, which means not a secret at all. Put that together, and if you pool a few thieves and whores, you can figure out the entire power structure of the Sa'kagé. That's been fine for the last fourteen years, because things have been so stable."

"Was that stability because of your leadership, or just luck?" Jarl asked.

"My leadership," she said honestly. "I had the last king killed and put Aleine on the throne, so we haven't had pressure from above, and I've handled all the pressures from within. But the normal state of any Sa'kagé is upheaval, Jarl. Thieves and murderers and cutpurses and whores don't tend to stay united. Assassinations are common. During your life it's been far more peaceful than ever before.

"The first five years I was Shinga, we lost eight 'Shingas.' Six were assassinations from outside. Two I had to have killed myself because they tried to take my power. Only two seats on the Nine remained unchanged. For the last fourteen years, Pon Dradin has been able to indulge his vices freely so long as he attended the meetings and kept his mouth shut and didn't step out of line. I never expected him to last so long."

"So only the Nine know who's really the Shinga?"

"And the wetboys, but they take a magically binding oath of service. The system does have its drawbacks. Pon is nearly as rich as I am just from kickbacks and bribes, and every new member of the Nine finds out that he's been sucking the wrong toes for however long it took to climb the ranks. It irritates some of them mightily, but it also keeps some people off the Nine who don't belong there. Best of all, it's kept me alive and in power."

"What does Roth mean to this?"

"Roth has just joined the Nine. He isn't in on the secret. That's why Pon will die sometime today or tomorrow. Roth thinks killing him will make him Shinga. But that actually exposes the greatest flaw in all my secrecy: if only eight people know who the real Shinga is, Roth only has to convince those eight that he is the Shinga now."

"If the rest of the Nine are so afraid of him, how do I take his power?" Jarl asked.

Momma K smiled. "Exactly that. You take it. I won't leave you defenseless, of course." She reached into her desk and pulled out a small book. "My spies. I hope I don't need to tell you that the longer it is before you burn this book, the less your life is worth."

He took the book. "I'll memorize it immediately."

She leaned back in her chair. "He's in a strong position, Jarl. People are terrified of him."

"So that's everything?" Jarl asked.

"You'll forgive me if I don't tell you where all my riches are stored. An old woman has to protect herself, just in case I live through this. Besides, if I die, you'll have plenty of time to find it all."

"Can I ask your advice?" he asked. She nodded. "I followed the men you asked about," Jarl said.

Momma K nodded. She didn't prod Jarl with questions. They'd worked together for long enough that she knew he would tell her everything.

"They were definitely wytches. They attempted an ambush on Regnus Gyre with a small retinue north of the city. Most of his men were wiped out, and all of them would have been except that he had a mage with him."

Momma K raised an eyebrow.

"I was viewing them from a distance, but Regnus and the mage quarreled afterward and rode separate directions. My guess was that Lord Gyre didn't know his man was a mage."

"This mage defeated three wytches?"

"Everything spectacular came from the wytches, but when the smoke cleared—and I mean that literally—he was the only one standing. The man fought with his wits. He stalled two of the wytches until Lord Gyre's soldiers could cut them down. He made a horse trample the third. I don't understand magic, so maybe there was more I didn't see, but that was what it looked like."

"Go on."

"Lord Gyre had only one man left after he and the mage quarreled. They took a circuitous route through the city and arrived at his manse after midnight. You've heard what was there?"

"Twenty-eight dead. Hu Gibbet was given free rein."

"Roth's orders?" Jarl asked.

She nodded. "Unfortunately, the wetboys' oath does have a number of loop holes."

"It was horrific. Anyway, Lord Gyre persuaded the men who came to arrest him to join him instead, and they are now hiding at a cousin's house, trying to quietly gather as much support as they can. The mage is Sethi, first name Solon. I couldn't find anything else yet. As of half an hour ago, he was staying at the White Crane."

"You never disappoint, Jarl."

He was about to ask a question when there was a knock on the door. A maid came in and handed a slip of paper to Momma K. She handed it to Jarl. "The cipher's in the front of your book."

In a minute, he had it decoded. "Pon Dradin's dead." Jarl looked up at her. "What do I do now?"

"That, my apprentice," she said. "Is your problem."

"Kylar, I want to talk about your future."

This should be brief.

Count Drake pulled his pince nez from his vest pocket and didn't put them on. He just waved them as he spoke. "I've got a proposal for you, Kylar. I've been thinking about this a lot, and Kylar, you're not cut out to be a wetboy. No, listen to me, I want to give you a way out, son. Kylar, I want you to marry Ilena."

"Sir?"

"I know it seems abrupt, but I want you to think about it."

"Sir, she's only fifteen."

"Oh, I don't mean now. What I propose is that, well, Kylar, that you get betrothed. Ilena's been infatuated with you for years, and I propose that we give it a couple of years to see if anything comes of it, while you're . . . well, while you're learning my business."

"I'm not sure I understand, sir. In fact, I'm sure I don't understand."

The count slapped his pince nez against his hand. "Kylar, I want you to—I want to give the chance to leave the life you're in. Learn my business and take it over for yourself someday. I've spoken with the queen, and with her permission, I've found out that we could transfer my title to you. You'd be a count, Kylar. It's nothing special, I know, but it would make you legitimate. You could be what you've been pretending all these years."

Kylar's mouth dropped open. "Transfer your title? What do you mean, *transfer* it?"

"Oh, Kylar, the title hasn't done me any good anyway. Bah! I don't have any sons to pass it on to anyway. You need it and I don't. Anyway, I want to do this, even if the whole betrothal with Ilena doesn't appeal with you. This would give you time, Kylar. Time to figure out what you want to do with your life. It cuts you free. Free of *them*."

Free. Out of the Sa'kagé. It was the most noble gesture Kylar had ever heard of—and after last night, it was too late.

Kylar looked at the floor and nodded. "It won't work, sir. I'm sorry. Believe me, I'm . . . You've been more than kind to me, far kinder than I deserve. But I don't think that"—he nodded toward the picnic Logan and Serah were sharing—"is for me."

"I know you're planning on leaving, Kylar."

That was the count. Right to it. "Yessir," Kylar said.

"Soon?"

"I meant to be gone already."

"Then maybe the God led me to speak with you now. Durzo told you not to listen to my preaching, I suppose?" Count Drake was looking out the window, but his voice was aggrieved.

"He said if I believed you, it'd get me killed."

"A fair enough statement, I suppose," Count Drake said. He turned and faced Kylar. "He used to work for me, you know."

"Excuse me? Durzo?"

That brought a small smile.

"Before he was a wetboy?" Kylar could hardly imagine that there had been a time before Durzo Blint was a wetboy, though he supposed there must have been.

The count shook his head. "No. He used to kill people for me. That's how we know each other. That's how he knew he could trust me with you. Durzo doesn't have much of a social life outside his work, you know."

"You? You ordered kills?"

"Not so loud. My wife knows, but there's no need to frighten the maids. I've tried to not preach at you with words, but rather let my life stand testimony to what I know, Kylar. But maybe I've erred in that. A saint once said, 'Preach at all times. When necessary, use words.' Can I take a minute of your time?"

Some part of him wanted to say no. Not only was it awkward to hear someone you respect try to sell you something that you knew you weren't going to buy, but Kylar was living on borrowed time. It seemed that at any minute news would arrive accusing Kylar of last night's theft, and this whole pretty picture would pop like a bubble. Logan would know him for what he was. Serah would have another chance to berate him. The count would get that disappointed look on his face that cut to the bone. Kylar knew the count would be disappointed in him, would never really know how much good Kylar had done last night and at what cost to himself. The count would be disappointed regardless of what Kylar did now, but Kylar didn't have to see it.

"Of course," he said. It was the right answer. This man had raised Kylar, had allowed him to live a life impossible for a guild rat. Kylar owed it to him.

"My father inherited a large fortune from his father, enough that he mingled with Gordin Graesin, Brand Wesseros, and Darvin Makell—I guess you wouldn't know about the Makells, they were wiped out in the Eight Years' War. Anyway, he tried to impress these sons of dukes by throwing money around. Lavish parties, gambling, renting out entire brothels. It didn't help that his own father died while he was still young. Of course, our family was soon in poverty. My father took his own life. So at the age of nineteen, I took control of a house on the brink of ruin. I had a good head for business, but I saw it as beneath me. Like many who have no reason for pride, that very lack of reason for it made me the prouder.

"But certain realities have a way of making themselves felt, and debt is one of them. Not surprisingly, one of my father's debtors had a way that I could make 'easy money.' I started working for the Sa'kagé. The man who recruited me was the Trematir. If he'd been better at his job, he would have only gotten me deeper and deeper in the Sa'kagé's debt, but I soon found out that I understood men and money and the ways they work together better than he did. Strangely enough, I had fewer qualms.

"I put my money into whatever made money. Specialty brothels to cater to any appetite, no matter how depraved. I started gambling dens and brought in experts from around the world to help me better separate my patrons from their money. I funded spice expeditions and bribed guards not to investigate the cargo. When one of my businesses was threatened, I had bashers take care of the problem. The first time they went too far and accidentally killed a man, I was shocked, but he wasn't someone I liked, and it was for my family, and I didn't have to see it, so that made it palatable. When I clashed with the Trematir, it was an easy decision to hire Durzo. I was naive enough that I didn't realize he went to the Shinga immediately to get permission first. They gave it to him, and I became the Sa'kagé Master of Coin."

Kylar was hearing every word, but he couldn't believe it. This couldn't be the Count Drake he had grown up with. Rimbold Drake had been on the Nine?

"I traveled a lot, setting up businesses in other countries with fairly good success, and it was then I had my horrible revelation. Of course, I didn't see the horror in it at the time. I could only see my own brilliance. In four years, I had paid off my family's debts, but now, I saw a way to make real money. I sold the Sa'kagé on the idea. It took us ten years, but we got our people in place and we legalized slavery. It was introduced in a limited form, of course. For convicts and the utterly destitute. People who couldn't care for themselves, we said. Our brothels filled with slave girls whom we no longer had to pay to work. We started the Death Games—another of my bright ideas—and they became a sensation, an obsession. We built the arena, charged the admission, monopolized the food and wine sold, ran the gambling, sometimes stacked the odds. We made money faster than we'd ever imagined possible. I hired Durzo so often that we became friends. Even he wouldn't take all the jobs I offered. He always had his own code. He'd take jobs on the people who were trying to take my business for themselves, but if I wanted someone dead who was just trying to stop me, I had to hire Anders Gurka or Scarred Wrable or Jonus Severing or Hu Gibbet.

"You have to understand with all this, I never considered myself a bad person. I didn't like the Death Games. I never watched, never went in the holds of the slave galleys where men lived and died chained to their oars, never visited the baby farms that sometimes became child brothels, never visited the scenes of Blint's work. I just said words, and money poured in like rain. The funny thing was, I wasn't even ambitious. I was richer than anyone in the kingdom with the exception of some upper nobility, the Shinga, and the king, and I was comfortable with that. I just couldn't stand incompetence. Otherwise, I'm sure the Shinga would have killed me. But she didn't have to, because I wasn't a threat, and Durzo told her that." The count shook his head. "I'm rambling, sorry, but I don't get to tell these stories anymore." He sighed.

"My mistake came when I fell in love with the wrong woman. For some reason, I was attracted to Ulana. Not just attracted, obsessed, and it took me a long time to figure out why. I even avoided her, it was so painful to be in her presence. But I finally figured out that it was because she was so unlike me. You see, Kylar, she was pure. And strangely, she seemed to love me, too. Of course she had no idea what I really was. I did none of my business under my own name, and few of the nobles had any idea of the kind of wealth that was becoming mine. The deeper I sank into the darkness, the more I loved her, and the more my shame grew. How can one love the light and live in darkness?"

The question lanced through Kylar. He felt ashamed.

"She started working on the slavery issue, Kylar, and she decided that she was going to visit the baby farms and the slave galleys and the fighting pits. I couldn't very well let her go alone, so for the first time, I saw my handiwork." The count's eyes grew distant. "Oh Kylar, how she moved among those wretches. In all the stench of human waste and despair and evil, she was a fresh cool breeze, a breath of hope. She was light in the dark places I'd made. I saw a champion pit fighter, a man who'd killed fifty men, weep at her touch.

"I was a man tearing in half. I decided to get out, but like most moral cowards, I didn't want to pay the full price. So I traveled to Seth, where slavery is so different. I came back and in secret helped pass a law that would free the slaves every seven years. The Sa'kagé allowed it to pass but tacked on a provision that made it effectively void. Then one day Ulana, who was then my fiancée, came to my estate, weeping. Her father and mother had been badly hurt in a carriage accident. She thought her mother was dying, and she needed me. At the same time, the Nine were meeting in my parlor because King Davin was on the verge of outlawing slavery again and that, of course, would cost us millions. Do you know whom I sent away, Kylar?"

"You sent away the Nine?" Kylar was aghast. Such an insult would mean death.

"I sent Ulana away."

"Damn. Um, sorry."

"No, that's how I felt. Damned. That's where the God found me, Kylar. I couldn't do it anymore. I was dead inside. I thought it would be the death of me to cut my ties to the Sa'kagé, especially when I realized that it wouldn't be enough to hand over my empire intact to someone who could continue it. Instead, I had to use all my cunning to hand it over to men who would tear it to pieces.

"So that's what I did. I used the money I had made to fund those who would rebuild the good I had destroyed and destroy the obscenities I had built. When I was done, I was penniless, my family was bankrupt, and I had dozens of powerful enemies. I went to Ulana, told her everything, and broke our engagement."

"What did she do?" Kylar asked.

"It broke her heart to learn what I'd been, Kylar, and to learn that she'd known so little of me when she thought she knew everything. It took time, but she forgave me. I couldn't believe that. But she really did. It took me longer to forgive myself, but a year later, after slavery was outlawed once more—in part because of my own efforts against it—we were married. I've had to work hard for the last twenty years. I've often been held back by my old reputation, and sometimes by my new one. You know how most of the nobles look on those of us who actually work. But my money is clean. And the God has been good. My family has enough. My children are a joy to me. Logan has proposed to Serah, and she's said yes. I get to have Logan as a son. How haven't I been blessed? Anyway, I should have told you this long ago. Maybe you already knew some of it through the Sa'kagé."

"No, sir. I had no idea," Kylar said.

"Son, I hope you see now that I do understand. I know what lies the Sa'kagé tells, and I know what it can cost to get out. The God was gracious to me. He didn't make me pay all that I owed, but maybe I had to be willing to pay the full price. That's how repentance is different from regret. I had been sorry about how slavery turned out, but I wasn't willing to take responsibility for it. Once I was, the God could work in me."

"But sir, how are you still alive? I mean, you didn't just leave, you destroyed a business that earned them millions!"

Count Drake smiled. "God, Kylar. The God and Durzo. Durzo likes me. He thinks I'm a fool, but he likes me. He's protected me. He's not a man to cross lightly."

Thanks for the reminder.

"The point is, Kylar, if you want to turn away from what you do, you can. You might miss your work. I imagine that you're excellent, and there is a joy in excellence. You can't pay for all you've done. But you aren't beyond redemption. There's always a way out. And if you're willing to make the sacrifice, the God will give you the chance to save something priceless. But I'm here to tell you, miracles do happen. Like this one," he pointed out the window and shook his head, incredulous. "My daughter, marrying a man as good as Logan. May the God be with them."

Kylar was blinking through tears, so he almost missed the count leaning forward further, looking toward the front gate. His eyes cleared as soon as he saw the soldiers push past the old porter. Kylar was on his feet in a moment, but the soldiers didn't come to the front door. They stopped when they reached Logan and Serah, and the count opened the window to hear the captain as he unrolled a scroll.

"Duke Logan Gyre, you are hereby under arrest for high treason in the murder of Prince Aleine Gunder."

46

Count Drake was out the door in an instant. Kylar hesitated at the very place he'd run into Logan ten years ago and started their friendship with a fistfight. He shouldn't go out. There was no time to think how much the guards knew, but if they thought Logan had been involved in the prince's death, who knew what else they thought? The king must be totally paranoid. Whatever was happening, it was never a good idea to bring yourself to the guards' attention.

But seeing the bewilderment on Logan's face dug into Kylar. He was just standing there as the smaller men disarmed him. He looked like a dog you'd kicked for no reason, eyes wide. Cursing himself for his stupidity, Kylar followed Count Drake.

"I demand an explanation," Count Drake said. Despite his limp, he somehow moved with authority. All eyes turned to him.

"We're, we're making an arrest, sir. I'm afraid that's all I can tell you," the captain said. He was a thick little man with yellow skin and almond eyes, but it seemed to take all of his determination just to stand before the count and not be blown away.

"You're attempting to arrest a duke, and you don't have the authority to do that, Captain Arturian. By the third amendment to the common law in the eighth year of the reign of King Hurol II, the arrest of dukes of the realm must be justified by habeas corpus, two witnesses, and a motive. Incarceration requires two of those three."

Captain Arturian swallowed and seemed to be holding his spine straight only by an act of will. "We, um, habeas corpus is holding the corpse? So I have to bring two witnesses or provide motive before you'll let me arrest the duke?"

"If you have the corpse," Count Drake said.

The man nodded. "We, uh, we do, sir. The prince's body was found last night at the Jadwin estate, and the motive is a matter of . . . uh. It doesn't bear speaking, sir."

"If you attempt to arrest Duke Gyre at my home outside the provisions of the law, as a noble of the land, I have the right and the obligation to protect him with the force of arms."

"We'd slaughter you!" one of the guards said, laughing.

"And if you did, you'd touch off civil war. Is that what you want?" Count Drake asked. The man who'd spoken fell silent, and Vin Arturian went gray. "Either produce a motive that would lead a man of known moral excellence like Duke Gyre to kill one of his best friends, or begone."

"Milord," Captain Arturian said, his eyes downcast. "Forgive me. The motive was jealousy."

For some reason, Kylar's eyes moved to Serah. She still looked stricken by the news, but as the captain grew more awkward, she seemed to shrink into herself, as if she knew what he was going to say next.

"Duke Gyre found out that the prince was having . . . sexual relations with your daughter."

"That's ludicrous!" Logan said. "That's the most ridiculous thing I've ever heard. For godsake, she hasn't even made love with me! Her fiancé! Aleine gets around, but he would never—"

Logan looked at Serah and never finished the sentence. "Serah, you . . . you didn't. Tell me you didn't." It was as if his soul had been stripped naked and all the darts in the world sank into it at once.

Serah keened, a sound of such woe it tore the heart, but none of the men moved. She ran away, back into the house, but they stood transfixed in Logan's pain.

Logan turned to the count. "You knew?"

Rimbold Drake shook his head. "I didn't know who, but she said she'd told you. That all was forgiven."

Logan looked at Kylar.

"The same," Kylar said quietly.

Logan took it like another dart. He struggled for breath. "Captain," he said. "I'll go with you."

The soldier who'd spoken before moved forward at the captain's signal and started putting the manacles on Logan's hands. "Damn, boy," he said quietly, obviously only for Logan's ears, but in the stillness of the yard his words were clearly audible. "You got fucked without even getting fucked first."

It was only the second time Kylar had seen Logan lose his temper, but the last time, he'd been a boy and he hadn't been nearly as powerful as he was now. Maybe a wetboy would have noticed the muscles tensing in Logan's shoulders and arm. Maybe a wetboy would have had the reflexes to dodge, but the guard didn't stand a chance. Logan ripped his hand away before the second manacle clicked shut and hit the guard in the face. Kylar didn't think he'd ever seen anyone hit so hard. Master Blint, with his Talent-strengthened muscles, could probably hit that hard, but he wouldn't have the mass behind the blow that Logan did.

The guard flew backward. Literally. His feet left the ground and he knocked over the two men behind him.

Kylar's Ceuran blade was in his hand before the guards hit the ground, but before he could wade into battle, he felt the count's fingers dig into his arms.

"No!" the count said.

Guards piled onto Logan, who roared.

"No," the count said. "It is better . . ." his face was as pained as Logan's, torn between sorrow and conviction. "It is better to suffer evil than to do evil. You will not kill innocent men in my house."

Logan didn't put up a fight. The men took him down to the ground, put the manacles on him behind his back, put a second set on his legs, and finally stood him up.

"Did the count say your name is Kylar? Kylar Stern?" Captain Arturian asked.

Kylar nodded.

"The crown charges you with treason, membership in the Sa'kagé, accepting payment for murder, and the murder of Prince Aleine Gunder. We have a witness, corpse, and motive, Count Drake. Men, arrest him."

The captain might have been sympathetic, but he wasn't a fool. Kylar had been so caught up in what was happening to Logan that he hadn't noticed the men circle behind him. At the captain's word, he felt two men take hold of his arms.

He swung his arms forward, only hoping to throw the men off balance so he could fall backward between them. But once again his Talent was there like a coiled viper, and he was suddenly stronger than he'd ever been. The men flew forward and crunched together, meeting along the blade of Kylar's sword. If he'd turned the blade, he could have gutted either of them, even through their boiled leather gambesons. Instead, he sheathed the sword—how had he done it that fast?—he was still falling backward from throwing the guards harder than he intended, and the sword was already sheathed.

Turning his fall into a back handspring was child's play. Kylar turned and ran toward a wall on one side of the count's small garden. He jumped to grab the lip of the twelve-foot-high wall, and found the wall approaching instead at the level of his knees. It sent him over the wall in a vicious spin, and only by rolling into a ball and some significant luck was he able to land on the other side without killing himself.

He stood and let the Talent go. There were cries coming from within the walls, but they'd never catch him. Kylar was a wetboy now in truth. He wondered what Blint would say. Kylar had achieved his lifelong dream, and he couldn't have been more miserable.

"How was it?" Agon asked Captain Arturian, as they walked through the halls of the castle toward the Maw.

"It was . . . awful. Absolutely awful, sir. I'd say it ranks with the worst things I've ever done."

"Regrets, captain? They say he killed one of your men."

"If I may be blunt, he rid me of a fool that I couldn't kick out because the man's sister is a baroness. The idiot had it coming. I know it's not my place to say, lord general, but you didn't see Logan's face. He's not guilty. I'd swear it."

"I know. I know, and I'm going to do everything I can to save him." They passed the guards who held the underground gate that separated the tunnels beneath the castle from those of the Maw. The nobles' cells were on the first level. They were small, but in relative terms, luxurious. Agon had Elene placed in one of these cells, though her status didn't afford it. He couldn't bear to have her put any lower, and if the king asked, he'd say that he wanted her kept close for further questioning.

Agon stopped outside Logan's cell. "Vin," he said. "Does he know about his family yet?"

The squat man shook his head. "I'd already lost one man, sir. I didn't know what he would do if we told him."

"Fair enough. Thank you." It wasn't the dismissal Agon would have given to one of his subordinates, but though the lord general's rank was the second only to the king's, the captain of the king's guards wasn't technically under Agon's command. Fortunately, though they weren't friends, they were on good enough terms that Captain Arturian took the cue and excused himself.

It wasn't going to be fun to tell a man who'd been jailed for a murder he didn't commit that his family had been slaughtered, but it was Agon's duty. He always did his duty.

Before he unlocked the door, Agon knocked as if he were coming for a visit. As if they were anywhere else besides the Maw. There was no response.

He opened the door. The nobles' cells were ten feet square, all rock polished smooth to prevent suicides. Each had a bare rock bench that served as a bed, and fresh straw was brought in every week. It was luxury only compared to the rest of the Maw, and even with fresh straw, nothing could erase the rotten-egg stench or the ripe tang of massed humanity in an enclosed space that wafted up from the rest of the cells. Logan looked oblivious. He looked like hell. Tears streamed down his bruised face. He looked up when Agon came in, but his eyes took a long time to focus. He looked lost, his big shoulders slouched, big hands open on his lap, hair askew. He wasn't alone. The queen was seated beside him, holding one of those limply open hands as one would hold a child's.

Bless the woman. She'd come to tell him herself.

King Aleine IX had totally missed with Nalia Wesseros. Nalia could have been one of his greatest allies. *What a queen she would have made for Regnus Gyre.* Instead, she'd accepted being pushed to the fringes of Aleine's Cenaria, even welcomed it, and had done everything she could to mother her four—now three—children. Agon had long suspected that the children were all that kept her alive.

"My queen. My lord," Agon said.

"Pardon me if I don't rise," Logan said.

"None necessary."

"They say that my father is dead, too. Or they say that he did it. That the king sent men to arrest him for killing my mother. What happened?" Logan asked.

"As far as I know, your father is alive. He arrived with only one or two men. He was attacked outside the city. Someone was trying to wipe out all the Gyres but you. Men were sent to arrest him, but not on the king's orders. I haven't found out who did give the orders. Not yet. Those men either fled the city, or they joined your father. I don't know which."

"Lord General, I didn't kill Aleine," Logan said. "He was my friend. Even if he did . . . what they say he did."

"We know. We—the queen and I—don't think you did it."

"He talked to me last night, you know? He knew I was going to propose to Serah. He tried to persuade me not to. He reminded me of the rumors about Serah getting around. He had this crazy idea that I marry Jenine. I thought it was strange, but that he was being magnanimous. It wasn't magnanimity. It was guilt. Damn him!"

Logan looked at the queen. "I'm sorry. I shouldn't talk this way, but I'm so, so angry—and I feel so guilty for it at the same time! I would have forgiven them, Your Majesty. I would have. Gods! Why didn't they just tell me?"

They cried silently together and the queen just squeezed Logan's hand.

After a minute, Logan looked up at Agon. "They say Kylar did it. At Count Drake's, I saw him move. He was fast. Too fast. But are you sure?"

Gods. The boy had just been betrayed by his fiancée and the prince. Now he wanted to know if he'd been betrayed by his best friend as well. Agon didn't know if he would survive it—and he needed him to survive it—but Logan deserved the truth. It wasn't in Agon to give him less. "I'm sure Kylar was upstairs when Aleine died. I'm sure he's a wetboy. I doubt his real name is Kylar or that he's a Stern, but I won't know that for two weeks. We've sent a rider to their estates but it's a week's ride each way.

I can't put everything together in any other way, son, and I've been trying."

"Your being here is a kindness," Logan said. His back straightened. "And I don't want to take that away from you, but I'm guessing that you want something from me or you wouldn't both have come here. Not now. Not so soon."

The queen and the lord general looked at each other. Something passed between them, and the general said, "You're right, Logan. The truth is, the kingdom's in peril. I wish that we could be sensitive to your grief. You know that your father is one of my dearest friends and what happened to your house is more than a tragedy. It's a monstrosity.

"But we have to ask you to put your feelings aside, for a time. We don't know how bad the threat is, but I believe that it's dire. When the king decided to get rid of your father one way or another ten years ago, it was I who suggested Screaming Winds. I knew that your father would make the garrison there a real stronghold, and I believed that Khalidor would invade sooner or later. Perhaps because he did such an excellent job, that invasion hasn't come. Most people want to believe that it won't come, because they know that if the might of Khalidor marches, we don't stand a chance.

"I believe that the prince, your mother, and your servants were the first casualties in a war. A new kind of war that uses assassins instead of armies to gain its will. We can stop armies, we've been preparing for that. Assassins are a different story."

"Begging the queen's pardon," Logan said, "why should I care if the king's head rolls? He's been no friend to the Gyres."

"A fair question," the queen said.

"On a personal level," Agon said, "you should care because if the king dies, you'll either stay in prison forever or you'll be killed. On a national level, if the king dies, there will be civil war. Troops will be called back to the respective houses to which they are loyal, and Khalidor's armies will pour over our borders. Even united, our country couldn't stand against Khalidor's might. Our only strategy has been to make it so costly to take us that the price would be too high. With our armies scattered, we'd be defenseless."

"So you think an assassination attempt is coming?" Logan asked.

"Within days. But Khalidor's plans rest on certain assumptions, Logan. So far, they've been valid assumptions. They knew that you would be arrested. No doubt they've already planted rumors to stir up the people against the king, suggesting that everything that's happened has been his fault or his plan. We have to do something beyond anything Khalidor has considered."

"And what's that?"

The queen said, "Khalidor has hired Hu Gibbet, perhaps the best wetboy in the city. If he wants to kill Aleine, he probably can. The best way to save the king's life is if the taking of it won't gain Khalidor anything. Maybe it's the only way. We have to assure the line of succession. In a time of peace or if she were older, Jenine might take the throne, or I might, but now. . . . That simply wouldn't be possible. Some of the houses would refuse to follow a woman into war."

"Well, what are you supposed to do? Have another son?"

Agon looked queasy. "Sort of."

The queen said, "We need someone who's popular enough to win the people's trust back to the throne, and whose claim to the crown would be beyond dispute."

Logan looked at him and sudden understanding washed over him. Emotions warred on his face. "You don't know what you're asking."

"Yes, I do," the queen said quietly. "Logan, has your father ever spoken of me?"

"Only in terms of highest praise, Your Majesty."

"Your father and I were betrothed, Logan. For ten years, we knew we were going to marry. We fell in love. We named the children we would someday have. The king was dying without heirs, and our marriage was to have secured the throne for House Gyre. Then my father betrayed Regnus and broke his word to your grandfather by marrying me in secret to Aleine Gunder. There were only enough witnesses present to ensure the legality of the marriage. I wasn't even allowed to send a message to your father beforehand. The king lived for another fourteen years, long enough for me to have children, long enough for your father to marry and have you, long enough for your father to take control of House Gyre. Long enough for House Gunder to fabricate some ridiculous history that supposedly gave Aleine the right to be called Aleine IX, as if he were a legitimate king. When King Davin died, your father could have gone to war to take the throne. He could have won it, but he didn't, for my sake and the sake of my children.

"I was sold into a marriage I despised, Logan, to a man I never loved, and for whom I could never make love grow in my breast. I know what it is to be sold for politics. I even know my literal price in the lands and titles my family secured after the king's death." There was iron in her as she spoke, clearly, calmly, every inch the queen. "I still love your father, Logan. We've barely spoken in twenty-five years. He had to marry a Graesin after I married a Gunder, just to keep House Gyre from becoming isolated and wiped out like the Makells were. He accepted a marriage that I've heard had little love in it. So if you think it pleases me to do to you what was done to me, you couldn't be more mistaken."

Logan's father had never spoken of such things, but his mother—it was suddenly so clear—his mother had been reminding Regnus of it for years. Her sidelong comments. Her constant suspicions that Regnus had other lovers, though Logan knew he hadn't. His father's angry remark once that there was only one woman she had any right to envy.

"I have hope that your marriage will not be the agony mine has been," Queen Gunder said.

Logan put his face in his hands. "Your Majesty, words can't express the . . . fury I feel toward Serah. But I gave her father my word that I would marry her."

"The king can legally dissolve such bonds for the good of the realm," Agon said.

"The king can't dissolve my honor!" Logan said. "I swore! And dammit! I still love Serah. I *still* love her. It's all playacting, isn't it? What's the plan, that the king adopt me? That I be his heir until you bear him another son?"

"This *playacting* gets us through a crisis, son," Agon said. "And it keeps your family from being destroyed. You have to stay alive if you want that to happen. It also happens to save you from disgrace and prison, even if we're wrong about the plot."

"Logan," the queen said, her voice again quiet. "It isn't playacting, but we've convinced the king that it is. He is a despicable man, and if it's up to him, he will never let Regnus's son take the throne."

"Your Majesty," Agon interrupted. "Logan doesn't need to—"

"No, Brant. A person ought to know what they're being asked to give." She looked him in the eye, and after a moment, he looked down. She turned to Logan. "My hope has been my children, Logan, and I lay Aleine's death at my husband's feet. If he'd not gotten involved with that Jadwin whore . . ." She blinked her eyes, refusing to let tears fall. "I have given the king all the sons he will have from me. I will not share his bed again. Ever. He will be told that if he seeks to force me to his bed or replace me as queen, we have retained the services of a wetboy to make sure he finds an early grave. The fact is, Logan, if you say yes, you will one day be king."

He said nothing.

"Most men would leap at the chance for such power," Agon said. "Of course, most men make terrible kings. We know you wouldn't ask for this, but you aren't only the right man for it; you're the only man for it."

"Logan was the name Regnus and I had decided on for our first son," the queen said. "I know what I'm asking, Logan. And I'm asking."

47

The game wasn't going well. The pieces were spread out before Dorian like armies. Except that they weren't like armies; they were armies, though in this game, few of the soldiers wore uniforms. Even those who did moved with reluctance. The Fool King shamed the Commander. The Reluctant King was kneeling somewhere at this moment. The Mage in Secret's secret had split him from the King Who Might Have Been. The Shadow that Walks and the Courtesan couldn't decide which side they were on. The Rent Boy was moving fast, but too slow, too slow. The Prince of Rats had marshaled his vermin, and they would rise from the Warrens, a tide of human filth. Even the Rogue Prince and the Blacksmith might play a part, if. . . .

Blast! It was hard enough, just envisioning the pieces as they were. From there, he could often focus on one piece and see the choices it faced: the Commander as a drunk king shouted in his face, the Shadow that Walks as he faced the Apprentice in a honeymoon chamber. But just as he was fixing the pieces in space, setting their relative positions, he'd start seeing one or more at a different time. Seeing where the Blacksmith would be in seventeen years, stooped over a forge, urging his son back to work, didn't do him any good in figuring out how to keep Feir alive until that day.

He went back to work. Now where was the Kidnapped?

Sometimes he felt as if he were but a breath of wind over the field of battle. He could see everything, but the most he could hope to do was blow one or two killing arrows off course. Where is that Mage in Secret? Ah.

"Open the door, quick," Dorian said.

Feir looked up from the little table where he was seated, dragging a whetstone across the face of his sword. They were in a little house they'd rented off Sidlin where Dorian said they would be left alone. Feir rose and opened the door.

A man was just disappearing past it, walking determinedly down the street. His hair and gait were familiar. He must have seen something out of the corner of his eye—of course, the blond mountain that was Feir was hard to miss—because he turned on his heel, his hand dropping to his sword.

"Feir?"

Feir looked almost as surprised as Solon was, so Dorian said, "Both of you, inside."

They came in, Feir giving a customary grumble about how Dorian never told him anything, and Dorian just smiling. *So much to see, so much to know.* It was easy to miss things right under your nose.

"Dorian!" Solon said. He embraced his old friend. "I

ought to wring your neck. Do you know how much trouble your little 'Lord Gyre' bit cost me?"

Dorian laughed. He knew. "Oh, my friend," he said, holding onto Solon's arms. "You did well."

"You look well, too," Feir said. "You were fat when you left. Look at you now. A decade of military service has done you right."

Solon smiled, but the smile faded fast. "Dorian, seriously, I have to know. Did you mean that I needed to come serve Logan, or did you mean Regnus? I thought you'd said Lord Gyre and not Duke Gyre, but when I got here, there were two lords Gyre. Did I do the right thing?"

"Yes, yes. They both needed you, and you saved both of them several times. Some you know, some you don't." Perhaps the most important thing Solon had done was something he would never appreciate: he had encouraged Logan's friendship with Kylar. "But I won't lie to you. Keeping your secret was something I didn't foresee. I thought you would have shared it years ago. Down most paths I see now, Regnus Gyre will lose his life."

"I'm a coward," Solon said.

"Pah," Feir said. "You're many things, Solon, but you're not a coward."

Dorian kept silent, and let his eyes speak empathy. He knew differently. Solon's silence had been cowardice. Dozens of times he'd tried to speak, but he could never summon the courage to risk his friendship with Regnus Gyre. The worst of it was that Regnus would have understood and laughed about it, if he'd heard it from Solon's own lips. But discovering deceit in a friend felt like betrayal to a man who'd had his fiancée sold out from under him to another man.

"Your powers have grown," Solon said.

"Yes, he's truly insufferable now," Feir said.

"I'm surprised the brothers at Sho'cendi let you come here," Solon said.

Dorian and Feir looked at each other.

"You left without permission?" Solon asked.

Silence.

"You left against their direct orders?"

"Worse," Dorian said.

Feir barked a laugh that told Solon he'd been put into another plan of Dorian's that he couldn't believe.

"What did you do?" Solon asked.

"It belonged to us, really. We're the ones who found it again. They didn't have any right," Dorian said.

"You didn't."

Dorian shrugged.

"Where is it?" Solon asked. From the bland looks on their faces, he knew. "You brought it here?!"

Feir walked to the little bed and threw back the blankets. Curoch lay sheathed on the bed. The scabbard was white leather, inlaid with gold Hyrillic script and capped with gold.

"That's not the original scabbard, surely."

"It's work like this that makes me want to never be a sword smith," Feir said. "The scabbard is the original. Woven thick with magic as fine as Gandian silk, and I think all that's just to preserve the leather. It won't stay dirty, won't take a mark. The gold inlay is real, too. Pure gold. Hardened to where it would stand against iron or even steel. If I could figure out that technique alone, my heirs would be rich to the twelfth generation."

"We've barely dared unsheathe the sword, and of course we haven't tried to use it," Dorian said.

"I should hope not," Solon said. "Dorian, why would you bring it here? Have you seen something?"

He shook his head. "Artifacts of such power skew my vision. They themselves and the lusts they invoke are so intense that it fogs my sight."

Suddenly, he was drifting again, but drifting was too gentle a word for it. His vision latched onto Solon and images streamed past him. Impossible visions. Solon against incredible odds. Solon as a white-haired old man, except not old, but—blast, the image disappeared before he could understand it. Solon Solon Solon. Solon dying. Solon killing. Solon on a storm-tossed ship. Solon saving Regnus from a wetboy. Solon killing the king. Solon dooming Cenaria. Solon propelling Dorian into Khalidor. A beautiful woman in a chamber of a hundred portraits of beautiful women. Jenine. Dorian's heart lurched. Garoth Ursuul.

"Dorian? Dorian?" the voice was distant, but Dorian grabbed onto the sound and pulled himself back to it.

He shook himself, gasping as if emerging from a cold lake.

"It's getting worse as you get stronger, isn't it?" Solon asked.

"He trades his mind for the visions," Feir said. "He won't listen to me."

"My sanity isn't necessary for the work I must do," Dorian said simply. "My visions are." The dice were in his hand, not just two dice, a whole handful of dice, each with a dozen faces. *How many twelves can I throw?* He would be throwing blind; he could see that Solon already was thinking he should leave, that no matter how good it was to see his old friends, he had to try to save Regnus Gyre. But Dorian had a feeling. That was the damnable thing. Sometimes it was as logical as a sesch game. Sometimes it was just an itch.

"Anyway, where were we?" he asked, playing the oblivious seer. "Feir doesn't have enough Talent to use Curoch. If he tried, he'd either burn or explode. No offense, friend, you have finer control than either of us. I could use it, but only safely as a meister; my mage powers probably aren't strong enough. Of course using it with the vir would be a total disaster. I don't even know what I'd do. Of us, Solon, you're the only mage in the room, or the country for that matter, who could hope to even hold it without dying, though it would be a near thing. You'd die if you tried to use more than a fraction of its power. Hmm." He gazed into space as if he were suddenly caught by another vision. The line was set.

"Surely you didn't bring it all this way for nothing," Solon said.

Set and sprung.

"No. We had to get it away from the brothers. It was our only chance. If we'd waited until after we returned, they would have known they couldn't trust us. It would have been kept far from us."

"Dorian, you still believe in that one God of yours, don't you?" Solon asked.

"I think he sometimes confuses himself with Him," Feir said. It was uncharacteristically bitter and it struck Dorian deeply. It hurt because it was deserved. He was doing it right now.

"Feir's right," Dorian said. "Solon, I was setting you

up to take the sword. I shouldn't treat you that way. You deserve better and I'm sorry."

"Damn," Solon said. "You knew I was thinking of taking it?"

Dorian nodded. "I don't know if it's the right thing or not. I didn't know you'd walk in our door until a second before you did. With Curoch, everything gets twisted. If you use it, Khalidor may well take it from us. That would be a disaster far greater than losing your friend Regnus, or even losing this entire country."

"The risk is unacceptable," Feir said.

"What good does it do anyone if we don't use it?" Solon said.

"It keeps it out of the hands of the Vürdmeisters!" Feir said. "That's good enough. There's only a handful of mages in the world who could hold Curoch without dying, and you know it. We also know that there are dozens of Vürdmeisters who could. With Curoch in their hands, what could stop them?"

"I have a feeling about this," Dorian said. "Maybe the God is nudging me. I just think it's right. I feel like it's connected to the Guardian of Light."

"I thought you'd given up on those old prophecies," Solon said.

"If you take Curoch, the Guardian will be born in our lifetimes." Even as Dorian said it, he knew it was true. "I've been living so long saying I had faith, but it isn't really faith when you just do what you see, is it? I think the God wants us to take this crazy risk. I think he'll bring good out of it."

Feir threw up his hands. "Dorian, the God is always your out. You run into a wall rationally and you say the

God is speaking to you. It's ridiculous. If this one God of yours created everything like you say, he also gave us reason, right? Why the hell would he make us do something so irrational?"

"I'm right."

"Dorian," Solon said. "Can I really use it?"

"If you use it, everyone in fifty miles will know it. Maybe even the ungifted. You run all the normal risks of drawing too much power, but your upper limit is higher than its lowest threshold. Things are happening too fast for me to see much, but I'm going to tell you this, Solon. The invasion force was headed for Modai." *Until Kylar didn't kill Durzo Blint.* "So they were prepared for a different kind of war. The boats arrive tonight. They have sixty meisters."

"Sixty! That's more than some of our schools," Feir said.

"There are at least three Vürdmeisters capable of calling forth pit wyrms."

"If I see any little men with wings, I'll run," Solon said.

"You're mad," Feir said. "Dorian, we need to leave. This kingdom's doomed. They'll capture Curoch; they'll capture you, and then what hope will the rest of the world have? We need to pick a battle we can win."

"Unless the God is with us, we won't win any battles, Feir."

"Don't give me that God bullshit! I won't let Solon take Curoch, and I'm taking you back to Sho'cendi. Your madness is taking you."

"Too late," Solon said. He scooped up the sword from the bed.

"We both know I can take that away from you," Feir said.

"In a swordfight, sure," Solon agreed. "But if you try to take it, I'll just draw power through it and stop you. Like Dorian said, every meister within fifty miles will know we have an artifact here, and they'll all come looking for it."

"You wouldn't," Feir said.

Solon's face took on an intensity Dorian hadn't seen since he'd left *Sho'fasti* wearing his first blue robes. Now, as then, the slab of a man looked more like a soldier than like one of the foremost mages of the day. "I will do it," Solon said. "I've given ten years of my life for this backwater, and they've been good years. It's been damn good to stand for something rather than just watch from the side and criticize everyone who's actually doing something. You should try it. You used to, you know? What happened to the Feir Cousat who went and took this sword in the first place? I'm going to do something here. Don't spoil my chance to make it be useful. Come on, Feir, if we *can* fight Khalidor, how could we *not?*"

"Once you make your mind up, you're about as easy to move as Dorian," Feir said.

"Thank you," Solon said.

"I didn't mean it as a compliment."

48

$\mathcal{T}$he man who had ordered soldiers to arrest Regnus hadn't been much use. They'd captured him coming out of an inn after lunch. His interrogation had been short if not kind. He'd given them his commanding officer's name, one Thaddeus Blat.

Thaddeus Blat was currently being entertained upstairs in a brothel called the Winking Wench. Regnus and his men were waiting downstairs, seated at various tables, and not doing a good job of remaining inconspicuous.

It all made Regnus nervous. He didn't know this man, but soldiers tended to visit brothels in the middle of the afternoon only when they knew something big was going to happen. Something from which they might not return. He also didn't like being out in public. Years ago, he wouldn't have been able to go anywhere without people recognizing his face. He had been presumed to be the next king, after all. But that had been years ago. Few people looked at him twice now. He was a big, threatening man in the Warrens. Apparently, that outweighed the fact that he was a rich nobleman in the Warrens.

Finally the man came downstairs. He was swarthy, with a single thick black eyebrow and a face etched with a permanent glower. Regnus stood after the man walked past and followed him to the stable. They'd already paid the stable boy to abandon his post, and by the time Regnus got there, Thaddeus Blat was bleeding from his nose and the corner of his mouth, disarmed, held by four soldiers, and cursing.

"That's not what I want to hear coming out of your mouth, Lieutenant," Regnus said. He gestured and the men kicked the back of Blat's knees so he dropped in front of the trough. Regnus grabbed a handful of hair and pressed his head under water.

"Tie his hands. This may take a few minutes," Regnus said.

Blat came up gasping and flailing, but the soldiers bound his hands in short order. Thaddeus Blat spat toward Regnus, missed, and cursed him.

"Slow learner," Regnus said, and heaved. The man went under and this time Regnus waited until he stopped flailing. "When they stop fighting," he said to his men, "it means they understand for the first time that they might actually die unless they really concentrate. I think he'll be a little more polite this time."

He pulled Blat up, his dark hair plastered to his forehead down to his single brow, and Blat saved his air for breathing for a long moment. "Who are you?" he asked.

"I'm Duke Regnus Gyre, and you're going to tell me everything you know about my people's death."

The man cursed him again.

"Turn him a little," Regnus said. They did, and he drove his fist into the man's solar plexus, driving the wind from his lungs. Thaddeus Blat only had time to suck in half a breath before he went under.

Regnus held him below the water until bubbles burst on the surface, then he dragged Thaddeus up, but only for a moment. Then he pushed him back down again. He repeated the process four times. When he pulled Blat up the fifth time, he released his head.

"I'm running out of time, Thaddeus Blat, and I've got nothing to lose by killing you. I've already killed my wife and all my servants, remember? So if I have to put your face under that water one more time, I'm going to hold it there until you're dead."

Real fear was painted across the lieutenant's face in dripping watercolors. "They don't tell me anything—no, wait! I swear it. I don't get my new orders until tonight. But this one goes all the way to the top. To the top of the Kin, you know?"

"The Sa'kagé?"

"Yeah."

"Not good enough. Sorry."

They plunged his head back under the water and he thrashed like a demon, but on his knees, with his hands tied, there was nothing he could do. "You set a limit, and then you break it," Regnus said. "Most people can hold out if they've been given a limit. They tell themselves, 'I can hold out that long.' Let him up."

The man spluttered as he came up, spitting out inhaled water and wheezing. "You think of anything else?" Regnus asked, but he didn't give Thaddeus time to respond.

He dunked the man again. "Sir," one of the soldiers

said, looking a little queasy. "If you don't mind my asking, how do you know all this?"

Regnus grinned. "I got captured by the Lae'knaught during a border raid when I was young. But we don't have the time to use everything I learned from them. Up."

"Wait!" Thaddeus Blat cried out. "I overheard them saying that Hu Gibbet's next deader was the queen. Her and her daughters. That's all I know. Gods, that's all I know. He's going to kill them tonight in the queen's chambers after the banquet. Please don't kill me. I swear that's all I know."

They had promised Kaldrosa Wyn a man-o'-war and put her on a sea cow instead. The Sethi pirate hadn't been able to say no to the money. *Damn the mother who whelped me, why didn't I say no?* Looking over the port side, she barked an order and men scurried to adjust the sails to catch another cupful of wind. *Sails? Bedsheets, more like.* The sails were too small. The ship and its sister were too fat and ungainly to outrun a rowboat piloted by a one-handed monkey. In short, the Cenarian warships would be on them in minutes, and there wasn't a damn thing Kaldrosa Wyn could do about it.

"If you're going to do something, now might be a good time," she told the circle of wytches sitting on the barge's deck.

"Wench," the leader of the wytches said, "no one tells a meister his work. Understood?" The man's eyes didn't rise from her bare breasts until the last word.

"Then to hell with ya," Kaldrosa said. She spat over the side, not betraying the queasiness that rose in her at the touch of that wytch's eyes. The bastards had been staring at her breasts for the entire trip. Normally around foreigners, she'd have covered herself, but she liked making the Khalidorans uncomfortable. Wytches were another matter.

Kaldrosa reefed the sails and had the men below decks start rowing, but even that was hopeless. Khalidoran craftsmanship. They'd even designed the oars poorly. They were too short. Even with the hundreds of men she was carrying, she couldn't translate their strength into speed because not enough men could man the oars at once, nor was there room below for full sweep. She cursed her greed and the wytches—quietly.

In minutes, the three Cenarian warships were on them. It was a shame. In all the ocean, Cenaria couldn't have had more than a dozen ships in her navy, and Kaldrosa had found the three best ships of it. In her *Sparrowhawk* or any Sethi ship with a Sethi crew, she'd be safe.

The wytches finally stood as the first Cenarian ship drew within a hundred paces. They were going to ram her sea cow at an angle and sheer off the oars. Eighty paces. Seventy. Fifty. Thirty.

The wytches had their hands twined. They were chanting and it seemed darker on deck than it had been a moment before, but nothing was happening. The sailors and soldiers on the Cenarian ship were shouting to each other and at her, getting ready for the collision and the battle to follow.

"Damn you," she yelled, "do something!"

Out of the corner of her eye, she thought she saw something immense pass by, under the ship. She turned to brace for the impact, but instead only got a face full of water. There was a tremendous crack, and when her vision cleared, she saw pieces of the Cenarian ship flying through the air. But not many pieces. Not enough to account for an entire ship.

Then she saw the rest of the ship through the shallow blue waters. Somehow, it had been sucked down in an instant. The flying pieces were merely what had broken off the decks and the sails as the water broke over the ship.

The sea went black, as if a thick cloud had passed in front of the sun, but it undulated. It took Kaldrosa a moment to realize that something enormous was passing beneath her ship. Something absolutely immense. She saw the wytches chanting, more than their hands intertwined now. It seemed as if the black tattoos that all of them wore had torn free of their hands and were holding each other, pulsing with power. The wytches were sweating as if under tremendous strain.

Water swelled as if an immense arrow were passing just under the surface of the sea—and then stopped as it reached the second Cenarian warship. The men on its deck, fifty paces away, were shouting, shooting arrows into the water, brandishing swords, the captain trying to turn the ship.

For five seconds nothing happened, then two gray massive somethings slapped against the Cenarian ship's deck. They were too big for Kaldrosa to even guess what they could be for a moment—each one covered nearly a quarter of the ship's hull. Then the ship bounced ten paces out of the sea, straight up, and Kaldrosa saw that they were fingers of a massive gray hand. Then the hand went down and the entire ship disappeared under the waves, bursting apart as the water closed over it, throwing splinters in a wave.

Then the black shape was moving again. It was too big to be real. And this time, the men on the last Cenarian ship were screaming. Kaldrosa heard orders being shouted, but there was too much chaos. The ship drifted, even though it had closed the distance with her sea cow while the other ships had been being destroyed, and was now almost touching it.

The sea swelled again, but this time there was no pause. The leviathan swam beneath the Cenarian ship at incredible speed, rising high enough in the water that spines from its back rose thirty feet in the air.

The spines cut the ship in half and two flicks of a gray tail smashed each half into the ocean. The Khalidoran soldiers who'd crowded the deck—Kaldrosa hadn't even noticed them emerging—cheered.

She was about to begin ordering them back to their places when the cheering suddenly stopped. The soldiers were pointing. She followed their gaze and saw that swell rising again, this time pointed straight for them. The wytches were sweating freely, open panic on their faces.

"No!" a young wytch shouted. "That won't work. Like *this*."

Something rippled out from the wytches toward the leviathan. It met the oncoming beast, and nothing happened. The soldiers cried out in horror.

Then the huge shape turned and went out to sea.

The soldiers cheered and the wytches collapsed on the deck. But something wasn't finished. Kaldrosa saw that immediately. Even as she ordered the oars pulled and the sails raised once more, she kept an eye on the wytches.

The leader was speaking to the young man who—if Kaldrosa guessed correctly—had taken control and saved all of their lives. The young man shook his head, staring at the deck.

"Obedience unto death," she heard him say.

The leader spoke again, too low for Kaldrosa to make out, and the other eleven wytches gathered around the two men. They laid their hands on the young man who'd saved them all, and Kaldrosa saw his tattoos rise from below his skin. They swelled and swelled until his arms were black, and then they burst—not outward, away from the wytch's body, but in, as if they were veins that had been overfilled and now leaked through the rest of his body. The ruptured tattoos bled beneath the young man's skin and he collapsed to the deck, twitching violently. In moments, his entire body was black. He thrashed and choked, and in moments he was dead.

Everyone else on the ship was studiously ignoring the wytches. Kaldrosa found herself the only one watching the exchange. The leader of the wytches said a word, and the other wytches tossed the corpse overboard. Then he turned and watched her with too-blue eyes.

Never again, Kaldrosa swore to herself. *Never again.*

"Do you know the secret of effective blackmail, Durzo?" Roth asked. He was seated at a fine oak table incongruously placed in a typical Warrens hovel. Durzo stood before him like a chastened courtier standing before the king. Roth's chair was even raised. The presumption.

"Yes," Durzo said. He wasn't in any mood for games.

"Refresh me," Roth said, looking up from the reports he'd been reading. He was not amused.

Durzo cursed himself and cursed fate. He'd done everything to avert this, paid every price of misery, and yet it had come. "Use your hold to get a better hold."

"You've made that difficult for me, Durzo. You've convinced everyone that you don't give a damn about anything."

"Thank you." Durzo didn't smile. It wasn't in him to play the abased servant.

"The problem is, I'm more clever than you are."

"Cleverer."

Roth's close-set eyes narrowed at Blint's blithe monotone. Roth was a lean young man with an angular face obscured by an oiled black goatee and long hair. He disliked making words for their own sake. He disliked people. He stuck out an open hand. Waited.

Durzo tossed him the bit of pretty silver glass.

Roth looked at it briefly and threw it back, unamused. "Don't toy with me, assassin. I know there was a real one there. We have two spies who saw someone bond it."

"Then they should have told you someone got there first."

"Really."

Roth was mimicking Momma K's tendency to state questions. He probably thought it made him seem authoritative. Roth was out of his league if he thought mimicking Momma K would be enough to hold power. Part of Durzo wanted to tell Roth that Momma K was the Shinga. Roth obviously didn't know, and Momma K had betrayed Durzo, but Durzo had no taste for using rats to do a man's work. If he killed Gwinvere, he'd do it with his own hands. *If? I'm going soft. When. She betrayed me. She must die.*

"Really," Durzo answered, with no intonation.

"Then I think it's time for you to meet another of my *cards.*" There was no signal that Durzo could see, but an old man stepped into the hovel instantly. The creature was short and bent still further by more years than a mortal frame should endure. He had piercing blue eyes and a fringe of silver hair combed over a bald dome of head.

The man gave a toothless grin. "I am Vürdmeister Neph Dada, counselor and seer to His Majesty."

Not just any wytch. A Vürdmeister. Durzo Blint felt old. "How exalted. I thought you called your dog kings His Holiness," Durzo said.

"His Majesty," Neph Dada said, "Roth Ursuul, ninth aetheling of the Godking." He bowed to Roth.

By the Night Angels. He wasn't kidding.

Neph Dada grabbed Durzo's chin with a frail hand and pulled it down toward himself until Durzo looked into his eyes. "He knows who took the Globe of Edges," Neph said.

There was no denying it. Not with a Vürdmeister here. Vürdmeisters were supposed to be able to read minds. It wasn't true, but it was close enough. Most of them couldn't do it, Durzo knew. Even those who could didn't actually read minds. The way Durzo had heard it explained, longer ago than he liked to remember, was that they could see hints of images that their subject had seen. The best Vürdmeisters could intuit a lot of truth from a few images, though. It was almost the same thing at this point. *How can I take advantage of the differences between what I've seen and what I know?*

"It was my apprentice," Durzo said.

Roth Ursuul—*by the Night Angels, Ursuul?*—raised an eyebrow.

"He doesn't know what it is," Durzo said. "I don't know who sent him. He never does jobs without telling me."

"Perhaps you should not be so sure of this?" Neph said.

"I'll get the ka'kari for you. I just need some time."

"Ka'kari?" Roth asked.

Roth had never used the word. It was a stupid mistake. Totally uncharacteristic. Durzo was falling apart.

"The Globe of Edges," Durzo said.

"I've given you a chance to be honest with me, Durzo. So what I'm going to do is your own fault." Roth motioned to one of the guards at the entrance to the hovel. "The girl."

Several moments later, a little girl was carried in. She was drugged, whether chemically or magically, and the guard had some trouble carrying her limp body. She was maybe eleven years old, skinny and dirty, but not the skinny and dirty of a street rat—healthy skinny, healthy dirty. Her black hair was long and curly, and her face had the same angelic-demonic cast that her mother's had had. She would be even prettier than Vonda, some day. She took her height from Durzo, but thank the gods, everything else from her mother. Uly was a damn fine-looking kid. It was the first time Durzo had seen his daughter.

It made him ache somewhere that was already sore.

"You've already chosen not to cooperate enthusiastically, Durzo," Roth said. "So usually, I'd make an example of you. We both know I can't do that. I need you too much, at least for the next few days. So maybe I should,

say, cut off her hand as a warning, and let the little girl
know that it's because you won't stop it. That you are
choosing to hurt her. Perhaps something like that would
help gain your cooperation?"

Durzo was frozen, just looking at his daughter. *His
daughter! How had he put her in the hands of this man?*
She had been the king's leverage, and Roth had taken her
right out from under the man's nose.

"How about this?" Roth said. "We'll cut off a hand or
you cut off a finger."

There was a way out. Even now, there was a way. One
of his knives was poisoned. He'd put the asp poison it. For
Kylar. It would be painless, especially for such a small
person. She'd be dead in seconds. Maybe Roth would be
surprised enough that Durzo could get away. Maybe.

He could kill his daughter and probably be killed himself, and Kylar would live. Or this Roth Ursuul would
demand he kill Kylar and get the ka'kari. That would
have been easy enough to fake, if Roth didn't have a
Vürdmeister.

Could he kill his own daughter? He'd be letting them
kill Kylar if he didn't.

"She didn't do anything," Durzo said.

"Spare me," Roth said. "You've got too much blood on
your hands to cry about the suffering of innocents."

"Hurting her isn't necessary."

Roth smiled. "You know, from anyone else, I'd laugh.
Do you remember what happened the last time you called
an Ursuul's bluff?" Durzo couldn't keep his expression
blank; grief flashed through him. "Who'd have thought,"
Roth said. "My father takes the mother and I take the
daughter. Have you learned your lesson, Durzo Blint? I

think you have. My father will be pleased that I'm closing the circle. He tried to blackmail you for a false ka'kari and failed. I'll blackmail you for a true ka'kari and succeed." Neph's eyes flashed when Roth said that. It was clear he didn't appreciate the prince's presumption, but Durzo was still reeling. He couldn't see any way to take advantage of that tiny split between the men.

"Here's how blackmail is going to work for you, Durzo Blint: if I think you're resisting me, your daughter will die. And there are other, shall we say *indignities,* that she will suffer first. Let your imagination work on what those might be—I know I'll let mine. She'll be a husk by the time we're finished. I will spend months eking out every drop of suffering from her mind and body before we kill her, and I enjoy such work. I am one of Khali's most dedicated disciples. Do you understand me, Blint? Am I being clear?"

"Perfectly." His jaw was tense. He couldn't kill her. By the Night Angels. He just couldn't do it. He'd think of something. He always had before. There was some way out of this. He would find it, and he would kill both of these men.

Roth smiled. "Now tell me everything about this apprentice of yours. And I mean everything."

49

$\mathcal{K}$ylar stepped out of the shadows of the Blue Boar's office and grabbed Jarl around the throat with his arm, putting a hand over his mouth.

"Mmm mmmph!" Jarl protested against Kylar's hand.

"Quiet, it's me," Kylar whispered in his ear. Wary of Jarl shouting, he released his friend slowly.

Jarl rubbed his throat. "Damn, Kylar. Take it easy. How did you get in here?"

"I need your help."

"I'll say. I was just going to come looking for you."

"What?"

"Look in the top drawer. You can read it as fast as I could tell you," Jarl said.

Kylar opened the drawer and read the note. Roth was Roth Ursuul, a Khalidoran prince. He'd just been elected Shinga. Kylar was a suspect in the prince's murder. The king's men were looking for him. Kylar tossed the note aside.

"I need your help, just one more time, Jarl."

"Are you telling me you knew all that?"

"It doesn't change anything. I need your help."

"Is this going to get me killed?"

"I need to know where Momma K is hiding."

Jarl's eyes narrowed. "Do I need to ask why?"

"I'm going to kill her."

"After all she's done for you? You—"

"She betrayed me, Jarl, and you know it. She manipulated me into trying to kill Durzo Blint. She's so good, I thought it was my own idea."

"Maybe you should get her story before you kill her. Maybe murder shouldn't be your first resort against the people who've helped you," Jarl said.

"She convinced me that to save a friend, I had to kill Hu Gibbet, except that it wasn't Hu. It was Durzo. She betrayed us. She made me ruin a friend and take away everything he loves."

"I'm sorry, but I can't help you."

"I'm not asking," Kylar said.

"Are you going to beat it out of me?" Jarl asked.

"I'll do what I have to."

"She's hiding out," Jarl said, unafraid. "She had a terrible fight with Blint not long ago. I don't know what it was about. But she's helped me, and I won't betray her."

"You know she'd give you up in a second, Jarl."

"I know," Jarl said. "I might sell my body, Kylar, but I do what I can to keep the rest of me. I've only got a few shreds of dignity left. If you take those, you won't just be killing Momma K."

"It's one thing to say you'll keep a secret to the death. It's quite another to go through with it," Kylar said. "I've never tortured anyone, Jarl, but I know how."

"If you were going to torture me, you'd already have started, my friend."

They stared at each other until Kylar looked away, defeated.

"If you need help with anything else, I'll do it, Kylar. I hope you know that."

"I do." Kylar sighed. "Just be ready, Jarl. Things are going to happen faster than anyone expects."

There was a knock at the door.

"Yes?" Jarl asked.

A bodyguard poked his bald head in. "D—Durzo Blint to see you, sir." He looked terrified.

Kylar tried to draw on his Talent to cloak himself in shadows the way he had done when he came into the Blue Boar.

Nothing happened. *Oh, shit.* He practically dived behind Jarl's desk.

"Sir?" the bodyguard asked Jarl, not seeing Kylar through the crack of the door he had opened.

"Uh, show him in," Jarl said.

The door closed and soon opened once more. Kylar didn't dare to look. If he exposed enough of his face to be able to see Durzo, Durzo would see him.

"I won't waste your time or mine," Kylar heard Durzo say. Steps whisked softly across the floor and the desk groaned as someone sat on it. "I know you're Kylar's friend," Durzo said, only inches above Kylar.

Jarl made a sound of acknowledgment.

"I want you to get a message to him as soon as possible. I already sent him the message, but I need to make sure he gets it. Tell him I must speak with him. I'll be at the Tipsy Tart. I'll be there for the next two hours. Tell him it's *arutayro*."

"Spell that," Jarl said, moving to his desk and grabbing a quill from the inkpot.

Durzo spelled it, and then Jarl made a strangled sound of protest as Durzo must have grabbed him.

"Get it to him fast, rent boy. It's important. I'll hold you responsible if he doesn't get it." The desk protested again as Durzo got off it and walked out.

After the door closed, Kylar crawled out from under the desk.

Jarl's eyes widened. "You were under the desk?"

"Can't always be fancy."

Jarl shook his head. "You're unbelievable." As he wadded up the paper that had his note on it, he said, "What does *arutayro* mean?"

"Bloodless. It means we don't kill each other while we're meeting."

"And you trust him? After you tried to kill him last night?"

"Blint will kill me, but he'll do it professionally. He thinks I deserve that much. Mind if I use your window? I have a lot to do before I see him."

"Help yourself."

Kylar threw open the window, then turned to his friend. "I'm sorry. I had to try. I have to kill her and you were the fastest way to find her."

"Sorry I couldn't help."

Crawling out the window, Kylar moved out of Jarl's line of sight, then tried to draw the shadows again. This time it worked easily. *Perfect.* He couldn't even tell what he had done differently from what he did in the office.

By the Night Angels. Kylar figured that learning to control his Talent would have been hard enough if he had Durzo to explain it to him. Figuring it out on his own would be well-nigh impossible.

He moved back to the window. After a minute, Jarl checked the window, then walked to his desk and scrawled a quick note. He summoned a boy to his office and handed him the note.

Kylar circled around the building, and followed the boy after he came out a side door. He'd known Jarl wouldn't tell him—and he hoped his friend never figured out that Kylar had used him anyway.

The messenger boys were of uneven quality. Some of them made their passes so well that Kylar could barely follow them. Others simply held the letter out to the next boy.

It took a half hour for them to get to a small house on the east side. Kylar recognized the guard who took the message from the last boy. He was a Ymmuri with almond-shaped eyes and straight black hair. Kylar had seen the man at Momma K's house before. It was good enough. Momma K was here. Kylar would deal with her later.

He headed to the Tipsy Tart.

Durzo Blint was seated against a wall, with a wrapped bundle on the table. Kylar joined him, removed the sash from his waist, and set each of his weapons in it: the dagger and wakizashi that had been tucked into the sash, the Ceuran hand-and-a-half sword across his back, two daggers from his sleeves, throwing knives and darts from his waistband, and a tanto from one boot.

"That all?" Blint asked sardonically.

Kylar rolled up the sash and set it beside Blint's, which was just as large. "Looks like we'll both be working soon."

Blint nodded and set down mug of a foul Ladeshian stout exactly in the center of a board so that it didn't cross any of the cracks.

"You wanted to speak with me?" Kylar said, wondering why Blint was drinking. Blint never drank when he had to work.

"They have my daughter. They made threats. Credible threats. This Roth is a real twist."

"They'll kill her if you don't give them the ka'kari," Kylar guessed.

Blint only drank in response.

"So you have to kill me," Kylar said.

Blint stared him in the eye. It was a yes.

"Is it just the job, or did I fail?" Kylar asked, butterflies roaring in his stomach.

"Fail?" Blint looked up from the stout, snorted. "A lot of wetboys go through what we call the Crucible. Sometimes it's designed deliberately for journeymen wetboys who have some serious problem—anything that hinders a gifted apprentice from becoming a gifted wetboy. Sometimes, it happens to a wetboy after he's a master. It's one of the reasons there are so few old wetboys.

"My Crucible was Vonda, Gwinvere's little sister. We thought we were in love. We thought certain realities didn't apply to us. I became a wetboy with an obvious weakness and Garoth Ursuul kidnapped her. He was looking for a ka'kari, as he still is. So was I."

"I don't know what-all it does. I can't even use my

Talent all the time. Can I use the ka'kari when I don't even have it in my possession?"

"Stop interrupting. This story has a point, and you should know better than to expect me to give you a tutorial on the very day I'm going to have to kill you," Durzo said. "Suffice it to say that the power of a ka'kari is vast. I'd been working for years to get one. Garoth Ursuul had been doing the same. He thought a ka'kari would give him an edge over the princes and the Vürdmeisters so he could become Godking. So he took Vonda and told me where he was holding her, and told me that if I went for the ka'kari, he'd kill her."

"You've never done well with threats," Kylar said.

"I think I've *always* done well with them," Durzo said. "The thing was, there was going to be a limited time to get the ka'kari. The man who'd allegedly bonded the ka'kari was on his death bed, so the time to get it would be immediately after he died. Naturally, Garoth had Vonda held way outside of town. I knew that the Sa'kagé was going to poison the man that night. I guessed that Garoth knew it too. I couldn't be two places at once, so I had to make a choice.

"I knew Garoth Ursuul. He's a master of traps. He's smarter than I am. More devious. So I guessed that if I went for Vonda, either the traps or meisters of his would kill me. I knew of one trap he'd used before that would use my entrance as a trap's trigger that would kill her. That was like him, turning my attempt to save Vonda into the very thing that killed her. Getting the ka'kari would just make a sweet deal sweeter for him. That was my Crucible, Kylar. Would I fling myself into a trap in an attempt to be a hero, or would I use my mind, give up Vonda for lost, and get the ka'kari?"

"You chose the ka'kari."

"It was a fake." Durzo studied the tabletop, and his voice shook. "Afterward, I sprinted, stole a horse, ran it to death, but it was half an hour after dawn when I got to the house where Vonda was. She was dead. I checked all the windows, but couldn't find any sign of traps. I'll never know if it's because he had someone remove them, or if they were purely magical, or if they were never trapped at all. The bastard. He did it on purpose." Blint took a long pull from his stout. "I'm a wetboy, and love is a noose. The only way to redeem my choice was to become the best wetboy ever."

Kylar felt a lump in his throat.

"That's why we can't have love, Kylar. That's why I did everything I could to keep you out of it. I made one mistake, let myself be weak one time, and now after all these years, it's come back to haunt me. You're not going to die because you failed, Kylar. You'll die because I did. That's the way things work. Others always pay for my failures. I failed, Kylar, because I thought you only go through the Crucible once. I was wrong. Life is the crucible."

From what Kylar could see, Durzo's choice had never stopped haunting him. The man was a shell. He was a legendary wetboy, but he'd sacrificed everything to that god. Kylar had always wanted to be Durzo, had always held his skills in awe. Durzo was the best, but where was the man beneath the legend?

"So my Crucible was Elene." Kylar chuckled on the hollowness inside him. "There's no way you'll fight with me, against them?"

"And let Roth torture and kill my daughter? Here's my choices, kid: You die or my daughter dies." Durzo pulled a gold gunder from a pouch. "Crowns Roth wins, castles I lose."

He flipped the coin. It bounced on the table and, impossibly, landed on edge.

"There's always another choice," Kylar said, slowly releasing his Talent. *Damn, it actually worked.*

Blint centered and re-centered his empty mug on the table. "I worked for almost fifteen years to get the Globe of Edges, Kylar. I didn't know where it was. I didn't know if it was bonded to someone. I didn't know what kind of magical defenses protected it. I knew people like you were supposed to call the ka'kari, and that your need for it would make the call stronger. That's why I took you on jobs in every corner of the city. How could I have known King Gunder had it and thought it was just jewelry? No one talked about it because no one knew it was special. No one cared. And I thought maybe I was wrong, that you just had a block. That if I pushed you enough, you'd use your Talent. After working for fifteen years, you think it'd be easy to just hand it over? You think it's easy to give away fifteen years of your life?"

"But you were going to." Kylar was amazed.

"Hell no. Once I had it, I'd never have given it away," Durzo said. But Kylar didn't believe him. Blint had been planning to give him the ka'kari all along—until Roth.

"Master, work with me. Together we can take Roth."

Durzo was silent for a few moments. "You know, I used to be like you, kid. For a long time. You should have known me back then. You would've liked me. We might have been friends."

I do like you, master. I'd like to be your friend, Kylar said, but only in his mind. Somehow those words wouldn't force their way past his lips. Maybe it didn't matter. Durzo wouldn't believe him anyway.

"Roth's a Khalidoran prince, kid. He's got a Vürdmeister. Soon he'll have more wytches than all the southlands have mages and an army to boot. He owns the Sa'kagé. There's no hope. There's no way to oppose him now. The Night Angels themselves wouldn't try it."

Kylar threw up his hands, fed up with Blint's fatalism and his superstitions. "Here I thought they were invincible."

"They're immortal. It's not the same thing." Blint popped a garlic clove. "You can take what you need from my place. I wouldn't want you to die just because I've got better gear."

"I won't fight you, master."

"You'll fight. You'll die. And I'll miss you."

"Master Blint?" he said, remembering something Dorian had said. "What does my name mean?"

"'Kylar'? You know the word *cleave?*"

"To cut, right?" Kylar asked. "Like a meat cleaver."

"Yes, but it has another meaning, too. In old wedding ceremonies, a husband and wife were commanded to cleave together."

"Like cleavage?"

Blint smirked, but the dark cloud over him didn't shift. "Right. *Cleave* means both 'to come together' and 'to split apart.' Two opposite meanings. Your name's like that. It means one who kills and one who is killed."

"I don't understand," Kylar said.

"You will. May the Night Angels watch over you, kid. Remember, they have three faces."

"What?"

"Vengeance, Justice, and Mercy. They always know which to show. And remember the difference between vengeance and revenge. Now get out of here."

Kylar stood and stashed his weapons expertly. His hip brushed the table as he stood and the balanced coin wobbled and fell before he could reach out with his Talent again and stop it. He ignored it, refused to see it as an omen. "Master Blint," he said, looking his master in the eye and bowing, "*kariamu lodoc.* Thank you. For everything."

"Thank you?" Master Blint snorted. He picked up the coin. It was castles. *Castles I lose.* "Thank you? You always were the damnedest kid."

50

Kylar had an hour before Durzo came after him. He knew that because he'd watched Durzo drink a full mug of stout, and Durzo Blint wouldn't work when he had alcohol in him.

It was the perfect time to go to Master Blint's safe house. He might get lucky and be able to figure out how Master Blint intended to kill him from what tools were missing.

To be careful, he used the back alleys to get to the safe house. In short order, Kylar disarmed the trap on the lock, then searched for the second trap. If he'd been fully visible, he would have felt exposed, but his Talent obeyed him this time and covered him with shadows. He still had no idea how well he was concealed, but in the heavily shadowed and rarely traveled street, he felt comfortable taking his time. The second trap was embedded in the doorframe opposite the latch. Kylar shook his head. And Blint said he was no good at traps. Setting a trap which used the release of pressure from the bolt itself for a trigger was no easy feat.

Having disarmed that trap, Kylar started picking the lock. Blint had always told him that setting more than two traps on a door was a waste of time. You should get someone with the first trap, but if it was set so poorly that it made them overconfident, you might get them with a perfectly placed second trap. After that, only an idiot wouldn't check the door over so carefully that they'd find anything you could hide.

Kylar didn't have to fumble with the rake. He'd practiced on this door for years, so he pressed the tumbler in place almost instantly. Then he felt something wrong. He threw his fingers apart and dropped the rake just as the spring released. A black needle darted out between his spread fingers, grazing his knuckle and almost breaking the skin.

"Whew." The black compound on the needle was henbane and kinderperil. It wouldn't have been fatal, but it would make a person ill for days, and he wouldn't have had time to get far before the poison did its work on him. It was a nasty bit of business—and its presence meant that Master Blint was still testing him. *"Only an idiot wouldn't check the door over carefully after two traps."* Gods.

Kylar stepped inside carefully. This safe house wasn't as spacious as the one where he'd spent his first months with Master Blint, and with the animals in it, it had been terribly noisy, smelly, and dirty.

Now the animals were gone. Kylar scowled. A cursory examination told him they'd been here this morning.

Moving further in, Kylar saw a letter sitting on Durzo's desk. He drew a knife in each hand and opened the letter without touching it. He doubted Durzo would use a contact poison in the paper, but he hadn't thought the wetboy would put a third trap on the door, either.

"Kylar," it read in Durzo's tight, controlled script:

"Relax. Killing you with contact poison would be terribly unsatisfying. I'm glad the third trap didn't get you, but if you had used what you thought you knew about me instead of checking, you'd have deserved it.

"I'll miss you. You're the closest to family I'll ever have. I'm sorry I brought you into this life. Momma K and I did everything we could to make you a wetboy. I suppose it's to your credit that we failed. You mean more to me than I ever thought another person could."

Kylar blinked back tears. There was no way he could kill the man who'd written this. Durzo Blint was more than his master; he was his father.

"Tonight it ends," the letter continued. "If you want to save your friend, you'd better find me. —A Thorne"

A thorn? Well, Blint was certainly prickly enough to call himself a thorn, but he was also usually a good speller. And what did he mean about saving my friend? Did Durzo know where Elene was? Why was he threatening her? Or was he talking about Jarl? The blood drained from Kylar's face.

The animals were gone. Everything else Blint owned was still here, so he wasn't moving.

The animals would look fine to a cook, and the taste tester who tried the foods wouldn't be affected for hours—long enough for the foods to be served at a dinner.

Blint only drank after he finished a job.

The animals were gone. All of them. There weren't many places that could take all of them.

"Oh shit." Blint was poisoning the nobles at the Midsummer's banquet. Elene wouldn't be there, of course. Neither would Jarl. Blint must have known something he didn't. It must mean that Logan would be there.

Roth was attempting his coup. Tonight.

Kylar felt dizzy. He threw a hand down on the table to steady himself and set the glass vials and beakers to clinking against each other. His eyes raised to one he'd stared at for years. The asp poison was there. It was low. Blint had really meant the threats. For a while after talking with him at the arutayro, after seeing the letter, Kylar might have thought Blint wouldn't kill him. But he would. It was all professional for Blint. He'd crossed a line years ago when he let Vonda die, and there was no going back.

It was classic Durzo Blint. He was giving Kylar a chance now, giving him enough information so that he would show up, enough motivation so he'd fight, but when it came to the fight, Blint would do everything in his power to win. He always had.

Kylar's body knew what to do even though his mind was far away. He threaded cotton through the tiny holes on a tiny poisoner's knife and dripped asp venom on it.

Logan didn't like rabbit, so Kylar prepared the antidotes for the poisons they'd fed the pheasants and starlings and hoped that Logan didn't touch the pork. Alone, it wouldn't be fatal, but there was no antidote for it. If Logan got really sick, there was no way Kylar could carry him.

He scoured his body without soap so as to have as little scent as possible. He strapped knives to his bare forearms and a tanto to one calf. Pulled on his trousers and tunic, both tight, mottled black, made of Gandian cotton. Buck-

led his weapons harness. Checked the belt for his poisons
and grappling hooks. Slid home the poisoner's knife in
its special sheath. Slapped home daggers and his Ceuran
hand-and-a-half sword.

Then he saw Retribution. Blint had left the big black
sword on the wall. He'd left his favorite sword for Kylar.
Doubtless, he'd make some quip about either taking it off
his body, or if things went the other way, not needing it
anymore.

He really means it. This is really to the death. Kylar
lifted the sword reverently and strapped it to his back. It
was heavier than he was used to using, but with his Talent,
it would be perfect.

Finally ready, he walked to the door, then stopped. He
put his head against the wood and just breathed, breathed.
How had it come to this? Tonight, either he or Master
Blint would die. Kylar didn't even know what he was
going to do when he got to the castle. But if he didn't do
something, Logan would die.

51

*D*urzo crept along the rafters supporting the roof of Castle Cenaria's Great Hall, cloaked in shadows. His work had a lot of variety. He'd always liked that. But he'd never wanted to be a maid.

Yet somehow, he found himself pushing a damp rag over wood, scooping up dust meticulously, scooting forward slowly as he cleared each inch. Strangely enough, hovering fifty feet over the floor of the hall, the rafters hadn't been dusted recently. And Durzo hated being dirty.

Still, no matter how careful he was, he couldn't help but dislodge little clumps of dust from time to time—clumps that would puff out like clouds heavy with snow and drift downward, marking his otherwise invisible progress.

The nobles below, mercifully, weren't exactly staring at the ceiling. The festivities were in full swing. The events of the night before had brought out everyone. Voices drifted up to the rafters in a dull roar as men and women celebrated Midsummer's and gossiped about what the king could possibly be doing. Obviously, the biggest morsel was what Logan was doing at the high table. Everyone knew he'd been arrested, and they couldn't keep their eyes off him. Why was he here?

For his part, Logan was sitting like a man doomed—which was exactly what Durzo suspected he was. Knowing Aleine, the king had summoned Logan so he could publicly humiliate him in front of all the peers of the realm. Maybe he'd announce Logan's death sentence. Maybe he'd have it carried out at the table.

Durzo moved again and dislodged a large clump of decades-old dust. He watched, helpless, as it spiraled down toward one of the side tables. Part of the clump broke apart in the air, but part of it hit the arm of a gesticulating noblewoman.

She brushed her arm and continued her story without a pause.

Brushing more dust and still moving slowly, Durzo gritted his teeth. He was slipping. Of course, he always told himself he was slipping. It kept him sharp. Maybe this time, though, he really was. Too much was happening. It was all too personal.

Durzo reached a joint where several beams came together to support the roof. There was no way to stay on top of the rafter and get past. He would have to go around or under. Whoever had designed these rafters hadn't had convenient skulking in mind.

Setting climbing hooks around each of his wrists, Durzo wedged his fingers where two beams came together at an angle. It was painful, but a wetboy learned to ignore pain. He swung out over space, letting his feet release the beam. He wondered what the fat noblewoman below him would think if her dinner were suddenly crushed by a falling shadow. He held his entire weight by his fingertips and used his weight to wedge his fingers deeper into the painful crack, then released his right hand and swung to grab the other side of the joint, past the solid surface where all the beams came together.

He had only his long reach to thank for making it. He got three fingertips into the crack on the far side of the beam. As he shifted his weight, the dust in the crack was just enough to slide his fingertips off.

Blint rolled his wrist forward as his fingers slipped. He dropped three inches, and then the wrist hook caught in the crack his fingers had just left. The hook held. Blint released his left hand and his body swung again—now he'd fall directly on the woman, instead of on her food. He pulled against the iron hook biting into his wrist and was able to reach high enough to grab with his fingers. He swung again, pulled out the hook, and grabbed the edge of the beam with his other hand.

He hung there, fingertips holding his entire weight from the same side of the beam, and the grip slick with an inch of dust. Had he thought he liked his work?

But with practiced grace, he swung sideways and caught the edge with a foot. Deftly, he wriggled back up onto the beam, ignoring the dust he pushed off the beam as he did so. Some risks you can't help.

And some you can. I haven't exactly minimized my risks, have I? Durzo tried not to think about it, but scooting along the beam acting like a cleaning lady didn't take his full attention. He'd given Kylar all the hints he needed to interrupt what Roth had planned here. And he'd given him motive to make sure he came here rather than leaving town. *It's bad luck, old boy.* But what was bad luck to him now? He was going to lose no matter what.

At the head table, the king stood. His face was flushed and he wobbled. He raised his glass. "My friends, my subjects, today is Midsummer's Eve. We have much to celebrate and much to mourn. I—words have abandoned me in light of what's happened in the last day. Our kingdom has endured the grievous loss of Catrinna Gyre and her entire household at the hands of her murderous husband, and the loss of our beloved prince." The king choked out the words and his emotion was so obvious that not a few eyes brimmed with equal tears. The prince had been young and dashing if unwise, and the Gyres had been respected for decades personally and for generations familially.

"Today we gather to celebrate Midsummer's. Some might wonder why we celebrate in the shadow of such dark deeds. I'll tell you why. We wish to celebrate the lives of our loved ones, not yet mourn their deaths." On the king's left hand, Lord General Agon was nodding his head with grim approval. Durzo wondered how much of this speech was Agon's. Most of it, he suspected.

The king drank from his glass, forgetting that he was in the middle of a toast. The nobles throughout the room looked confused. Should they drink, or was the king not finished? Half chose each, but the king continued, gaining volume. "I'll tell you why we're here. We're here because *the bastards who murdered my boy aren't going to stop me.* They aren't going to get me. They aren't going to stop me from doing whatever the hell I please!"

Lord General Agon looked alarmed. Aleine IX had

slipped into the first person singular from the royal plural. He must have had more to drink than was apparent.

"And I'll tell you what is our sovereign pleasure. There are schemers, plotters—traitors!—here tonight. Yes! And I swear to you traitors, you will die!" The king had gone purple with rage. "I know you're here. I know what you're doing! But it's fucking not going to fucking work!"

Well, look who learned a new word.

"No, sit down, Brant!" the king shouted as the lord general stood.

The nobles were stricken silent.

"Some of you have betrayed us to Khalidor. You've murdered our prince! You've killed my boy! Logan Gyre, stand!"

Serah Drake was sitting near the back according to her rank, but even from above, Durzo could see the terror on her face. She thought the king was going to have Logan executed publicly, and she wasn't alone.

Logan Gyre stood, shaken. He was handsome, and from what Durzo knew, formidable, and popular with both the assembled nobles and the small folk of the city.

"Logan," the king shouted, "You've been charged with my son's death. And yet here you are tonight, celebrating! Did you kill my boy?"

Several nobles cried out in alarm, shouting that Logan would never be involved in such a thing. The king's soldiers looked scared. They looked to Captain Arturian for guidance. He nodded and two guards stepped up beside Logan.

Well, Durzo thought, finally coming directly over the head table where the king and Logan were seated, if threats don't make Kylar want to kill me, this will. The innocent always lose.

"Let him speak!" the king roared. He let off a stream of curses, and the crowd quieted. The tension hung thick over them.

Logan spoke loudly and clearly. "Your Majesty, your son was my friend. I deny all charges."

The king was silent for a long moment. Then he said, "I believe you, Duke Gyre." He turned to the nobles. "Lord Gyre has been found blameless in our sight. Logan Gyre, will you serve your country at all costs?"

Durzo paused, as stunned as the nobles were.

"I will," Logan spoke clearly, but there was obvious tension in his face. His eyes had locked on Serah Drake's.

What the hell is going on? This had the feel of something scripted.

"Then Lord Gyre, we pronounce you Crown Prince of Cenaria, and we announce your marriage of this afternoon to our own daughter, Jenine. Logan Gyre, you shall be our heir until such time as an heir is born to our royal house. Do you accept this duty and this honor?"

"I do."

The apprehension in the Great Hall had turned to disbelief, then awe.

Jenine Gunder moved to stand beside Logan, looking as awkward as a fifteen-year-old can. Durzo heard a little cry from Serah Drake. Her hands flew up to her mouth. Then she fled. But nobody besides Logan and Durzo noticed, because even as she ran for the exit, a cheer broke out, rapidly spreading to every throat.

The king tossed off his wine, and the nobles joined his

toast, saluting Logan. "Prince Gyre! Prince Gyre! Logan Gyre!"

The king sat, but the cheering continued. All eyes were on Logan and Jenine. The king looked irritated. That the nobles were chanting "Prince Gyre" instead of the traditional "Prince Logan" might have been simply because it was easier to chant, but it also drove home that Logan wasn't a Gunder—and everyone was happy about it.

Logan graciously if somewhat woodenly accepted the applause, nodding to his friends, then he blushed as his new wife took his hand. Her face glowed with embarrassment at her own boldness and adoration for her husband. The nobles loved it. But as the approval roared to a crescendo, the king looked more and more vexed.

And still, the cheering continued. The servants were cheering. The guards were cheering. It was as if the nobles felt a black cloud lifting from their futures. Not a few were saying, *"What a king Logan Gyre will make!"* Hurrahs rang out.

Aleine Gunder was turning purple again, but no one was paying him the slightest attention.

"Prince Gyre! Prince Gyre!"

"Long live Prince Gyre! Hurrah!"

The king jumped to his feet, apoplectic. "Now go! Go consummate this marriage," he shouted at Logan, who wasn't five paces away. Lord General Agon stood, but the king shoved him away roughly.

Logan looked at Aleine, shocked. The nobles quieted.

"Are you deaf?" the king shouted. "Go fuck my daughter!"

The princess turned white. So did Logan. Then she flushed red, mortified. She looked like she wanted to sink through the floor. At the same time, barely controlled rage washed over Logan's face in a crimson wave. The honor guards on either side of him looked stunned. Durzo wondered if the king had gone mad.

The nobles didn't make a sound. No one even breathed.

"Out! Get out! Go fuck. GO FUCK!" the king yelled.

Trembling, livid, Logan looked away and led his wife from the hall. The nervous guards followed.

"And the rest of you," the king said, "Tomorrow we mourn my son, and I swear that I'll find out who killed my boy if I have to string up the lot of you!"

The king sat abruptly and started weeping like a child. Durzo had frozen in place for the entire exchange. The nobles looked baffled, horrified. They slowly sat, staring at the king in silence.

Durzo's mind was racing. Roth hadn't foreseen this. Couldn't have. But Durzo was sure that Roth was in the castle, maybe in this very hall. A guard with one of the minor nobles was their signal man. If he took off his helmet, the coup was off.

It gave him a moment to digest what had just happened—not the king's madness, but Logan's marriage. It was a brilliant bit of intrigue. Now if the king were killed, instead of four houses having equal claims while Logan Gyre rotted in the Maw, Logan Gyre would clearly be the king. With his reputation and the endorsement of the Gunders, he would get quicker obedience from the noble houses than even King Gunder had.

It was a brilliant move, but it was too late. Roth had men throughout the castle. He probably couldn't afford to try again later. If the coup had been planned for tomorrow,

Logan's marriage might have changed everything. As it was, Logan and Jenine would just be added to the list of those who had to die.

As Durzo waited, it appeared that Roth agreed. A servant approached the signal guard and spoke with him. The man nodded and kept his hands off his helmet. The coup was on.

Whatever Roth would have to fix, it would involve killing Prince Logan Gyre now—who would be conveniently tucked away in the north tower where he'd be easy to find. Roth would probably want to assign that job to Durzo, but Durzo had no intention of giving the Khalidoran the chance. He would do what he had promised, but he wouldn't kill Kylar's friend.

During the first course, the nobles had already eaten the rabbits Durzo had prepared. He'd been feeding those rabbits hemlock for a year. The amount in a portion was a small enough dose that nothing would happen to the diners unless they'd also eaten the starling appetizers. In less than a half hour, the nobles would feel ill. Hemlock poisoning started peacefully enough. Already, the nobles' legs should be losing feeling. If anything, they might notice that their legs felt heavy. Soon, the feeling would spread up. Then they'd start vomiting. Anyone unlucky enough to have eaten seconds would begin convulsing.

The timing now was tricky. Poisoning wasn't an exact science, and someone might notice something amiss at any time. Durzo needed to act before that happened.

He secured one end of his rope to the beam. It was black silk—ridiculously expensive, but the slenderest and least visible rope Durzo owned. Fixing the harness he'd designed specifically for this mission, Durzo wrapped the rope through it and slid off the beam.

Steadying his swaying against the beam, Durzo looked down at his target. The king was directly below him. Durzo tucked in his knees and folded over. The harness bit into his shoulders, and he let out slack, slipping down toward the floor, head first.

Now timing was everything. In one hand, Durzo held the rope. By adjusting its position and tension against the harness, he could dive quickly toward the floor or stop easily. When he moved, he would need to move quickly: he was shrouded in shadows so that he was barely visible, but he couldn't shroud the rope.

In a room this cavernous, a rope swaying above the king as if holding weight would be noticed. The king's guards were good. Vin Arturian made sure of that.

With his other hand, Durzo pulled out two tiny pellets. Both were compounds from various mushrooms. Durzo had been able to make the pellets tiny, but they didn't dissolve quickly and for this job he couldn't use a powder.

The nobles were still silent. The king was barely crying now, but he noticed the nobles looking at him.

"What are you staring at?" he shouted. He cursed them roundly. "This is my daughter's wedding feast! Drink, damn you! Talk!" The king drained his wine again.

The nobles pretended to be talking, and soon that pretense became a furor of speculation. Durzo imagined that they were wondering if the king had lost his mind. He wondered the same himself.

He wondered what they'd think after the king drank his next goblet of wine.

A servant came and filled the king's goblet. The king's

cupbearer sipped the wine first and swished it around his mouth. Then he gave it to the king who set it down on the table with a thump.

"Your Majesty," Lord General Agon said at the king's left hand. "May I have a word with you?"

The king turned and Durzo pushed the rope forward. He dropped like a bolt. Ten feet above the table, he pulled the rope back and jerked to a stop. Ten feet was still a long way to drop something so light, but he'd been practicing. But as he tightened the rope, it twisted, and suddenly, he was spinning. Not fast, but spinning.

It didn't matter. There was no time to try again.

The first pellet splashed solidly in the center of the king's goblet. The second hit the edge and tinged off. The pellet rolled several inches across the table by the king's plate.

Durzo coolly drew another pellet and dropped it in.

The king picked up the goblet and was about to drink when Lord General Agon said, "Your Majesty, perhaps you've had enough to drink." He reached a hand to take the goblet from the king.

Durzo didn't waste time seeing what the king would do. He drew a short tube from his back and looked beyond Agon to the king's mage, Fergund Sa'fasti. He saw the man, but the rope spun him away before he could shoot the blow dart.

He was trying for a leg shot. His hope was that the hemlock would have deadened the mage's legs enough that he wouldn't even notice the sting. But on the next rotation, he didn't have a clear shot because the king and the lord general were gesticulating wildly.

Damn robes! The mage's robes left barely six inches

of his calf visible. Durzo came around again and abandoned the calf shot. The mage had shifted his feet and Durzo only had one of the darts—whatever they were bated with, it was a Khalidoran secret that was supposed to disable the mage's magical abilities.

Durzo puffed on the blowgun. The dart stuck into the mage's thigh.

He saw a brief flash of irritation on the man's face. The mage reached down toward his thigh—and was jostled by the Sa'kagé servant. "Sorry, sir. More wine?" the man asked the mage, snatching the dart. He was good. With hands like that, he must be one of the best cutpurses in the city. But of course, Roth would only use the best.

"Mine's full, you idiot," the mage said. "You're supposed to serve the wine, not drink it."

Durzo flipped over and scrambled up the rope, not an easy feat with silk. He rested when he got onto the beam. He had no idea if the king had drunk the wine or not. But his part was done. The only thing to do now was wait.

52

"Drink yourself blind, then," Agon said. He didn't care if the king heard him. He didn't care if the king killed him.

Just when I thought I could deal with this bastard. He disgraces his own daughter and shames a man who's given everything he loves to serve the throne.

Agon had been able to steer the king through the marriage of Logan Gyre and Jenine Gunder, but the king had hated the idea. He was jealous of Logan's looks and intelligence, jealous of how much people approved of his choice, and angry that Jenine had been excited to marry Logan rather than resigned to it.

But if Agon had done one valuable thing in his ten years of serving this hell-spawned brat, it had been convincing the king to appoint Logan crown prince.

Not that Logan would ever forgive him, but it was for the good of the realm. Sometimes duty required a man to do things he would do almost anything to avoid. It had been duty that had compelled Agon to serve Aleine IX, and only duty. Like Agon, Logan wasn't a man who would shirk his duty, but also like Agon, that didn't mean he had to like it.

Logan would probably hate Agon for it for the rest of his life, but Cenaria would get a good king. With Logan's intelligence, popularity, and integrity, the country might even become something more than a den of thieves and murderers. Agon was willing to pay the price, but it didn't sit well with him. He'd seen himself in Logan's eyes—realizing he was pledged to a destiny he would never have chosen. He'd seen the look on Serah Drake's face. Logan would live with the guilt of that betrayal for the rest of his life. The sight had seared him. Agon had barely been able to touch his food tonight.

The king tossed back the rest of his wine. The nobles were still buzzing. It wasn't the pleasant hum of conversation usual at Midsummer's Eve. Their tones were hushed, their glances furtive. Everyone offered an opinion on what the king was doing, why he would appoint an heir and then insult him in the same breath.

It was madness.

Slowly, the king emerged from his tears and silence. He stared around the Great Hall with hate-filled eyes. His lips moved, but Agon had to lean close to hear what he was saying. He wasn't surprised to hear the king muttering curses, one after another, droning on and on, mindless in his rage.

Then the king burst out laughing. The hall quieted once more, and the king laughed louder. He pointed at one of the nobles, an unassuming count named Burz. Everyone followed the king's finger and stared at Count Burz.

The count stiffened and reddened, but the king said nothing. His attention wandered and he stared cursing to himself again. For long moments, nobles continued staring at Count Burz, then looked at the king.

Then Chancellor Stiglor, who was seated at the head table, stood up with a cry and shouted, "There's something in the food!" The chancellor tottered and collapsed back into the chair, his eyes rolling up in his head.

Next to him, a man the king had always hated, Lord Ruel, suddenly slumped forward. His face smacked into his plate and he lay still.

The king laughed. Agon turned to him. The king wasn't even looking at Lord Ruel, but the timing couldn't have been worse.

Someone cried, "We're poisoned!"

"The king has poisoned us!"

Agon turned to see who had shouted, but he couldn't tell. Had a servant said it? Surely no servant would dare.

Another voice took up the shout, "The king! The king's poisoned us!"

Laughing, the king jumped to his feet and stumbled drunkenly. He shouted obscenities as the Great Hall erupted in chaos. Chairs squeaked as lords and ladies stood. Some of them wobbled and fell. An old lord started retching onto his plate. A young lady collapsed, vomiting.

Agon was on his feet, shouting orders to the soldiers.

The side door by the head table burst open and a man in Gyre livery pushed in, holding his hands up to show he was unarmed. His livery was torn and bloody. A gash bled beside his eyes, streaming blood down his face.

Gyre livery? None of Logan's servants were here tonight.

"Treachery!" the servant shouted. "Help! Soldiers

are trying to murder Prince Logan! The king's soldiers are trying to murder Prince Logan! We're outnumbered. Please help!"

Agon turned to the king's guards, drawing his sword. "There has to be some mistake. You, you, and you, come with me." He turned to the bleeding messenger, "Can you take us to the—"

"No!" the king bellowed, his laughter instantly turning to rage.

"But sire, we have to protect—"

"You will not take my men. They will stay here! You will stay here! And you, Brant! You're mine. Mine! Mine!"

To Agon, it seemed he saw the king for the first time. He'd seen Aleine IX as a foul, wicked child for so long that he'd forgotten what a foul, wicked child with a crown could do.

Agon looked to the king's guards. Disgust was written on their faces. He could tell they ached to go defend Logan, their prince, but duty forbade them from disobeying their king.

Logan, their prince.

Suddenly, it became so simple. Duty and desire became one for the first time in years. "Captain Arturian," Agon barked in his command voice, so that every royal guard heard him. "Captain! What's your duty if the king dies?"

The squat man blinked. "Sir! My duty would be to protect the new king. The prince."

"Long live the king," Agon said.

The king was staring at him, confused. His eyes widened as Agon's sword swung back.

Aleine was halfway through a curse when Agon's sword struck his head off.

King Aleine Gunder IX's corpse hit the table and knocked over chairs before coming to rest on the floor.

Before any of the guards could attack him, Agon raised his sword over his head with both hands.

"I'll answer for this, I swear. Kill me if you must, but now your duty is to the prince. Save him!"

For a second, none of them moved. The rest of the panic in the hall seemed far away. The ladies screaming, men shouting, servants armed only with meat knives trying to defend their retching lords, shouts of "Treachery!" and "Murder!" ringing in the air.

Then Captain Arturian shouted, "The king is dead; long live the king! To the prince! To King Gyre!"

Together, Agon, the king's guards, and a dozen knife-wielding nobles ran from the Great Hall.

Before Kylar got within sight of West Kingsbridge, he slowed to a walk. He willed himself to be a shadow, and looked at himself. He looked like a raggedly cut piece of darkness. That was good; Durzo had told him that the ragged edges obscured the humanness of his figure and made a wetboy harder to recognize. Kylar thought that his Talent would also be muffling his steps—he wanted it to—but he had no idea if it was. He couldn't afford to find out the hard way.

He rounded the corner and saw the guards. West Kingsbridge was controlled with a large gate like the castle's own gates. Hand-thick oak reinforced with iron, twenty feet high and spiked along the top, with a smaller gate inset. The big, mailed guards looked nervous. One was fidgeting, awkwardly turning his whole head to look to the sides. The other was more calm, pointedly staring every direction except down to the river. Kylar came closer. He recognized the men despite their helmets, and not only because the twins had matching lightning bolt tattoos on their faces. They were bashers, and good ones: Lefty—he was the one with the crooked nose—and Bernerd.

Kylar looked where Bernerd wasn't looking. In the darkness, an unwieldy barge squatted on the river like a beached sea cow. Its doors were open, but no one held any lights. But darkness no longer affected Kylar's eyes. If he'd had more time, he would have marveled about that—as night fell, if anything his vision improved as the shadows became more uniform.

Through the open doors of the barge, he saw rank upon rank of soldiers. Each wore Cenarian livery, but with a red kerchief tied around one arm. Common soldiers with kerchiefs on their left, officers with them on their right.

The soldiers weren't Cenarian. Under their helmets, secreted in the shadows of the night, Kylar saw the stark, cold features of northmen: hair as black as a raven's wing and eyes as blue as frozen lakes. They were big, raw-boned men, weathered and hardened from exposure to the elements and battle. So they weren't just Khalidorans. They were Khalidoran highlanders, the Godking's fiercest, most elite troops. All of them.

In daylight, that would be obvious to any Cenarian in the castle. But at night, it would take time for the Cenarian soldiers to realize that they were being attacked by a foreign enemy. The Cenarian soldiers would figure out that the armbands were what the Khalidorans were using to identify each other, but it would take time. Each new group that encountered the Khalidorans would have to learn it for themselves.

Kylar saw another barge pulling up the river, only a hundred paces away. Khalidoran highlanders tended to be broader and deeper of chest than most Khalidorans, and while a few free tribes still held out in the mountains, those who had been absorbed into the empire had become its most feared fighters.

Four or five hundred highlanders. Kylar couldn't tell, but he guessed that the other barge was full of the elite soldiers too. If so, Khalidor meant to take the castle tonight. The rest of the country would crumple like a body deprived of its head.

Several wytches were talking as they climbed the switchbacks from the water up to the bridge. They were scanning the sky over the castle, apparently looking for some sign.

Indecision held Kylar frozen. He had either to get inside to save Logan—surely Roth would have either Hu or Durzo kill all the dukes, especially after all of Logan's fighting on the Khalidoran border. Just as surely, the murder would happen shortly, if it hadn't already. Kylar could go inside and try to stop the hit, or could try to oppose the Khalidorans out here.

By myself? Madness.

But just watching the barge pull closer to the bridge made him furious. He knew he should feel no loyalty to Cenaria, but he was loyal to Logan and Count Drake. If this army got into the castle, it would be a massacre.

So he needed to fight inside and outside. Great.

Kylar looked at the Sa'kagé impostors manning the

bridge. Bashers wouldn't know or care about the bridge's defenses, much less have the discipline to dismantle them. All they had done was turn the crank that lifted the massive iron river gate.

Then, in the sky above the castle, Kylar saw a long arc of blue-green flame. He started walking.

The wytches looked pleased. They conferred with an officer, who started barking orders. One of the Khalidorans raised a torch and waved it twice. Lefty and Bernerd took torches of their own, walked to either side of the bridge, and waved twice.

All clear. Right.

Kylar drew Retribution. As it hissed out of the scabbard, the bashers turned. Lefty blinked and leaned forward. With the torches in their hands blotting out their night vision, all they saw was a thin strip of dark metal bobbing and floating through the air. Then it moved with terrible speed.

In a moment, both men were dead. Kylar replaced the torch he'd plucked from Bernerd's hand and checked the men on the barges. They had already formed up and were walking, single-file, up the narrow switchbacks that led to the bridge.

Grabbing the keys off Bernerd's body, Kylar opened the gate and slipped through the inset door. The crank and the release for the river gate were there. The gate itself was simply a massive, counterweighted portcullis that could drop into the water. In this case, onto a ship.

Kylar threw the release. The river gate dropped two feet—and didn't crunch. It *clanged*. Kylar looked over the side of the bridge. The river gate had slammed down onto magical stops that glowed and sparked in the darkness. Wytches were on the deck of the first barge, shouting.

He ran into the guard station. There was a fire pit with a cauldron full of stew, cooking paraphernalia, a helmet, several cloaks, chests for the men's personal belongings, and a set of knucklebones on the low table. There was a closet full of old broad carpets stuffed in fat buckets.

Kylar rushed out of the guard station. Surely the king wouldn't have left his military bridge with only that defense. The pilings of the bridge were wood sheathed in iron—impervious to fire. The sheathed wood still got wet, but couldn't breathe and release the water it absorbed, so every beam rotted within years and had to be replaced.

Why would the king be so particular about fire?

And then Kylar saw why. Along either side of the bridge were long wooden beams set on pivots. On the end of each beam was a huge clay globe as wide as Kylar was tall. At least part of the clay was molded over iron because a mooring rope was tied to an iron loop at the top of the globe. Several small handles also protruded from the sides.

Pulling on one handle, Kylar found a bracket. As he slid it out, a wash of oil fumes swept over his face.

It took him several precious seconds of staring at the entire contraption to understand. The arms would swing out over the side of the bridge, holding the globes full of oil, then drop them onto any boat passing underneath—and hopefully set it on fire in spectacular fashion.

He rushed back to the gate and grabbed the torches the guards had been carrying. He closed and locked the gate quickly. The advance party of Khalidorans were almost to the bridge.

What am I doing?

The first barge was just starting under the bridge. There was no time. Kylar kicked a safety latch holding the beam in place and pushed on it. It didn't move. He stumbled and almost tripped over taut ropes at his feet, cursed, and flung himself against the beam again. Hadn't the damned soldiers ever greased this thing?

Finally it occurred to him to use his Talent. He felt power flowing through him—he could lift a wagon on his back. He pressed against the beam and could feel himself shimmering, the ragged black covering and uncovering his skin as he redirected his Talent.

If I'm lucky, they won't even know I'm here until it's too late.

A ball of crackling green wytchfire flew over the globe, missing it by a yard. Yells sounded from below. Whether the wytches saw Kylar or just his torches, they weren't pleased.

Kylar pushed against the beam, but with nothing to brace his feet against, he just slid across the planks. The beam barely moved.

A ball of wytchfire caromed off the globe and ricocheted up into the sky. Kylar ignored it. Something white was blooming above the deck of the barge—now directly under him. A small creature took shape in front of a red-haired wytch and started flying up like a hummingbird. The wytch chanted, his vir-marks thick with power, directing the creature.

Kylar heaved and the ropes at his feet tripped him hard.

The homunculus took shape as it zoomed toward Kylar. It was small, barely a foot tall, and pasty pale. It wore the likeness of the red-haired wytch like ill-fitting clothes. It landed on the globe gently and then rammed steely claws into the iron as if it were butter. It turned to Kylar and hissed, baring its fangs.

Kylar scuttled back and almost fell off the edge of the bridge.

A concussion thudded below. The air in front of the red-haired wytch rippled like a pond absorbing the shock of a thrown rock. Something was moving as if it were just under the surface of the air. Something huge. Reality itself seemed to be stretching—

And tearing. Kylar saw hell and rushing skin as reality itself ripped under the pressure of the wyrm's passage.

It was coming for him.

Twenty feet from him, reality frayed and tore. Kylar had one glimpse of a gigantic, lamprey-like circular mouth. It seemed to throw its mouth inside out in a spiny cone. Then the narrowest ring of teeth hit the homunculus and the teeth snapped in the opposite direction, tearing into the pasty creature. Each successive circle of teeth pulled and snapped onto everything surrounding the homunculus with hideous strength, the cone inverting, sucking everything in.

The last, widest row of teeth snapped closed on the widest part of the iron globe and the pit wyrm whipped back into its hole as suddenly as it had emerged. The air rippled again and then faded as if nothing had happened.

The homunculus was gone. So was three quarters of the globe, clay crunched and iron sheered off as if it were lard. Oil dribbled onto the water beside the barge. The soldiers cheered. The first barge had passed the bridge, and the second barge was just emerging.

Feeling weak, Kylar scooted back and almost fell on ropes again. He cursed loudly. Then his eyes followed the ropes. They were connected to a pulley system—attached to the beam.

"I'm an *idiot!*" Grabbing a rope, Kylar pulled it hand over hand as fast as he could. The arm supporting the second globe swung out over the side of the bridge smoothly and easily. Kylar heard a yell, and two green missiles flew past.

Next to the pulley, there was another rope. Thin. Probably important.

Kylar yanked it and the beam holding the clay globe suddenly dropped. The globe dropped with it. For a moment, Kylar was afraid that he'd just dropped his only weapon straight into the water, but the mooring rope swung the globe like a pendulum a foot above the river. The globe slammed into the second barge at the waterline.

There was no explosion. The side of the boulder that struck the barge was iron beneath a patina of fired clay. It burst through the side of the barge as if the hull were birchbark and blasted through crowded ranks of highlanders.

The rest of the globe was clay. It disintegrated. The oil that filled the globe splashed violently over men and their gear, soaking the wood decks.

Kylar looked at the barge from above. A nice hole gaped at the waterline and the men inside were screaming, but he'd hoped for something more impress—

BOOM!

The barge exploded. Flames leaped out of the hole the globe had made and tore it to three times its original size. Fire burst from the portholes. The doubled and redoubled screams of men were swallowed in the sudden roar of flames.

Men who'd been standing on the deck of the ship were thrown off their feet, and not a few of them into the water. Their armor dragged them hopelessly under the gentle waves.

As quickly as it had sprung up, the gush of fire disappeared. Smoke continued to roll out of the portholes, and men were streaming up onto the deck. The barge listed heavily. An officer, bleeding from a gash on his head, was bellowing orders, but to no avail. Soldiers leapt from the deck to swim for the shore that looked so close—and dropped like rocks. The water wasn't deep, but with heavy armor, it was deep enough.

Having paused for several moments to turn from feeding on oil to feeding on wood, the fire advanced again like an insatiable beast. Fire roared up out of every deck on the ship, and even as the barge drifted forward, Kylar saw that it wasn't going to make it to shore. A few men had the sense to tear off their armor before they leaped overboard, and others were clinging to bridge pilings, but at least two hundred highlanders would never fight on Cenarian soil.

The gate behind Kylar shook as something struck it. He cursed himself. He shouldn't have stayed, shouldn't have watched while he could have been running.

No Cenarian soldiers had come running during his battle, and weren't coming even now, two minutes after the first signal. However bad this was, whatever was happening at the castle must be worse.

The gate blew apart and wytches aglow with power strode through its smoking remains.

Kylar ran for the castle.

53

With Neph Dada and a dozen soldiers in Cenarian livery trailing behind him, Roth sprinted across the catwalk. He reached a small room, turned right, and pounded up a narrow set of stairs.

It was a dizzying maze of corridors, walkways, and service stairs, but it would get Roth and his men to the north tower twice as fast as any other route. Time was of the essence. So many plans that Roth had planted, watered, and coaxed into bloom over the past years were bearing fruit tonight. Like a greedy child, he wanted to taste every one and let the bloody juices spill down his chin.

The queen and her two younger daughters were dying right now, Roth realized with regret. It was too bad. Too bad he wouldn't get to see it. He hoped nobody would move the bodies before he could come inspect them. He'd given orders, but though he trusted Hu Gibbet to carry them out meticulously, this was a war. There was no telling what would happen.

There was no help for it, though. There was no way he would have missed watching the king die.

How exquisite that was! If Roth hadn't been dodging around corners, he'd have burst out laughing.

He'd planned to have a bolt cranked in his crossbow and pointed at the king's forehead all night. He'd planned to be the one to kill the king himself, but Captain Arturian's security had been too tight. Roth had been able to get into the Great Hall, but he hadn't been able to bring a weapon. It had been a small disaster. If Durzo Blint hadn't come through for him, the entire plot would have failed. Father would have killed him.

But it didn't fail. Durzo had come through for him, and what a virtuoso performance it had been. The poisoning of the guests had been brilliant. Roth had been in the kitchens as the food tasters had tried every dish, and not a one had even been ill. The delivery of the king's poison had been a marvel of athleticism. The concoction itself had worked even better than Blint had promised. Roth would find more work for that man. With Durzo as his tool, Roth would dispense such exquisite agonies as he'd never before imagined. Herbs! He'd never even thought of their potential. Durzo would be just the one to guide him in all their uses. Who would have imagined that herbs given to the king would push Agon over the edge?

He had positively giggled when the lord general had relieved the fool king of his head. It had been better than doing it himself. He'd never had the particular thrill of watching a man commit what he himself must have seen as treason. There was something very fine about seeing a man damn himself.

Roth and his men had tarried in the Great Hall just long

enough to see that the lord general and his men had taken the bait and were on their way, and then they had run.

If he had planned this right—and Roth planned everything right—he'd taste even finer fruits than Agon's betrayal tonight. Father would be so pleased.

Six hundred of the Godking's elite highlanders were to arrive at the castle within the next half hour. A thousand more would arrive at dawn. The king had told Roth that he wanted to lose less than half of those by the time he arrived with an occupying army the next day.

Roth thought he would lose less than a quarter. Perhaps far less. He'd pass his *uurdthan* brilliantly. The Godking would appoint Roth King of Cenaria, and take the title of High King for himself. In time, he'd pass the entire empire to Roth.

Pushing future glories from his mind, Roth came to a stop in the last narrow corridor as his men caught up. The door before him would open on unseen hinges into the stairway at the bottom of the north tower. Roth motioned to his men.

They slammed the hidden door open and burst into the hall, swords flashing. The two honor guards posted at the base of the tower didn't stand a chance. They barely had time to register surprise before they were dead.

"We hold this door. Agon doesn't go upstairs," Roth said. "The prince and princess are next." He checked his crossbow.

Logan sat on the edge of the bed, waiting. He closed his eyes and rubbed his temples. He was, for the moment, alone in the bedchamber at the top of the north tower. Jenine Gunder—no, Jenine *Gyre*—had left him to get ready.

To get ready.

Logan felt ill. He'd fantasized about lovemaking, of course, but he'd done his best to confine his desires to one woman—and that woman wasn't Jenine.

When Serah had accepted his proposal, he'd thought his fantasies were going to come true. They'd been planning their wedding just this morning.

Now this.

He heard the soft scuff of bare feet on rug and looked up. Jenine's hair was down, curling luxuriantly halfway down her back. She wore a silky, translucent white gown and an anxious smile. She was breathtaking. Every hint her evening gown had given last night—gods! was that only last night?—was fulfilled, every sensuous promise exceeded. Logan's eyes drank in her curves, her hips sweeping to a narrow waist, waist swelling to those perfect breasts, curve yielding to curve with the sweetness that inspired art. He feasted on the gold of her skin in the candlelight, the darker circles of her nipples showing faintly through her gown, the flutter of her pulse at her throat, the bashfulness in her stance. He wanted her. He wanted to take her. Lust roared through him, dimming the rest of the room, swallowing all the world except the beauty before him and his thoughts of what he was about to do.

He looked away. Ashamed. A lump swelled in his throat and cut off his breath.

"Am I so ugly?" she asked.

He looked up and saw her arms crossed over her

breasts, instant tears in her eyes. Pained, he looked away again.

"No. No, my lady. Please, come here."

She didn't move. It wasn't enough.

Logan met her eyes. "Please. You're so pretty, so, so beautiful you bewilder me. You make me ache. Come sit with me. Please."

Jenine sat next to him on the bed, close, but not touching him. Logan had known little about her before today. Even his father had considered her too rich a match for him. He only knew that she was well-liked, "sunny," "settling down," and not yet sixteen. Logan could understand "sunny." She'd practically glowed at dinner—until her father had spoken. The bastard. Logan understood now a little of how his father must have felt, seeing the woman he loved married to that.

The term "settling down" had been applied to Jenine's brother, too. For the prince, it had meant that people thought he was finally leaving off his more obvious wenching and starting to assume some of the responsibilities of ruling. But Logan imagined that for Jenine, "settling down" probably meant she didn't play tag in the castle anymore.

She was so different from Serah—and she was his wife.

"I'm—I was engaged to another woman this morning. A woman I loved for years . . . I still love her, Jenine. Can I call you that?"

"You may call me whatever pleases you, my lord husband." Her voice was chilly. He'd hurt her. She was hurt, and for all the wrong reasons. Damn, she was young. But then, he hadn't been the only one who'd been handed a lot of surprises in the last day.

"Have you ever been in love, Jenine?"

She considered his question with more gravity than he would have expected from a fifteen-year-old. "I've . . . liked boys."

"It's not the same," Logan snapped. He regretted his tone instantly.

"Are you going to cheat on me?" She shot right back. "With her?"

It hit Logan between the eyes. This couldn't be easy for Jenine, either. How must she feel, liking him, marrying him, knowing he was in love with someone else? Logan put his face in his hands. "I swore our wedding vows because the king asked me to, because the nation needed it. But I swore those vows, Jenine. I will be faithful to you. I will do my duty."

"And your duty to produce an heir?" she asked.

The chill hadn't thawed at all. He should have known better, but he answered. "Yes."

She flopped on the bed, pulled her gown up roughly, and spread her legs. "Your duty awaits, my lord," she said, turning her face away, staring at the wall.

"Jenine—look at me!" He covered her nakedness and—thank the gods—looked only at her face as he spoke, though even now her body cried out to him. It made him feel like an animal. "Jenine, I will be as good a husband as I can. But I can't give you my heart. Not yet. I look at you and, and I feel wrong for wanting to make love to you. But you're my wife! Dammit, it would be easier if you weren't so—so damn beautiful! If I could just look at you without wanting to—to do what we're supposed to do tonight. Do you understand?"

She obviously didn't, but she sat back up and folded her legs under her. Abruptly she was a girl again, blushing for what she'd just done, but her eyes intent.

Logan threw his hands up. "I don't blame you. I don't understand it myself. It's all so twisted up. Nothing makes sense since Aleine—"

"Please, don't talk about my brother tonight. Please?"

"I've lost everything. Everything's . . . everything's wrong." How could he be so selfish? He'd lost a friend, but she'd lost her big brother. She must be aching, too. "I'm sorry," he said.

"No. I'm sorry," Jenine said, her eyes teary but her gaze steady. "I've known for my whole life that I'd be married to whomever the country needed me to marry. I've tried not to even have crushes because I knew that my father might tell me any day that he needed me. I've been trying *not* to like you for two years. I know you think I'm a silly girl, but do you know who some of my potential husbands were? A Ceuran prince who likes boys, another who's sixty, an Alitaeran who's six, a Lodricari who doesn't speak our language and already has two wives, Khalidorans who treat their women as chattel, and a Modaini who's been twice widowed under suspicious circumstances.

"Then there was you. Everyone likes you. A good king would have made the match to heal the split between our families, but my father hates you. So I had to watch you, hear stories about you from my brother and from all the other girls, hear that you're brave, you're honorable, you're loyal, you're smart. My brother told me that you were the only man he knew who wouldn't be intimidated by my mind. Do you know what it's like to have to use small words and pretend not to understand things so you don't get a *bad reputation?*"

Logan wasn't sure he understood. Surely women never had to pretend not to be stupid. Did they?

"When I found out I was marrying you," Jenine said, "it felt like all my little-girl dreams were coming true. Even with my father behaving like—and Serah—and Aleine . . ." She took a deep breath. "I'm sorry, my lord husband. You've been honest with me. I know you didn't ask for this. I'm sorry you had to lose her so I could have you. I know you've had a lot of bad surprises recently." Her chin raised and she spoke like a princess. "But I'm going to do all I can to be a good surprise, my lord. I'm going to strive to be worthy of your love."

By the gods, what a woman! Logan had looked at Jenine last night and seen breasts. He had seen her giggling with her friends and seen a child. He was a fool. Jenine Gunder—Jenine Gyre—was a princess born to be a queen. Her poise, her deliberate self-sacrifice, her *strength* awed him. He had hoped his wife might grow to become a good match for him. Now, he hoped that he might grow to become a match for this woman.

"And I'll do all I can to make our love grow, Jenine," Logan said. "I just—"

She put a finger on his lips. "Will you call me Jeni?"

"Jeni?" Logan touched the soft smooth skin of her cheek, and let his eyes roam over her body. *I'm allowed to do this. I can do this. I should do this.* "Jeni? May I kiss you?"

She abruptly became an uncertain girl again, until their

lips met. Then, even with all her hesitations, uncertainty, and naïveté, to Logan she was all that was warm and soft and beautiful and loving in the world. She was all that was woman, and she was altogether lovely. His arms circled her and he pulled her close.

Some minutes later, Logan pulled away from her on the bed, turning his head toward the door.

"Don't stop," she said.

Hob-nailed boots pounded up the stairs outside the door. Lots of boots.

Not even pausing to pull on his clothes in the darkness, Logan rolled off Jenine and caught up his sword.

54

Regnus Gyre ducked back into a hallway as Brant Agon ran past with a dozen royal guards, and inexplicably, a few fat nobles.

"Long live the king! To the prince!" one of them yelled.

To the prince? The rumors must have been wrong then. Regnus had heard that Aleine Gunder had been murdered last night.

Had the lord general been alone, Regnus would have called out to his old friend, but not with Vin Arturian there. Vin was duty-bound to arrest Regnus, and he would, even if he didn't like it.

There was shouting in the distance, toward the center of the castle, but Regnus couldn't make out any words. Having so much happening that he didn't understand made him anxious, but he could do nothing about whatever was happening elsewhere in the castle. He only had six men, none of them in armor. It had been hard enough to smuggle themselves in as servants and still bring swords. All he could hope to do was find Nalia and get her out of here.

The queen's chambers were on the second floor of the castle in the northeast quarter. Regnus and his men had been walking through the castle nonchalantly, in two groups of three, trying not to attract the servants' attention, but now he gestured sharply. His men gathered around him, and he started jogging.

They got to the queen's chamber without running into a single servant or guard. It was unbelievably good luck. Against even a pair of royal guards, who would be armed and armored, Regnus and his unarmored men might all have died.

Regnus pounded on the great door, and then opened it. A lady-in-waiting who'd been about to open the door fell back in surprise.

"You!" she said. "Milady, run! Murderer!"

Nalia Gunder was seated in a rocking chair, embroidery obviously untouched in her lap. She stood immediately, but waved the servant off. "Don't be a fool. Begone." Her two younger daughters, Alayna and Elise, both looked like they had been crying. They stood uncertainly, neither old enough to recognize Duke Gyre.

"What are you doing here?" Queen Nalia asked. "How did you get here?"

"Your life's in danger. The man who attacked my estate last night has been hired to kill you tonight. Please, Nal—please, my queen." He looked away.

"My lord," she said. It was how a queen might greet a favored vassal. It was also how a lady might address her husband. In those two words, Regnus heard her say, "I've never loved anyone but you." "My lord," she said again. "Regnus, I'll go wherever you lead, but we can't go without them. If I'm in danger, they are too."

"Your girls can come along."

"I mean Logan and Jenine. They wed this afternoon."

Long live the king! To the prince! The nobles' brief cries suddenly made sense. They'd abbreviated it: The king is dead; long live the king. They meant long live the new king. The prince. Logan.

King Gunder was dead. Logan was the new king.

A better man would have had other thoughts first, Regnus knew—a better husband would have had other thoughts first—but his first thought was that Nalia's husband was dead. The hateful little man who'd caused so much misery was gone; his own wife was gone, too. He and Nalia were both suddenly, miraculously freed from twenty-two years of bondage. Twenty-two years, and what he'd thought was a life sentence had suddenly been commuted.

He'd consigned himself to the satisfactions of a proud father and an able commander, never believing that he'd have anything but marital agony to come home to. Now, happiness wasn't just a dim possibility, it was here, one step away, beaming at him, eyes full of love. What a difference it would be to come home to Nalia, to share her home, her conversation, her life, her bed.

If she would have him, he could marry Nalia. He would marry her.

The other implications came to him more slowly. Logan was the new king? The genealogists would have nightmares if Regnus and Nalia had children. He didn't care.

He laughed aloud, his heart was so light. Then he stopped. Agon, the guards, and the nobles had been running to his son, armed with dinner knives.

Logan was in danger. Those men had been running to

save him. Logan was in danger, and Regnus had turned aside.

There wasn't time to explain everything, to tell Nalia that she was free, that Aleine was dead. Regnus had to act. He had no idea how much time they had left.

"They're in trouble! Follow me!" Regnus shouted, lifting his sword. "We—" something hot lanced through his back and then was gone.

Regnus turned and rubbed his chest, irritated. He saw something black flit into the shadows as blood suddenly bloomed from one of his men's throats. As if they were marionettes whose strings had been cut, his men fell one after another in rapid succession, dead. Regnus's hand came away from his chest sticky.

He looked down. Blood was spreading on the front of his tunic over his heart. He looked up at Nalia. The shadow was behind her, holding her. One black hand held her chin up, the other held the long thin short sword that had killed Regnus, but Nalia's eyes were fixed on him and wide with horror.

"Nalia," he said. He dropped to his knees. His vision was going white. He tried to keep his eyes open, but then he realized his eyes *were* open, and it didn't matter any more.

Lord General Agon and his ragtag band of nobles and royal guards were not making good time. Through the centuries, the castle had undergone several expansions, and no simplifications. Twice the general's men had been stopped by a locked door, argued the relative merits of hacking it down or going around, and decided to go another way.

Now they ran down the last hallway to the north tower—the royal guards sprinting, Agon running, and several of the nobles wheezing their way down the long hall. The nobles had long since given up their earlier enthusiastic cries of "to the prince" and "long live King Gyre!" They were saving their breath now.

Agon entered the tower's antechamber to the sound of men cursing and beating at the door to the stairs.

One of the royal guards, Colonel Gher, was standing at the entrance to the antechamber. "Hurry, my lords," he urged the last two paunchy nobles.

Scanning the room, Lord Agon let the younger, more athletic men attack the thick door to the stairs. The room wasn't large, barely twenty feet square, sparsely furnished, with ceilings so high they were lost in the darkness, and just two doors: one to the stairs and one to the hall. There was no going around this door.

Something wasn't right. That the door was locked meant that the guards posted here had either been killed or subverted.

Lord General Agon looked over his shoulder to where Colonel Gher was ushering the last nobles into the room. Agon pushed past Logan's cousin, the fat lord lo-Gyre, and started to shout a warning, but before he could get a word out, Colonel Gher's mailed fist caught him in the chin.

Falling backward, Agon could only watch from the floor as Colonel Gher slammed the doors and threw the bolt.

One of the royal guards threw his shoulder into the door an instant later, but it held, and a moment later, Agon heard the door being barred.

"Trapped," Lord Urwer said helpfully.

For a moment, everyone in the room stopped. As the

Lord General stood with the assistance of one of the royal guards, he could see the implications hitting the men.

If they'd just been betrayed by one of their own, then the attempt on the prince's life wasn't isolated or poorly planned. Everything in the last few days had been orchestrated—from Prince Aleine's death to their own arrival at this dead end. Their odds of surviving weren't good.

"What do we do, sir?" one of the guards asked.

"Get through that door," Lord Agon said, pointing to the door guarding the stairs. It was probably too late. They would probably find enemy soldiers and dead royals up those stairs. But Agon had long ago learned not to waste time on the battlefield lamenting what you should have done, what you should have seen. Recriminations could come later, if there was a later.

The guards had renewed their assault on the door when the twang-hiss of a crossbow bolt rang out.

A royal guard went down, his mailed chest pierced as easily as if he'd been wearing silk. Agon cursed and stared around the room for murder holes in the walls. He could see none.

The men looked around wildly, trying to guard against an enemy that attacked from nowhere.

Twang-hiss. Another guard stumbled into his comrades and fell dead.

Agon and the men looked up into the darkness. A low-hanging chandelier destroyed their chances of seeing beyond it. A low laugh echoed out of the gloom it hid.

Guards and nobles alike scrambled for whatever cover they could find, but there was precious little to be had.

One soldier rolled behind a thickly stuffed wing-backed

chair. A noble tore a portrait of Sir Robin from a wall and held it before himself like a shield.

"The door!" Agon barked, though his heart was clouding with despair. There was no way out. The man or men shooting them not only had numbers and traitors in the castle, they also knew the castle's secrets. The paranoid King Hurlak had honeycombed his expansion of the castle with secret rooms and spy holes. Because he knew where they were, this assassin had merely to sit in place and murder them all. There was no way to stop him.

Twang-hiss. The soldier sitting behind the great chair stiffened as the bolt tore through the chair's back and penetrated his. The assassin was letting them know the hopelessness of their plight.

"The door!" Agon shouted.

With the kind of courage many commanders would demand but few would get, the rest of the guards jumped up and began hacking at the door. They knew that some of them would die doing it, but they also knew it was their only way out, their only hope for life.

Twang-hiss. Another royal guard crumpled in the middle of a swing at the door. Lord Ungert, weakly holding the portrait before himself, wailed like a little girl.

Twang-hiss. A soldier seemed to leap sideways as a bolt punched through his ear hole and threw him bloodily into the doorframe.

A rent appeared in the door. One of the remaining three royal guards gave a shout of triumph.

An arrow flew in through the gash in the door and buried itself in his shoulder. The man spun around once before a bolt from above clove his spine.

Both of the last two guards snapped. One dropped his

sword and fell to his knees. "Please," he begged. "Please no. Please no. Please . . ."

The last was Captain Arturian. He attacked the door like a man possessed. He was a strong man, and the door shuddered and rocked under his blows, the gap widening, stretching to reach the latch.

He dodged as two arrows sped through the hole and past his head, then attacked once more. Another arrow streaked past Vin Arturian, and Agon saw his head whip back. His cheek had been grazed, cut in a neat line, his ear sliced in half.

Screaming, Captain Arturian threw his sword through the hole like a spear. He grabbed the latch and tore it out of the door, jerking as an arrow went into his arm and out the other side. Ignoring it, he seized the door and heaved, tearing it from the frame.

Five Khalidoran archers wearing Cenarian livery stood on the stairs with arrows drawn. Six swordsmen and a wytch stood behind them. Another archer lay at their feet, the guard's sword sprouting from his stomach. The five archers released their arrows simultaneously.

Riddled with arrows, Captain Vin Arturian dropped backward. His body landed next to the guard on his knees, who shrieked.

Twang-hiss. The shriek ended in a gurgle and the young man fell, drowning in his own blood.

Then came one of those eerily normal moments in the chaos of battle that Lord Agon had seen before but could never get used to.

One of the archers handed his bow off, stepped into the room, and grabbed the door. "Excuse me," he said to the captain he'd just helped kill. His voice wasn't sarcastic, simply polite. He pulled the door out of the captain's death-clenched fingers, stepped back into the stairwell and propped the door in place as Lord Agon and the nobles watched him.

In that no-time before reality came crushing back into place, Lord Agon looked at the nobles. They looked at him. These were the men who'd been willing to put their own lives at stake to rescue the prince. Brave men, if some of them fools, he thought as he looked at Lord Ungert shielding himself with a painting. These were the men he'd led to death.

The trap was clever. The "Gyre servant" who'd announced the attack on Logan had doubtless been one of the usurper's men. The ploy not only split the royal guard, taking most of them away from the Great Hall, it also neatly separated the wheat from the chaff. The lords who had come with Agon weren't even exactly the men he himself would have expected to defend Prince Logan, but they were all men who had shown their loyalties in the only way that mattered—with their actions.

By killing these men, the Khalidor would eliminate the very men most likely to oppose them. Brilliant.

Under the sound of the dying soldier's gurgling and rasping breath, Agon heard another sound. His ears identified it immediately. It was a crossbow's windlass being cranked.

Click-click-clack. Click-click-clack.

"So you know whom to curse as you die," a voice, darkly amused, said from his hideout above them. "I'm Prince Roth Ursuul."

"Ursuul!" Lord Braeton cursed.

"Oh, it's an honor then," Lord lo-Gyre said.

The bolt caught lo-Gyre through his fat stomach and struck with such force that it tore out of his back, taking a good part of his viscera with it. He sat roughly against a wall.

Several of the lords damned Ursuul as he had invited. Some went to comfort Lord lo-Gyre, wheezing and shaking on the floor. Lord General Agon remained standing. Death would find him on his feet.

Click-click-clack. Click-click-clack.

"I want to thank you, Lord General," Roth said. "You have served me well. First you killed the king for me—a nice bit of treason, that—and then despite that, you were able to lead these men to my trap. You will be rewarded well."

"What?" old Lord Braeton asked, looking at Brant with alarm. "Say it's not true, Brant."

The next bolt went through Lord Braeton's heart.

"It's a lie," Lord Agon said, but Lord Braeton was dead.

Click-click-clack. Click-click-clack.

Lord Ungert looked at Agon, terrified. The canvas shook in his hands. "Please, tell him to stop," he begged Agon as he saw that he was the last noble standing. "I didn't even want to follow you. My wife made me."

A small hole appeared in Sir Robin's painted shield and Lord Ungert staggered backward. For a long moment, he stood against the wall, grimacing, canvas still in hand. He looked disgusted, as if the canvas should have stopped the crossbow bolt. Then he fell on the painting, breaking the frame to splinters.

Click-click-clack. Click-click-clack.

"Bastard," Lord lo-Gyre said between thin gasps, staring at Lord General Agon. "You bastard."

The next bolt hit Lord lo-Gyre between the eyes.

Lord General Agon raised his sword defiantly.

Roth laughed. "I wasn't lying, Lord General. You'll have your reward."

"I'm not afraid," Lord General Agon said.

Click-click-clack. Click-click-clack. The bolt hit Agon's knee and he felt bones shatter. He stumbled to the chair and fell. Moments later, another bolt tore through his elbow. It felt like it had torn his arm off. He barely held himself sitting on the floor, clutching the arm of the chair like a man drowning.

"My wetboy told me I could trust you to run blindly into this trap. After all, you were stupid enough to trust him," Roth said.

"Blint!"

"Yes. But he didn't tell me you'd betray your king! That was delicious. And marrying Lord Gyre into the royal family? Friend of yours, isn't he? You cost Logan his life with that. I know you're not afraid to die, Lord General," Roth said. "The reward I give you is your life. Go live with your shame. Go on, now. Crawl away, little bug."

"I'll spend the rest of my sorry life hunting you down." Agon said between gritted teeth.

"No, you won't. You're a whipped dog, Brant. You could have stopped me. Instead, you helped me every step of the way. My men and I are going upstairs now. The prince and princess will die because you didn't stop me. So why would I kill you? I couldn't have done this without you."

Roth left the lord general there, gasping on the floor. Shattered.

55

Sergeant Bamran Gamble drew the Alitaeran longbow with the broad muscles of his back. It didn't matter if you were as strong as an ox; you couldn't draw an Alitaeran longbow with your arms. This bow was thick yew, seven feet long unstrung, and it could punch through armor at two hundred paces. He'd heard of men hitting a four-foot target at over five hundred paces, but thank the God, he didn't need to do that.

He stood on the roof of the guardhouse in the castle yard. They'd been barricaded in by a traitor, but the coward had either not had the stomach or not had the torch to set fire to the guardhouse with them inside it. Gamble's men had knocked a hole in the roof and lifted him out.

The wytch's first bolt had flown high past the sergeant's head before he'd even strung his bow. The wytch was the only meister in the yard, stationed to keep an eye on things, evidently. From Gamble's perch, he could see that more troops were streaming over the East Kingsbridge even now, but he had eyes only for the wytch. It was a woman, her hair red, skin pale. She was breathing heavily, as if the last bolt had taken something out of her, but she was already pulling herself together, chanting, the black vir on her arms straining.

If he missed, he wouldn't get a second shot. The wytch would aim this shot low, and it would set fire to the thatch roof of the guardhouse. More than forty of Sergeant Gamble's men would die.

His back flexed and the broadhead slid back. Three fingers slid toward his face; the gut string touched his lips. There was no aiming. It was purely instinctive. A ball of fire ignited between the wytch's palms. The broadhead jumped right through the flame, and the power that would have carried the arrow through armor had no trouble piercing ethereal flame or a young woman's sternum. She was blasted off her feet as if tied to a horse at full gallop. The arrow pinned her body to the great door behind her.

Sergeant Gamble wasn't conscious of having drawn another arrow. If he'd had a choice, he would have chosen to get off the roof and let his men out, but suddenly, battle was singing in his veins. After seventeen years as a soldier, he was fighting for the first time.

The arrow touched his lips and leapt away. This one hit another wytch leading a file of highlanders across the bridge. It was a brilliant shot, one of the best shots of Gamble's entire life. It flew between three rows of running soldiers and hit a wytch in the armpit as she pumped her arms while running. It blew her sideways off the edge of the bridge. She tumbled, limp, into the waters of the Plith.

The highlanders didn't even slow. That was when Sergeant Gamble knew they were in trouble. Two archers and a wytch peeled off from the group and began looking for him, but all the other men proceeded across the bridge. As the archers drew their arrows, the wytch touched each and fire attached to each arrowhead.

Gamble slid down the roof and dropped into the yard as two burning arrows sank into the thatch. The fire spread unnaturally fast. By the time he unbarred the door, there was already smoke pouring out of the inside of the barracks.

"What do we do, sir?" one of the men asked as they crowded around him.

"They can't take us all at once, so they're trying to separate us. I'd guess there's two, maybe three hundred of them. We gotta get to the lower barracks." There would be two hundred men there. That would be even odds, at least, not that Sergeant Gamble thought even numbers would even anything, not against Khalidoran highlanders and wytches.

"To hell with that," a young guard said. "I'm not dying for Niner. We still got East Kingsbridge. I'm outta here."

"You head for that bridge, Jules, and it's the last thing you'll do," Sergeant Gamble said. "This is what they pay us for. Anything less than our duty is betrayal, just like Conyer locking us in the barracks to die."

"They don't pay us shit."

"We knew what they paid when we signed up."

"You do what you gotta do, sir." Jules sheathed his sword and turned confidently. He started jogging for the bridge.

Every man of his thirty-nine was looking at Sergeant Gamble.

He drew, whispered a prayer for two souls as the string

touched his lips, and sent an arrow through the back of Jules's neck. *I'm turning into a regular war hero, aren't I? Skilled at killing women and my own men.*

"We're going to fight," he said. "Any questions?"

Kylar sprinted through the servants' quarters unseen. Still no soldiers had come running. Things had to be bad somewhere for the soldiers not to have organized any resistance.

Abruptly, he was on a fight. At least one detachment of highlanders must have come in another way, because twenty of them were busy slaughtering twice as many Cenarian soldiers.

The Cenarians were on the verge of breaking, even as their sergeant was bellowing orders at them. The sight of the man's face stopped Kylar. He knew that sergeant. It was Gamble, the guard who'd come into the north tower the day of Kylar's first kill.

Kylar joined the fray and killed Khalidorans as easily as a scythe cuts wheat. It was simple labor. There was no joy in killing men who could barely see him.

At first, no one noticed him. He was a smear of darkness deep in the bowels of a castle constructed of dark stone and lit with flickering torches. Then he saved Gamble's life, beheading one Khalidoran and eviscerating another as they cornered the officer.

Kylar didn't even slow. He was a whirlwind. He was the first face of the Night Angels; he was vengeance. Killing was no longer an activity, it was a state of being. Kylar became killing. If every drop of guilty blood he spilled might blot out a drop of innocent blood, he would be clean tonight.

The feeling of mail parting, of leather parting, of flesh parting along the icy judgment that was Retribution was the best feeling in the world. Kylar was lost in a madness, a kind of bizarre meditation, spinning, thrusting, lunging, cleaving, piercing, battering, smashing, ruining faces, snuffing futures. It passed all too quickly. For in what couldn't have been more than half a minute, every last Khalidoran was dead. None was even dying. The killing wrath was nothing if not thorough.

The effect on the Cenarians was monumental. These sheep-in-guards'-armor stood, gaping, at the ragged darkness that was Kylar. Their weapons weren't even raised. They didn't stand in ready positions. They just marveled at Death's avatar among them.

"The Night Angel fights for you," he said. He'd already paused too long. Logan could be dying right now. He ran deeper into the castle.

All the doors were closed, and the halls were eerily quiet. He could only assume that the servants were huddled in their rooms or already fleeing.

The pounding of many footsteps keeping time brought him up short. Kylar sank into a shadowed doorway near a corner. He might be safe from the eyes of men, but there were things more dangerous than men in the castle tonight.

"There must be a good two hundred of their soldiers trapped downstairs," one of the officers was saying to a man whose narrow build gave him away as a wytch even though he wore armor and a sword. "It'll hold for maybe fifteen minutes, meister."

"And the nobles in the garden?" the wytch demanded.

His answer was lost in the tramp of the highlanders' feet as they wound past Kylar and into the distance.

So the nobles were trapped in the garden. Kylar had never been to the garden before—indeed had avoided the castle as much as possible—but he'd seen paintings of the garden, and if the artists hadn't taken too much license, Kylar supposed he could find it. He guessed that was as good of a place as any to look for Logan and Durzo.

As he wound deeper into the castle toward the garden, dead men began to clutter the halls, their blood slickening the floors. Kylar didn't even slow as he ran past. The dead were mostly nobles' guards.

Poor bastards. Kylar didn't have much sympathy for men who took up the profession of arms and then didn't train themselves, but these men had been massacred. Well over forty guards were dead and dying, kicking and frothing in pain. Kylar only saw eight highlanders dead.

Following the blood and the corpses led Kylar to double doors of walnut, barred from the outside. He lifted the bar and eased the door open.

"What in the hell?" a gruff voice with a Khalidoran accent said.

Retreating from the crack to stand behind yet another picture of Niner standing in a heroic pose, Kylar saw several highlanders guarding a room full of nobles. There were men, women, and even a few children in the group. They were disheveled and frightened. Some were crying. Some were throwing up, poisoned.

Footsteps tapped across the floor from beyond Kylar's line of sight, and the highlanders he could see readied their weapons. The point of a halberd hooked the corner

of the door and pulled it open, revealing a squat Khalidoran officer as thick as he was tall.

The officer pulled the other door open with the halberd,
then he beckoned and two men jumped into the hall, back
to back, swords raised. They looked right at the statue,
right at Kylar, who'd pressed himself against the statue's
back, putting his arms behind its arms, his legs behind
its legs.

"Nothing, sir," one said.

Inside the garden, which wasn't nearly as grand as it
looked in the paintings, were ten guards and forty or fifty
nobles—none of them armed. Mercifully, the highlanders
had no wytches with them. Kylar assumed wytches were
too valuable to be wasted guarding prisoners.

The nobles included some of the highest in the land.
Kylar recognized more than a few of the king's ministers. That they were all here meant that Roth believed he
would take over the castle quickly, and he wanted to be
able to personally decide whom to kill and whom to add
to his own government.

The men and women looked dazed. They didn't seem
to believe what had happened to them. It was beyond their
comprehension that their world could turn so completely
upside down so quickly. Many were obviously ill. Some
were torn and bloodied, but others were absolutely untouched. Some ladies whose hair was still perfectly coifed
wept while others bearing gashes and torn skirts seemed
poised and calm.

Behind Kylar a soldier said, "Bleeding mercy, Cap! It
didn't just unbar itself!"

"We're here to guard this room, and we stay here."

"But we don't know what's out there . . . sir."

"We stay," the squat captain said in a voice that brooked no argument.

Kylar almost felt bad for the young highlander. The young man's instincts were right. One day he'd have been a good officer.

But that didn't stop Kylar from dropping the shadows a pace away from him.

He told himself he wasn't becoming visible to be fair. He'd need his strength later.

The young Khalidoran's sword had barely cleared its scabbard when Kylar disemboweled him. Then he danced past the man, throwing a knife with his left hand, parting hardened leather armor and ribs with an upward cut, and guiding a sword hand past his side and the sword into another soldier's body in a smooth motion. Kylar jerked his head forward into a highlander's face and spun with the man quickly. The man's back absorbed the captain's halberd with a meaty crunch.

Kylar dropped under a slash and stabbed up into a highlander's groin with his wakizashi. On his back, he knocked the man backward with a kick, and used the force of the kick to spring to his feet.

Six men were dead or down. Four remained. The first was impetuous. He charged with a yell, something about Kylar killing his brother. A parry and riposte, and brother joined brother. The last three moved forward together.

A quick cut deprived one of sword and sword hand, and the next crossed swords with Kylar five times before he didn't dodge back far enough and fell eyeless from the slash across his face. Kylar jumped over the sweeping halberd and turned to face the officer. He reversed his grip on his sword and stabbed behind him, impaling the one-armed soldier.

The officer dropped the halberd and drew a rapier. Kylar smiled at the extremes of the man's weapon choices and then looked over the officer's shoulder. The man started to turn, frowned, and didn't look back.

A pretty noblewoman smashed the back of his head in with a planter. Flowers and soil flew everywhere, but the planter itself didn't so much as crack.

"Thank you for saving us," she panted, "but damn you for looking at me. You could have gotten me killed." She was one of the women whose hair and makeup hadn't been the least disturbed by whatever violence had brought her here. She looked completely unruffled by having just crushed a man's skull. She merely brushed dirt from her dress and checked to see if she'd dragged it through any blood. Kylar was surprised that she hadn't spilled out of her low-cut dress when she'd run. He recognized her.

"He didn't look back, did he?" Kylar asked Terah Graesin, glad for the black silk kerchief over his face. He'd worn the mask out of habit, but if he hadn't, some of these nobles would have recognized him.

"Well, I never—"

There was a knock on the door, and she and everyone else froze. Three knocks, two knocks, three, two. A voice called out, "New orders, Cap! His Majesty says to kill 'em all. We need your soldiers to help quell resisters in the courtyard."

"You need to leave immediately," Kylar said loudly enough that all the nobles could hear him. "There's at least two hundred more highlanders coming over West Kingsbridge. They're probably the ones fighting in the courtyard right now. If you want to live, collect whatever weapons you can and free the soldiers who are trapped downstairs. Others are already heading there. With them, you can make it out of the castle. You can start a resistance. You've already lost the castle; you've lost the city. If you don't move fast, you'll lose your lives."

The news hit the nobles crowding around Kylar like cold water. Some of them shrank even more, but a few of them seemed to find their backbones as he spoke.

"We'll fight, sir," Terah Graesin said. "But some of us have been poisoned—"

"I know those poisons. If you've lived this long, you've taken a small enough dose that you'll recover within a half hour. Where's Logan Gyre?"

"Excuse me, I'm Terah Graesin, now Queen Graesin. If you—"

Kylar's eyes narrowed. "Where's. Logan. Gyre?"

"Dead. He's dead. The king's dead. The queen's dead. The princesses are dead, all of them."

The world rocked. Kylar felt as if he'd been clubbed in the stomach. "Are you sure? Did you see it?"

"We were with the king in the Great Hall when he died, and I found the queen and her younger daughters in their chambers before I got caught. They were . . . it was awful." She shook her head. "I didn't see Logan and Jenine, but they must have been the first to die. After the king announced their marriage, they'd not left the Great Hall ten minutes before the coup started. The lord general took men to try to save them, but he was too late. These men were just bragging about how they slaughtered the royal guards."

"Where?"

"I don't know, but it's too—"

"Does anyone know where Logan went?" Kylar shouted.

He saw from the looks on their faces that some of them knew, but they weren't going to tell him because they were afraid he would leave them. The cowards. He heard a moan further back in the garden and he pushed through the standing nobles to see a pasty pale man sweating on his back. His mouth was crusted with froth and there was a puddle of vomit near his head. He looked so bad that Kylar almost didn't recognize him. It was Count Drake.

Kylar knelt by the count and grabbed leaves from his herb pouch and began stuffing them in the count's mouth.

"You have an antidote?" one of the sick but standing nobles asked. "Give it to me."

"Give it to me!" another demanded. They began pushing forward. Kylar whipped Retribution out and put the point on a noble's throat.

"If any of you touch me or him, I'll kill you. I swear."

"He's only a count!" a fat, quivering noblewoman said. "He's poor! I'll give you anything!"

The hard, vengeful part of Kylar wanted to withhold the antidote just to repay their meanness, their pettiness. Instead, he grabbed the bag of antidote and tossed it to Terah Graesin. "Give it to those who need it most. It won't save anyone who's already unconscious, and anyone still standing doesn't need it."

Her mouth opened at being so frankly commanded, but she obeyed.

Time was slipping through Kylar's fingers. He was here. He was in the castle, but he had no idea where in the castle he needed to be. He looked down at the count, wondering if he was too late to save him.

The count stirred. His eyes opened, slowly focused. He was going to make it. "North tower," he said.

"That's where Logan went?"

The count nodded and then lay back, exhausted.

"It's too late for them," Terah Graesin said. "Fight with us. I'll give you lands, titles, a pardon—"

But heedless of the nobles' gasps, Kylar wrapped himself in shadows and ran.

Roth's men pounded up the stairs and kicked open the door to the bedchamber. Roth and Neph Dada followed as the eleven men pressed into the room amid grunts and cries. Even though the double doors were wide enough for three abreast, with four ranks of men in front of him, Roth couldn't see what was happening, except to know that it wasn't good. There was the sound of flesh hitting flesh, the sound of a sword cutting through mail, the sound of a skull bursting like a melon.

Beside him, Neph Dada had extended his vir-marked arms. He muttered and a quarter of the vir wriggled. An eerily silent concussion blew men in every direction. Even Roth's men were blasted off their feet.

The three directly in front of him hurtled backward, but as Roth braced for the impact, they smacked against an invisible barrier Neph had erected to protect him.

Neph spoke again and the room filled with light. Roth stepped inside with Neph as everyone recovered.

Logan tried to jump to his feet, too, but his limbs were anchored to the floor as if by a great weight. He was naked and furious. Roth sheathed his sword as eight of his men collected their scattered weapons. Six men lay on the floor, all bleeding from deep wounds. Three of them were dead, three would be soon. Apparently Logan Gyre was no slouch with a sword.

On the bed, wearing a hiked-up translucent nightgown, lay the princess. She was thrashing, terrified, but she couldn't cover herself. Neph had immobilized her, too.

Roth sat down on the bed next to the girl and let his eyes roam over her nubile body. He licked a finger, put it at the base of her neck, and traced it down her body.

"I hope I'm not interrupting anything," he said.

Jenine Gunder's eyes flashed. She was blushing from his casual perusal, but she was furious, too.

Roth put a finger to her lips and shushed her before she could say anything. "I just came to congratulate you on your recent nuptials, my dove," he said. "How is everything? Are you satisfied with the wealth of your husband's endowments?" he asked.

He looked over at the naked Logan and scowled. "Well, I suppose you are. And my dear Duke Gyre—stand him up," Roth ordered. "Or should I say Prince Gyre? Don't lose heart. I've seen her mother naked, and in time she'll—"

Logan lunged forward, but his bonds held. One of the men hit him across the face.

Roth continued as if there had been no interruption. He clucked his tongue. "In time. There's the rub. In time, the princess might grow into these rather admirable breasts and hips." He smiled at her and pinched a cheek. Roth stood, and Neph's magic lifted Jenine from the bed to stand, trembling, next to her husband.

"But you don't have time. I hope you've enjoyed your marriage. And Logan, friend, I hope you've not been wasting your time with foreplay—because your marriage is over."

The moment drew out. There was nothing Roth loved so much as watching bewilderment turn to dread turn to despair.

"Who are you?" Logan asked, his eyes betraying no fear.

"I'm Roth. I'm the man who ordered your brother's death, Jenine." Ignoring Logan, Roth watched the words break over the girl like a wave. But he didn't stop, didn't let her voice a denial.

"I'm Roth, the Shinga of the Sa'kagé. I'm the man who ordered your father's death, Jenine. Not ten minutes ago, I watched his head roll off the high table.

"I'm Prince Roth Ursuul of Khalidor. I'm the man who ordered your sisters' and your mother's deaths, Jenine. If you listen, you might hear their cries." He put a finger to his ear and an attentive look on his face, mocking.

"You two are all that's left between me and Cenaria's crown, Jenine. And I'm going to take that crown. I'm afraid I'm going to have to kill you. Do you want to choose which of you dies first?"

With each revelation, he watched her eyes, fed hungrily on her dying hope, gorged himself on her ripening despair. Roth drew a knife and turned her so she faced Logan.

Logan cried out wordlessly, but Neph had gagged him. He bucked and strained against the bonds, his muscles taut, swelling huge, but escaping Neph's magic was impossible. He could sooner tear stars from the heavens.

"My lord," a soldier called from the hall. "One of the barges has been destroyed. The meisters need you to help quell the resistance."

Watching the hope bloom in the young girl's eyes gave Roth a shiver of excitement. "Resistance," he said. "Maybe they'll save you! But wait, your hero is already here. Logan, are you just going to stand there? Aren't you going to save her?"

The muscles in Logan's arms and legs bulged and the magical bonds shifted and thinned until Neph spoke again and they redoubled. The prince couldn't move.

"I guess not," Roth said, turning back to Jenine. "But you're the princess! Surely the royal guards will come. Why, I bet even now the lord general is leading men here to rescue you!" He brushed his hair back over a mangled ear. "But I killed Agon and all the royal guards. There are no more heroes. No one can save you, Jenine."

Roth stepped behind Jenine and trailed his free hand up her slender stomach. He ripped her nightgown open, tore it off, and cupped a breast in his hand. As a tear rolled from her eye, he bent and kissed her neck like a lover. His eyes locked on Logan's, mocking.

Then, where he'd kissed her, he cut her throat.

Roth gave her a shove, and Jenine stumbled into Logan's arms, the right side of her neck a fountain of blood. Neph loosed Logan's bonds enough that he could hold the girl, but not enough to reach up to try to stop the bleeding.

Logan's eyes were wells of horror and pity. A sound like beatific music to Roth's ears, the sound of a soul at its utmost limit of suffering, escaped Logan's lips. He held the small, gasping girl to his chest. Roth devoured his horror, trying to lock this memory into his mind, knowing he would need this on the long dark nights.

But then Logan pulled back, turned so Roth couldn't see his face, and looked into Jenine's face.

"I'm here, Jeni," Logan said, holding the girl's eyes with his own. "I'm not going to leave you." The gentleness in his voice infuriated Roth. It was as if Roth didn't matter anymore. With his soothing voice, Logan was pulling Jenine and himself out of this world of darkness, walling them off somewhere Roth couldn't go.

As Jenine stared into Logan's eyes, Roth could see her relax—not into death, but from despair. "You really would have loved me, wouldn't you?" she said.

Roth knew he should have cut deeper, should have slashed her windpipe and not just that single artery. He struck Logan across the face, but his blow might have been the buzzing of a gnat for all it did. The big man didn't even lose eye contact with the princess.

"Jeni. Jeni," he said quietly. "I already love you. I'll be with you soon."

"You're dying!" Roth shouted, not a pace away, but he might have been a summer breeze. Jenine's knees trembled and Logan pulled her back into his embrace, closing his eyes and whispering in her ear as her life bled out against his chest.

"My lord, they need you now," the messenger said, more urgently.

Logan didn't even look at Roth as Jenine shuddered against his chest. He just kept whispering assurances. She sucked in three more labored breaths, and then sighed her life out in Logan's arms, her eyes fluttering closed. Neph released the bonds holding her slowly and she crumpled to the floor.

"No! No!" Roth yelled. She wasn't even *afraid*. He'd done everything right and she wasn't even afraid to die. Who wasn't afraid to die? It wasn't right. It wasn't fair.

He slapped Logan. Once and again. And again. And again. "You won't die so easy, Logan Gyre," Roth snarled. He turned to his men. The muscle in his jaw twitched. "Take him to the Maw and give him to the sodomites."

"My lord!" the messenger said, rushing into the room again. "You must—"

Roth grabbed a handful of the messenger's hair. He stabbed at the man's face in a fury, wildly, again and again. He flung the man sideways and tried to cut his throat, but caught him above the ear instead. The knife turned and a fat strip of hairy scalp came off in Roth's hand. The man wailed until Roth grabbed him again and cut his throat.

Meanwhile, Neph had opened the hidden door out of the chamber. He lifted the princess's body with magic and floated it before him.

"Neph, what are you doing?"

"The Godking wishes to have the heads of all the royal family displayed. Whatever you're planning, I'd advise you to hurry."

He didn't address Roth by his title. Everything was going wrong and Father would be here soon. Roth turned, panting, the gory strip of hair and flesh in his fist. He trembled with rage and the men holding Logan went as white as paste. "Bring me his head when they're finished. But before you give him to the sodomites, cut his cock off and bring me his sack for a purse. I want him to bleed to death as they fuck him."

56

The antechamber at the base of the north tower stank overwhelmingly of blood and feces released in death, the bitter tang of urine threaded through the stench. Kylar gagged as he opened the barred door.

A quick glance told the story. The men had been trapped in the room, ambushed by a crossbowman. Kylar scowled. A crossbowman? In a room this small?

Then he saw the narrow platform by the ceiling, plainly visible in the shadows that now welcomed Kylar's eyes. From the way the bodies were scattered, it had just been the one man, shooting the royal guards and nobles like fish in a barrel.

So this was what happened to the men who'd come to save their prince. From the streaks of blood going out the door, it looked like only one man had survived to drag himself away.

Sickened, Kylar ran up the stairs. He found six dead Khalidorans at the entryway. The rest of the story was clear enough. Caught in bed with his wife—Logan's clothes were scattered around the room—Logan had sprung up and fought. He'd killed six fully armed Khalidorans, but from the burn marks on the floor, he'd been hurt or disabled with magic.

Then, from the wide, sticky puddle of blood, it was obvious that Roth had either killed Logan slowly so that he bled copiously, or had killed both him and his wife. Neither body was in the room. The Khalidorans would want Logan's body along with the rest of the royal family's bodies so the whole kingdom could see they were dead, the line of succession wiped out.

A torn nightgown lay on the floor. The princess, young and beautiful as she was, was probably in a room somewhere being raped until she died of it.

Kylar tried to interpret it another way. His mind analyzed the scene, trying to ward off the shock of despair. Was it possible the princess had been killed and Logan was alive?

But soldiers wouldn't keep Logan alive and kill a princess whom they could rape. Logan was a warrior, a renowned swordsman, and the heir to the throne. The assassinations of the rest of the royal family had been carried out brutally but precisely, carefully. If the Khalidorans were going to make an exception and spare one life for any length of time, it wouldn't be Logan's.

Grief hit Kylar like a physical blow. Logan was dead. His best friend was dead. Dead, and the blame could only be placed on Kylar.

He could have stopped it. Kylar could have killed Durzo last night. Durzo's back had been there, a target he couldn't miss. Dorian had told him. Told him!

What pain hadn't he inflicted on Logan? He'd allowed

the murder of Logan's friend Aleine, concealed the truth about Serah's and Aleine's affair, got him sent to prison for murder, and forced him to break his engagement. Now Logan had been forced to marry a girl he didn't know and had been murdered, his wife of less than an hour raped and killed.

Sinking to the floor, Kylar wept. "Logan, I'm sorry. I'm sorry. It's all my fault." He reached a hand to steady himself, and found it in the puddle of blood. He looked at his bloody, bloody hand. Bloody as it had been bloodied in this very chamber, five years ago when he'd finished his first solo kill. Bloody as it had been bloody continually since he murdered his first innocent. This was where murder had brought him. It had brought him full circle, his murder of one innocent leading inexorably to the murder of more. In the last five years, he'd done exactly what he'd intended to do: he'd become more and more like Durzo Blint. He'd become a killer. He slept uneasily, so he slept light, so he was ever more dangerous. He was always on edge, and the blood that first covered his hands in this very room had never been washed clean. It had only been added to. It was no mistake that Logan's blood was on his hands now, no coincidence.

The Drakes liked to talk about a divine economy: the God turning weeping into laughter, sorrow into joy. A wetboy was the merchant prince of the satanic economy. Murder begat murder, and as Durzo had said, others always paid the price.

Must others always pay for my failures? Is there no other way? The blood on his hands said no, no. *This is reality; it's hard, uncomfortable, hateful, but it's true.*

"I'm breaking my own rules," a blur of shadows said.

Kylar didn't look up. He didn't care if he died. But the man said no more. After a long moment, Kylar asked bitterly, "'Don't play fair. A kill is a kill'?"

Durzo stepped out of the shadows. "Kylar, I have one last rule to teach you."

"And what's that, master?"

"You're almost a wetboy now, Kylar. And now that you've learned to win almost any fight, there's one more rule: Never fight when you can't win."

"Fine," Kylar said. "You win."

Durzo stood there a long moment. "Come, apprentice. Here is your Crucible."

"Is that all your life is?" Kylar asked, finally looking up. "Tests and challenges?"

"My life? That's all *life* is."

"That's not good enough," Kylar said. "These people shouldn't be dying. Khalidor shouldn't be winning. It's not right."

"I never said it's right. My world isn't cut into black and white, right and wrong, Kylar. Yours shouldn't be either. Our world only has better and worse, shadows lighter and darker. Cenaria couldn't win against Khalidor no matter what happened tonight. This way, a few nobles die rather than tens of thousands of peasants. It's better this way."

"Better? My best friend's dead and they're probably raping his wife! How can you stand by and do nothing? How can you help them?"

"Because life's empty," Durzo said.

"Bullshit! If you believed that, you'd have died a long time ago!"

"I did die a long time ago. All the good passes by and all the evil passes by, and we can't do a damn thing to change anything or anybody, Kylar. Least of all ourselves. This war will come and go, there will be a victor, and people will die for nothing. But we'll be alive. Like always. At least, I will."

"It's not right!"

"What do you want? Justice? Justice is a fairy tale. A myth with soft fur and reassuring strength."

"A myth you believed in, once upon a time," Kylar said, gesturing to the word JUSTICE etched into Retribution's blade.

"I used to believe a lot of things. That doesn't make them true," Durzo said.

"Who's better off? Logan or us? Logan could sleep at night. I hate myself. I dream of murder and wake in cold sweat. You drink yourself oblivious and blow your money on whores."

"Logan's dead," Durzo said. "Maybe he'll wear a crown in the next life, but that doesn't do him much good now, does it?"

Kylar looked at Durzo strangely. "And you're the one who says life is empty, meaningless. That we don't take anything of value when we take a life. Look how you hold on to yours. You fucking hypocrite."

"Every man worth a damn is a hypocrite." Durzo reached into a breast pocket and pulled out a folded scrap of paper. "If you kill me, this is for you. It explains things. Consider it your inheritance. If I kill you . . . well, when I die, I'll take a break on my way to the lowest plane of hell and stop to talk."

Durzo tucked the paper in a breast pocket and drew a huge sword with a long red ribbon dangling from its hilt.

It was a longer, heavier blade than Retribution, but with his Talent, Durzo could wield it with a single hand.

"Don't do this," Kylar said. "I don't want to fight you."

The wetboy closed on him. Kylar stood still, making no move to defend himself. "Did you already give him the Globe of Edges?" Kylar asked.

The wetboy stopped. He reached into a pouch and pulled out the silvery globe. "This?" he said. "This is nothing. Another fake." He hurled the globe through at the window. Glass broke as it punched through the window and sailed out into darkness.

"What have you done?" Kylar asked.

"By the Night Angels!" Durzo said. "You bonded my ka'kari. You stole it from me. You still don't understand?"

It was like he was speaking another language. *Bonded?* Kylar thought he'd bonded the ka'kari—must have, because his Talent worked now. And Durzo said it was glass?

"Unbelievable," Durzo said, shaking his head. "Draw your sword and fight, boy."

"It's my sword now, is it?" Kylar asked.

"Not for long. You aren't worthy to succeed me." Durzo raised his blade.

"I don't want to fight you," Kylar said, refusing to draw the blade. "I won't fight you."

Durzo struck. At the last second, Kylar drew Retribution and blocked. Talent-strengthened blow met Talent-strengthened blow. The blades shivered from the impact.

"I knew it was in you," Durzo said. He smiled fiercely.

Any delusion Kylar might have had that Durzo would take it easy on him because he hadn't had time to learn to use his Talent dissolved instantly. Durzo launched into a blistering attack so fast it should have been impossible.

Kylar staggered backward, blocking some blows and jumping back to avoid more. Durzo used every weapon in his arsenal. His sword blurred through combinations, whipping the hilt ribbon into a scintillant red stream. The ribbon's purpose was to pull an opponent's eyes from the point of danger. Anyone who let his attention wander would find a steel reminder in his ribs.

But it wasn't just the sword that confused Kylar. Durzo would follow a cut at Kylar's head with a kick at his knee then a spinning backhand with his free hand at his face. Combinations followed and flowed into each other in a raging river of deadly motion.

Blocking and dodging, Kylar retreated back and back. Durzo didn't give him time to think, but Kylar was aware of the room. It took up the entire top floor of the tower, so it formed a large circle flattened at one end for the entrance and at the other for a closet.

The very familiarity of fighting against Durzo slowly calmed him. Of course, he'd always lost, but things would be different this time. They had to be.

The surge of power flowed through his arms with a rush of tingles that made him feel like every hair on his body was standing on end. He parried a thrust and Durzo's blade was slapped aside as if it weighed a quarter of what it did. Blint recovered in a blink, but he stopped advancing.

Kylar was standing a yard from the wall with a cherry-wood bureau next to him. Blint's sword flicked toward his eyes, but it was a feint. Blint's real attack was a kick at Kylar's leading knee. Kylar dropped backward toward the wall and lashed out with a foot, halting Blint's foot as it came forward. Expecting his sword to meet resistance, Blint slashed too hard. His heavy blade slashed deeply into the bureau.

The stone wall slapped against Kylar's back as he stumbled and levered himself upright again. But instead of trying to drag his sword out of the bureau, Durzo reached over his shoulders and grabbed twin hook swords. Each bore a crescent-shaped blade over the knuckles, but was otherwise a normal sword with a hooked point for catching an enemy's sword.

"I hate those," Kylar said.

"I know."

Kylar attacked, still trying to adjust to the Talent's effect on his fighting. So far as he could tell, it could make his muscles move more quickly and more powerfully, but there was a limit to how fast even two Talented fighters could fight. The Talent didn't help you make decisions faster, so it wasn't a simple matter of accelerating regular fighting. Kylar had to be more careful—and he still had no idea if the Talent would defend his body itself. If Blint got through Kylar's defenses with a Talent-aided kick, would it crush his ribs like twigs, or were they strengthened as well?

The only way to find out was no way to find out.

Blint let Kylar come forward, using the hook swords defensively. Then, as they neared the bed, he started using the hooks. As Kylar struck, Durzo turned his blade down to the hook and wrenched Retribution aside. He followed with an overhand slash with the other sword.

Leaping backward, Kylar found himself being driven toward one of the tower's broad windows. Durzo strode in and caught a slow slash, but instead of sweeping it aside, he caught it with his other hook, trapping Kylar's blade.

As Kylar lunged forward, Blint guided the blade past his head and wrenched it free. Retribution clattered on the floor behind Kylar. Blint kicked him in the chest, his foot barely slowed by the arms Kylar brought up as he drew daggers.

Kylar slammed into the window and felt glass break, wood splinter, and the latch burst. He had the sickening sensation of launching into space.

Clawing for something, anything, Kylar turned, twisting with the desperate grace of a falling cat. Abandoned to gravity, his daggers spun away, glittering in the moonlight.

Kylar punched his fingers through a delicate windowpane. His hand clamped on wood and jagged glass as his momentum swung the window open.

His face met the tower wall with a crunch. Glass glided through the flesh of his fingers then ground against bone as his hand slipped. Held.

Blinking, he dangled by one hand. Blood coursed down his arm. Blood coursed down his face. He hung two hundred feet over the basalt of the castle's foundation and the broad expanse of the river. Steam escaped from the single volcanic vent that opened on Vos Island and obscured a barge pulled up to the shore. The steam shone in the moonlight, and far below, by the ship, Kylar saw men talking. Even from this height, he could hear the ringing of steel, and catch glimpses of Khalidoran invaders overwhelming foot soldiers in the castle courtyard.

Then Sergeant Gamble emerged from the front gate. He was leading the nobles and more than two hundred Cenarian soldiers. They were trying to escape the castle, just as Kylar had told them, but even as they pushed toward the east gate, the Khalidorans were reinforced by more than a hundred highlanders coming from the opposite side of the castle.

In seconds, the courtyard had become the frontline of the battle and the war for Cenaria. The castle and the city were lost. If the nobles were slaughtered, so was all of Cenaria. If the nobles could press through the massed highlanders and get across East Kingsbridge, they could begin a resistance.

It was the dimmest sort of hope, but hope had never come in the blinding bright variety in Cenaria.

Something popped and Kylar dropped four inches. He scrambled up the window frame as the next hinge tore out of the sill. The last hinge protested and popped out.

Kylar hurled himself at the storm shutter tied back against the tower wall. His fingers raked over slats. Caught. Three slats broke and then finally arrested his fall.

The window sailed peacefully below him, turning end over end in the whistling wind. It hit the rocks just paces short of the river—exactly where Kylar would land if he fell. The window exploded into splinters and slivers of glass.

Kylar looked up. The shutter's hinges were straining, slowly pulling out of the rock.

Perfect.

Durzo Blint stood in the carnage and saw none of it. Bodies were strewn about the bedchamber. Freshly cut lilies bloomed next to the royal bed—white lilies flecked red with blood.

A delicate, once-white nightgown lay soaking in a wide pool of crimson near his feet. The floor mosaic was scorched in a black circle. The acrid tang of wytchfire smothered the hint of perfume in the air.

But Durzo saw only the open window in front of him. His pockmarked face looked stricken. Wind howled through the window, sending the curtains fluttering and his gray hair into his eyes.

His fingers flipped a blade end over end in his right hand. Finger to finger to finger, stop. Finger to finger to finger, spin. He noticed what he was doing and jammed the dagger into a sheath. His face set and he pulled his mottled gray and black cloak around his shoulders, covering a belt full of darts, daggers, and numerous tools and pouches.

It wasn't supposed to end like this. It wasn't supposed to be so empty. He turned his back to the window, then stopped. His head cocked to the side as he heard something over the screaming wind.

Kylar willed himself to release the shutter with his bloody right hand. His hand found empty sheaths for daggers that matched the empty scabbard on his back. Grunting, he contorted himself to draw a tanto from his calf. His fingers were deadened, lacerated, weak. The tanto almost slipped out of them.

The ropes tying the shutter against the wall parted easily. Rusty hinges creaked loudly. Kylar stiffened, but there was no help for the noise. He took two quick breaths, then launched off the tower wall with both feet. He swung back toward the open window and heaved his body up with the force of his Talent as if he swinging on a giant swing.

The shutter tore away from the tower in his hands, and he barely made it high enough not to slam into the wall, instead sliding into the bedchamber along the floor.

His body swept Durzo's feet out from under him and the wetboy fell on top of Kylar, one of his hook swords going flying out the window. The shutter was between them, trapping Durzo's hands in an awkward position. Kylar slapped the shutter into Durzo's face.

"I don't—" Kylar slammed the shutter into Durzo's face with all of his strength and Talent. The man flew off him.

Kylar rolled aside and jumped to his feet.

But Blint was already up. He kicked a footstool at Kylar. Kylar blocked it with a foot, but it caught him off-balance and tripped him. He landed face-first on a decorative rug.

Running forward like lightning, Blint raised the hook sword. Instead of trying to stand or roll aside, Kylar grabbed the rug and yanked.

Durzo lurched forward faster than he expected and cut only air as his knees collided with Kylar's shoulder. He flipped over headfirst.

Durzo's heavy curved sword was still lodged in the bureau next to the window, but Retribution was closer. Kylar grabbed it and turned.

"—want to—"

The wetboy lunged to grab the hook sword off the ground.

"—fight you!" Kylar jumped on the hook sword.

Durzo pulled up with all the strength of his Talent. For an instant, it seemed the iron core of the blade would hold. Then the sword snapped an inch from the hilt.

"You might not want to, son, but there's something in you that refuses to die," Durzo said. He threw the broken blade aside, but didn't draw any other weapon.

"Master, don't make me fight you," Kylar said, pointing the blade at Durzo's throat.

"You made your choice when you disobeyed me."

"Why'd you do it?"

"I wouldn't have apprenticed you, but I thought you were something you're not. May the Night Angels forgive me."

"I don't mean me!" Kylar's hands shook on the sword. "Why'd you make me betray my best friend?"

"Because you broke the rules. Because life's empty. Because I broke the rules too." Durzo shrugged. "It catches up."

"That's not good enough!"

Durzo tented his hands and pursed his lips. "Logan died screaming, you know. Pathetic."

Kylar lashed out. The sword streaked for Durzo's neck. But Durzo didn't flinch. The blade slapped into his palm and stopped as if it didn't even have an edge.

But Durzo's hands were still tented in front of him. The hand holding Kylar's sword was made of pure magic.

It flung Retribution out of Kylar's grip. Other hands bloomed in the air, striking at him. Kylar blocked and stumbled back as Durzo walked forward calmly, surging with Talent.

There was nothing Kylar could do. He blocked faster and faster, but the hands came faster still. Dimly, a few hands of his own Talent bloomed in front of him and blocked some of the attacks, but it wasn't enough. Durzo drove him back and back.

Finally, hands latched onto each of Kylar's limbs and pinned him to the wall. He couldn't move an inch.

"Ah, kid," Durzo said. "If I could have taught you to use your Talent, you'd have been something really special."

Durzo drew a throwing dagger. Spun it in his fingers. Brought it up. He paused as if to say something, then shook his head.

"I'm sorry, Kylar."

"Don't be. Life's empty, right?"

Durzo sighed. He was staring at Retribution, gleaming blackly at Kylar's feet, as close as the moonlight and as far away as the moon. The look on his scarred face was anguish, regret.

Following his gaze, Kylar stared at the black sword that Durzo had carried for so many years, and remembered—

Scowling, Durzo had snatched the pouch away from him and turned it over. The Globe of Edges fell into his hand. "Damn. Just what I thought," he said, his voice harsh in the quiet of the Jadwin hallway.

"What?" Kylar asked.

It was a fake, another fake ka'kari.

But Durzo wasn't in any mood to answer questions. "Did the girl see your face?"

Kylar's silence was enough.

"Take care of it. Kylar, that's not a request. It's an order. Kill her."

"No," Kylar said.

"What did you say?" Durzo asked, incredulous. Black

blood was dribbling down Retribution, pooling on the floor.

"I won't kill her. And I won't let you."

"Who is this girl that she's worth being hunted for the rest of your short—" he stopped. "She's Doll Girl."

"Yes, master. I'm sorry."

"By the Night Angels! I don't want apologies! I want obedien—" Durzo held up a finger for silence. The footfalls were close now. Durzo blurred into the hall, inhumanly fast, his sword flashing silver in the low light.

His sword flashed *silver?* Retribution's blade is black.

There was the sound of something metallic rolling across marble toward Kylar. He raised a hand and felt the ka'kari slap into his outstretched palm.

"No! No, it's mine!" Blint yelled.

The ka'kari pooled like black *oil in an instant.*

What had Durzo just said? The silver was another fake. You stole *my* ka'kari. Not a silver ka'kari at all. A black ka'kari. The ka'kari Durzo had been carrying for years, hidden covering the blade of Retribution.

The ka'kari choose their own masters. For some reason, the black ka'kari had chosen Kylar. Maybe had chosen him years ago, the day Durzo had beaten him for seeing Doll Girl again. That day, when a blue glow had surrounded the black blade. When Durzo had shouted, "No, not that! It's mine!" as incandescent blue fire had burned into Kylar's fingers. Durzo had thrown it away from Kylar so Kylar couldn't complete the bond, because once Kylar completed the bond, Kylar wouldn't call the silver ka'kari for Durzo. Now they knew he hadn't called it because it had been a fake. There had never been any ka'kari in the city except Durzo's black.

And Durzo had known from that very day that if he let Kylar live, the black ka'kari was lost to him forever. Durzo had even left it for him tonight so that Kylar would have a chance.

But now it was too late.

Durzo looked like there was more he wanted to say to Kylar, some way he wanted to vent his anguish. But he'd never been a man of words.

Instead, mere paces away, he hurled the knife at Kylar's face.

Time didn't slow.

The world didn't contract to the point of the spinning knife.

But despair flash-boiled in the heat of an insane hope in Kylar's heart. He didn't even notice his hand come up, didn't know how it had broken free, couldn't say how the ka'kari had gone from the blade on the floor into his hand. It was just there.

In that unslowed fraction of a second, black goo flipped from his fingertips and splattered across the knife spinning toward his chest like spit against pavement.

When Kylar looked again, the knife was just *gone*.

Ting.

Kylar looked down to see what had made the sound. The ka'kari was rolling across the floor coming toward him. It wobbled as it rolled and when it climbed up his boot and dissolved into his skin, Kylar felt a rush of power.

With a mental shrug, Kylar burst through the phantasmal hands holding him to the wall. Settling smoothly on his feet, he extended a hand toward his old master and released the power arcing through him.

Durzo was hurled away as if all the force of a hurricane had been unleashed in his face. He tumbled end over end, sliding and rolling across the room until he slapped against the wall.

With the Talent, Kylar caught up Retribution and brought it to his hand.

"Don't fight when you can't win," Kylar said. "And don't fight when you don't want to win. Right?"

Durzo struggled to his feet and stood, weaponless. He took a ready position and smirked. "Sometimes you have to fight."

"Not this time," Kylar said. He raised the sword and came forward at a run. Durzo didn't move; he just looked Kylar in the eye, ready. At the last second, Kylar dodged to the side and dove through the window into the moonlit air whipping the north tower.

One of those men on the boat had been Roth.

57

Logan had no intention of letting *anyone* use his sack for a coin purse, much less Roth Ursuul. In fact, he intended to kill the bastard. He wasn't worried that he was unarmed and still naked—Roth had supposed it would strip him of his dignity—rage gave him power. All the cruelty and depravity and horror Logan had seen in the last day had transformed him. He would be a man again, later. Now he was hard, crystal-clear frozen rage. Logan figured that even with his hands bound he could kill both guards. With the fury that was arcing through his body, he didn't think there was much of anything that could stop him.

Except magic. Roth had known it, too, and he'd sent his wytch, Neph Dada, to escort Logan to the dungeon. Neph had obviously memorized the layout of the castle, because he threaded through servants' hallways and back staircases and cellars effortlessly.

The city of Cenaria had only one gaol, connected to the castle by a single tunnel—now overrun with Khalidoran highlanders—and separated from the rest of the city by the two forks of the Plith River. Prisoners were taken to the gaol by barge. Few left. The felons who came here might as well have been devoured by the earth herself.

Or, the sliver of Logan that wasn't rage thought as a peculiar smell assaulted his senses, maybe it was called The Maw for different reasons. Fumes were constantly escaping from the north side of Vos Island and filling the air of the prison with the smell of brimstone before finally finding the open air.

Neph Dada paused before an iron gate while one of the men guarding Logan fumbled for a key. Neph glared at the man and waved a hand in front of the lock, the tendrils of black on his arm not quite moving in time with his arm. The lock clicked.

The guard produced the correct key and smiled weakly.

"I've other matters to attend to," Neph said. "Can you handle him by yourselves from here?"

"Yes, sir," the guard said, looking at Logan nervously.

Logan's heart smiled. Fighting two armed men while naked wasn't exactly good odds, but with Neph's magical bonds holding his arms motionless and giving his legs barely enough space to shuffle, there was *nothing* he could do.

"Good. The bonds will hold for ten minutes," Neph said.

"Plenty of time, sir," the guard said.

With a snort, Neph left them. The big-nosed guard locked the iron gate, giving Logan time to adjust to the dim room. To the right and left were heavy doors with iron-barred windows.

"In case you're wondering," Nose said. "These are the

nicest suites in the place. Real sweet places. For nobles. Not for you, though." He chuckled.

Logan looked at the man flatly.

"Ramp up there goes to the surface. Not for you, either."

The weasel-faced guard looked at Nose, "You always taunt dead men?"

"Always," Nose said, stuffing a finger up his nose. "What?" he said as Weasel looked at him. "I was scratching."

"Shut up," Weasel said. "We down on three?"

"Yeah, all the way to the Howlers. Let's make it quick." Nose tapped on the fourth door as he passed it. "I'll be right back for ya, sweetheart!"

There was a little cry from the cell, but the woman inside didn't look up.

"That bitch makes me hot," Nose said. "You seen her?"

Weasel shook his head, so Nose continued, "Got more scars on her face than a highlander's got fleas, but who needs to look at her face, huh?"

"The prince will rip your throat out if you touch her," Weasel said.

"Ah, how's he gonna know?"

"He's coming down tonight. Wants to free our Sa'kagé boys and check on that wench and some little kid they dragged in," Weasel said.

"Tonight? Hell, she won't take me five minutes," Nose said. He laughed.

They wended their way through two levels of manmade tunnels, the smells of massed humanity thickening and mingling with potent brimstone, sewage, and other smells

Logan couldn't identify. He tested his bonds periodically, but there was no change. He was barely mobile. Nonetheless, he kept his eyes open for his chance. Simple escape wouldn't be good enough. He had to kill both guards, get the keys, and remember the way out.

The Howlers were on the third floor, but as they came into the natural caves, merely widened with tools, Logan heard no howling.

"We don't want to go no further," Nose said, pausing in front of a double-banded iron door. "These bastards here will do all we need. I'm not gonna even try to get him out of the Hole. I don't go near those animals."

"The Hole?" Logan asked.

Nose leered, but seemed eager to terrify him. "Hell's Asshole. For the rapists, killers, and twists so bad that hangin's too good for 'em. They drop 'em in there and let 'em devour each other. They hafta get their water off the rocks, and the guards never throw in enough bread. Sometimes they piss on it first."

"So who's going to . . . you know?" Weasel asked, drawing his blade awkwardly. "Those bonds won't hold forever."

"Who's going to what?" Nose asked.

"You know. Cut 'em off."

Logan tested the bonds, but they were still strong. His arms were locked at his sides, his torso held ramrod straight, and his feet could only move a few inches at a time—and the guards knew it. *Oh gods.* He was running out of time.

"I'll do it," Nose said with a snarl. He grabbed a catchpole and draped the noose over Logan's neck, then handed the pole to Weasel. "You hold him. We can't take any chances. Gimme that."

Weasel handed his knife to Nose. It was just an ordinary knife, but Logan's eyes fixed on it. Fear began to mix with rage, and he felt that ice thawing. Melting. *They're going to do it. Gods, no.* He thrashed, thrashed his arms and legs like an animal. But no matter how he shook or twisted or turned, he barely moved an inch.

Nose laughed, and Weasel just tightened the rope on his throat until Logan was turning purple. He didn't care. *Let them kill me now. Oh, gods!* Nose said, "It's too bad you haven't worked with me longer."

"Why's that?" Weasel asked, nervously holding the catchpole with both hands.

Nose rammed the knife into Weasel's eye. The man stood up on his tiptoes and twitched violently, then fell.

"Because I would have tried to cut you in, instead of cutting you off," Nose said. He laughed to himself and cut the noose off Logan's neck. Logan stared at him, stunned to silence, his rage and fear slow to fade.

Nose didn't pay him any attention. "When you can move, put these on. Sorry they didn't send someone more your size," Nose said, stripping the clothes off Weasel's corpse.

"Who the hell are you?" Logan asked.

"Don't matter," Nose said, throwing Weasel's breeches at Logan. "What matters is who I work for." He lowered his voice so the prisoners wouldn't overhear him. "I work for Jarl. A friend of a friend of yours."

"Who?"

"Jarl said to say he's the friend of a friend." Nose cut

away Weasel's underclothes with the knife. "I'm just telling you what I was told to—"

"What the hell are you doing?" Logan interrupted.

"Cutting his sack off."

"Oh, shit!" Logan shut his eyes, and would have turned away if the magical bonds had allowed it.

Nose ignored him and cut. "Damn! Well, it ain't pretty, but it'll do. Good for us his hair's the same color as yourn, eh?" He stood and shook a piece of flesh at Logan. "Look, pretty boy, this wasn't my idea. But if Roth finds this sack after you and I are conveniently 'killed during the uprising,' we might both stay alive. Understand?"

"No."

"Too bad. We don't have time. That shite I was talking about on our way down here was true. There's a woman and a little girl up in the first set of cells. Jarl wants us to get 'em out. He wants to know why Roth wants 'em. Looks like those bonds are weakening. Grab a leg."

Logan found he could move his arms if he pushed hard enough, and his feet were almost loose. He grabbed one of Weasel's feet—avoiding looking at his crotch—and started dragging him with Nose.

"So you said all that just so I'd know it?" Logan asked.

Nose scowled at the long iron bars set over a dark gap in the floor. The Hole was deep enough that in the meager torchlight Logan couldn't see the bottom of it. Nose grabbed a key and unlocked a small grate at the near side of the bars. Snuffling noises and grunts that Logan would barely call human drifted up from the Hole.

"And to see if he knew anything I didn't before I killed

him," Nose said. "Help me dump him in. Don't worry, it's plenty deep and the sides are sheer."

Logan moved forward reluctantly to help. He still couldn't move enough to squat to grab the grate, so Nose dragged it open and Logan shoved Weasel into the Hole.

Demonic cries of glee pierced the air and a fight promptly broke out below.

Shivering, Logan stepped away from the Hole. "What's the plan now?"

"The plan?" Nose looked down into the darkness and shook his head. "We get the hell out. If Roth wins tonight, he'll be hot to find you. Jarl will have several men report seeing your body. Someone else will have seen me dead and will finally admit to having looted my body. He'll show your 'coin purse' to Roth."

"That's pretty thin," Logan said. "Will you shut that damn grate?"

"There's hundreds of men dying upstairs. Trying to find out what happened to any one of them will be impossible. Roth knows that. Anyway, it's the best we can do and keep your head on your shoulders at the same time. Jarl will have to decide if the 'coin purse' bit is too much."

Nose stared back into the Hole, where the unmistakable sounds of feeding could be heard. He turned to Logan and smirked. "Kinda makes ya wonder, don't it?"

Logan shook his head, sickened. He looked back at Nose in time to see a thin lasso sail out of the Hole. It dropped neatly over Nose's shoulders.

In a blink, Logan saw that the rope was braided of sinews and he had an inane thought: *What animal down here is big enough that they could make a rope of its sinews?*

Nose's eyes filled with terror, then the lasso jerked tight and yanked him off his feet. He smacked full-length across the open grate and spread his arms and legs to keep from falling in. But raising his arms brought the noose off his shoulders and around his neck. A wild cackle sounded from the Hole. Logan staggered forward, moving faster than he had for half an hour, but he was too slow.

Nose's eyes bulged as pressure mounted on the rope around his neck. There must have been five men pulling it. His arms weakened as he blinked at Logan, eyes bulging grotesquely.

Then his arms folded and he slid into the Hole.

Logan tried to grab for the man. Instead, he stumbled, tripped against the last vestiges of his bonds and found himself rolling toward the Hole himself.

He gripped the bars and found himself staring down. He could vaguely make out the forms of men in a knot, limbs rising and falling, screeching and tearing at each other and Nose, who was flailing and screaming.

For a full minute, Logan was stuck there, unable to move his arms and legs far enough to push himself away. Nose gradually stopped shrieking and the dark forms retreated from each other to feed.

Then one of the men saw Logan and shouted.

Logan flung himself to the side as hard as he could. He felt the weakened magic strain and snap. He flopped on his back on the jagged stones, then sat and flipped the grate closed.

The key had fallen out of Nose's hand when the rope had jerked him from his feet, but Logan was shaking too badly to lock the grate. Unsteadily, he got to his feet and walked up the hall.

Logan pulled on Weasel's clothes, stretching them over his taller, more muscular body. He was lucky that the man's clothing had been baggy or it wouldn't have fit him at all. After pulling on boots that pinched his feet terribly, Logan stood.

He tried to find the strength to go back and lock the grate. If he never saw a prison again, he knew he would still have nightmares of this day for the rest of his life. The last thing he wanted was to go back down the long hallway to the Hole.

But he couldn't let animals like that have even the slimmest chance of escape.

He walked down the long hall carefully, slowly, even though he knew he should hurry. Several paces from the grate, he stopped. It was undisturbed, but he could still hear the sounds of men tearing meat. He wanted to vomit.

The sound of approaching voices came to Logan from above. The long rock halls carried their words.

"Hey, you!" a voice with a Khalidoran accent demanded.

One of the men in the last set of cells before the Hole answered, but Logan couldn't distinguish his words.

"Did a couple of soldiers and a prisoner come this way?"

Logan froze as the prisoner murmured something.

"See?" the voice said. "They didn't come this way. And believe me, you don't want to go down to the Hole."

Logan silently blessed the prisoner who'd lied probably more out of the habit of lying to authorities than to save him.

"And you think a prisoner is going to tell you the

truth?" a man with a cultured Khalidoran accent asked. "The prince demanded confirmation that Logan Gyre is dead. All your men are cooperating and searching the rest of this dungeon. Are you trying to hinder us?"

"No, sir!"

An unnatural, unflickering red light illuminated the long hallway.

A wytch! Oh shit, where can I go?

In the feeble torchlight, Logan examined the hallway again. But there were no niches, no crawl spaces. It was a dead end.

Have I been spared from death so many times just for this?

Logan considered a mad rush at the men. With only a knife, it would be tight, but if he could kill the wytch first he might have a chance.

"This is a place of power; I feel dizzy with it," a different voice said.

"Indeed," the first wytch answered, "I've not felt so much evil in one space since—well, since I last met with our liege."

For some reason, they found that humorous. Logan's heart broke as he heard at least six men laughing.

Six men. Maybe five wytches. At least two. Even if it were two wytches and four soldiers, Logan was lost. And the red light was growing brighter; they were only steps away.

With dread, Logan looked down at the grate. It was the only way. Count Drake had told him that life was precious, that suicide was a coward's way out, a sin against the God by flinging his gift back in his holy face.

What was it Kylar had told him once? They had been

propositioned by black-black market prostitutes, girls who operated outside of the Sa'kagé's control and protection. The girls, neither more than twelve, had offered themselves specifically for degrading practices Logan hadn't even heard of. Kylar had just said, "You'd be surprised at what you'd do to stay alive."

You'd be surprised at what you'd do to stay alive.

Logan opened the grate and slipped inside. He hung on the iron bars by one hand while he locked it. Then he tucked the key back into a pocket, drew his knife, and dropped into hell.

58

It wasn't until Kylar was flying through the air that he realized just exactly how far down it was to the river. He had no excuse, really. He'd been dangling out of this very window, looking at this very view, not five minutes ago. Except now the view was enlarging. Rapidly. He was going to clear the rocks. That was good. He was also going to hit the river at incredible speed, face first. Maybe a trained diver could have taken such a plunge without harm, but Kylar wasn't a diver.

The river filled all his vision and he flung his hands out. A thin wedge of Talent wrapped around him.

Then he plunged into the river. His outstretched hands did nothing, but the wedge of Talent protected him and drove him under the river's skin like a splinter.

The wedge collapsed an instant after he hit and the water slapped him as brutally as if a giant had clapped his hands together over the whole of Kylar's body.

He was dreaming again, if it was called a dream

when. . . . *When what?* The thought dribbled through Kylar's fingers and he lost it.

It was the dream he dreamt whenever he'd seen death for the last ten years. Like always, for a brief moment, he knew it was a dream. He knew it was a dream, but by the time he realized what dream it was, he couldn't pull away. It swelled around him, and he was eleven again.

The boat repair shop is dark, abandoned, cold in the silver moonlight. Azoth is terrified beyond terror even though he planned this. Now he turns and Rat is behind him, naked.

Azoth edges toward the hole where boats once were lifted from the filthy waters of the Plith, edges toward rope and the rock tied to it and the noose he knotted on the end.

"Kiss me again," Rat says, and he's right in front of Azoth, hands grabbing at him lustfully. "Kiss me again."

Where's the noose? *He'd put it here, hadn't he? He sees the rock that was supposed to drag Rat to a watery death but where's the—Rat pulls him close and his breath is hot on Azoth's face, and his hands are pulling at Azoth's clothes—*

Kylar hit the bottom of the river with a bump. His eyes flicked open and he saw Retribution inches away from his face. In the shock of hitting the water, it had been torn from his grasp. He was lucky he hadn't cut himself to pieces with it. He was lucky that the silver blade had plunged straight to the bottom with him.

Suddenly aware of the burning in his lungs, Kylar grabbed Retribution and pulled for the surface.

How long have I been down here? It couldn't have been more than a moment, or he would have drifted away and drowned. Seconds later, Kylar was surprised to find himself breathing air again and uninjured, at least from the fall. His nose and fingers were still bleeding, though, briefly staining the waters around him. The current jostled him up against a rock and he pulled himself up.

He'd washed up on the rocks on the Vos Island side under East Kingsbridge, directly across the river from the Jadwin estate. The bank of the river where he stood was also the foundation of the castle wall, so to go upstream, he had to half climb and half swim. It took him ten exhausting minutes to get to a point where he could climb out of the water again.

The docks where he'd seen Roth were at the northern tip of the island. To get there, he'd have to either continue through the water and the boulders along the river, or he'd have to go through the squat, stinking building that covered the Vos Island Crack.

Kylar didn't think he could make it over the rocks for another ten or twenty minutes. Even if Roth were still there when he arrived, Kylar was too weak to go that way. His nose had finally stopped bleeding, and he'd wrapped his hand so it wasn't bleeding too badly, but if he tried to swim, it would bleed again. His hand throbbed and his whole body felt weak from the blood he'd lost.

If it were any other night, Kylar would have left. He was in no shape to attempt an assassination. But logic didn't mean much. Not tonight. Not after what Roth had done.

The building on the Vos Island Crack was built of stone in a square, thirty paces on a side and only a single story above ground. It was supposed to be a marvel of engineering, but Kylar knew little about it. He supposed nobles weren't impressed by a marvel that smelled like rotten eggs.

It was stupidity to go on. Kylar was so exhausted he could barely even think of using his Talent. It took a certain kind of strength of its own to do that. He propped himself against the heavy door, gathering his strength. He was still holding Retribution. Looking down at the blade, he stared at the word etched into the blade. JUSTICE. Except it didn't say "justice" now. He blinked.

MERCY, it said in the same silver script, exactly where it used to say JUSTICE in black. On the hilt, perpendicular to that, now also silver where it had been ka'kari-black, it said VENGEANCE.

The ka'kari was gone. Kylar was so tired-stupid that for a moment he despaired. Then he remembered where it had gone. *It went into my skin?* Just how tired was he? Surely that must have been his imagination. A hallucination.

He turned his hand over and black sweat suddenly poured from his palm like oil, fluid for an instant, then suddenly congealing into a warm metal sphere. It was midnight black now, utterly featureless. A black ka'kari. Logan's stories had mentioned only six: white, green, brown, silver, red, and blue. Emperor Jorsin Alkestes and his archmagus Ezra had given them to six champions, slighting one of Jorsin's best friends, who then betrayed him. After the war, the six ka'kari had been objects of great lust, and those who carried them died quickly.

Kylar tried to remember the name of the betrayer. It was Acaelus Thorne. Jorsin hadn't slighted him after all. By pretending to slight him, Jorsin had given his best friend a way to escape—and keep an artifact out of enemy hands.

Because no one had known of the black's existence, Acaelus hadn't been hunted. Acaelus had survived.

Durzo had signed his letter "A Thorne."

"Oh, gods," Kylar breathed. He couldn't think about it now, couldn't stop or he wouldn't be able to start moving again. "Help me," Kylar said to the ka'kari. "Please. Serve me." He squeezed the ka'kari and it dissolved, rushing along his skin, up over his clothes, over his face, over his eyes. He flinched, but he could still see perfectly—still see through the dark as if it were natural. He looked down at his hands, his black sword, and saw them shimmer with magic and disappear. They weren't just cloaked in shadows, as wetboys cloaked themselves. They disappeared. Kylar wasn't a shadow like before. He was invisible.

There was no time to marvel; he had work to do. It had been ten minutes or more since he'd seen Roth on the dock. If Roth was going to die tonight, Kylar needed to move. He picked the lock and stepped inside.

The inside of the building was stiflingly hot. Wooden catwalks surrounded a mammoth central chimney fifteen paces in diameter. It was made of broad sheets of metal riveted together and supported by an external wood frame. The chimney descended at least four stories into the ground to meet the natural crack in the earth's crust.

Looking into the shadowed depths of the Crack, Kylar understood why people called this a marvel. The men who worked here not only harnessed the power of the hot air that blew out of the earth itself, they also kept the Plith River from spilling into the earth.

If that happened, the river would boil; the fish would die; the fishermen would be wiped out; and Cenaria would lose its major source of food.

Even now, oblivious to the chaos not a quarter of a mile away, men were working: servicing ropes, checking pulleys, greasing gears, replacing sections of sheet metal.

Kylar crossed a long catwalk, took a few turns, and found himself at a crossroads where he could go to a door below ground level or go up to a maintenance door by the outlet of the chimney on the north side of the building—where Roth would be.

He went down. The door was set beside double doors used for bringing in huge pieces of equipment. Kylar eased it open a crack.

A young wytch was standing outside, her hair pulled back and vir-marked arms folded. She was looking up a long stone ramp. Someone was talking to her, but Kylar couldn't see the other person. Beyond her were a dozen others, dressed similarly.

Kylar eased the door shut. He went back to the other branch of the catwalk and opened the door set into the horizontal section of the chimney.

Bent sideways, the chimney was more like a steam tunnel here. It was fifteen paces across until it pinched down to four paces at the last fan. The floor was sheet metal reinforced underneath so the workers could stand inside it as they worked on either the massive fan set just before the chimney turned straight down, or the much smaller last fan before the hot air escaped into the Cenarian night. The northern fan spun slowly enough that Kylar should be able to see Roth through it.

He stepped inside carefully, testing the floor to see if it would squeak as he put his weight on it. It didn't. But even before Kylar closed the door behind himself, he had a vaguely uneasy feeling.

Cooled from its long journey up the metal chimney, sulfuric smoke poured sluggishly through the tunnel into the night air outside. Heavy smoke filled the bottom third of the tunnel, curling and rolling. The only light came from the moon outside but was filtered through the spinning fan. Between the dense smoke and the dancing shadows, Kylar's vision was no better than any other man's.

There's someone here.

59

Durzo's heart had just leapt out that goddam window. He walked to the window and watched until he saw Kylar surface.

Amazing. *In all my years, I never tried anything so dumb, and here he does it on his first day—and it works.* Kylar clambered onto shore and began working his way north. Durzo knew where he was headed. The stubborn fool. He'd always had that streak, from the time he'd refused to accept that he'd failed in Rat's murder and had gone and killed the twist in the next three hours.

Kylar did what he thought was right, and to hell with the consequences, to hell with what anyone thought, even Durzo. He reminded Durzo of Jorsin Alkestes. Kylar had chosen his loyalty to Durzo, had clung to it despite Durzo. He'd put faith in Durzo Blint as Jorsin had put faith in him. Kylar was just a damned kid, but he'd also put his faith in a much worse man than Acaelus Thorne.

The pain resonated along every string in Durzo Blint's life. He'd been a thousand kinds of fraud in his years, so everyone who had believed in him during his deceptions could be written off, but Jorsin had known him. Kylar had known him. Not for the first time in seven centuries, existence ached. All the world was salt and Durzo Blint was an open wound. *Where did I go wrong?*

He moved, because like every man Acaelus Thorne had been, Durzo Blint was a man of action. His Talent puddled around his hands and feet—funny that it still worked like that, despite losing the ka'kari—and he stepped out of the window. He didn't fall.

The magic around his feet gripped the stone and he pitched forward, catching himself with his hands so that he hung face down on the castle wall like an insect. Kylar hadn't learned all of Durzo's tricks. Hell, he hadn't even seen all of Durzo's tricks.

He knew where Kylar was headed, and he knew how to get there faster than Kylar could, so he was in no hurry. The clash of arms in the courtyard attracted his attention. He cloaked himself in shadows and crawled down to the courtyard.

The battle was deadlocked. Two hundred Cenarian guardsmen and the forty or more useless nobles with them couldn't budge the hundred Khalidorans who were blocking the gate to East Kingsbridge. The Khalidorans had half a dozen meisters with them, but this late in the battle, they weren't doing much except psychologically. They'd used pretty much as much magic as they were able to.

With eyes long honed in battle and the arts of assassination, Durzo picked out the cornerstones of the battle. Sometimes that was simple. Officers were usually important. Meisters always were, but sometimes there were simple soldiers in the lines who were strength for the men around them. If you killed the cornerstones, the whole battle would shift. On the Khalidoran side, the cornerstones were two officers and three of the meisters and one giant of a highlander. On the Cenarian side, there were only two: a sergeant with an Alitaeran longbow and Terah Graesin.

The sergeant was a simple soldier, probably in his first battle despite his age, and Durzo knew the look on his face. He was a man who had joined the military to find his measure and had finally found it in battle. He had passed his own Crucible, and approved of himself. It was a potent thing, that approval, and every man around the sergeant felt it.

Terah Graesin, of course, would have stood out in any crowd. She was all tits and haughtiness, a vision in a torn cerulean gown. She believed no harm would dare step into her presence. She believed everyone around her would obey her, and the men felt that, too.

"Sergeant Gamble," a familiar voice said, just below Durzo. The sergeant loosed another arrow, killing a meister, but not one of the important ones.

Count Drake emerged from the front gate and grabbed the sergeant. "Another hundred highlanders on their way," Count Drake said, his voice almost swallowed by the clash of arms and the press of men back and forth in the courtyard.

The sight of the count packed the wound Kylar had opened with more salt. Durzo had thought the count was staying home, but here he was, still ill from Durzo's poison, about to die with all the rest.

"Dammit!" Sergeant Gamble cursed.

Durzo turned away from them. The Cenarians would

be slaughtered. It was out of his hands. He had his own date with judgment.

"Night Angel," the sergeant yelled. "If you fight with us still, fight now! Night Angel! Come!"

Durzo froze. He could only guess Kylar had already intervened in the castle somehow. *Very well, Kylar. I'll do this for you, and the count, and for Jorsin, and for all the fools who believe that even a killer may accomplish some good.*

"Give me your bow," Durzo said. It was a hard, menacing voice, pitched with Talent to carry. Sergeant Gamble's head whipped around and he and Count Drake looked at the shadow over the gate. The sergeant threw him his bow and a fresh quiver of arrows.

Durzo caught the bow in his hand and the quiver with his Talent. As he drew one arrow, he pulled another from the quiver with his Talent. He squatted against the vertical face of the wall and in an instant locked his deaders into his mind's eye.

The giant highlander went down first, an arrow catching him between the eyes. Then the meisters, every last one of them, then the officers, then a wedge of the highlanders directly in front of the bridge. Durzo emptied the quiver of twenty arrows in less than ten seconds. It was, Durzo thought, some damn fine shooting. Of course, Gaelan Starfire had been quite a hand with the longbow.

Durzo tossed the bow back to Sergeant Gamble, who didn't seem to comprehend yet what had happened. Count Drake was a different matter. He didn't even look at the courtyard as the Cenarian line surged forward into the gap. He wasn't surprised at the sudden hesitation in the Khalidoran ranks that within seconds would turn into a rout. He was looking toward Durzo.

Sergeant Gamble uttered an awed curse, but Count Drake's mouth opened to bestow a blessing. Durzo couldn't take it. He was already gone.

No more blessings. No more mercy. No more salt. No more light in my dark corners. Let this end. Please.

60

Fear flashed through Kylar. He dropped into the smoke. A thunk and a metal whine resounded above him. He rolled and saw one knife sticking out of the door and one sticking through the sheet metal of the chimney.

"So you figured out that it will make you invisible, huh?" Durzo Blint said from somewhere in the darkness near the huge fan at the south end of the tunnel.

"Dammit, Blint! I told you I don't want to fight," Kylar said, then moved away from where he'd been standing when he spoke.

He scanned the darkness. Even if Durzo weren't fully invisible, in the smoke and flickering interplay of light and shadow he might as well be.

"That was quite a dive, boy. You trying to become a legend yourself?" Durzo asked, but his voice oddly strangled, mournful. Kylar stumbled. Durzo was now by the smaller fan at the north end of the tunnel. He must have passed within a pace of Kylar to get there.

"Who are you?" Kylar asked. "You're Acaelus Thorne, aren't you?" Kylar almost forgot to move.

A knife sailed a hand's breadth from Kylar's stomach and pinged off the wall.

"Acaelus was a fool. He played the Devil and now I draw the Devil's due." Durzo's voice was raw, husky. He'd been weeping.

"Master Blint," Kylar said, adding the honorific for the first time since before he'd taken the ka'kari. "Why don't you join me? Help me kill Roth. He's outside, isn't he?"

"Outside with a boatload of meisters and Vürdmeisters," Durzo said. "It's over, Kylar. Khalidor will hold the castle within an hour. More highlanders arrive at dawn, and an army of Khalidoran regulars is already marching for the city. Anyone who could have led an army against them is dead or fled."

There was a distant gong, reverberating up the raw throat of the chimney. Warm air started blowing up from the depths.

Kylar felt sickened. His work had been for nothing. A few soldiers killed, a few nobles saved—it hadn't changed anything.

He padded over to the small north fan, which was now turning faster. Through its blades, he could see Roth conferring with the wytches.

Durzo was right. There were dozens of wytches. Some were getting back into their boat, but at least a score were accompanying Roth, who also had a bodyguard of a dozen gigantic highlanders.

"Roth killed my best friend," Kylar said. "I'm going to kill him. Tonight."

"Then you'll have to go through me."

"I won't fight you."

"You've always wondered if you'd be able to beat me when it came down to it," Durzo said. "I know you have. And you have your Talent and the ka'kari now. As a boy, you swore you wouldn't let anyone beat you. Not ever again. You said you wanted to be a killer. Have I made you one or not?"

"Damn you! I won't fight you! Who's Acaelus?" Kylar shouted.

Durzo's voice rose, chanting over the sound of fans and hot wind:

> "The hand of the wicked shall rise against him,
> But it shall not prevail.
> Their blades shall be devoured
> The swords of the unrighteous shall pierce him
> But he shall not fall
> He shall leap from the roofs of the world
> and smite princes . . . "

Blint trailed off. "I never made it," he said quietly.

"What are you talking about? What is that? Is that a prophecy?"

"That isn't me, just like the Guardian of Light wasn't Jorsin. It's you, Kylar. You are the spirit of retribution, the Night Angel. You are the vengeance I deserve."

Vengeance stems from a love of justice and a desire to redress wrongs. But revenge is damning. Three faces has the Night Angel, the avatar of Retribution: Vengeance, Justice, Mercy.

"But I don't have anything to avenge. I owe you my life," Kylar said.

Durzo's face grew somber. "Yes, this life of blood. I served that goddam ka'kari for almost seven hundred years, Kylar. I served a dead king and a people who weren't worthy of him. I lived in the shadows and I became like the shadow-dwellers. I gave all I was for some dream of hope that I never understood in the first place. What happens when you strip away all the masks a man wears and you find not a face beneath them but nothing at all? I failed the ka'kari once. *Once* I failed in seven hundred years of service, and it abandoned me.

"I didn't age a day, Kylar, not a day, for seven hundred years. Then came Gwinvere, and Vonda. I loved her, Kylar."

"I know," Kylar said gently. "I'm sorry about Vonda."

Durzo shook his head. "No. I didn't love Vonda. I just wanted—I wanted Gwinvere to know how it felt to have someone you love sharing other people's beds. I fucked them both and I paid Gwinvere, but it was Vonda I made a whore. That was why I wanted the silver ka'kari at first— to give it to Gwinvere, so she wouldn't die as everyone I've loved has died. But King Davin's rock was a fake, so I left it for Garoth Ursuul's men to find. The only way to save Vonda would have been to give them my ka'kari. I balanced her life against my power and my eternal life. I didn't love her, so the price was too high. I let her die.

"That was the day the ka'kari stopped serving me. I began to age. The ka'kari became nothing more than black paint on a sword that mocked me with the word JUSTICE. Justice was that I get old, lose my edge, die. You were my only hope, Kylar. I knew you were a ka'karifer. You would call the ka'kari to you. There were rumors that there was another in the kingdom. The black ka'kari had rejected me, but maybe the silver would not. A slim hope, but a hope for another chance, for redemption, for life. But you only called my ka'kari. You began to bond it that day I beat you, the day you risked your life to save that girl. I was insane. You were taking from me the only thing I had left. Reputation gone, honor gone, excellence fading, friends dead, the woman I loved hating me, and then you took my hope." He looked away. "I wanted to end you. But I couldn't." He threw a garlic clove in his mouth. "I knew that first kill wasn't in you. Not even that twist Rat. I knew you couldn't kill someone for what he *might* do."

"What?" Kylar's skin prickled.

"The streets would have devoured you. I had to save you. Even if I knew it would come to this."

"What are you saying?" Kylar asked. *No. God, please no. Don't let it fit.*

"Rat didn't mutilate Doll Girl," Durzo said. "I did."

The smoke half-filled the tunnel now. The huge fan turned slowly and the smaller fan was spinning as fast as Kylar's heart was beating. The moonlight was chopped into pieces and scattered wantonly through the roiling smoke.

Kylar couldn't move. Couldn't breathe. Couldn't even protest. It was a lie. It had to be a lie. He knew Rat. He'd seen his eyes. He'd seen the evil there.

But he'd never seen Durzo's evil, had he? Kylar had seen his master kill innocents, yet he'd never let himself see the evil there.

The big fan spun quickly now. Its whup-whup-whup chopped time into pieces, marked its passage as if time had significance.

"No." Kylar could barely force the word through the stranglehold of truth tightening his throat. Blint would do it. *Life is empty. Life is empty. A street girl is worth exactly what she can get for whoring.*

"No!" Kylar shouted.

"It ends now, Kylar." Durzo shimmered and disappeared, the darkness embracing him. Kylar felt rage, stark, hot rage rush through him.

Under the sounds of the protesting fans and the hot wind, Kylar barely heard the footsteps. He wheeled and dived.

The smoke swirled as the shadowy wetboy ran past him.

He heard a sword clearing a scabbard and he drew Retribution. A shadow appeared, too close, too fast. They clashed and Kylar's sword went flying. He dove backward.

Kylar came to his feet slowly, silently, straining his senses, crouching low in the smoke. The rage overcame his fatigue, and he channeled it, forced it to bring clarity.

He looked for any advantage, but there was little to be found. He could stand close to the huge southern fan and it would protect his back, but Blint could easily knock him into the spinning blades. They weren't so sharp or turning so fast that they'd sever a limb, but they'd certainly stun him. In a fight against Durzo, that would mean death.

Handholds were set into the walls and ceiling of the tunnel at intervals so the workers could replace sections. But where Kylar stood, the handholds were at least ten feet over his head.

A brief jolt of his Talent coursed through him as he leapt. He found a rung in his grip. As his right hand flexed, he almost fell. He'd forgotten that the window had slashed his hand open.

Kylar swung and looped his feet behind another rung to stabilize himself. His right hand was too weak to hold his weight, so he drew the tanto with that hand. The gong sounded again as Kylar looked at the tanto. It was straight, eight inches long, and had an angled point for punching through armor. With his hand as weak as it was, he couldn't slash with this knife.

He sheathed the tanto, popped the catch on a special sheath, and drew out a short curving knife only half the size of the tanto. Four tiny holes up the spine of the blade were stuffed with cotton. The sheath was wet. Kylar didn't know if the white asp poison had been washed off by the river or not. But he had no choice.

The wind slowed and then stopped abruptly. The great fans still spun, rattling on their greased axles.

Kylar held still and waited. The smoke was gradually drifting lower again, no longer filling the entire tunnel. The next time Durzo moved through the smoke, Kylar would be able to see the disturbance even if he couldn't see the wetboy himself.

The fans rattled down to a bare whisper and soon Kylar could hear no other sound but the pounding of his pulse in his own ears. He was straining now, not just to see or hear the wetboy, but merely to hold himself in place—and hold himself there silently.

If Durzo heard him, Kylar was totally exposed. With his feet locked behind the rung, he wouldn't be able to move quickly. And he made a huge target.

His only advantage would be surprise. But Durzo had

taught him that that was the most important advantage of all.

A minute passed.

The fans went completely silent. Even the low mutter of voices from outside was gone. The smoke, cooling once more, settled back into its cradle along the bottom of the tunnel.

Agonizingly slowly, Kylar turned his head, careful that not even his collar rustled. Surely with the smoke this low, drifting slowly as it did to the north, he should be able to see something, some eddy, some curl out of place.

He breathed the way he moved: slowly, carefully. His nose, bloodied earlier against the tower wall, allowed air to pass only through one nostril. His left arm was burning; his legs ached, but still he made no move, no sound.

Dread grew in his heart as he hung there. How could he fight Durzo? How many men had his master killed? How many times had Durzo beaten him in every test, every challenge? How could Kylar fight now, injured and weak as he was? Durzo could wait on the bottom of the tunnel forever. He'd probably placed himself by the smaller north fan. With the light at his back, he'd see as soon as Kylar dropped and be on him in a second.

Who was Kylar to kill a legend?

He tried to still the racing of his heart. His throat was tight. The hot emotions that had fueled him throughout the night cooled. He was cold. Empty. Durzo was right, justice had no place in this world. Logan was dead. Elene had been beaten, and the men who had done all the evil Kylar could imagine were winning. They always had. They always would.

He couldn't hold on much longer. Durzo would hear

the sound of his heart, thudding as it was against his chest. He forced himself to breathe slowly.

Patience! Patience.

He drew a slow breath again and paused. There was the slightest tang on the air.

Garlic! Both master and apprentice had had the same thought. Durzo was hanging exactly as Kylar was, mirror-image, inches away, poised watching the smoke for the slightest eddy.

Kylar jerked his head up and lashed out with the little knife. He must have made a sound, because the smear of darkness that had been just one rung above him was moving too.

His knife cut cloth and he blocked an attack with his other hand as they both dropped off the ceiling.

Kylar hit the floor heavily, splashing in the puddle gathered in the tunnel's bottom and hitting the metal so hard that he felt a sting in his neck. He rolled and jumped to his feet. He heard the ring of a sword clearing its scabbard.

Durzo winked back into visibility. Kylar let himself become visible too. He was too tired to maintain invisibility for another second. He felt like a wrung-out rag. He stared at three feet of steel in Blint's hand and the four inches in his own.

"So it comes to this," Durzo said. "I don't suppose you have any more tricks like that one up in the tower?"

"I don't even know how that happened," Kylar said. "I've got nothing left."

"Good thing I didn't let you go after Roth then, isn't it?" Durzo said, that infuriating little smirk on his lips.

Kylar didn't have it in him to get angry. He was a shell.

"I don't see how it matters," he said. "But I'd rather my blood was on his head than yours."

He sheathed the dagger.

"You used the asp venom, didn't you?" Durzo said. He laughed. "Of course you did." Durzo saluted Kylar and sheathed his sword.

Then he sagged and had to grab onto a rung on the wall to keep from falling. "I always wondered how it really felt," Durzo said. He reached up to the gash in his tunic. Kylar had thought he'd only cut cloth, but Durzo's chest bled from a shallow cut.

"Master!" Kylar rushed to him and kept him from falling as he swooned again.

Blint chuckled, his face was a cadaverous white. "I haven't worried about dying in a long time. It's not so bad." He winced. "It's not so good either. Kylar, promise me something."

"Anything."

"Take care of my little girl. Save her. Momma K will know where they've got her."

"I can't," Kylar said. "I would, but I can't."

He turned his head and pulled Durzo's dart out of his neck. At first, he'd thought the twinge in his neck was from hitting the ground, but as soon as he moved, he knew better. It was a poisoned dart. Kylar was dying, too.

Durzo laughed. "Lucky throw," he said. "Get me out of this tunnel. I'll have to smell brimstone soon enough."

Kylar pulled the two of them out of the door of the tunnel. He helped Durzo sit on the walkway and then sat across from him. Kylar was exhausted.

Maybe the poison on the dart was king snake venom with hemlock, then.

"You really love that Elene girl, don't you?"

"I do," Kylar said. "I really do." Oddly, that was his only regret. He should have been a different man, a better man.

"I should be dead by now," Durzo said.

"The knife got wet." Was that touch of dizziness the poison?

Durzo tried to laugh, but eyes filled with sorrow instead. "Jorsin told me, 'Six ka'kari for six angels of light, but one ka'kari stands watch in the night.' The black has chosen you, Kylar. You are the Night Angel now. Give these petty, ungrateful people better than they deserve. Give them hope. This is your master's piece: Kill Roth. For this city. For my daughter. For me." His fingers dug painfully into Kylar's arm. "I'm sorry, son. Sorry for all of it. Someday, maybe you can forgive. . . . " his eyes dipped drowsily and he fought to open them, to stay focused.

Durzo wasn't making sense. He knew Kylar was dying. It must have been the poison. "I do forgive you," Kylar said. "May our deaths not be on each other's heads."

Durzo's eyes lit suddenly and he seemed to rally against the poison in his veins. He smiled. "I didn't poison . . . the dart. . . . The letter . . ." Durzo died in mid-breath, a slight tremor passing through his body, his eyes still fixed on Kylar.

Kylar closed Durzo's eyes. A hollow enormity swallowed his stomach. A cry was stuck somewhere inside him, lost in the dark emptiness in his throat. Kylar stood woodenly, not taking enough care. The corpse slid from his lap, its head smacking roughly on the iron walkway. Its limbs were loose, graceless, lying in an uncomfortable position. Unmoving. Just like any corpse. In life, every man was unique. In death, every man was meat. Durzo was like any deader.

Numb, Kylar reached into the corpse's breast pocket and pulled out the letter Durzo had said was his inheritance. It was just under where Kylar had cut the wetboy's chest.

The letter was soaked with blood. Whatever words had been scrawled on the paper were illegible. Whatever Durzo had meant to excuse, whatever he had meant to explain, whatever gift he had meant to give Kylar with his last words had died with him. Kylar was alone.

Kylar dropped to his knees, all his strength gone. He took the dead wetboy in his arms and wept. He stayed there for a long time.

61

*D*awn found Kylar stumbling through the streets to one of his safe houses. Before he'd finally left, he'd erected a cairn over Durzo's body on the northern tip of Vos Island. At that hour, no one had been in sight. Kylar had stolen a rowboat from the dock and let the current carry him to the Warrens, too exhausted to paddle.

He'd docked at the shop where he'd killed Rat. It was still dark and inconspicuous, perfect for his kind of work. He wondered if Rat was still anchored in the muck, his unquiet spirit staring up at Kylar's little boat with the hatred and evil that had once lived in his adolescent heart.

It was a morning for lonely meditations. Kylar disabled the traps on his door automatically and stumbled inside. Blint had been right. It would have been suicide to go after Roth last night. Kylar had been so exhausted he'd thought it was poison working on him. He probably wouldn't have made it through a single meister.

It might be worth it to trade life for life to rid the earth of Roth Ursuul, but Kylar wasn't going to die for nothing. He locked the door, then stopped and turned back. He locked each of the three locks three times. Lock, unlock, lock. *For you, master.*

He took the pitcher of water and filled the basin with water and took the soap and began cleaning the blood from his hands. The face in the mirror was cold, calm as he washed the last vestiges of his master's life away. Blood marred the handle of the pitcher, just a little. Just a small, dark smear from the blood on his hands.

Kylar snatched the pitcher up and hurled it through the mirror. Both pitcher and mirror shattered, spraying glass and porcelain and water against the wall, into the room, onto his clothes, onto his face. He dropped to his knees and wept.

Finally, he slept. When he woke, he felt better than he had any right to. He washed himself and felt refreshed. As he scraped off his stubble, he caught himself grinning in one of the shards of the mirror. *Blint didn't mean to kill me at all, but he couldn't resist putting a dart in me just to show that he could. The old bastard. Kylar laughed. The* really *old bastard.*

It was gallows humor, but he needed whatever he could find.

He got dressed and armed, thinking mournfully of the gear he'd lost last night. Daggers, poisons, grappling hooks, throwing knives, tanto, poisoner's knife—he'd lost all of his favorites except for Retribution. *Mourning my gear, but not Logan or Durzo or Elene.* It was so ridiculous that Kylar laughed again.

He was, he decided, a little off. Maybe it was natural. He'd never lost anyone he really cared about before. Now he'd lost three in one night.

The streets were crowded in the late afternoon when Kylar finally emerged from his safe house. Rumors were flying about what had happened at the castle in the night. An army had appeared from thin air. An army had boiled up out of the Vos Island Crack. An army of mages from the south had come. No, they were wytches from the north. Highlanders had killed everyone in the castle. Khalidor was going to raze the entire city.

Few of the rumormongers seemed worried. Kylar saw a few people with their belongings loaded onto carts or wagons and heading out of the city, but there weren't many. No one else seemed to believe that anything bad could happen to them.

Momma K's hideout was still being guarded by the sinewy Cewan pretending to fix the fence. Kylar didn't bother becoming invisible. He approached the man unhurriedly, leaned over to ask directions and put a hand on the man's concealed short sword. The man tried to draw too late and found the sword locked in Kylar's grip. Kylar broke the man's sternum with an open-handed strike, leaving him gasping, his mouth working like a fish's.

Kylar took the keys from the man's belt and opened the door. He locked it after himself and embraced the shadows.

Invisible, he found Momma K in the study looking over reports from her brothels. He read them silently over her shoulder. She was trying to piece together what had happened at the castle.

The needle sank into the sagging flesh at the back of her arm. She cried out and clawed at it. She pulled the needle out then turned her chair slowly, looking ancient.

"Hello, Kylar," she said. "I expected you yesterday."

He appeared in the other chair, a lounging young Death. "How'd you know it was me?"

"Durzo would have used a poison that would leave me in agony."

"It's a tincture of ariamu root and jacinth spoor," Kylar said. "The agony's coming."

"A slow poison. So you decided to give me time. What for, Kylar? To apologize? To cry? To beg?"

"To think. To remember. To regret."

"So this is retribution. There's a new young killer on the streets doling out what old whores deserve."

"Yes, and you deserve to lose the very thing that made you betray Durzo."

"And what's that, oh wise one?" She smiled a serpent's smile.

"Control." Kylar's tone was flat, apathetic. "And don't reach for the bell rope. I've got a hand crossbow, but it's not accurate. I might hit your hand rather than the rope."

"Control, is that what you call it," Momma K said, her back ramrod straight, not making it a question. "Do you know that rapes aren't spread out evenly, even among working girls? Some girls get raped again and again. Others never do. The ones who get raped are the victims. The rapist bastards can somehow tell. It's not 'control,' Kylar. It's dignity. Do you know how much dignity a fourteen-year-old has when her pimp won't protect her?

"When I was fourteen, I was taken to a noble's house and enjoyed for fifteen hours by him and his ten closest friends. I had to make a choice after that, Kylar, and I chose dignity. So if you think giving me a poison that makes me shit myself to death is going to make me beg, you're sadly mistaken."

Kylar was unmoved. "Why did you betray us?"

Momma K's defiance slowly faded as Kylar sat there with a wetboy's patience. She didn't answer him for a minute, five minutes. He sat with all the patience of Death. By now, he knew, she had to be feeling queasy.

"I loved Durzo," she said.

Kylar blinked. "You what?"

"I've slept with hundreds of married men in my life, Kylar, so I never saw the most flattering portrait of marriage. But if he'd asked me, I would have married Durzo Blint. Durzo is—was, I suppose you killed him? Yes, I thought so. Durzo was a good man in his way. An honest man." Her lips twitched. "I couldn't handle honesty. He told me too many unlovely truths about myself, and that hard, dark thing that lives in me couldn't bear the light."

She laughed. It was a bitter, ugly sound. "Besides, he never stopped loving Vonda, a woman utterly unworthy of him."

Kylar shook his head. "So you thought you'd kill him? What if he'd killed me?"

"He loved you like a son. Once you bonded the ka'kari, he told me. A life for a life, he said. The divine economy, he called it. He knew then that he'd die for you, Kylar. Oh, he fought it sometimes, but Durzo was never as unprincipled as he wanted to believe. Besides, he changed when Vonda died.

"I warned him, Kylar. She was a lovely, careless girl. The kind of woman born without a heart, so she couldn't imagine breaking anyone else's. Durzo was exciting for her. He was nothing more than her rebellion, but she died before he ever saw through her, so she was always perfect in his sight. She was forever a saint, and I was always spit-in beer."

"He didn't love her," Kylar said.

"Oh, I knew that. But Durzo didn't. For every other way that he was unique, Durzo thought excitement plus fucking is the same thing as love, just like every other man." She suddenly hunched over in pain as her stomach spasmed.

Kylar shook his head. "He told me he was trying to make you jealous, make you feel how he felt when you were with other men. When she died, he thought you could never forgive him. Gwinvere, he loved you."

She snorted in disbelief. "Why would he say such a thing? No, Kylar. Durzo was going to let his daughter die."

"That's why you betrayed him?"

"I couldn't let her die, Kylar. Don't you understand? Uly is Durzo's daughter, but she's not my niece."

"Then who's her m— . . . No."

"I couldn't keep her. I knew that. I always hated taking tansy tea, but that time, I couldn't do it. I sat with the cup growing cold in my hands, telling myself something like this would happen—and still I couldn't drink. A Shinga with a daughter, what more perfect target could there be? Everyone would know my weakness. Worse, everyone would see me as just another woman. I could never hold my power if that happened. So I left the city, had her in secret, and hid her away. But how could he let Uly die, even thinking she was Vonda's? How could he? Roth threatened him, but Durzo called his bluff. You don't know Roth. He would have done it. The only way I could save Uly was for Durzo to die first. If Durzo was dead, Roth wouldn't have to carry out his threat. I had to choose between the man I've loved for fifteen years and my daughter, Kylar. So I chose my daughter. Durzo wanted to die anyway, and now I do too. You can't take anything from me that I won't gladly give."

"He didn't call their bluff."

Momma K couldn't seem to grasp it. "Uh-uh," she said, shaking her head. He could see the edifice of suppositions she'd built crash down brick by brick. A Durzo who let himself be blackmailed was a Durzo who cared for a daughter he'd never seen. A Durzo who could do that was a Durzo who could love. She'd hardened her heart against him because she thought he didn't care, and couldn't.

So for fifteen years she'd been hiding her love for a man who had been hiding his love for her. That meant she'd betrayed the man who loved her. In pitting Kylar against Durzo, she'd killed the man who loved her. "Uh-uh. Uh-uh. No."

"His dying wish was that I save her. He said you'd know where she is."

"Oh gods." The words barely squeezed out, a strangled sound. Another spasm passed through her and she seemed to welcome the pain. She wanted to die.

"I'll save her, Momma K. But you need to tell me where she is."

"She's in the Maw. In the nobles' cells with Elene."

"With Elene?" Kylar stood bolt upright. "I have to go back." He got to the door, then turned and drew Retribution. Momma K looked at him hollowly, still absorbing his words.

"I used to wonder why Durzo called this 'Retribution' and not 'Justice,'" Kylar said. He drew the ka'kari off the sword and exposed the word MERCY on the steel beneath it. "Or, if this is what was under JUSTICE, why not call it MERCY? But now I know. You've shown me, Momma K. Sometimes people shouldn't get what they deserve. If there isn't more in the world than justice, it's all for nothing."

He reached into his pouch and pulled out a tiny vial of the antidote. He set it on Momma K's desk. "That's mercy. But you'll have to decide if you want to accept it. You've got half an hour." He opened the door. "I hope you'll take it, Momma K," Kylar said. "I'd miss you."

"Kylar," she called out as he reached the door. "Did he really—did he really say he loved me?"

Her mouth was set, her face tight, her eyes hard, but tears rolled down her cheeks. It was the only time he'd ever see her cry. He nodded gently and left her then, her back bent, sunk on the cushions of her chair, cheeks wet, her eyes fixed grimly on the bottle of life.

62

$\mathcal{K}$ylar hurried to the castle. Even going as fast as he could, he might be too late. The effects of the coup were being felt throughout the city. The Sa'kagé's bashers had been among the first to figure out the most practical consequence of a coup: with no one to report to, and no one to pay them, the city guards didn't work. No guards, no law. The corrupt guards who had worked for the Sa'kagé for years were the first to start looting. After that, the looting spread like plague. Khalidoran highlanders and meisters were stationed on Vanden Bridge and on the east bank of the Plith to keep the looting confined to the Warrens. Apparently, Khalidor's invasion leaders wanted the city intact, or at least they wanted to do the more profitable looting themselves.

Kylar killed two men about to murder a woman, but otherwise didn't pay any attention to the looters. He cloaked himself and snuck across the river, dodging meisters who should have been more attentive.

When he got to the east side, he stole a horse. He was thinking about the Night Angels. Blint had talked about them over the years, but Kylar had never paid any attention to him. He'd always thought them just another superstition, some last vestige of old, dead gods.

Then Kylar thought about how Elene would take it even if he did rescue her. The thought made him ill. She was in gaol because of him. She thought he'd killed the prince. She hated him. He tried to plan how he was going to kill Roth—a man who would be guarded by meisters, Khalidoran highlanders, and maybe the odd Sa'kagé basher. That didn't make Kylar feel any better. The more he thought, the worse he felt.

He didn't even know if meisters could see him when he was cloaked, but the only way he could test that had serious drawbacks. He had, however, finally used his head and taken a look at himself in a mirror to see if the ka'kari was as effective as he thought. He'd been amazed. Wetboys bragged about being ghosts, about being invisible, but that was all it was: braggadocio. No one was invisible.

The only other wetboy Kylar had seen go stealthing looked like a big blob of an indeterminate something. Blint had looked like a six foot smear of mottled darkness— good enough for all practical purposes when the light was poor. And when Blint held still, he dwindled to a shadow of a shadow.

But Kylar was *invisible*. All wetboys became more visible when they moved. When Kylar moved, there wasn't so much as a distortion in the air.

It almost irritated him that he'd spent so much time learning to sneak without his Talent. It seemed like wasted effort. Then he thought of having to sneak past the wytches. Maybe the effort wasn't wasted after all.

He rode up Sidlin Way to Horak Road, then veered

around the Jadwin estate, leaving his horse and cloaking himself with the ka'kari. The sun was setting as he scouted East Kingsbridge.

As he'd expected, the security was daunting. A score of Khalidoran regulars were stationed in front of the gate. Two meisters paced among them. Two more talked together on the other side of the gate. At least four boats patrolled Vos Island, going around it in measured circles.

It was a good thing Kylar wasn't planning on getting into the castle. It was a good thing he'd come with a small arsenal. Dodging from rock to rock, tree to shrub, Kylar moved to the bridge. He unlimbered the heavy crossbow from his pack. He hated crossbows. They were unwieldy, slow, and could be shot by any idiot who could point.

Kylar fitted the special bolt in place, checked the silk spool and braced his body against the side of the bridge. What was it that Blint used to tell him? That he should practice more with weapons he didn't like?

Scowling, Kylar aimed. Thanks to the iron sheathing on the bridge pilings, his target was tiny. He'd have to hit the last piling above the iron sheathing where the wood was exposed, a target four inches wide from forty paces away, with a slight breeze. This crossbow's accuracy at that range was within two inches. So he had two inches to spare.

If he erred, he had to make sure he erred right. Up or down and the bolt would hit iron—and the sound would wake the dead. Left and the bolt would fly past the bridge and hit the rocks of the castle, and probably rebound to splash in the river.

Kylar hated crossbows.

He waited until the boat was almost directly underneath the bridge. If he made the shot—*when* he made it—he'd take advantage of the boatmen having just left the brilliance of the dying sun and coming into the shadow of the castle. Their vision wouldn't be good. He exhaled half a breath and pulled smoothly, riding the release point until the catch gave.

The bolt sped from the crossbow, the spool whizzing faintly—and the bolt sailed four inches to the right of the last piling.

Kylar grabbed the still-unreeling rope as it went taut. The bolt jerked to a stop not three feet from the castle wall.

The bolt started falling and Kylar pulled it in hand over hand as fast as he could. The rope draped over one of the crossbeams to the right of the piling he'd aimed for. It swung back toward the piling. Kylar dragged in rope as fast as he could, but the bolt pinged off the iron sheathing.

The hooks on the bolt caught and Kylar drew the rope taut, flush against the underside of the bridge.

A meister stepped to the edge of the bridge, holding onto the railing nervously. He looked down and saw the boat passing under the bridge. "Hey!" he called. "Watch it!"

A lightly armed boatman looked up, squinting in the gloom. "Right, you piece of—" He swallowed his words as he realized he was speaking to a meister.

The meister disappeared and the boatman starting haranguing his rowers. Both boatman and wytch thought the other had made the sound.

Without pausing to consider how lucky he was, Kylar secured his end of the line and hid the crossbow. The next boat was still a good distance away. Kylar threw a leg over the line, approached the precipice that sloped off to the river, and slipped out into space.

For a long time, he thought he was going to die as the silk rope drooped toward the river. *It's come free!* But he held on, and the rope finally accepted his weight. He climbed across the chasm almost upside down, pulling himself with his hands, his legs crossed over the rope. The droop of the rope meant that after he crossed the halfway point he was climbing sideways and up.

Instead of fighting it, Kylar just pulled himself as far as the second-to-last piling. He looked at the iron sheathing. It was pitted with age and exposure. It was also vertical. Not exactly the best climbing surface.

There was no good choice. Kylar had to get off the rope before the next boat came. He was invisible, but the drooping rope wasn't.

He flung himself from the rope to the piling—and fell. He slapped all of his limbs around the iron sheathing, but its diameter was so great that his arms couldn't reach around it. The uneven iron surface didn't provide enough friction to stop his descent, but it was enough to tear at the skin on the insides of his arms and his inner thighs.

He hit the water slowly enough that the splash was quiet. He clambered back up to the surface and held himself against the piling as the next boat passed.

With the number of weapons he was wearing, he couldn't swim, but when he pushed himself off the piling, he sank close enough to shore that he was able to walk along the river bottom and pull himself out of the water before he drowned. Barely.

He moved north, along the same route he'd followed the night before. Kylar was glad Blint was dead. The wetboy would never have let him live this down. Between the missed shot and the undoubtedly embarrassing cuts he'd have on his inner thighs, Blint would have had gibes for a decade. Kylar could hear it now: "Remember that time you tried to hump the bridge?"

Kylar found a perch inside the boathouse and cleaned his weapons. He'd have to assume that all of his poisons had washed away—for the second day in a row. He wrung out his clothes, but didn't dare take the time to let them dry fully. Now that he was here, he wanted to get in and get out, fast. He looked around the boathouse. It wasn't guarded. Evidently the Khalidorans thought their patrols were enough.

Two men guarded the long ramp down that led to the Maw. They were tense, obviously uncomfortable with their assignment. Kylar didn't blame them. Between the stink, the periodic cries, and the occasional rumblings in the earth, he wouldn't have been comfortable either.

Retribution slashed left and right and the men died. He pulled their bodies into the brush and took the keys to the door.

The entrance to the Maw was designed to terrify the men and women incarcerated there. On opening the gate, Kylar saw that the ramp down did indeed look like a tongue leading down a gigantic throat. Hooked teeth were carved out of the black volcanic glass around him, and torches were set behind red glass to look like two flickering, demonic eyes.

Nice. Kylar ignored everything except for the sounds of men. He glided down the tongue and turned down a hall toward the nobles' cells. From Durzo's friends he'd gained a rough idea of the layout of the place, but he'd certainly never had any wish to visit.

He found the cell he was looking for, checked the door

for traps, and spent a moment waiting in the hallway, just listening. It was insane—he was afraid to open the door. He was more afraid to face Elene and Uly than he was to sneak past wytches and fight the Sa'kagé.

Gods! He was here to save Elene, and he was scared what she would say. Ridiculous. Or maybe what she wouldn't say, just how she'd look at him. He'd given everything for her! But she didn't know that. All she could know was that she'd done nothing and now she was in jail.

Well, it wasn't going to get any better by waiting.

Kylar picked the lock, released the ka'kari's cloaking, and pulled down his black mask.

The ten-by-ten cell was occupied by a pallet and a pretty little urchin sitting on Elene's lap. Kylar hardly noticed the little girl. His eyes were glued on Elene. She stared back at him, stunned. Her face was a mask—more literally than Kylar would have liked, since both of her eyes were blackened from when he'd hit her. She looked like a scarred raccoon.

If it wasn't his fault and it were someone else, Kylar would have chuckled.

"Father!" the little girl cried out. She squirmed out of Elene's lap. Still staring at Kylar, Elene barely noticed her go. Uly threw her arms around Kylar and hugged. "Mother said you'd come! She swore you'd save us. Is she with you?"

Tearing his gaze away from Elene, whose eyes had suddenly narrowed, Kylar tried to pry the little girl loose. "Uh, you must be Uly," he said.

Mother? Did she mean Momma K? Or her nurse? He'd straighten out this "father" business later. What was he going to say? "*Sorry, your mother's probably dead and*

I'm the one who killed her but I changed my mind about it and gave her the antidote so it's not my fault if she is dead, and I killed your father last night, too. I'm his friend. Sorry."

He bent down so she could look him in the eye. "Your mother isn't with me, Uly. But I am here to save you. Can you be very very quiet?"

"Quiet as a mouse," she said. The kid was fearless. Either she had no sense, or Elene had done a helluva job calming her fears.

"Hello, Elene," he said, standing.

"Hello, whatever your name is."

"His name's Durzo, but we can call him Zoey," Uly said. Kylar winked at her, glad for the interruption. Even if children were generally intolerable, she'd averted a conversation he wasn't interested in having—especially not now, not here.

Elene glanced at Uly then back to him, her eyes asking, *Is she yours?* Kylar shook his head. "You coming?" he asked.

She scowled. He took it for a yes.

"Follow me," he told Uly. "Quiet as a mouse, right?" Best to get moving, and fast. Messy emotional issues could wait until later, or never.

They followed as he walked, visible and nervous, to the ramp. Elene walked holding Uly's hand and stopped as Kylar went ahead. When they got to the carvings of teeth, Elene pulled Uly close and began speaking to her in soothing tones.

Kylar walked up the ramp and eased the door open a crack.

The door shook as three arrows smacked into the wood.

"Shit!" Kylar said.

It had been too easy. Kylar should have known. He'd been counting on the chaos to throw everyone off. Locking the door again, Kylar snapped the key off in the lock. *Let the bastards break it down.*

"Back up the tunnel!" he said, pulling Elene into a jog. "You won't see me, but I'll be here. I'll protect you. Just listen for my voice," he said as the black ooze of the ka'kari bubbled out of his pores.

If Elene were startled to have him disappear before her eyes, she hid it well. She jogged, pulling Uly along. "Do I need to run?" she asked the empty air.

"Just walk fast," Kylar said.

The gate that led underground to the castle was unguarded. Thank the gods for that. Maybe the chaos of taking over an entire country would help him. Maybe a patrol outside had just stumbled across the bodies.

Kylar locked the gate and broke off the other key. They climbed a staircase slowly and emerged in a service hallway in the castle proper.

From the hallway, they quickly came upon an intersection. Down one hall, off-duty Khalidoran soldiers were slouching against a wall and sharing a joke. Kylar stopped Elene and walked toward them, then heard one of them call something to someone inside the open room behind them.

If he killed them, whoever was in that room would sound an alarm. He could make it, but Elene and Uly wouldn't. He went back to Elene.

"Go when I say," he said. "Now."

Elene threw her shawl over her head and struggled

across the hallway, her back bent and her face down, one foot turned in and dragging along the floor. She looked like an old crone. And she blocked most of Uly from view.

It took her longer to get across the opening, but when one of the soldiers saw her, he didn't even say anything to the others.

"Nice trick," Kylar said, catching up with her as she resumed her normal fast stride.

"Where I grew up, stupid girls don't stay virgins," Elene said.

"You grew up on the east side," Kylar said. "It's not exactly like the Warrens over there."

"You think it's safer to work around oversexed nobles?"

"Where are we going?" Uly asked.

"Shh," Kylar said as they approached another inter-section. The hallway they had been following led to the kitchens. From the raucous voices there, though, that wasn't the way to take Elene and Uly. The door to the right was locked, and the hall left was clear.

Kylar pulled out his picks, risking the possibility of someone stepping out of the kitchens. He didn't like the idea of following the path of least resistance.

The lock came open quickly, but something heavy had been wedged against the door on the other side. Probably a servant had done his best to block it during the coup.

"Where are we going?" Uly asked again.

Kylar had known her cuteness would grate on him; he'd just hoped it would take longer than this. He let Elene hush her this time.

With his Talent, he could kick through the door and whatever was blocking it—but the noise would bring whoever was in the kitchens, and Kylar felt a sense of urgency. He didn't want to leave the girls here while he scouted.

"Left," he whispered.

This corridor twisted and rose up several flights of steps. Kylar heard the jingling of mail and the slap of feet in hobnailed boots behind them.

"Hurry!" he said. The men behind them were moving at a slow jog, so they weren't chasing escaped prisoners but just responding to orders. Kylar dropped back to the staircase and caught a brief glimpse of at least twenty men.

He ran to catch up with Elene and Uly. They were passing doors, and heedless of who might hear, Kylar started testing the latches. Every one was locked.

"Why are we going to the throne room?" Uly asked.

Kylar stopped. Elene stared at Uly, looking as surprised as he felt. "What?" he asked.

"Why are we going—"

"How do you know where we're going?" Kylar asked.

"I live here. Mother's a maid. Our room's just—"

"Uly, do you know a way out? A way that doesn't go to the throne room? Quick!"

"I'm not supposed to come up here," she said. "I get in trouble."

"Dammit!" Kylar said. "Do you know a way out or not?!"

She shook her head, frightened. *That would have just been too easy, wouldn't it?*

"Great with children, aren't you?" Elene said. She touched Uly's cheek and squatted on her heels to look her in the face. "Have you come up here, Uly?" Elene asked gently. "We won't be angry if you have, I promise."

But Uly was too frightened to say anything.

The footsteps were getting closer.

"Move!" Kylar said, grabbing Elene's hand to get her running, making her drag the brat.

He didn't like this. It was too tidy. Too convenient that there was only one path.

One path. That's it! There's never just one path in this castle. Kylar scanned the walls and ceilings as he ran. He didn't even try the doors that they passed. They turned another corner. Kylar skittered to a stop.

He shimmered back into visibility. "Elene, do you see that third panel?" He pointed up.

"No," she said. "But what do I need to do?"

"Push on it. I'll lift you. There are secret corridors throughout the castle. Find your way out. Maybe Uly can help you."

She nodded and Kylar squatted against the wall. Elene hitched up her skirts and stepped on his thigh. She scowled as she realized that climbing up on him would drape her skirts over his head, but she didn't hesitate to step up to his shoulders and finally into his hands. She walked her hands up the wall for balance. Then Kylar stood and extended his hands, lifting her high into the air.

Elene pushed the panel open and slipped inside a crawl space. She had turned around by the time Kylar picked up Uly.

"Can you catch?" he asked.

"I'd better," she said. The footsteps were almost on top of them.

Kylar tossed Uly up in the air easily. *Damn but the Talent is useful.*

Elene caught her and started to slip until her own

shoulders were sticking out over space. Then she must have braced herself against something inside the crawl space, because she stopped. She grunted, and with Uly wiggling to help, was able to pull the girl up with her.

"*Oh,* I've been here," Uly said.

Kylar took out a dagger and tossed it up to Elene.

She caught it. "What am I supposed to do with this?"

"Aside from the obvious?" he asked.

"Thanks. Now come on. There's room. Hurry."

Kylar didn't move. *Dorian said, 'If you do the right thing twice, it will cost you your life.' Blint said, 'There are things more valuable than life.' The count said, 'You can't pay for all you've done. But you aren't beyond redemption. There's always a way out. And if you're willing to make the sacrifice, the God will give you the chance to save something priceless.'*

He looked at Elene. *Something priceless indeed.* He smiled at her. She looked at him like he was crazy.

"Kylar, hurry!"

"It's a trap, Elene. If they lose me here, they'll search the hidden passages. I can't protect you in the crawl-spaces, they're too cramped. Get out of the castle. Go to Jarl at the Blue Boar, he'll help you."

"They'll kill you, Kylar. If it's a trap you can't—"

"I did look," he interrupted. He smirked. "And you've got great legs."

He winked—and disappeared.

63

$\mathcal{V}$ürdmeister Neph Dada damned Roth Ursuul for the hundredth time of the day. Serving an aetheling of the Godking was supposed to be an honor. Like all the Godking's honors, this one came with strings attached. If an aetheling failed his *uurdthan,* his Vürdmeister was punished with him. And obedience was required. Total obedience, except in things that might displease the Godking.

Which was why Neph was cursing. He wasn't precisely disobeying Roth, but he was undoing something the prince had begun. Something, in fact, that Roth believed he had accomplished. Something that it was taking all of Neph's abilities to stop. Mercifully, Roth had been too busy securing the castle and the city to ask where his Vürdmeister was. Besides, he had sixty meisters to command now, three of them Vürdmeisters almost as powerful as Neph. If Roth had sent men after him, the small servant's room Neph had commandeered was isolated enough that they had never been able to find him.

His work—his petty deceit, and rebellion, and gamble

for the Godking's favor—lay stretched out on the bed. She was a beautiful girl—not that the Godking needed another beautiful girl—but she had spirit. Fiery, intelligent, and best of all a widowed, virgin bride, and a princess. Jenine Gyre was a prize indeed. A prize to crown the Godking's harem. A prize Neph had snatched from the very jaws of Death.

Every Vürdmeister as old as he was knew volumes about preserving life, of course. It was in their own self-interest as they grew old. *But I am a genius. A genius.*

His plan had crystallized as Roth had ranted, meaningless words exploding from the boy like diarrhea. As usual. His cut had been fortunate. Just one side of the neck, not so deep that it cut the windpipe. Neph let her bleed until she was losing strength, then tickled a little tendril of magic against her diaphragm to push the air from her lungs, two more to close her eyes, a fourth to seal the wound on her neck, some quick movement to take attention away from her body so no one would notice that she was still breathing, and the girl had been his.

He'd killed seven serving girls looking for the right kind of blood for her. *Sloppy work.* He should have done better, but it had been enough. He'd decided to leave the scar. It gave the princess a certain something. And as a finishing touch, he'd found a girl in the city who looked like the princess and had her head mounted over the east gate with the rest of the royal family's. If you got the right color of hair and styled it correctly, all you had to do was beat the face enough, and it could look like anyone's head. Still, he thought, he'd done brilliant work, even if it had been exhausting.

Tomorrow morning, the Godking would arrive and

he'd dispense either favor or punishment to Roth Ursuul. Either way, Neph would prosper.

Something made him pause before he went out the door. Something felt odd outside. He walked to his window, threw open the wooden shutters—no glass for the servants' rooms—and stared through the hole into the ghastly Cenarian statue garden.

The meisters had set up their camp there, figuring it to be a center of power. Vürdmeister Goroel had always enjoyed thumbing his nose at the conquered countries' gods and dead kings. It was pure playacting not to take rooms in the castle, but when the meisters went to war, Goroel liked to show the Godking that they were roughing it. *Insufferable.*

A man climbed up onto one of the statues. Neph couldn't see his features clearly, but he certainly wasn't Khalidoran. *Sethi? What's a Sethi man with a sword doing climbing a statue in the middle of a war?* A giant of a blacksmith with blond hair stood below him, looking around anxiously. Neph shook his head. Vürdmeister Goroel wouldn't take such an insult lightly.

"Wytches of the Godking!" the man shouted, his voice booming, amplified a dozen times over with magic. *A mage?* "Wytches of the false Godking, hear me! Come to me! This day, on this rock, you will be shattered! Come and let your arrogance find its reward!"

Had he not spoken heresy, the wytches might have let Vürdmeister Goroel deal with him, but heresy would be stopped. Must be stopped. Instantly. Fully thirty meisters drew on their vir.

Neph's magical senses exploded. He lurched against the wall and collapsed. It felt like a thousand demons were screaming in unison into each of his ears. Magic like a bonfire—like a second sun—exploded through the castle. Neph felt his vir tingling, burning as magic washed toward him. He hadn't been holding his vir, and that was surely the only thing that saved him. The power pouring through the castle was more magic than he'd ever imagined. More magic than the Godking himself could wield.

Specks of magic leapt up to meet it. The meisters, Neph could tell. The meisters who hadn't already been holding their vir grabbed it. They might as well have been flies trying to extinguish a bonfire with the wind from their wings. The magic sought them out, wrapped around them, burned them to pillars of ash. He could feel the tendrils of their power snapping, bursting apart one by one.

The conflagration was in the courtyard, in that odd Cenarian statue garden. Should Neph stay here and live? Did he dare go face that fire? What would this titan of a mage do if Neph dared to confront him? What would the Godking do to him if he didn't?

An odd, detached thought came to Kylar as he opened the last door and walked toward the throne room. *That's why those guards outside the Maw were nervous—they were bait. Now I am, too.*

His next thought was of Durzo's creed: Life is empty. It was a creed Durzo himself had betrayed, an empty creed. It neither saved life nor made it better. For a wetboy, it made life safer because it obliterated his conscience. Or tried to. Durzo had tried to live that creed and had found himself too noble for it.

Kylar wondered what had brought him to this. He was

ready to die. Was it pride, that he thought he could defy any odds? Was it duty to Durzo, that he thought he had to pay back the debt of his life by saving Uly? Was it revenge, that he hated Roth so much that he would die to kill him? Was it love?

Love? I'm a fool. He felt something for Elene, it was true. Something intense and intoxicating and unreasonable. Maybe it was love, but what did he love, Elene or an image of her, glimpsed from afar, pieced together with the glue of assumption?

Maybe it was just some last vestige of romanticism that had brought him here, some sludge left over from the stories of princes and heroes Ulana Drake had read to him. Maybe he'd spent too long with people who believed in false virtues like valor and self-sacrifice that Durzo had tried to teach him to despise. Maybe he'd been infected.

But why he was here didn't really matter. This was the right thing to do. He was worthless. If his empty life could ransom Elene's life, then he would have accomplished something good. It would be the only thing he had ever done that he could be proud of. And if he gave Uly a chance too, so much the better.

He'd have his own chance, too: his chance at Roth. Kylar had gone into other fights feeling confident, but this was different. As he stepped into the short hall to the throne room, Kylar felt at peace.

A high-pitched whine cut the air. The men who'd been standing in the room looking to the door adjusted their grips on their weapons.

A magical alarm to tell them I've arrived, then.

There were highlanders, of course. He'd expected that.

But he hadn't expected thirty. And there were wytches. He'd expected that, too. But not five.

The doors at the dead end where he'd lifted Elene and Uly banged open and another ten highlanders poured in behind him.

Taking a few quick steps, Kylar leapt into the throne room at the level of the floor, hoping to make it past the first attacks. The room was huge, the ivory and horn throne set above the seats of the assembly by two broad sets of seven steps separated by a flat landing. Roth sat in the throne, flanked by two wytches. The others stood on the landing. The highlanders were spread around the perimeter of the room.

The leap took him past the whirring swords of two highlanders who were cutting blindly at the air in front of the door, hoping to get lucky and hit the invisible wetboy.

Drawing Retribution from its back scabbard, Kylar rolled to his feet.

A swarm of tiny hands appeared in the air as the wytches chanted. The hands were looking for him, plucking at him. They seethed over the ground leaping and clawing at each other as they groped for him.

He jumped away, cutting at the hands, but his sword passed through them harmlessly; there was nothing for him to cut.

They swarmed over him and the hands thickened, strengthened as two of the wytches chanted in time with each other. Then, as the hands pulled him upright, Kylar felt something else seize him. He felt like a baby caught in giant's fingers.

It tore at him and he felt the ka'kari's cloaking strip

open. He let it go. It wouldn't do him much good to be partly invisible if he couldn't move.

Well, that was glorious. In all the history of stupid men intentionally springing traps set for them, that was probably the lamest result ever.

Kylar had hoped—hell, expected—that he'd at least take a few guards with him. Maybe a wytch. Two would have been nice. Durzo would be shaking his head in disgust.

"I knew you'd come, Blint," Roth crowed from the throne. He hopped to his feet and waved to the wytches. Kylar was lifted off his feet and shot forward, carried magically up the stairs and deposited on the landing below the throne.

Blint? Gods. I sprang a trap that wasn't even set for me.

The magic fingers tore away Kylar's mask. "Kylar?" Roth said, astonished. He burst out laughing.

"My prince, beware," a red-haired wytch at Roth's right said. "He has the ka'kari."

Roth slapped his hands together and laughed again, as if unable to believe his luck. "And just in time! Oh, Kylar, if I were another man, I'd almost let you live."

The witty riposte dried on Kylar's tongue as he saw into Roth's eyes. If most of his deaders had a cupful of darkness in their souls, Roth had a river, boundless and bleak, a roaring, devouring darkness with a voice like thunder. Here was a man who hated all that was lovely.

"Captain," Roth said, "where are the girl and the scarred wench?"

One of the men who'd entered after Kylar said, "We've lost them, Your Majesty."

"I'm disappointed, Captain," Roth said, but his voice was jubilant. "Unlose them."

"Yes, Your Highness," the soldier said. He grabbed his ten highlanders and headed back into the hall.

Roth turned back to Kylar. "Now," he said. "Dessert. Kylar, do you know how long I've been looking for you?"

Kylar blinked and tore himself away, somehow shut his senses off to the evil in the man before him. He forced nonchalance into his voice. "Since I'm the man who's going to kill you, I'd guess—oh, since you first looked in a mirror and realized just how damn ugly you are."

Roth clapped his hands. "How droll. You know, Kylar, I feel like you've been in my shadow for years, opposing everything I've done. Stealing my ka'kari really irritated me."

"Well, I aim to vex," Kylar said. He wasn't really listening. Opposing him for years? Roth really was crazy. Kylar didn't even know him. But let the man rant as long as he wanted. Kylar surreptitiously flexed against the bonds of magic.

They were like steel. This was not going well. Kylar didn't have a plan. He didn't even have the beginning of a plan. He didn't think that there was a plan that might have worked even if he'd been smart enough to think of it. The Khalidoran soldiers had encircled him, the wytches were watching him like vultures, their vir wiggling faintly, and Roth looked altogether far too pleased with himself.

"And vex you do. You seem to turn up at the most inopportune moments."

"Just like that rash you picked up from the rent boys, huh?"

"Oh, *personality*. Excellent. I haven't had a really satisfying kill since yesterday."

"If you fell on your sword, we'd all be satisfied."

"You had your chance to kill me, Kylar." Roth shrugged. "You failed. But I didn't know you were a wetboy. I only got your real name yesterday, and killing you had to wait while I gained a kingdom for my father."

"I won't hold it against you." *I had my chance?*

"So gracious in defeat. Did Durzo teach you that?"

Kylar had no response. It was probably stupid at this point to feel irked that he seemed to have lost a point in the battle of wits, but then if Kylar had been smarter, he wouldn't have been here in the first place.

"I must say," Roth said. "I've not been impressed with this generation of wetboys. Hu's apprentice was as much of a disappointment as you are. I mean, *really*. Durzo would have at least killed one of my men before we caught him, don't you think? I'm afraid you're a poor shadow of your master, Kylar. By the way, where is he? It's not like him to have an inferior do a job that concerns him."

"I killed him last night. For working for you."

The prince clapped his hands with glee and giggled. "I think that's the most lovely thing I've ever heard. He betrayed me by saving you, and you betrayed him for working for me. Oh, Kylar," Roth came down the steps to stand in front of him. "If I could trust you damn wetboys, I'd hire you in a heartbeat. But you're too dangerous. And, of course, you've bonded my ka'kari."

Roth's wytch shifted, obviously nervous to have Roth standing so close to Kylar.

The wytch must know something I don't, Kylar thought. He couldn't move a muscle. He was totally helpless.

Wait. That's it. That's exactly *why he's nervous. He thinks the ka'kari's a threat. And if he thinks it is, maybe it is.*

Roth drew a beautiful long sword from a hip scabbard. "I'm disappointed with you."

"Why's that?" Kylar asked, racking his brain to think of how he might use the ka'kari. What did he know about it? It enabled his Talent. It made him see through shadows. It made him invisible. It came out of his skin, and hid him more perfectly than any wetboy could hide.

But how?

"I'd hoped this would be fun," Roth said. "I was going to tell you how hard you made my life. But you're like Blint. You don't even care if you live or die." Roth raised the sword.

"Sure I do," Kylar said, showing fear. "How hard have I made your life?"

"Sorry, I'm not going to give you the satisfaction."

Oh, come on! "Not for me," Kylar said. "You know your father's meisters and soldiers are going to report everything they've seen and heard to him. Why not give them the whole story?" It was clumsy, but with his life on the line, it was harder to think quickly than he would have imagined.

Roth paused, thinking.

It was useless. The ka'kari just did what it did. It had eaten *a knife last night, for the God's sake! There was no telling by what logic it operated—if any. It was just magic.*

Absorbs. Eats. That's *what it does!* He'd felt a huge jolt of power after it had absorbed the knife. *The Devourer.* Blint had called it the Devourer. He was close, maybe.

"Sorry," Roth said. "I don't perform for anyone. Not even you. This is just between us, Azoth." Roth handed his sword to the wytch to his left and smoothed his long hair back over his ears—

Except he didn't have ears. The left ear looked like it had been melted off. The right ear had been cut off.

Azoth had been pushed to his knees in the middle of the boat shop. It had been hard to get Rat to come into the dark shop, but he'd done it. Now Rat's foot was squarely in the middle of the noose Azoth had laid on the floor, but Azoth couldn't move. He couldn't draw a full breath. Rat was inches away, terrifying in his nakedness, giving an order. He clouted Azoth. Azoth tasted blood. He found himself moving. He grabbed the noose and snugged the knot tight against Rat's ankle. Rat shouted and raised his knee sharply into Azoth's face.

He landed on the big rock and scraped his back, falling between the rock and the hole in the floor where boats had once been lowered into the river's foul waters. He scrambled and braced his thin arms against the rock, and lifted his eyes, expecting the older boy to be already to be on him.

Rat looked at Azoth, at the hole, at the rock, at the rope, at his ankle. Azoth would never forget the look in Rat's eyes. It was terror. Then Rat lunged, and Azoth shoved the rock into the hole.

The rope went tight and Rat was pulled to the side in midlunge. He scrambled, grabbing for Azoth, missing. His fingers raked the rotting wood floor as he slid and disappeared into the hole. There was a splash.

But moments later, Azoth heard crying. He walked to the edge of the hole.

Rat was holding on by his fingertips, begging. It was impossible. Then Azoth saw that his rock had landed on one of the lattice-like support beams that held the shop up over the river. It was balanced precariously, but as long as Rat held tension on the rope, it wouldn't drag him into the depths.

Azoth walked to Rat's pile of clothing and found his dagger. Rat was pleading, tears coursing down his pimply cheeks, but Azoth heard only the roar of blood in his ears. He squatted by Rat, careful but fearless. Even now, Rat's arms were shaking from holding his weight; he was too fat to hold himself for long, too fat to let go with one hand and grab Azoth.

With a quick motion, Azoth grabbed his ear and sliced it off. Rat screamed and let go.

His body hit the rock, dislodged it. The last thing Azoth saw was his terrified face as he was pulled under the water, then even that was obscured by his hands churning, reaching for something, anything—finding nothing.

Azoth waited and waited, and then staggered away.

The pimples were gone. He'd grown a beard to cover the few pits they'd left. The build was right, though he'd lost weight since he left the Warrens, but that jaggedly cut ear, and his eyes—*gods! how didn't I notice those dead eyes?*—the eyes were the same.

"Rat," Kylar breathed. His plan burst into a thousand shards. His heart stopped. He felt like a child again, waiting in line for Rat to beat him, too cowardly to do anything but weep.

"I'm dead, right? Funny, that's what they told me about you." Roth shook his head, but his voice was low. This was just for him. "Neph burned off my other ear to punish me for what you did. You cost me three years, Azoth. Three years before I became a guild head again. I held my breath for—gods it seemed like forever. Forever working at the knot you tied on my ankle, bleeding my life out into that filthy water until Neph finally pulled me out. He watched the whole thing, said he was debating letting me die. Neph had to kill one of my bigs—you remember Roth, don't you?—and put him in my place before your master came. I had to move to some shitty guild on the opposite side of the Warrens and start all over. You almost made me fail my father." He was shaking with rage. He exposed his melted ear again. "This was the *least* of my punishments. And then you conveniently 'died.' I never believed it, Azoth. I knew you were out there, just waiting for me. Believe me, if I had time, I would torture you for years, I would push you to the end of human endurance and beyond. I'd heal you just to make you hurt again." He closed his eyes and lowered his voice once more. "But I don't have that luxury. If I leave you alive, my father might come up with other plans for you. He might do something else with the ka'kari. I paid for that ka'kari, and I intend to bond it immediately." He smiled grimly. "Any last words?"

Kylar had lost his focus, gotten distracted. Fear and horror had made his mind wander from the puzzle, when nothing should have been as important. Durzo had taught him better. Fear was to be acknowledged, then ignored. Where had he been? Devourer? Magic? "Shit," he said, not realizing he spoke aloud.

Roth arched an eyebrow. "Hmm. Boring, but accurate enough." His grip turned on his sword, and his shoulder rolled back. The blade was coming up. The man was going to cut his head off. Everything in Kylar cried out for help.

A boom sounded somewhere below the range of human hearing, but Kylar felt it wallop his stomach like a thunder crack. His vision went blue-white with magic. He could see the magic streaming through the air as fast as an arrow, a wall of magic.

The castle itself rocked and everyone fell. Everywhere he looked, Kylar saw the same stunned looks. Roth was sprawled on the stairs, his sword still in hand, mouth wide.

Kylar suddenly felt one of the magic bonds holding him snap. He looked toward the others and saw that the magic—it looked like a storm of blue-white rain falling sideways, flying invisibly through walls and people—was spattering against the bonds, collecting around them. The bonds were as black as the wytches' vir, and the blue magic hissed and spat wherever it touched the black.

Then the blue magic latched on to the wytches' magic and roared up the black tendrils like wildfire climbing a hill to the wytches holding them.

Shrieks burst from three of the wytches and the bonds holding Kylar disappeared as three living blue torches lit the room. But Kylar's eyes were drawn to himself. The ka'kari was covering him like a black skin, and everywhere the blue magic pelted him, the magic danced like a puddle in the rain, then disappeared—and the ka'kari swelled more powerful.

The Devourer ate magic, too.

Then the magical shockwave was gone.

There was the briefest silence, then Roth screamed at the wytches who hadn't been using the vir—the two wytches in the room still alive, "Get him!" Roth plucked his sword from the stairs and swung it at Kylar's face.

Incredibly, the wytches obeyed instantly. Bonds leapt into place around Kylar's arms and legs. Everywhere the bonds touched Kylar, in response to his will, the ka'kari swelled, twisted through them, shifted, sucked, and devoured them.

Kylar threw himself back against the bonds even before they were completely dissolved. He burst through them with all the strength of his Talent as Roth's sword slashed the air inches from his throat.

He tore through the shriveling bonds and flew back clumsily, his feet tearing free last, tripping him. He twisted in the air and threw a knife with his off hand.

A soldier grunted and hit the floor.

Kylar landed below the second flight of steps, flat on his back. The impact knocked the wind out of him, but even as he slid across the floor his sword was moving. Highlanders stood to the left and right of him and his sword flashed twice, cutting through boots and ankles on either side of him.

Three highlanders had fallen, but others were already attacking. Kylar flipped his feet over his head and stood, gasping but ready to fight.

64

Solon tried to climb down from the statue. King Logan Verdroekan had been one of the earliest kings of Cenaria, perhaps mythic, and Solon couldn't remember what he'd done, for all that it must have been heroic to have Regnus Gyre name his son after him. And he must have been special to get a statue of such size, holding his sword aloft in defiance. Solon had chosen it not for its metaphoric significance but simply because he wanted every meister in the garden to see him. Every meister that had used vir within five hundred paces in the few seconds he'd been able to hold Curoch was dead.

Curoch lay on the stones beneath him. Feir was snatching it up and wrapping it in a blanket. He was shouting at Solon, but Solon couldn't make out the words. He still felt as if he were on fire. Every vein in his body was tingling so fiercely it was hard to even feel Verdroeken's stone sword under his fingers. Solon had perched on the dead king's shoulders and held onto the stone sword for balance, holding Curoch aloft the same way when he'd released the magic. He shifted his grip, his legs shaking, and suddenly fell.

Feir didn't quite catch him, but he at least broke his fall.

"I can't walk," Solon said. His brain was burning, his vision flaring every color in the rainbow, his scalp felt afire. "It was amazing, Feir. Such a tiny piece of what it can do . . ."

Feir grabbed him and threw him over his shoulders as a lesser man might lift a child. He said something, but Solon couldn't quite make it out. He said it again.

"Oh, I got about fifty of them. Maybe ten left," Solon said. "One on the east bridge." He was trying to remember what Dorian had told him. Something urgent. Something he hadn't let Feir hear.

Don't let Feir die. He's more important than the sword.

"I'm going to have to set you down," Feir said. "Don't worry. I'm not leaving you."

In outrageous hues of green and blue, Khalidoran soldiers were swarming in front of the east gate. Solon couldn't even remember leaving the garden. He laughed at what he saw. Feir was using Curoch as a *sword*.

Watching Feir with a sword was more than amazing; it was a privilege. Feir had always been a natural, deceptively quick, unbelievably strong, his movements as precise as a dancer's. In hues of green and blue and red, Feir demolished the soldiers. There was no extended swordplay. At most, each soldier had time to swing his own weapon once, miss or have it parried, and then die.

Feir cursed, but when Solon tried to follow his gaze, the riot of colors was too intense. The big man lifted him, threw him over a shoulder again, and started running. Solon saw the wood of the bridge beneath Feir's feet.

"Hold on tight," Feir said.

Not a moment too soon, Solon latched onto Feir's belt on either side of the man's broad back. Feir dodged to the side and his great shoulders rolled. With his feet sticking out in front of Feir and his head merely bobbing along behind him, all Solon saw was a brief flash of Curoch. Feir spun—the right way so Solon wasn't flung off—and Curoch came up again, then he was running full speed once more. Solon saw three bodies behind them, lying on the bridge. The man had killed three men while holding Solon over his shoulder. Astounding.

Feir said, "Dorian told me our hope is in the water, but not to jump. Look for a rope!"

Solon lifted his head, as if he would be much help in finding a rope while bouncing on Feir's back. He didn't see a rope, but he did see a meister behind them, conjuring a ball of wytchfire. He tried to yell, but couldn't draw breath.

"Damn you, Dorian!" Feir was shouting. "What goddam rope?"

"Down!" Solon said.

With the reflexes of the sword master he was, Feir dropped instantly. Wytchfire crackled over their heads and burst against a dozen Khalidoran soldiers holding the far gate in front of them. Solon went sprawling and was almost brained by one of the great fire pots that guarded the bridge.

The old wytch behind them—from his thickness of his vir Solon guessed he was a Vürdmeister—was drawing magic once more. Feir grabbed Solon's collar and threw him behind the fire pot. The move put Solon in a safe place, but exposed Feir. This time it wasn't wytchfire, but something else Solon had never seen. An angry red beam didn't so much fly as streak through the air toward Feir. He threw up a magical shield and ducked.

The shield barely deflected the beam—again into a soldier running to join the fray—but the force of the magic blew Feir's shield apart and flung him to the other side like a rag doll. Curoch spun from his grasp.

Drawing on strength he didn't know he had, Solon grabbed Feir and pulled him into the shadow of the fire pot with him.

Two more meisters were running to join the Vürdmeister and soldiers were behind them. The gate at the far end of the bridge opened and soldiers were pouring through.

Feir sat up and looked out at Curoch, twenty feet away, exposed. "I can use it," he said. "I can save it."

"No!" Solon said. "You'll die."

The soldiers and the meisters had paused, regrouping, advancing slowly now, cautious and orderly.

"I don't matter, Solon. We can't let them have it."

"You wouldn't even live long enough to use it, Feir. Not even if you were willing to trade your life for one second of power."

"It's right there!"

"And so is this," Solon said, motioning to the edge of the bridge.

Feir looked. "You've got to be joking."

Over the edge, a black silk rope had been tied to the underside of either end of the bridge. It only extended out below them when the wind blew. Feir was looking not at the rope but at the fall.

"Hey, it's prophecy, right? It has to work," Solon said. If only the world would stop flashing yellow.

"It never works out exactly like Dorian says!"

"If he told you that you were going to do this, would you have come?"

"Hell no. And don't you nod knowingly to me. I get enough of that from Dorian." Feir looked at the approaching soldiers and meisters. "Right. You first."

He's going to go after Curoch. The heroic idiot.

"I can't," Solon said. "I'm not strong enough to grab the rope. I'll die if I go alone."

Feir stood. "Just let me try—" he reached out with his Talent and grabbed the sword. Instantly, hands of vir crackled visibly over his magic and started climbing toward him. Solon slashed the magic loose with his own.

Spots exploded in front of Solon's eyes. "Oh, don't do that. Don't do that, please. Oh."

"Let me ride pony-back, Feir." Solon didn't have time to explain. The meisters were close.

"I'm crazy, and you're fat," Feir said. But he picked up Solon and put him on his back.

"Magically too. I've got a plan. And I am not fat."

For all that he second-guessed plans when they were all safe, Feir knew to obey in battle. He opened himself quickly, and Solon dipped into Feir's Talent. He lashed himself onto Feir's back with magical bonds. Then he quickly readied five thin weaves. It still hurt, but not nearly as much as using his own Talent.

"Now," he said. "Jump."

Feir leaped over the side of the bridge. The rope was in the perfect place—not because of the wind or the power of prophecy, but because Solon pulled it there with magic. As Feir grabbed the rope, Solon activated the other weaves.

Holes were torn in the sides of each of the fire pots and air inside them suddenly compressed, jetting the oil in the pots out onto the bridge. The last weave dropped a little spark in middle of the oil.

There was a satisfying whoosh. The river suddenly lit orange and white and heat washed over the falling mages.

Then things were happening too rapidly to follow. Feir had caught the rope with both hands and a leg. He immediately flipped upside down. The sudden change in direction caught Solon's arm across Feir's shoulder and snapped it. If it weren't for the magical bonds holding him, he would have dropped like a stone. The rope, anchored on both sides of the bridge, first stretched, bowing down toward the middle. Because Feir and Solon hadn't made it to the middle of the bridge, that meant they zipped headfirst for fifteen paces. Then the rope tore loose at the castle end.

Solon was watching light explode over them, distantly aware that they were swinging with terrific speed toward the river. The bridge was engulfed in flames leaping merrily into the night. Or maybe that was pain exploding in his head. Then they slapped into something cold and hard.

He took a breath. It was bad timing. The cold hard stuff had become cold wet stuff. They were under water. He coughed as Feir came to the surface, and Solon thought dimly that the man was either a hell of a swimmer or something was dragging them out.

Feir was on his knees in the shallows, holding up his

hands. From his perch on the man's back, Solon saw that Feir's hands had been torn to bloody pieces by the rope. He could see bone.

"Ah, you're better off than I thought you'd be," Dorian's voice was saying as his magic hauled them out of the river. "Stop lollygagging, you two. We need to get going if we're going to make it to Khalidor in time."

"Lollygagging?" Solon asked, glad to find that he had strength to be outraged.

"Khalidor?" Feir said.

"Well, that is where my bride is waiting. I can't wait to find out who she is. I think Curoch is going to find its way there, too."

Feir cursed, but Solon—broken arm, purple vision, and all—just laughed.

65

As they came within the arc of his sword or the reach of his lashing feet or striking fists, men went down like grain in a summer storm. To Kylar, who had always been gifted at fighting, battle suddenly made sense. The chaos unfolded into beautifully intricate, interlocking, and logical patterns.

Just by looking at a man's face, he could judge instantly: parry left, hesitate, lunge, clear. A man died and fell far enough away that he didn't impede Kylar's movements. Next, sweep right, roll in, bear fist to nose. Spin, hamstring, throat. Parry, riposte. Stab.

Parsed to the individual percussion of each chamber of his heart, battle had a rhythm, a music. Not a sound was out of place. The tenor of ringing steel layered over a bass of the fists and feet hammering flesh—soft to hard, hard to soft—and the baritone of men's curses, punctuated by the staccato percussion of rending mail.

With his Talent singing, Kylar was a virtuoso. He fought in a fine frenzy, a dancer possessed. Time never slowed, but he found his body reacting to sights he didn't consciously see—turning, dodging under blows his mind never registered, striking with the awesome speed and grace of that angel of death, the Night Angel.

The highlanders sought to overwhelm him by force of numbers. Their blades caught the air within an inch of Kylar's ear, within half an inch of his stomach, a quarter of an inch from his thigh. He rode the front of each beat, cut the margins closer and closer, until the bodies he was killing were being pushed forward instead of falling back, and pressing in closer on him.

He sheathed Retribution and grabbed the hand holding a blade aimed at his belly and yanked a skinny highlander across the circle to stab his fellow. Reaching around his own back with a knife, he diverted a sword thrust while his other knife found an eye socket.

Two spears came for him and he dropped to the floor, yanking both forward. As each impaled a body, he swung up, destroying another highlander's face with a kick.

But the situation was hopeless. Within a cage of tangled weapons and thrashing, dying men, he'd be trapped in moments.

Light as a cat, he sprang to the back of a man dying on his knees and vaulted off the shoulder of one of the impaled spear bearers.

As he flipped sideways through the air, a ball of green wytchfire the size of his fist streaked through the air at him. It caught his cloak and broke into pieces. He landed on his feet and ducked under a sword cut. His cloak burst into green flame. Kylar tore the cloak off as he dove between two spears.

Holding one edge of the cloak, he came to his feet and

wrapped the cloak around another of his attackers. The green flame raced for the man's skin, and there burned a fierce blue as he screamed.

Another ball of wytchfire sizzled through the air and Kylar dove behind one of the pillars supporting the high ceiling.

There were two beats of rest. Kylar had killed or disabled more than half the Khalidorans, but now the others played to their strengths. Point, counterpoint.

"To the captain! Keep a meister in view!" Roth shouted. Men streamed to the captain to form a wedge between Kylar and Roth, who had retreated to the throne to watch.

But Kylar wasn't wasting his time as he stood in the protection of the pillar. He knew that if he wanted a chance at Roth, he had to kill the wytches. Both of them were eyeing the spaces between the pillars where he would have to run.

He pooled the ka'kari in his hand, and keeping the feel of those fingers of magic in his mind, willed it to dribble down the length of his sword. Seeming to sense his urgency, the ka'kari coated the steel instantly. Both ka'kari and steel shimmered out of visibility.

Kylar dodged out from the pillar and the fingers were on him instantly. He cut in a quick circle and felt them shrivel and die out of existence. Grabbing the edge of one of the long tapestries that covered the walls of the throne room, Kylar moved toward the pillar, but not before wytchfire leaped from a wytch's fingers.

If he'd had time to think about it, Kylar wouldn't have tried to block with his sword—it was insanity to try to block magic—but it was his ingrained response. The flat of his blade hit the green globe of fire. Instead of bursting, the fire whooshed *into* the blade.

Kylar dodged around a pillar with the tapestry in one hand and a sword now visible because of the green flame crackling through it. With all the strength of his Talent, he leaped.

He soared into the air in the middle of the throne room, and then as the tapestry met a pillar, it abruptly changed his trajectory and launched him up the steps.

The other wytch must have thrown wytchfire that Kylar hadn't seen, because the tapestry gave way and tore a moment before Kylar was going to release it. He hit the landing between the flights of stairs with eight feet of burning tapestry in his hands. He hurled it toward the highlanders and slashed at the wytch chanting not two steps away.

The top of the wytch's head opened, exposing his brain. The man spun, but his lips completed his incantation. The thick black tendrils that had been squirming under the skin of his arms fattened grotesquely like rippling muscles and tore free of the wytch's arms, bursting through his skin.

Power roared from the dying wytch and he staggered, trying to find Kylar. Kylar jumped behind him. He kicked the wytch so hard that the man lifted off the ground and crashed into the highlanders.

The flailing black tendrils ripped into the men, sucking them in like greedy hands and chewing through them with a sound like logs in a sawmill.

Even as the black tendrils were tearing through the soldiers, Kylar felt more than saw the white light forming behind him. He turned in time to see the homunculus streaking through the air. It dodged under his desperate slash and stabbed tiny claws into his chest.

He was already jumping to the side when he felt the concussion and saw the air ripple. Reality bubbled in a line toward him. The rippling air curved, following him as he ran. Then the air tore open. He vaulted all the way to the wall and nearly caught another ball of wytchfire with his face.

The pit wyrm lunged forward into reality, barely missing him. It thrashed, furious, tearing the hole open wider and hooking fiery claws around two of the pillars, mere feet away. Kylar ripped the homunculus from his chest and slapped it onto a soldier's face.

As the pit wyrm lunged again, Kylar leapt straight up. Its lampreylike mouth shot out, latched onto the screaming man, and sucked him back into the pit. By the time Kylar landed, both pit wyrm and soldier were gone.

Kylar turned and jumped for the top of the stairs, but he was too slow. Even as he left the ground, he saw a blur of light streaking toward him. There was no time to draw a throwing knife. Kylar hurled his sword at the last wytch.

The bolt of magic blasted his left shoulder. As the momentum of his leap carried him up and forward, the blast made him flip end over end backward. He crunched into the marble floor at the foot of the throne and felt his left knee shatter.

For a long moment, his eyes refused to focus. He blinked and blinked and finally cleared the blood away. He saw Retribution buried to the hilt through a wytch ten paces away, its blade black with his ka'kari.

He realized that he was viewing the dead wytch

through a pair of legs. His eyes followed the legs up to Roth's face.

"Stand up," Roth said. He plunged his long sword through Kylar's lower back.

Kylar gagged as Roth twisted the blade in his kidney. Then the hot metal lifted away. Something pulled Kylar to his feet.

The pain was like a cloud making everything fuzzy and indistinct. Confused, Kylar stared at the dead wytches. *Who picked me up?*

"All the aethelings of Godking Ursuul are wytchborn," Roth said. "Didn't you know?"

Kylar stared at Roth dumbly. Roth was Talented? The invisible hands released him and he folded as he put weight on his destroyed left leg. The marble floor jarred him once more.

"Get up!" Roth said. He stabbed Kylar's groin and cursed him. Kylar dropped his head onto the marble as Roth's screaming became inarticulate. The sound of Roth's voice faded to a murmur next to the roaring voice of pain.

The pain flashed in another bar through his stomach as Roth stabbed him again. Then he must have picked Kylar up again, because Kylar felt his head lolling to one side. If he'd felt pain before, now it became agony.

Every part of his body was being scoured with fire, dipped in alcohol, packed with salt. His eyelids were lined with crushed glass. His optic nerves were being chewed by little teeth. And after his eyes, every tissue, sinew, muscle, and organ marinated in misery in its turn. He was screaming.

But his mind cleared.

Kylar blinked. He was standing before Roth, and he was aware. Aware and dismayed. He must have landed on his left knee when he'd crashed to the marble, because it was demolished. He was bleeding inside—his intestines leaking slow death into his viscera, stomach acids scorching his intestines, a kidney pouring black blood. His left shoulder looked like it had kissed a giant's hammer.

"You won't die easy," Roth said. "I won't allow it. Not after what you've done. Look what you've done! My father will be furious."

There it was. He was dying. Kylar could perch unsteadily on his one good leg, but he had no weapons. His sword and the ka'kari were ten paces away—they might as well have been across the ocean. No weapons, and Roth was—even now—careful not to come within range of his hands. Kylar didn't have so much as a belt knife.

"Are you ready to die?" Roth said, his eyes glowing malevolence.

Kylar was staring at his right hand. Of all the beaten, sliced, and smashed places on his body, his fingers were healthy, perfect, healed. Wasn't that the hand he'd cut on the window last night? "I'm ready," he said, surprising himself.

"Any regrets?" Roth asked.

Kylar looked into Roth, and understood him. Kylar had always had enough darkness in his soul to understand evil men. Roth was trying to wring anguish from him. Roth wanted to kill him while he thought of all the things he hadn't done. Roth reaped despair. "Dying well is easy," Kylar said, "it only takes a moment of courage. It's living well that I couldn't do. What's death compared to that?"

"You're about to find out," Roth spat.

Kylar smirked, and then smiled as rage washed over Roth.

"Killing Logan was more fun," Roth said. He rammed his sword into Kylar's chest.

Logan! The thought cut through Kylar more cruelly than the sword in Roth's hand. Kylar had lived by the sword. Dying by it was neither unexpected nor unjust. But Logan had never even wanted to hurt anyone. Roth killing Logan wasn't right. It wasn't fair. It wasn't just.

Kylar stared at the steel stabbed through his chest. He took Roth's hand in his own and pulled, pulled himself up the sword, impaling himself to the hilt. Roth's eyes widened.

"I am the Night Angel," Kylar said, gasping on the steel through his lung. "This is justice. This is for Logan."

There was a ting and the sound of metal rolling on marble. The ka'kari leaped for Kylar's hand—

And was caught squarely by Roth. Triumph lit his eyes. He laughed.

But Kylar grabbed Roth's shoulders and stared him in the eye. "I am the Night Angel," Kylar repeated. "This is justice. This is for Logan." Kylar lifted his right hand.

Roth looked confused. Then he looked at his left hand. The ka'kari was turning to liquid and gliding through his fingers. His hands scrambled as they'd scrambled across the wood floor of the boat shop, and found nothing. The ka'kari slapped into Kylar's palm and formed an enormous punch dagger on his fist.

Kylar slammed his fist into Roth's chest.

Roth looked down, his disbelief turning to horror as Kylar drew the dagger out, his horror turning to fear as his heart pumped blood directly into his lungs.

Roth shrieked a shrill denial of his own mortality.

Kylar released the prince and tried to step away, but his limbs refused to obey him. His knee buckled and he crashed to the ground with the Khalidoran prince.

Roth and Kylar lay eye to eye on the marble at the foot of the throne, staring at each other, dying. Each trembled as uncontrollable twitches ran through his limbs. Each breathed terrible, labored breaths in time with the other. Roth's eyes brimmed with fear, panic so intense it paralyzed. He seemed to no longer see Kylar lying inches away. His gaze grew more distant and filled with soul-deep terror.

Kylar was content. This Night Angel had apportioned death—and death was his portion. It wasn't nice, but it was just. This sentence was deserved. Watching Roth's eyes finally glaze in restless death, Kylar wished there were something more beautiful to find in death than justice. But he didn't have the strength to turn away from this life, this death, this terrible justice.

Then someone turned him over. A woman. She came into focus slowly. It was Elene. She pulled Kylar into her lap, stroked his hair. She was crying. Kylar couldn't see her scars. He reached a hand up, touched her face. She was angelic.

Then he saw his hand. It was perfect, whole, and amazingly, unbloodied. For the first time in his life, his hands were clean. *Clean!*

Death came. Kylar yielded.

66

Terah Graesin had just paid a fortune to one of the prettiest men she'd ever seen. Jarl said he spoke for the Shinga, but he carried himself with such assurance, she wondered if he might not be the Shinga himself. She hadn't liked handing over so much money to the Sa'kagé, but she hadn't had any choice. The Godking's army would arrive with the dawn, and she'd already spent too long in the city.

The coup had not gone according to the Godking's plan. The Khalidorans controlled the bridges, the castle, and the city's gates, but some of them had only skeleton crews. That would change when the rest of the army arrived, and Terah Graesin and her nobles needed to be gone when that happened. If she hadn't paid half her fortune to Jarl, she would have had to leave behind all of it. A queen made the hard decisions, and with everyone else dead, a queen was what she was, now.

It was midnight. The wagons were packed. The men were waiting. It was time.

Terah stood outside her family's mansion. Like the other

ducal families' homes, theirs was old, a veritable fortress. A looted fortress now. A looted fortress smelling of the barrels and barrels of oil they had poured in every room, over the precious heirlooms too heavy to carry, and into the grooves they'd cut in every centuries-old beam. It was time. Jarl's wetboys were supposed to slaughter the Khalidorans holding the city's east gate at midnight. All the other nobles were huddled outside their own houses. From her elevated front porch, she could see some of them up and down Horak Street, waiting to see if she'd really do it.

She locked the mansion in her mind. After she returned, she would rebuild this for her family, twice as splendid as before.

Terah Graesin walked to the street and took the torch from Sergeant Gamble. The archers gathered around her. She personally lit every arrow. At her nod, they loosed them.

The mansion went up in flame. Fire poured from the windows and reached for the heavens. Queen Terah Graesin didn't look. She mounted her horse and led her column, her pathetic army of three hundred soldiers and twice as many servants and shopkeepers into the street toward the east gate.

Across the east side, the great houses lit up one by one. They were the funeral pyres of fortunes. Not only were the nobles losing everything, but so too were all those who depended on them for their employment. But the fires of destruction were also beacons of hope. You may have won, Cenaria was saying, but your victory is no triumph. You can force me from my home, but you will not live in it. I will leave you nothing but scorched earth.

In response to those great fires, across the city,

smaller fires rose, too. Shopkeepers set fire to their shops. Blacksmiths stoked their furnaces so hot they would crack. Bakers destroyed their ovens. Millers sank their millstones in the Plith. Warehouse owners set fire to their storehouses. Livestock owners slaughtered their herds. Captains confined to the Plith by wytches' magic scuttled their own ships.

Thousands joined the exodus. The trickle of nobles and their servants became a flood. The flood became a host, an army marching out of the city—marching in defeat, but marching. Some drove wagons, some rode, some walked barefoot with empty hands and empty bellies. Some cursed; some prayed; some stared over their shoulders with haunted eyes; some wept. Some left brothers and sisters and parents and children, but every one of Cenaria's orphaned sons and daughters carried a small, dim hope in their hearts.

I shall return, it vowed. *I shall return.*

Neph stood as far to one side as he could among the meisters, generals, and soldiers waiting to greet Godking Garoth Ursuul as he rode across West Kingsbridge with his retinue. The Godking wore a great ermine cloak that accentuated the paleness of his northern skin. His chest was bare aside from the heavy gold chains of his office. He was robust, thick-bodied but muscular, vigorous for his age. The Godking pulled his stallion to a halt before the courtyard gate. Six heads on pikes greeted him. A seventh pike stood empty.

"Commander Gher."

"Yes, my liege—uh, my god, Your Holiness, sire." The

former royal guard cleared his throat. Things were not good. Though Roth's and Neph's plans had seemed to go without a problem, somehow the Godking's armies had sustained far heavier losses than they'd planned. A boatload of highlanders dead. Many of the nobles who ought to be dead escaped. Great swathes of the city aflame. The heart of Cenaria's industry and economy reduced to ashes.

There was no resistance yet, but with so many nobles still alive, it would come. The meisters that were supposed to have been a devastating spearhead into the heart of Modai were now dead. More than fifty meisters dead, at a stroke, without any explanation except rumors of some mage with more Talent than anyone since Ezra the Mad and Jorsin Alkestes. The Ceuran invasion ended before it began. The Godking's son murdered just as he completed his uurdthan.

The Sa'kagé would have to be brought to heel, fires literal and figurative would have to be put out. Someone would have to answer for it. Neph Dada was trying to figure out how to make sure it wasn't him.

"Why is there an empty pike on my bridge?" the Godking asked. "Anyone?"

Commander Hurin Gher shifted in his saddle, stupidly looking at the empty pike. "We haven't found prince's—I mean, the pretender's—um, Logan Gyre's body yet, sire. We, we do know that he's dead. We have three reports confirming his death, but in all the fighting. . . . We're, we're working on it."

"Indeed." Godking Ursuul didn't look at Hurin Gher. He was studying the faces of the royal family above him. "And this *Shadow* that killed my son? He's dead, too?"

Neph felt a chill at the quiet menace in the Godking's

query. When the Khalidorans had first gone into the throne room, they thought some elite unit must have wiped out all the Khalidorans in the room, but Neph had been able to revive a man who'd had his feet cut off. He swore he'd seen most of the fight before he passed out. It was one man. A shadow. The Night Angel, he called him. The story was already getting out among the men.

A man who walked unseen, who could kill thirty highlanders and five meisters and one of the Godking's own aethelings. A man impervious to steel and to magic. It was nonsense, of course. With all the blood they'd found, the man must be dead. But without a body. . . .

"Someone dragged his body away, sir. We followed the blood trail through the hidden passages. It was a lot of blood, sire. If it really was just one man, he's dead."

"It seems we have a lot of dead people without bodies, Commander. Find them. In the meantime, put up another head. Preferably one that looks like Logan Gyre's."

It wasn't fair. Ferl Khalius had been among the first highlanders on Cenarian soil. He'd been one of the few to get off the burning, sinking barge, and that only because he'd had the wits to throw off his armor before jumping in, so he didn't drown like so many others had. He'd joined another unit and fought barehanded until he could arm himself from the highlanders who died in the first assault on the courtyard. He'd personally killed six Cenarian soldiers and two nobles, six nobles if you counted children, which he didn't.

And what had he been given to recognize his heroism, his cunning? The shit duty. Certain units were being given looting privileges—the good units on the west side, what

the barbarians called the Warrens, and the best units looting the remains of the east side with the officers. Ferl's
unit was all dead, so he got assigned with clearing the
rubble on the east bridge.

It wasn't only dirty—it was dangerous. The wytches
had extinguished the fire, but many of the planks were
weak, some of them cracking or breaking if you stood on
them. The pilings were fine: sheathed in iron, they were
impervious to the fire, but you couldn't stand on the pilings, so a fat lot of good that did.

The worst part of the job was the bodies. Some of them
were like seared steak, crusted black on the outside, but
cracked and oozing inside. And the stench of burnt flesh
and burnt hair! He was picking through the bodies, taking whatever looked promising and dumping the bodies
over the side of the bridge. Some of the units would be
glad to have their dead back for proper burial, but Ferl
wasn't going to carry the damned stinking things across
this bridge. To the abyss with them.

Then he saw a sword. It must have been under one of
the bodies when the fire had started, because it was untouched. There wasn't even smoke damage on the hilt. It
was a beautiful blade, the hilt carved with dragons. It was
the kind of sword that befitted the leader of a warband. Or
a warlord. With such a sword, Ferl's clan would hold him
in awe. Awe he deserved. He was supposed to bring anything unusual he found to one of the Vürdmeisters. *Sure,
after how well they've treated me.*

Looking at the other men working on the bridge and
seeing that none were watching, he drew his sword, set it
aside, and slid his prize into its sheath. Not a perfect fit, but
good enough for the moment. The hilt was a problem, what

with those dragons, but he'd wrap leather bindings around it soon enough. He was good with his hands. Give him a few hours, and this sword would look like any other.

The sword brightened his outlook considerably. It wasn't really enough to repay his valor, but it was a start.

The meister walked down the last corridor to what the Southron barbarians called Hell's Asshole. The nauseating-intoxicating wash of torment engulfed her. She missed a step and stumbled against the wall. The soldier accompanying her turned. He looked scared.

"It's nothing," she said. She walked to the grate covering the hole. A few words and red light burned in front of her.

The creatures in the Hole squinted and shrank back. She spoke again and the light descended into the Hole. She examined each prisoner. Ten men, one woman, and one simpleton with filed teeth. None of them could be the usurper.

She turned, slightly dizzy, and walked out, trying not to flee.

A minute later, a big man rolled out from an overhang carved in the stone.

The woman looked at him and shook her head. "You're a fool. Nothing they could do to you would be as bad as staying here. Look at you. You're soft. The Hole will break you, Thirteen."

Logan stared at her flatly, a grimy woman with gaping holes in her dress, short a few teeth. The look on her face was the only thing approaching human kindness that was to be found in this hole. "Though all the detritus of humanity pass through this hole and all the fires of perdition rise from it, I will not be broken," Logan said.

"He use a lotta big words, don't he?" the big man named Fin said. He smiled a smile full of bloody gums, one of the first symptoms of scurvy, and wrapped his sinew rope back around his body. "Lotta meat on that big fucker. We'll eat real good."

Scurvy meant food deficiencies. Food deficiencies meant Fin had lived long enough to get sick from food deficiencies. Fin was a survivor. Logan turned his eyes to him and pulled out his knife—literally his only edge against these animals. "Let me make this real simple," he said, having to stifle the impulse to say "really" instead of "real." "You will not break me. The hole will not break me. I will not break. I. Will. Not. Be. Broken."

"What's your name, love?" the woman asked.

Logan found himself grinning. Something fierce and primal was rising inside him. Something inside him said, where others have failed, have faltered, have fallen, I will be triumphant; I am different; I am cut of a new cloth; I will rise. "Call me King," he said, and he smiled a fuck-you through the angst and the sorrow, and he was potent.

That was it. That was survival. That was the secret. That was the living flame hidden in the ashes of his burned-out heart. If only he could hold it.

Epilogue

*E*lene knocked on the door of the cooper's shop, her hair covered, back bent, and foot twisted sideways in the dust. The Khalidoran army had arrived yesterday and King Garoth Ursuul was rewarding his troops for their valor by allowing selected soldiers to take what they desired. It wasn't a good day to be a pretty woman on the streets of Cenaria.

It had taken her two harrowing days to find this place. The cooper unbolted the door and signaled her in, gesturing to the back of the shop. Jarl was at a table covered with papers, fat sacks of money at his feet. "I've found your way out," he said. "A Khalidoran caravan master has agreed to take you. You'll have to lie in a compartment used to smuggle barush tea and worse things until you get outside the gates, but it's big enough to hold you and the girl. You leave at nightfall."

"You can trust this smuggler?" Elene asked.

"I can't trust anyone," Jarl said, exhausted. "He's Khalidoran and you're beautiful. But because he's Khalidoran, he has the best chance of getting through the gates. And he's worked with us for twenty years. I've made it in his best interest to take you safely."

"You must have paid him a fortune," Elene said.

"Only half of one," Jarl said, the shadow of a smile coming to his lips. "The other half he gets when you send me word that you've made it safely."

"Thank you."

"It's the least I could do for Kylar." Jarl looked down, ashamed. "It's also the most I can do."

Elene hugged him. "It's more than enough. Thank you."

"The girl's downstairs. She won't leave his bo—she won't leave him."

He recognized this place. The white-gold warmth suffused him; his flesh gloried in the light. He moved through the tunnel with sure and easy steps. Eagerness without hurry.

Gentle fingers closed his eyes.

A child shrieked. Regrets. Sorrow. Darkness. Cold.

He blinked away the nightmare. Breathed. Let the white-gold light hold him again.

"Grab his arm, Uly. Help me."

Cold stones slid under his back. Discomfort. Pain. Hopelessness.

Then even the cold and the jostling faded.

He walked forward unsteadily in the tunnel. Broke into a jog. This was where he belonged now. Here, without pain.

A tear splashed on his face. A woman spoke, but he couldn't make out the words.

He stumbled and fell. He lay there, terrified, but the nightmare didn't come back. He got up to his knees, stood. At the next step he smacked up against . . . nothing.

He put his hands out and felt the invisible barrier. It was as cool as iron and as smooth as glass. Beyond it, the warmth increased, the white-gold light beckoned him. Were those people up ahead?

Something was pulling him aside, away. He felt twisted, and slowly a chamber came into focus—not the chamber, for the chamber itself remained indistinct, it seemed full of people intensely curious to see him, but he couldn't make them out. All that was truly in focus was a man seated before him on a low throne, and two doors. The door at his right hand was of beaten gold. Light leaked around every edge, the same warm white-gold light Kylar had just been in. The door to his left hand was plain wood with a simple iron latch. The man's face was dominated by lambent, lupine yellow eyes. He wasn't tall, but he exuded authority, potency.

"What is this place?" Kylar asked.

A toothy smile. "Neither heaven nor hell. This, if you will, is the Antechamber of the Mystery. This is my realm."

"Who are you?"

"It pleased Acaelus to call me The Wolf."

"Acaelus? You mean Durzo?" Kylar asked.

"Before you, there is a choice. You may proceed through one door or the other. Choose the gold, and I will release you back to where you just were, and you will have my apology for interrupting your journey."

"My journey?"

"Your journey to heaven or hell or oblivion or reincarnation or whatever it is that death holds."

"Do you know?" Kylar asked.

"This is the Antechamber of the Mystery, Azoth. You will find no answers here, just choices." The Wolf grinned, and it was a joyless grin, a predatory grin. "Through the wood door, you will go back to your life, your body, your time—or nearly so. It will take a few days for your body to heal. You will be the Night Angel in truth, as Acaelus was before you. Your body will be immune to the scourge of time as Acaelus' was—something that perhaps one must become old to appreciate. You will also heal at a rate beyond that of mortal men. What you call your Talent will grow. You can still be killed; the difference is, you will come back. You will be a living legend."

It sounded wonderful. Too good, even. *I'd be like Acaelus Thorne. I'd be like Durzo.* The latter thought gave him pause. The burden of immortality—however it worked—or the power of it or sheer press of so much time was what had turned Acaelus Thorne, the prince, the hero, into Durzo Blint, the hopeless, bitter murderer. He remembered his snide remark to Durzo:

"Here I thought the Night Angels were invincible."

"They're immortal. It's not the same."

"Why would you do this for me?" Kylar asked.

"Perhaps I don't do anything at all. Perhaps it is the ka'kari's work."

"What's the price?"

"Ah, Durzo has taught you well, hasn't he?" The Wolf looked almost mournful. "The truth is, I don't know. I can only tell you what I have heard from those more enlightened than I. They believed that coming back from death as you would was such a violation of the natural order of things that this unnatural life cost the afterlife. That for his seven centuries of life, Acaelus traded all eternity. But they might be wrong. It might have no influence on eternity whatsoever—or there may be no eternity to influence. I'm the wrong . . . man . . . to ask, for I have chosen this life myself."

Kylar walked toward the golden door. It was so beautiful there. He'd had such peace. What fool would trade the eternal peace and happiness in that gold light for the blood and gore and dishonor and despair and duplicity of the life he'd led?

As he stepped closer to it, the door changed. The gold melted, puddled to the ground in an instant and a raging inferno leapt up, eager to devour Kylar. Then it was gone, and the gold door was back. Kylar shot a look at the Wolf.

"Eternity," the Wolf said, "might not be a pleasant place for you."

"You did that?"

"A simple illusion. But if you sat in judgment of Kylar Stern, would you give him eternal paradise?"

"You're not exactly disinterested in my choice, are you?"

"You've become a player, Night Angel. No one is disinterested in your choice."

How long Kylar stood there, he didn't know. All he knew was that if he made the wrong choice, he might have a very very long time to regret it. The mathematical formulae were no help; they were full of infinities and zeroes, with no way of knowing on which side of the equation they landed. There was no hedged bet when you might be throwing away eternity in paradise or avoiding eternity in hell or taking an eternal existence on earth with all its flaws, weighed against merciful oblivion. Kylar didn't have Count Drake's faith in a loving God or Durzo's faith that there was no such God. He knew that he had done a lot of evil, by anyone's definition. He knew that he had done some good. He'd given his life for Elene.

Elene. She filled his mind and his heart so utterly that it ached. If he chose life, even if she accepted him, she would grow old and die in the smallest fraction of his life. The odds were that she never would accept him, never could.

All the ifs and maybes rose and fell in great towers of foundationless suppositions, but Elene remained. Kylar loved her. He had always loved her.

Elene was the risk he would take every time.

He made his choice and ran toward the plain door. He screamed—

—and jerked upright.

Elene screamed. Uly screamed.

Taking huge, gasping breaths, Kylar ripped open his blood-encrusted tunic.

His chest was smooth, the skin perfect. He touched his demolished shoulder. It was whole, as healthy as the fingers of his right hand. There wasn't a scar on his body.

He sat there blinking, not even glancing at Uly or Elene, who were frozen, staring at him.

"I'm alive. I'm alive?"

"Yes, Kylar," Momma K said, coming into the room. Her calm was surreal.

Kylar sat stupidly for a moment. It had all been real. He said, "Unbelievable. Kylar: one who kills and is killed. Durzo knew all along."

Uly, seeming to take her cue from the calm Kylar and Momma K were showing, seemed to be fine with Kylar sitting up and talking when he'd been dead a moment before. Elene was not doing as well. She stood up abruptly and walked out the door.

"Elene, wait," Kylar said. "Wait, just tell me one thing." She stopped and looked at him, confused, terrified and hopeful at the same time, her eyes full of tears. "Who was it who gave you those scars? It wasn't Durzo, was it? It was Rat, right?"

"You come back from the dead to ask me that? Of course it was Rat!" She fled.

"Wait! Elene, I'm sorry!" He tried to move, but it seemed he'd used up all his strength to sit up. She was gone. "Wait, what the hell am I sorry about?"

Uly looked at Kylar accusingly. "You aren't going to let her go, are you?"

Kylar held onto the edge of the bed like a lifeline. He looked at Uly, and raised a hand helplessly—and had to quickly put it down to keep from falling over. "How can I stop her?"

Uly stomped her foot and stormed out of the room.

Momma K was laughing, but it was a different laughter than he'd heard from her before, deeper, fuller, truly happy, as if with the same act of will that had made her choose life, she'd set aside her cynicism. "I know what you're thinking, Kylar. Durzo lied to you when he told you he'd hurt Elene. Of course he did. It was the only way he could save you. You had to kill him to succeed him.

The ka'kari couldn't complete the bond until its former master died."

They sat there in silence, Kylar thinking of how Durzo's death cast his life in a completely different light. It was disconcerting to think how wrong he'd been about his master, thinking him so hateful—actually believing Durzo was capable of mutilating Doll Girl—but Kylar liked the picture that was emerging. Durzo Blint, the legend, had been Acaelus Thorne, the hero. Kylar wondered how many other heroes' names his master had worn. He felt a stabbing pain, an emptiness in his stomach, a surge toward tears that he suppressed. "I'm going to miss him," he said, his throat tight.

Momma K's eyes mirrored his. "Me too. But it's going to be all right. I don't know why, but I really believe that."

Kylar nodded. "So you decided to live," he said, blinking tears away. He didn't want to break down in front of Momma K.

"And so did you." She arched an eyebrow at him, somehow holding both grief and happiness and amusement in her eyes all at once. "She loves you, Kylar. Whether she realizes it or not. She dragged you out of the castle by herself. She refused to leave you. Jarl's men found her. It was only when they got you here that Uly saw your wounds were healing."

"She's furious with me," Kylar said.

"Furious the way a woman in love gets. I know."

"Have you told Uly who her mother is?" Kylar asked.

"No, and I never will. I won't raise her into this."

"She needs a family."

"I was hoping you and Elene would be interested in the job."

Night came to the east shore of the Plith River in a smothering cloud. The city had been burning all day and the night winds wafted the smell over the entire city. Fires reflected in the Plith, and low-hanging clouds held the ashy air like a pillow against the face of the city.

A wagon clattered down a street, its driver hunched, face muffled against the malodorous air. He overtook a crippled woman with a bent back and a foot turned sideways.

"Want up?" his scratchy voice asked.

The woman turned expectantly. Her face too was muffled, but her eyes were young, though both eyes had been blackened.

Her Khalidoran driver was supposed to be dark-haired and fat. This man was white-haired, lean as a rail, stooped and almost lost in his clothes. She shook her head and turned away.

"Please, Elene?" Kylar asked with his own voice.

She flinched. "I should be scared of you, shouldn't I?"

"I'd never hurt you," he said.

Eyebrows above the eyes he'd blackened lifted incredulously.

"Well, not *really* hurt you."

"What are you doing?" she asked, looking around. There was no one else out on the streets.

"I'd like to take you away from here," Kylar said, brushing back his bleached hair and smiling through his makeup. "You and Uly both. We can go anywhere. I'm going to pick her up next."

"Why me, Kylar?"

He was dumbfounded. "It's always been you. I l—"

"Don't you say you love me," she said. "How could you love this?" She jerked the scarf down and pointed at her scars. "How could you love a freak?"

He shook his head. "I don't love your scars, Elene. I hate them—"

"And you'll never see past that."

"I'm not finished," he said. "Elene, I've watched over you since we were children. For a long time, you're right, I couldn't see past your scars. I'm not going to give you some crap that they're beautiful. Your scars are ugly, but you aren't, Elene. The woman I see when I look at you is amazing. She's smart, she's got a quick tongue, and she's got such a heart that it makes me believe that people can be good despite all I've seen to the contrary for my whole life."

His words were sinking into her, he could tell. *Oh, Momma K, tell me I learned something about words from you. Tell me I learned something despite myself.*

Elene's hands waved like little birds. "How can you say that? You don't know me!"

"Aren't you still Doll Girl?"

Her hands came down, the little birds fluttering to rest. "Yes," she said. "But I don't think you're still Azoth."

"No," he admitted. "I'm not. I don't know who I am. Right now, I only know I'm not my master and I won't live like he did."

Hope seemed to leach out of her. "Kylar," she said, and he saw that the name was a deliberate choice, "I will always be grateful to you. But we would be a disaster. You would destroy me."

"What are you talking about?"

"Momma K said your master intercepted all my letters."

"Yes, but I've had a busy afternoon catching up," Kylar said.

She smiled sadly. "And you still don't understand?"

Do girls ever make sense? He shook his head.

"When we were children, you were the one who protected me, who looked out for me. You were the one who put me with a real family. I wanted to be with you forever. Then when I was growing up, you were my benefactor who made me special. You were my secret young lord whom I loved so desperately and so foolishly. You were my Kylar, my poor nobleman that the Drake girls told me stories about. Then you were the one who came to save me in gaol."

He paused and paused. "You say that like it's a bad thing."

"Oh, Kylar. What happens to that silly girl when it turns out I'm not good enough for the man I've loved for my whole life?"

"*You*, not good enough?"

"It's a fairy tale, Kylar. I don't deserve it. Something will happen. You'll find somebody prettier or you'll get tired of me, and then you'll leave me, and I'll never recover, because the only kind of love I have to offer is stupid and blind and so deep and powerful that I feel like I'm cracking just to hold it in. I can't just swoon and fall into bed with you, because you'll hop right out and get on with your life, and I never will."

"I'm not asking you to make love with me."

"So I'm too ugly for—"

He couldn't say a damn thing right. "Enough!" he roared, emotion filling his voice so suddenly that it shocked her into silence. "I think you're the most beautiful woman I've ever seen, Elene. And the purest. And the best. But I'm not asking you to fuck!"

Consternation played over her features, but she obviously didn't like being yelled at.

"Elene," he said quietly. "I'm sorry I yelled. I'm sorry I hit you—even if it was to save you. I've thought I was dying twice in the last few days—maybe I did die, I don't know. What I do know is that when I thought I was dying, you were my regret. No! Not your scars," he said as she touched her face. "I regretted that I hadn't turned myself into the kind of man that you could be with. That it wouldn't be *just* for me to be with you, even if you wanted me. Our lives started in the same shit hole, Elene, but somehow you've turned into you, and I've turned into this. I don't like what I've done. I don't like who I've become. You don't deserve a fairy tale? I don't deserve another chance, but I'm asking you for one. You're afraid that love is too risky? I've seen what happens when you don't risk it. Momma K and my master loved each other, but they were too afraid to risk it and that destroyed them. We risk everything either way.

"I'm willing to risk it to see the world through your eyes, Elene. I want to know you. I want to be worthy of you. I want to look in the mirror and like who I see. I don't know what's next, but I know I want to face it with you. Elene, I'm not asking you to fuck. But maybe some day, I'll earn the right to ask you for something more permanent." He turned, and facing her was harder than facing thirty highlanders. He extended his hand. "Please, Elene. Will you come with me?"

She scowled fiercely at him, then looked away. Her eyes were shiny with tears, but it could have been from all the ash in the air. She blinked quickly before looking back up at him. She searched his face for a long moment. He met her big brown eyes. He had turned away from them so many times, afraid she would see what he really was. He had turned away, afraid that she couldn't bear the sight of his filth. Now he met that gaze. He opened himself to it. He didn't hide his darkness. He didn't hide his love. He let her gaze go all the way through him.

To his wonder, her eyes filled with something softer than justice, something warmer than mercy.

"I'm so scared, Kylar."

"Me too," he said.

She took his hand.

Acknowledgements

*I*t was all downhill after seventh grade. That was the year my English teacher, Nancy Helgath, somehow made me cool when she encouraged me to read Edgar Allan Poe to my classmates at lunch. They sat goggle-eyed as I read "The Pit and the Pendulum," "Berenice," and "The Raven." But I had eyes for only one: the tall, smart girl I had a crush on—and was terrified of—Kristi Barnes.

I soon started my first novel. I would go on to become an English teacher and a writer, and marry Kristi Barnes.

This book wouldn't have happened without my mother—for more than the obvious reason. I started reading late, and when I did, I hated it. This wasn't helped by a teacher who shouted "Choppy sentences!" at me for my inability to read aloud smoothly in the first grade. My mom took me out of school for a year to home school me (insert social awkwardness joke here), and her dedication and patience gave me a love for reading.

Thank you to my little sisters, Christa and Elisa, who

begged for bedtime stories. An enthusiastic and forgiving audience is a must for a budding teenage storyteller. Any princesses in my books are their fault.

It's one thing to love reading; it's another to write. My high school English teacher, Jael Prezeau, is a teacher in a million. She inspired hundreds. She's the kind of woman who could chew you out, cheer you on, make you work harder than you've ever worked for a class, give you a B, and make you love it. She told me I couldn't break the grammar rules she taught me until I was published. It was a rule up with which I could not put. She tried.

In college, I briefly considered politics. Horror. A few people turned me from disaster. One was an industrial spy I met in Oxford. On reading a story I'd written, he said, "I wish I could do what you do." Huh? Then my best friend Nate Davis became the editor of our college literary journal and held a contest for the best short story. Wonder of wonders, I won the cash prize, and realized I'd earned slightly better than minimum wage. I was hooked. (It was better than I would do again for a long, long time.) I started a new novel, and whenever I tried to do my homework, I could count on Jon Low to come knocking on my door. "Hey, Weeks, you got another chapter for me yet?" It was irritating and flattering at once. I had no idea I was being prepared for having an editor.

I must thank the Iowa Writers Program for rejecting me. Though I still sometimes wear all black and drink lattes, they helped me decide to write the kind of books I like rather than the books I ought to like.

My debt to my wife, Kristi, cannot be overstated. Her faith kept me going. Her sacrifices awe me. Her wisdom has rescued me from many a story dead end. To get published, you have to defy overwhelming odds; to marry a woman like Kristi, you have to knock them out.

My agent Don Maass has an understanding of story that I've not seen rivaled. Don, you've been a reality check, a wise teacher, and an encourager. You make me a better writer.

Huge thanks to the amazing editorial team at Orbit. Devi, thanks for your many insights, your enthusiasm, and your guidance ushering me through an unfamiliar process. Tim, thanks for taking a chance on me. Jennifer, you were my first contact at Orbit, and I have to tell you, the fact that I'd e-mail you a question and get an answer the same morning was a big deal. Of course, then you started sending me paperwork—and then I knew I wasn't dreaming. Alex, thanks for your brilliant Web page design, the beautiful billboards, full page scratch-and-sniff ads in the *New York Times,* and those nifty little cardboard display stands at Borders. They're fab. Lauren, thank you for taking my ones and zeros and making something real. Hilary, copyeditor extraordinaire, a special thanks for two words: bollock dagger. They made the novel.

I also want to thank all the other people at Orbit and Hachette who do the real work while we artists sit in cafés wearing black, drinking lattes. I'd mention you by name, but I don't know your names. However, I do appreciate what you do to take my words and make something out of them. So, layout people, art people (by the way, Wow!), office go-fers, accountants, lawyers, and the mail guy, thanks.

Crazy dreamers need a lot of encouragers. Kevin, your being proud of me is about the best thing a little brother can get. Dad, one of my first memories is of sharing my worry with you about the space shuttle poking holes in the atmosphere and letting out all of Earth's air. Rather than rushing to correct me, you listened—and still do. Jacob Klein, your encouragement and friendship over the years have been invaluable. You were there at the very beginning (4 A.M. in Niedfeldt, I think). To the Cabin Guys at Hillsdale College (Jon "Missing Link" Low, Nate "My Head Looks Like PK's Butt" Davis, AJ "My Girlfriend Will Clean It Up" Siegmann, Jason "I Love Butter" Siegmann, Ryan "Mystery Puker" Downey, Peter "GQ" Koller, Charles "Sand Vest" Robison, Matt "No Special Sauce" Schramm), I couldn't have shared a slum house with better wangs. Dennis Foley, you were the first professional writer who gave me time and guidance. You said you'd tell me if I should give up and get a real job—and that I shouldn't. Cody Lee, thanks for the unbridled enthusiasm; it still makes me smile. Shaun and Diane McNay, Mark and Liv Pothoff, Scott and Kariann Box, Scott and Kerry Rueck, Todd and Lisel Williams, Chris Giesch, Blane Hansen, Brian Rapp, Dana Piersall, Jeff and Sandee Newville, Keith and Jen Johnson—thanks for believing in us and helping make the years of work and waiting not just tolerable, but fun.

Thanks to everyone over the years who, on finding out I was a writer, didn't ask, "Oh, are you published?"

Last, thanks to you, curious reader who reads acknowledgments. You do realize the only people who usually read acknowledgments are looking for their own name, right? If you're quirky enough to read acknowledgments without knowing the author, you and I are going to get along fine. Picking up a book by an author you've never read is a leap of faith. Here's my offer: you give me a couple of pages, and I'll give you a helluva ride.

extras

www.orbitbooks.net

about the author

about the author

Brent Weeks was born and raised in Montana. After getting his paper keys from Hillsdale College, Brent had brief stints walking the earth like Caine from *Kung Fu*, tending bar, and corrupting the youth. (Not at the same time.) He started writing on bar napkins, then on lesson plans, then full time. Eventually, someone paid him for it. Brent lives in Oregon with his wife, Kristi. He doesn't own cats or wear a ponytail. Find out more about the author at www.brentweeks.com

Find out more about Brent Weeks and other Orbit authors by registering for the free monthly newsletter at www.orbitbooks.net

if you enjoyed
THE WAY OF SHADOWS
look out for

SHADOW'S EDGE

book two of the Night Angel trilogy

also by

Brent Weeks

1

We've got a contract for you," Momma K said. As always, she sat like a queen, her back straight, sumptuous dress perfect, hair immaculately coifed if gray at the roots. This morning she had dark circles under her eyes. Kylar guessed that none of the Sa'kagé's surviving leaders had slept much since the Khalidoran invasion.

"Good morning to you, too," Kylar said, settling into the wing-backed chair in the study. Momma K didn't turn to face him, looking instead out her window. Last night's rain had quenched most of the fires in the city, but many still smoked, bathing the city in a crimson dawn. The waters of the Plith River that divided rich eastern Cenaria from the Warrens looked as red as blood. Kylar wasn't sure that was all because of the smoke-obscured sun, either. In the week since the coup, the Khalidoran invaders had massacred thousands.

Momma K said, "There's a wrinkle. The deader knows it's coming."

"How's he know?" The Sa'kagé wasn't usually so sloppy.

"We told him."

Kylar rubbed his temples. The Sa'kagé would only tell someone so that if the attempt failed, the Sa'kagé wouldn't be committed. That meant the deader could only be one man: Cenaria's conqueror, Khalidor's Godking, Garoth Ursuul.

"I just came to get my money," Kylar said. "All of

Durzo's—my safe houses burned down. I only need enough to bribe the gate guards." He'd been giving her a cut of his wages to invest since he was a child. She should have plenty for a few bribes.

Momma K flipped silently through sheets of rice paper on her desk and handed one to Kylar. At first, he was stunned by the numbers. He was involved in the illegal importation of riot weed and half a dozen other addictive plants, owned a race horse, had a stake in a brewery and several other businesses, part of a loan shark's portfolio, and owned partial cargos of items like silks and gems that were legitimate except for the fact the Sa'kagé paid 20 percent in bribes rather than 50 percent in tariffs. The sheer amount of information on the page was mind-boggling. He didn't know what half of it meant.

"I own a house?" Kylar asked.

"Owned," Momma K said. "This column denotes merchandise lost in the fires or looting." There were checks next to all but a silk expedition and one for riot weed. Almost everything he had owned was lost. "Neither expedition will return for months, if at all. If the Godking keeps seizing civilian vessels, they won't come back at all. Of course, if he were dead—"

He could see where this was going. "This says my share is still worth ten to fifteen thousand. I'll sell it to you for a thousand. That's all I need."

She ignored him. "They need a third wetboy to make sure it works. Fifty thousand gunders for one kill, Kylar. With that much, you can take Elene and Uly anywhere. You'll have done the world a good turn, and you'll never have to work again. It's just one last job."

He wavered only for a moment. "There's always one last job. I'm finished."

"This is because of Elene, isn't it?" Momma K asked.

"Momma K, do you think a man can change?"

She looked at him with a profound sadness. "No. And he'll end up hating anyone who asks him to."

Kylar got up and walked out the door. In the hallway, he ran into Jarl. Jarl was grinning like he used to when they were growing up on the streets and he was up to no good. Jarl was wearing what must be the new fashion, a long tunic with exaggerated shoulders paired with slim trousers tucked into high boots. It looked vaguely Khalidoran. His hair was worked into elaborate microbraids capped with gold beads that set off his black skin.

"I've got the perfect job for you," Jarl said, his voice lowered, but unrepentant about eavesdropping.

"No killing?" Kylar asked.

"Not exactly."

"Your Holiness, the cowards stand ready to redeem themselves," Vürdmeister Neph Dada announced, his voice carrying over the crowd. He was an old man, veiny, liver-spotted, stooped, stinking of death held at bay with magic, his breath rattling from the exertion of climbing up the platform in Cenaria Castle's great yard. Twelve knotted cords hung over the shoulders of his black robes for the twelve shu'ras he'd mastered. Neph knelt with difficulty and offered a handful of straw to the Godking.

Godking Garoth Ursuul stood on the platform inspecting his troops. Front and center were nearly two hundred Graavar highlanders, tall, barrel-chested, blue-eyed savages who wore their black hair short and their mustaches long. On either side stood the other elite highland tribes that had captured the castle. Beyond them waited the rest of the regular army that had marched into Cenaria since the liberation.

Mists rose from the Plith River on either side of the castle and slid under the rusty teeth of the iron portcullises to chill the crowd. The Graavar had been broken into fifteen groups of thirteen each, and they alone had no weapons, armor, or tunics. They stood in their trousers, pale faces fixed, but sweating instead of shivering in the cool autumn morning.

There was never commotion when the Godking inspected his troops, but today the silence ached despite the thousands gathered to watch. Garoth had gathered every soldier possible and allowed the Cenarian servants and nobles and smallfolk to watch as well. Meisters in their black-and-red half-cloaks stood shoulder to shoulder with robed Vürdmeisters, soldiers, crofters, coopers, nobles, field hands, maids, sailors, and Cenarian spies.

The Godking wore a broad white cloak edged with ermine thrown back to make his broad shoulders look huge. Beneath that was a sleeveless white tunic over wide white trousers. All the white made his pallid Khalidoran skin look ghostly, and drew sharp attention to the vir playing across his skin. Black tendrils of power rose to the surface of his arms. Great knots rose and fell, knots edged with thorns that moved not just back and forth but up and down in waves, pressing out from his skin. Claws raked his skin from beneath. Nor were his vir confined to his arms. They rose to frame his face. They rose to his bald scalp and pierced the skin, forming a thorny, quivering black crown. Blood trickled down the sides of his face.

For many Cenarians, it was their first glimpse of the Godking. Their jaws hung slack. They shivered as his gaze passed over them. It was exactly as he intended.

Finally, Garoth selected one of the pieces of straw from Neph Dada and broke it in half. He threw away one half and took twelve full-length pieces. "Thus shall Khali speak," he said, his voice robust with power.

He signaled the Graavar to climb the platform. During the liberation, they had been ordered to hold this yard to contain the Cenarian nobles for slaughter. Instead, the highlanders had been routed, and Terah Graesin and her nobles had escaped. That was unacceptable, inexplicable, uncharacteristic for the fierce Graavar. Garoth didn't understand what made men fight one day and flee the next.

What he did understand was shame. For the past week, the Graavar had been mucking stables, emptying chamber pots, and scrubbing floors. They had not been allowed to sleep, instead spending the nights polishing their betters' armor and weapons. Today, they would expiate their guilt, and for the next year, they would be eager to prove their heroism. As he approached the first group with Neph at his side, Garoth calmed the vir from his hands. When the men drew their straws, they must think it not the working of magic or the Godking's pleasure that spared one and condemned another. Rather, it was simple fate, the inexorable consequence of their own cowardice.

Garoth held up his hands, and together, all the Khalidorans prayed: "*Khali vas, Khalivos ras en me, Khali mevirtu rapt, recu virtum defite.*"

As the words faded, the first soldier approached. He was barely sixteen, the least fringe of a mustache on his lip. He looked on the verge of collapse as his eyes flitted from the Godking's icy face to the straws. His naked chest shone with sweat in the rising morning light, his muscles twitching. He drew a straw. It was long.

Half of the tension whooshed out of his body, but only half. The young man next to him, who looked so alike he must have been his older brother, licked his lips and grabbed a straw. It was short.

Queasy relief washed over the rest of the squad, and the thousands watching who couldn't possibly see the short straw knew that it had been drawn from their reactions. The man who'd drawn the short straw looked at his little brother. The younger man looked away. The condemned man turned disbelieving eyes on the Godking and handed him the short straw.

Garoth stepped back. "Khali has spoken," he announced. There was a collective intake of breath, and he nodded to the squad.

They closed on the young man, every one of them—even his brother—and began beating him.

It would have been faster if Garoth had let the squad wear gauntlets or use the butts of spears or the flat of blades, but he thought it was better this way. When the blood began flowing and spraying off flesh as it was pummeled, it shouldn't get on the squad's clothing. It should get on their skin. Let them feel the warmth of the young man's blood as he died. Let them know the cost of cowardice. Khalidorans did not flee.

The squad attacked with gusto. The circle closed and screams rose. There was something intimate about naked meat slapping naked meat. The young man disappeared and all that could be seen was elbows rising and disappearing with every punch and feet being drawn back for new kicks. And moments later, blood. With the short straw, the young man had become their weakness. It was Khali's decree. He was no longer brother or friend, he was all they had done wrong.

In two minutes, the young man was dead.

The squad reformed, blood-spattered and blowing hard from exertion and emotion. They didn't look at the corpse at their feet. Garoth regarded each in turn, meeting the eyes of every one, and lingering on the brother. Standing over the corpse, Garoth extended a hand. The vir poked out of his wrist and extended, clawlike, ragged, and gripped the corpse's head. Then the claws convulsed and the head popped with a wet sound that left dozens of Cenarians retching.

"Your sacrifice is accepted. Thus are you cleansed," he announced, and saluted them.

They returned his salute proudly and took their places back in the formation in the courtyard as the body was dragged away.

He motioned the next squad. The next fourteen iterations would be nothing but more of the same. Though tension still arced through every squad—even the squads who'd finished would lose friends and family in other squads—Garoth lost interest. "Neph, tell me what you've learned about this man, this *Night Angel* who killed my son."